DATE DUE

THEORY
OF BASTARDS

Audrey Schulman

THEORY
OF BASTARDS

Europa
editions

Europa Editions
214 West 29th Street
New York, N.Y. 10001
www.europaeditions.com
info@europaeditions.com

Library of Congress Cataloging in Publication Data is available
ISBN 978-1-60945-437-1

Schulman, Audrey
Theory of Bastards

Book design by Emanuele Ragnisco
www.mekkanografici.com

Cover photo © Carlush/Shutterstock

Prepress by Grafica Punto Print – Rome

Printed in the USA

But sometimes a tool may have other uses that you don't know. Sometimes in doing what you intend, you also do what the knife intends, without knowing.
—PHILIP PULLMAN

Most of the experiments in this novel are based on actual experiments performed by real researchers. Information about them is provided in the Appendix.

The characters, however, bear no resemblance to any real researchers. They are utterly created by my imagination.

THEORY
OF BASTARDS

DAY 1

One

When Frankie's vehicle pulled in, she saw a whole group of them waiting for her, exactly what she hated. Dressed up, milling about, eager supplicants. Ten or eleven researchers in all, probably every Ph.D. at the Foundation.

When the door slid open and she stepped out, they blinked. A few glanced back inside the vehicle to search for another passenger, before returning to her. She didn't look much like her press photos these days.

Dr. Bellows—the executive director—was more prepared. Perhaps he had heard rumors or maybe her request for a wheelchair had been enough. He stepped forward to clasp her hands, saying how delighted, how truly honored he was to have her here. He'd read all her papers. The chair was pushed forward and Frankie sank into it. The group of them made lots of noise, talking all around her, each adding their tidbit of information: the Foundation's illustrious history, the past researchers, the freedom and facilities she would have. Frankie barely had to say a word.

They wheeled her along, into a courtyard with a large catered meal. A woman stepped in front for a moment, framing the shot with her fingers, ready to take a photo, calling out, Smile.

Jesus, Frankie said and held her hand in the way, Just take me to the animals. Let me see them. I haven't agreed to this job yet.

The silence awkward. The apologies profuse. They moved

her toward the exhibits. The crowds of tourists—pushing strollers and eating popcorn—parted like water in front of them. The exhibits were connected by a wandering path through landscaped gardens. They passed the gorilla and chimp enclosures. She did not even glance at them. The orangutans watched the parade go by, their jowly faces swiveling like radar dishes.

This level of attention being paid to her was relatively new. She'd heard afterward that the MacArthur committee was made up of very smart but busy experts. When asked to come up with names, they were likely to scan headlines, to Quark some searches. The press about her last study had hit during the spring, probably when they were making nominations. Up until then, she'd mostly been underfunded and ignored; she wanted very much to return to that. The desire wasn't out of kindness—a wish to make others comfortable. No, 33 years old and fresh from this last surgery, she had no use for other people's jealousy.

The doctors had been so careful in what they said, trying to be exact—85% chance of recovery, not from her disease, just the symptoms. Still she was so hungry for this opportunity. Waiting to see if the symptoms would return, there was the high-pitched hum of disbelief in her ears, like an extraterrestrial who'd finally cracked the door open, about to take that terrifying first breath. The medicine she craved was distraction.

They arrived at the bonobo enclosure, the area blocked off from the tourists. Today these animals were for her appreciation alone. Inside the plexiglass walls was a hill with a climbing structure on it and a small pond at the base of it, a few milk crates scattered about. Realizing something was up, the 14 bonobos were clustered near the glass, watching the path for whatever change was about to arrive, the crowd of them reminiscent of the researchers waiting for Frankie's car.

In appearance, they looked like the chimps she'd passed, only the bonobos were a touch skinnier and less muscled. Their fur softer. Their lips red. Their eyes thoughtful.

Think of a video montage where a human turns into a wild beast—hair sprouting, brow slanting, jaw jutting. If the chimp is the final image, the bonobo is a second earlier.

In front stood one bonobo. Her stance was not a chimp's: bandy-legged as a cowboy with the barrel-shaped chest heaved up, her torso ready at any moment to fall back onto all fours. No, she stood as a human does, comfortably upright, legs straight, her face turned to the researchers as though they'd just called her name.

And, unlike the rest of the bonobos, her body was balding and her head utterly hairless. Perhaps an autoimmune disease or the effect of aging. What little hair remained on her body was no longer thick enough to be called fur, closer perhaps to the sparseness of chest hair. She stood there, wiry and short, her skin the grey of putty, a naked Gandhi with jug ears, staring into Frankie's eyes.

Actually all of the bonobos were looking at Frankie. Staring not at the whole group of researchers, but at Frankie, her face. As though they'd followed the coverage in the *Wall St. Journal* and *New York Times*—the upswing in genetic testing, the outings of public figures and past presidents—and were surprised to spot her here.

It took Frankie a moment to realize the animals must know all the researchers who worked here. She was the only stranger. Studies had shown even a sheep could recognize up to 50 faces.

Dr. Bellows began to speak, his voice awkward, The particular . . . umm . . . behavior you'd be researching, the behavior that bonobos are famous for, happens primarily before mealtimes.

As though making excuses for them he continued, The

behavior is used to ease tensions, to calm down any conflict over the food. Would you like me to . . .

Feed 'em, she said.

Bellows nodded and a researcher obediently jogged off around the corner of the building.

Frankie waited. The animals continued to study her, in their half circle, positioned as though she was about to lecture them or they about to interrogate her.

She gestured with her chin at the bald bonobo's confident stance. She asked, Alpha female?

Yes, said Bellows, She runs the show. That's Mama.

Mama? Frankie asked, the rising lilt of her question making her sound like a needy child.

Mama, answered Bellows, letting the word fall heavy like the name of a mafia don.

From the silence around them, she guessed most of the researchers worked with other apes here at the Foundation and felt uncomfortable with what was about to happen.

She pointed her chin at the kiosk next to Bellows. It displayed a large photo of a bonobo waving hi. There was a panel with many buttons on it. She asked, What's that?

He said, Ahh, some of the bonobos were raised with sign language. This is a way to communicate with them.

Really? asked Frankie.

Seated, she couldn't see which two buttons he pressed but the avatar of a female bonobo appeared on the plexiglass between the humans and the bonobos—off to the side and a few feet up so she didn't block the exhibit. Her hands gestured in sign language as she spoke the words, saying, Human. Hello.

Her voice was loud, the condescending cheer of a kindergarten teacher.

The bonobos didn't glance at the avatar. Instead their dark eyes turned to Bellows.

Then behind them, a door opened up on the balcony, inside

the enclosure, and a staff-person in coveralls stepped out, lugging two buckets of food.

The bonobos turned, mouths gaping at their unscheduled luck.

The males rose to their feet, legs apart to show off their abrupt erections, pencil-thin but impressive. The moment following was when Frankie watched with the greatest attention. Just as she'd been told, all the animals reached for each other, for whoever was closest. Not one of them stepped around another to get to a preferred partner.

Frankie's eyes watered with gratitude. She blinked a few times, keeping her face turned toward the animals, hoping no one could see. Here was the distraction she needed, a worthwhile puzzle to dig into.

Meanwhile the rest happened, the part that the media was fascinated with: the wide variety of acts and positions, homosexual and hetero, the twosomes, the threesomes, the sheer creativity, oral sex, a hand job and what primatologists called penis-fencing. An imaginative juvenile began to hump the leg of an otherwise-occupied adult.

Dwarf hairy humans engaged in an orgy.

A researcher giggled nervously. Bellows's head swiveled and the giggle stopped.

Within seconds, the first bonobo began to climax.

Ah, the female huffed loudly, *Ahuh huh huh.*

Damn, whispered a woman under her breath, somewhere behind Frankie, impressed either with the speed with which the bonobo had reached this point or its obvious intensity.

Then the rest of the females began to call, *Ahh huh huh,* their mouths open.

The males' orgasms were less noisy and sounded a trifle disappointed in comparison.

The action stopped. They lay there, post orgasm, arms wrapped tenderly around each other. After a long quiet moment, one of them remembered the food and stood up. The rest followed, holding their hands out palms up, like beggars.

On the balcony, the staff-person was waiting. She picked fruit out of the buckets and began to lob pieces down to them.

Well, said Bellows, trying to recover his toothy smile.

For the first time since seeing the bonobos, Frankie turned to the humans. She said, Let me confirm some facts. They do this before every meal.

Yes, said Bellows.

Just that way? Copulating with whomever is closest?

Yes.

Then so far as any of you know, said Frankie raising her voice slightly to make sure they could all hear, It's just as likely that an ovulating female will end up mating with the least healthy male as the most healthy one? She is just as likely to mate with the weakest and dumbest as the strongest and smartest?

Yes, responded the group.

Alrighty, said Frankie. I officially accept the research position here. I have three conditions.

One, she said, I want an apartment on the Foundation grounds, with its own kitchen.

Two, she said, You can write as many grants as you want using my name and resume and I hope lots of funding comes from those grants, but understand my reason for being here is to do research. I will not be trotted out to wine and dine any potential funders. I will not be bothered or contacted unnecessarily. If I am, I will leave.

Three, she added, I require the help of one researcher, part time. Someone to answer questions about the bonobos and assist me as needed.

Of course, of course, said Bellows, May I recommend . . . He started to gesture toward a tall bearded man. Frankie recognized him from several of the Foundation brochures and conference pamphlets. The man had been eyeing her since she arrived—possessive and hungry—like a dog watching a biscuit.

No, Frankie said and pointed instead to the only person she could see who wasn't directly facing her—some guy who had hung back the whole time, looking like he wanted to be someplace else, probably doing his work. Pretty much the way she felt.

Him, she said.

DAY 2

Two

At 8 the next morning, the researcher she'd selected met her in the parking lot in front of the bonobo research building.

The way she looked today, she could star as the villain in a sci-fi movie: wheelchair, stretchy clothing and cavernous stare.

He, on the other hand, could play one of the Secret Servicemen standing in the background of any movie with the President. Buzzcut, white teeth and a rangy ease that said he could lope without effort for days.

Unlike most people, no Bindi glittered on his forehead, displaying its corporate logo. Instead he wore just an old Wristable. She hadn't realized they still made them, the device as bulky as a watch. She wondered if his salary was that low.

He stepped forward to shake her hand, his smile wide, his hand warm.

Probably not the sharpest knife in the drawer, she thought.

David Stotts, he said. It's an honor to meet you, ma'am.

I don't like praise, she said. Don't give me any.

He paused, considering her words, and nodded. He said, Sorry about that.

From the way he said this, she wasn't sure if he was apologizing for his words or just sad she couldn't appreciate praise.

She continued, Here's how your work with me is going to go. You'll assist me a little each day. Help me get around. Teach me about the bonobos. It won't take much of your day and the amount will decrease gradually. You'll still be able to do your own research. I will not waste your time.

At the moment in her bag was a jar of mayonnaise. Her meals the last few days consisted of a heaping spoonful of it. For a decade she had not been allowed this condiment—all the eggs and that oil. It was the richest joy in the mouth, the thrill of the forbidden. She licked it like ice cream, the mathematical accumulation of calories, no need to even chew.

Years ago she'd started dressing for herself, no one else. Currently she wore the sort of primary-colored smock and sparkly tights that suggested a child under five. Her favorites were clothes with embroidered animals on the breast and along the hem. It was her habit when concentrating to run her fingers over the grinning animals, feeling the smooth threads.

He wore a crisp button-down shirt and chinos—a uniform of anonymity.

His eyes lingered on a bright yellow chicken on her left breast. The Foundation had spent the last two months wooing her, trying to persuade her to do research here. Actual paper brochures FedExed daily, links to pertinent research papers and videos. Bellows left personal pleas on her Sim-mail. They'd never received a word back until two days ago when she'd Quarked to say she would arrive the next morning, no more notice than that.

The chicken had its beak open, its little sound bubble said *Cheep.*

Ma'am, he said, You clearly like to get to the point. Dr. Bellows asked me to say I might not be the best person for this job. I have only been working with the bonobos for six months and they are not what my degree is in.

His voice wasn't purposeful and clipped like hers—a New Yorker cutting through traffic. The rhythm of his words ambled along instead—a rural Missouri road, no car in sight.

Don't care, she said. If I require information you don't know, you'll learn it.

No reaction visible on his face. Again he nodded.

Good, she thought. He won't be a problem.

She said, Bring me to the bonobos. Do the research you normally do. I'll watch and occasionally ask questions.

Yes, ma'am. He stepped forward to push her wheelchair.

Army? she asked.

Ma'am?

You keep calling me ma'am. Were you in the Army or is this some sort of regional verbal tic?

The Reserves, he said. That's how I paid for school. I served in Syria.

You served remotely?

No, I actually went there.

How many years?

Four. Called up twice.

She said, Hopefully working with me will be easier.

She meant this as a small joke. He made no comment.

He wheeled her into the research building attached to the bonobo enclosure. Inside, it looked like any office hallway, white walls and gray carpet, offices on either side. Thirty feet down the hall was a second door with locks on it. A bright sign declaring, No Admittance to Unauthorized Personnel.

Entering this hallway, she gestured for him to halt and she got up out of the wheelchair.

He was getting used to the rhythm of their interaction, his pause a bit shorter, Ma'am?

She said, I have to walk a little further each day. The wheelchair is just for a few days.

He looked at her and then down the hallway. His unstated question clear.

If I need to, I'll sit down, she said. She inhaled through her nose and began to shuffle forward.

He walked alongside her, ready to catch her if necessary. He reduced his speed once to try to match her pace and then reduced it further. With that lanky body, he must engage in some marathon sport: running, biking, swimming. It took concentration for him to move this slowly, like watching a racehorse being walked to the gate. He looked down at his feet, might have been counting between each step.

Since the award, colleagues treated her differently. Some avoided her as much as possible and when they couldn't, they seemed on edge, as though she'd just insulted them or questioned their credentials. Others focused on her, like she'd said something profound even when she hadn't spoken. For this, her medical sabbatical, she'd been imagining Nepal or better yet Fiji. Some place far from everyone she knew, where she could retreat into insignificance, concentrate on work. There were, however, so many travel advisories, and they changed quickly. A few days ago, she'd decided Missouri was good enough. Compared to New York City, it was a foreign country: Republican, rural, creationist, poor.

Partway down the hall was a machine. It was colored brightly and looked a bit like the type of strength test found at a country fair, except displayed as its metric were various primate silhouettes from a bush baby all the way up to a mountain gorilla. Instead of a target to be hit with a mallet, there was a handgrip to squeeze.

Explain, she said.

He looked at her and then the machine. He said, It's a way of comparing your strength to other primates. No need to try it.

The handgrip was similar to the hand-strengthening equipment that ex-jocks squeezed while talking on the phone.

She had a hard time bypassing any challenge. Also her feet felt a little far away. The idea of grabbing onto something solid was attractive. Stopping, she wrapped her fingers round its molded grip, inhaled and compressed the spring as hard as she could. Determination was a quality she did not lack. She watched the needle swing upwards from *Bush Baby* to *Tarsier* and past *Tamarin*.

It stopped at *Ring-tailed Lemur—avg. weight, 5 lbs.*

They both looked at the result, neither saying anything. She let her hand fall to her side.

She asked, How much do the bonobos weigh?

The females, he said, About 70 pounds.

She turned to him and at her expression, he stepped forward, took hold of the handgrip and squeezed. She could see the effort rising into his shoulder. Being in the military left its impact on a person's posture and attitude. Stotts would stand out in a crowd, like a fox in a group of Pekingese. Alert, coiled and capable. There was the sense he wouldn't slouch on the sofa watching a movie, unaware of what was happening behind him. He could not do less than his best.

The needle stopped at *Macaque—avg. weight, 25 lbs.*

Rather than look upset, his eyes were pleased. He said proud, Once I made it all the way to mandrill.

She glanced at his left hand, saw the wedding ring.

You have kids, she asked.

He turned to her, The sweetest four-year-old on the planet. Why?

She said, Seemed like you should.

Given her well-known research, comments about reproduction could be taken many ways.

He filed this statement away for consideration and gestured to the machine.

Humans, he said, Have a fair amount of muscle fiber, but we're like . . . He paused, thinking, We're like a bank account where you can't take all the cash out in one day. The other primates can. Or at least that's the current theory, why you hear of chimps being able to rip a human's arm off. What they're doing is withdrawing all their money. Occasionally you hear of a human exhibiting sudden strength—a mom lifting a car off her kid—but it's rare.

He said, For other apes, it's automatic. They can do it any day of the week. Just afterwards they're very tired.

The word, *tired*, echoed in her ears and she touched her fingers to her sternum, feeling her breath.

He watched her. When he spoke again, his voice was quieter. Perhaps he thought she felt fear.

He said, Bonobos are different from chimps. They don't go to war with rival groups; they've never been recorded to kill. Even when they struggle for dominance inside their own group, there's almost no violence, just a lot of yelling and slapping things around. Worst I've ever seen was a male getting bit. Three drops of blood and they were all so *surprised*. Every one of them came over to inspect the cut several times.

Stotts the ex-soldier said with respect, They are the most gentle creatures.

The locked door was now perhaps 15 feet away. She swung her foot forward, aiming for it.

When she spoke, her voice echoed in her head as though from another room, Why were you pleased with the results?

The results?

She said, The strength test.

Ahh, he said.

He looked at the door ahead and answered, Ma'am, I like challenges. I am twice the size of the bonobos and I'm strong for a human. Yet even the smallest female could beat me up. I respect these apes. They keep me awake.

He continued, Every day I try that machine and I never get close to their strength.

Even as slowly as he walked, he was now half a pace ahead, while he considered how to make this point clear, momentarily inattentive of her progress or pallor.

He said, We keep them caged here, but they aren't like lab

rats where we can force them to do what we want. They are smart and very strong. You have to ask, to persuade. In the enclosure and research room, the rules aren't made by humans or bonobos. Instead they're somewhere in between, some compromise we all constantly negotiate.

At the word *negotiate*, the static rose, engulfing her hearing. Her vision tunneled. She had practice at this, had already let her knees go, was falling with some control. She sat down hard on the floor.

Her gut and the incision jarred.

A harsh light, sound whistling, space empty. This type of pain, she didn't mind that much. It didn't last. She leaned into the light and waited it out.

From some faraway universe he called, Dr. Burk, you're fainting. Put your head down.

She thought, No duh.

She felt him place one hand on the back of her head, folding her over, his other arm wrapped around her. Shivering, she could feel his warmth through her shirt.

Three

Frankie had been born in Hamilton, Ontario, and baptized Francine Burk. Francine was the name she went by until after college.

Her parents—Canadians—didn't discuss politics, sex or bowel movements. Their voices were carefully modulated, every consonant clear as a bell. They took a brisk walk once a day and ate a well-cooked vegetable with dinner. As Protestants, they considered a visit to the doctor somewhat suspect, a lack of fortitude. Their only medicine was an occasional aspirin taken with a glass of water, preferably out of sight of anyone except an observant child. When asked, they always replied they were doing well, thank you. In Hamilton, they blended in seamlessly with their neighbors, perhaps that was the point.

When she was seven, however, her father took a job with an American company and they moved to Manhattan. The cultural change was surprisingly large. The word *please* was not half as common. Strangers voiced their opinions with gusto. She remembered a dinner party early on where her father was seated beside aged Mr. Schwartz who (when asked how he was) began describing his prolapsed hernia. Both of her parents strove to keep whatever feelings they felt within the range of what they considered allowable. Within this narrow range, her father's expression was as shocked as if Mr. Schwartz had fondled himself at the table.

She was enrolled in second grade at P.S. 116 in Midtown.

First thing that first day, the whole class got to its feet, placed hands on hearts and recited the Pledge of Allegiance in one voice. She wasn't quite sure how she should act and so stood by her desk, her head lowered as though she were in church. Basically she was baffled. No one in Ontario ever pledged allegiance to anything and they were asked to sing *O Canada* so infrequently that, after the first stanza, most had to resort to indistinct humming.

She waited until recess to approach her new teacher, Miss Sanchez. In her crisp Ontario voice, Francine explained she was a citizen of another country and inquired what was the proper way to act while the rest of the class repeated the Pledge.

Put your hand on your heart and say the Pledge, said the teacher while putting her papers away.

Francine repeated for clarity, But I'm Canadian.

As fast as that Sanchez's eyes flashed. She leaned in and stated in a no-nonsense adult voice that so long as Francine was lucky enough to be in this great country, she would recite the Pledge each morning and be grateful for the opportunity.

Later Francine learned Sanchez's youngest brother had recently lost a leg in Iraq. Although easily a third of the students in the class were not citizens, every one of them was forced to pledge allegiance daily.

That afternoon it was Gerard from Haiti who taught Francine the preferred coping strategy.

From then on, she recited each morning along with the class, her hand over her heart, *I led the pigeons to the flag . . .*

This was her first lesson in the utility of lying.

*

After Frankie recovered from half-fainting, she had Stotts wheel her to the tourists' area in front of the bonobo enclosure and leave her there. It had the best view of the animals and she could rest.

She sat there, watching with attention. In order to see around the hips and elbows of the people, she rolled forward until her knees were pressed against the glass. In the first few minutes, a six-year-old girl tried to wiggle between Frankie's knees and the glass to get a better view of the bonobos. Frankie kneed her in the back just hard enough for the girl to regard her solemnly and then retreat.

A lot of the children ignored the bonobos in order to play with the sign-language kiosk. Whoever designed it had intended one person to press one button at a time, carefully building each sentence. *Me human. Look stick. Stick on ground.* Perhaps the designer had even imagined the bonobos responding by picking the stick up or signing back. A moment of inter-species communication.

Instead however the children clustered around the kiosk, slapping at the buttons, thrilled by the obedient toy, making the bonobo avatar on the plexiglass say sentences like, *Stick stick stick stick stick stick human human human. Stick stick stick stick stick ground.*

The voice was loud, even outside the enclosure. The bonobos ignored the avatar, aside from staying away from the immediate area near the speakers.

Frankie figured she could start working. She said, Ok Bindi, show desktop.

On her contact Lenses, appeared her desktop icons, arrayed around the periphery of her visual field—allowing her to still see the physical world in front of her. Applications on the left, files on the right, the trash can in the corner. Moving her right hand up so her Bindi could track it, she centered her index finger over the file for the 14 bonobos and double-tapped. The file opened up, centered in her vision. Her Bindi at this point monitored the area around her for any objects headed for her, clicking her desktop off in case of danger—too many cases those first few years of people stepping out in front of a moving car while on a Sim-call.

She flicked her finger through the pages. She wasn't self-conscious, because half the adults around her were tapping and flicking and talking to their Bindis.

The photo for each bonobo had a passing resemblance to a mug shot: a close-up of the face with the name and description below, hairy perpetrators in jail. If she clicked on a photo and tugged on its corners, the photo expanded, so large and high-res she could see every skin pore. Unaided, she'd never be able to keep a face this close and in focus at the same time. The colors also popped: the brown of the eyes, the grey of the face, the pink of the lips.

The problem Frankie found was, after a day of work on her Lenses, reality appeared a little disappointing. In comparison to their photos, the bonobos themselves seemed less real. And her Lenses weren't even the newest version. Technology had now reached the limits of human vision. Soon, she'd been told, the Lenses would bypass the eyes to connect straight to the visual cortex.

One by one, she stared at each photo, then pinched her fingers together, shrinking the photo down and flicking it up to the top of her Lenses, out of the way, so she could search for the bonobo who matched the photo.

Mama was easy to recognize because she was bald. Frankie assumed the juvenile who Mama held was Tooch, a two-year-old male, since he was listed as her youngest offspring. Tooch kept trying to sneak closer to the plexiglass, fascinated by the tourists. Mama stopped him each time, pursing her lips and making a noise in her throat that made him halt mid-stride. The fifth time he tried to sneak away, she simply picked him up by one foot and dangled him out in the air like a fish. Tooch squealed and wiggled and tried to climb his own leg, but soon gave up, hanging there limp, waiting for her to put him down. She lowered him into her lap where he sat, staring at the tourists with a wistful expression. Mama was not a mother to trifle with.

Of all the bonobos, the only one younger than Tooch was Id, a one-year-old female. She was easy to spot since she was tiny: all pencil-thin limbs, wispy fur and large eyes. She was bouncing maniacally on the trampoline of her mother's belly. From the document, Frankie learned the mother's name was Houdina. Her knees jumped involuntarily each time the baby Id landed. In comparison to Mama, Houdina was younger and hairier and didn't seem to be half as tough. She grunted with each bounce and held up her hands, protecting her tender areas.

Frankie tried to identify the other bonobos from their photos but couldn't. They all looked like hairy apes to her at this point. The only feature she could easily distinguish was gender since the nether regions were large and hairless and disturbingly on display. For most of the adult females, the area between the vagina and anus was hairless and swollen into something between a softball and a cantaloupe, advertising their potential fertility to all nearby males. The skin over this balloon appeared so tight and thin that, each time the females sat down, Frankie flinched.

After a while she gave up trying to tell which individual was which. She let herself watch them as a group, absorbing their actions, getting the feel for them, their bright eyes, their knuckled walk, the way they bathed in the pond, lying back in the water and letting their arms float, squirting water out of their mouths. Their voices reminded her of the finches she used to work with, high-pitched cheeps or squeaks.

They spent an enormous amount of time combing their fingers through each other's hair, bored hairstylists on a slow day, the face of the groomed bonobo slack with pleasure. Even though Mama had little hair, she was groomed the most. The others would approach her to clap their hands in front of her, requesting the honor. If she accepted, she would offer them part of her body. After finishing, the groomer would sometimes crouch low with pouting lips. If Mama felt generous, she would tilt her chin up and close her eyes so the groomer could give her a wet kiss on the chin. The scene reminded Frankie of a royal court, an inbred hive of shifting alliances, the lesser nobility approaching the Queen with gifts.

Every once in awhile the juveniles played what looked like tag, barreling after each other on all fours, a breathless charge, a blistering speed that didn't change at all even when the chase switched from running across the ground to bolting 30 feet straight up the side of the metal climbing structure. The athleticism was impressive since they weren't tiny like squirrel monkeys, but had real heft—the slaps of their palms on the metal audible even through the plexiglass.

Anytime more than one of the bonobos disappeared behind the concrete hill on the far side of the enclosure, Frankie would say, Ok Bindi, and with a few brisk gestures enlarge and center on her Lenses the video feed from the Foundation cameras on the other side of the hill. Considering the standards for video these days, the feed was remarkably grainy, intended only for the researchers working on the Foundation. However at least this way she could watch the hidden bonobos to make sure she didn't miss a mating or other interesting behavior.

After she'd spent a few hours watching the bonobos, someone jostled Frankie's wheelchair and she turned in irritation to the tourists behind her. For a moment she paused, surprised by her own species. It was like turning from a broadcast about Olympic gymnasts to look at the viewers sprawled on the couch.

Of course current events were partly to blame. The drought in California and across the southern U.S. still hadn't broken, and the escalating violence in the Middle East had doubled prices for petroleum. Prices for everything had skyrocketed. These days, a lot of Americans were relying on Fritos and soda, while working overtime at whatever jobs they could find.

The bonobos, on the other hand, ate almost entirely fresh

fruit flown in from the tropics. The cost of the fruit, along with vet bills, was the primary reason Frankie was here. With her recent award and publicity, the Foundation could attract more grants. Her award exchanged for mangos and medicine. These days everyone did whatever was needed in order to cope.

*

An hour before closing time, the bonobos became restless, crowding into the area in front of the balcony, competing for the best spot, staring upward, waiting.

Irritated with all the pushing, Mama grabbed one of the milk crates and slammed it on the ground—*whack*. She dragged it behind her as she galloped around, the rattle of it along the ground impressive, Tooch on her shoulder faced into the wind like a jockey. The bonobos quieted and cleared a wide space for her. She knuckled forward into the space, assuming her position in the front.

Then the keeper stepped out onto the balcony with the food, the same woman who'd fed them before, wearing Foundation coveralls.

The male bonobos stood up, knees apart to display their sudden erections, skinny and pink and pointing straight up. The bonobos began mounting each other, businesslike as salesmen shaking hands.

Id, standing on her mother's back, jounced around by all the action, occasionally reached down with curiosity to finger one pink area or another.

And the tourists fled—the stroller wheels wobbling with the speed, the parents singing out promises to their children about the Snack Shack and popsicles. A few older children remained for a moment, staring, before running after the adults, calling out questions.

Frankie leaned forward, intent. In a few days, once she had learned all the names of the bonobos, she would start keeping notes about each mating, checking that the choice of sexual partner was truly random. If it was, she would design a study investigating how the species continued to breed healthy off-spring. One of the most basic tenets of evolution was that there must be strong mating criteria—that a bonobo would step past whoever was closest to copulate with another who was healthier or smarter or stronger. However, from what she'd seen so far, these bonobos weren't even particular about gender.

Afterward, post orgasmic and calm, none of the bonobos had any interest in fighting for the food. Instead they simply held out their hands, palm up, their fingers flexing in an instinctive bonobo give-me gesture. The keeper lobbed chunks of fruit down to them, which they caught with one hand.

They did not gobble this food like dogs bolting down canned mush. Instead they delicately peeled back the skin and picked out the seeds before taking a bite that they rolled around in their mouths like wine, eyes closed, inhaling with joy.

When the keeper had thrown the last of the fruit, she held the buckets out so the bonobos could see they were empty. Most of the bonobos began looking around for any pieces that might have been dropped. Mama, however, continued to stand, her hand out, her fingers flexing, asking for something more. Tooch, against her chest, supplicated also with his tiny palm.

The keeper reached for an object by her feet and looked at Mama, waiting.

In response, Mama didn't repeat the bonobo gesture, but made a different one. She held her left palm up, flat as a table, then reached out with the other hand, wrapping her fingers around an invisible object on the table and raising it into the air. The gesture precise.

Frankie blinked.

The avatar spoke, translating the American Sign Language

gesture. The voice was clear, each consonant enunciated, a human voice emerging from the image of a bonobo's face. The avatar said, Bottle.

The keeper nodded and tossed the object in her hand. A baby bottle.

Mama caught it with the ease of an outfielder and handed it to Tooch. He took the bottle with both hands, rolled onto his back and started nursing. For the first time, Frankie noticed Mama's breasts were flat.

Like any mother, Mama was happy for a moment simply watching her baby drink, sucking in strength. Then lazily, she touched her fingers to her lips, extending her palm toward the keeper.

If Frankie hadn't seen the other sign she might not have recognized this as language.

The avatar translated the gesture automatically, Thank you.

Mama's hands were large and hairy and scarred from knuckle-walking. She scratched her butt with one of them, then picked up a chunk of pineapple from her pile of food and began to eat.

DAY 3

Four

The next morning, Frankie and Stotts tried again.

She managed to walk most of the hallway, nearly reaching the locked door, powering forward, The Little Engine That Could. Then she paused and reached a hand out in the direction of the wall.

He needed no other clue. He scooped her up, sat her down on the floor and folded her over like a lounge chair.

Facing the ground from just a few inches away, it looked so much less threatening than it had a moment ago.

He sat down beside her, one hand on her back. He relaxed, stretching out his legs, as though he was sitting on his favorite couch, like they were an old married couple watching the news. In Syria, he'd probably seen the carnage resulting from suicide bombers and I.E.D.s—automatic weapons used on school buses. Perhaps, like the N.Y.P.D., nothing could flummox him.

Unlike her, he was the kind of person who could touch others easily. He was used to assisting and did so without effort.

He said, Ma'am, you seem to like this hall.

She stared at the ground, blinking.

He asked, Anything you want to tell me about your medical condition?

She did her best to say, *Endometriosis.* There was a lot more air to the word than sound.

She inhaled and tried again, Stage Four. Surgery. Recovering.

Those five words had so much packed into them, a medical haiku.

She always learned about people from their reactions, not so much what they knew about endometriosis as what the depth of their experience was with disease in general. Basically, their reactions could be taken as a rough proxy for how many people they loved and with how much courage—grandparents, spouses, friends. Some people's eyes skittered or got flat. Others said—I'm sorry—a little loudly as though for someone else's benefit. These responses left her spotlit and alone.

Stotts, he stayed there with her, his hand warm on her back.

He said, Tell me what you need and I'll help.

Such a simple statement.

He looked around and offered, My office has a couch. Would you like to rest there?

She said, No.

He offered, I could bring some other researchers here. You could ask questions.

No, she said and pushed herself up to lean back against the wall, Take me to see the research.

He examined her expression.

She said, Let me see you work. It's the best medicine.

He took his hand off her back, but made no motion to get up.

She began to pat the ground around her. The difficulty of climbing to her feet might be overcome, she felt, if she could just get the placement of her hands right.

He said, No need to rush. Tell me about the birds. How'd you come up with the idea of putting hats on them?

Surprised she said, Bellows made you read my grad-school thesis?

Stotts nodded, Every one of your papers and then he quizzed me. Why the hats?

She could remember the zebra finches so clearly, their fluttering flight, the males' complicated mating call: Stravinsky on a squeaky toy. As a species, they were not beautiful. Their markings didn't work together like a tiger's or a puffin's. Instead they had a mish-mash of possible motifs: a few stripes here, a speckled corner there, the tuxedo front. Evolutionarily, they hadn't finished getting dressed, but paused in front of the mirror, unsure of which statement to make.

She said, I looked at the finches. It seemed clear what they were missing.

What did the other students think about what you were doing?

She said, No one cared. I was a nobody. It was lovely.

For lab space, she'd been assigned what at one point had been a closet, seven feet by six, no window—forced to consider only small species. Her budget so restricted, she'd skipped the lab animal catalog and visited the pet store instead. Her advisor had signed all her papers while on the phone. The first time he truly focused on her was at the end of the year when he reviewed her abstract, scanning it absentmindedly, then pausing to read it again with a tightness of attention. She led him to her closet to stare at the costumed birds and their pairings.

Stotts asked, How'd you get the hats to stay on?

They weren't hats, she said. Just red nylon fluff. I used a hot glue gun to connect the fluff to their existing feathers, the same way hair extensions are added. The idea came to me while I was getting a haircut one day.

He tucked his chin in, People use hot glue on their heads?

Oh, what the female will do, she answered, Darwin in action. I found a color that matched the birds' beaks. Took me a while to master the technique. The fluff stood up like a crest. The newspapers were the ones to call it a top hat.

How long did the hats last?

Long enough for me to see the results on courtship and parenting.

And you put stockings on them too?

She exhaled, You're trying to stall. So I don't stand up and faint.

Yup, he said.

She folded her legs up to her chest and rested her forehead on her knees, breathing in the heat of her body. The darkness comforting. The world, she thought, would be a better place filled with the bluntness of Missouri men.

What's your field, she asked, her voice muffled by her thighs.

Archeology with a specialty in lithic technology.

Lithic what?

I specialize in tools from the Stone Age and how they were constructed.

It took her a moment before she responded, You're an expert in rocks?

Yes, ma'am.

She pulled her head up, The government paid for that?

Even these days, ma'am, no politician can argue with a military scholarship.

She grunted. Look, I'm ready to get up.

Your skin is the color of oatmeal.

It's my natural color.

You're using the wheelchair.

No. I'm not.

Yes, ma'am, you are, he said and rose to his feet as easily—it seemed to her—as a ball bounces upward. He strode down the hall to retrieve the wheelchair.

I don't need it, she said as she attempted to stand. She made it only partway before she stopped, her eyes watering.

He returned with the chair and helped her up, not as a man helps his beloved, clasping her hands in his, but the way he would assist his grandma, his hands wrapped firmly around her upper arms. He lowered her into the seat.

(Just 33 years old and, these days, men touched her with as little thought as they would a child or a piece of furniture.)

In the seat, she gave up and sat back. She said, After this I'd like to lie down on that couch.

He answered, First smart thing you've said.

The word *smart* was ever so slightly emphasized. With a MacArthur comes a certain amount of teasing.

His humor wasn't clipped and pushy, no New-York cut of a fast-talking knife. Nor was it what she had imagined as Midwestern wit: knee-slapping guffaws, as intellectual as euchre.

The door had several large and complicated locks on it. A screen beside it declared *Entry Denied*.

Why all these locks, she asked.

He said, One of the bonobos, Houdina, is a bit of an escape artist. For a while we had to keep trying out new systems.

Frankie said, She's the mom with the baby Id?

That's her, he said, Most times we had no idea how she did it. We caught her on video once, back when we were experimenting with metal keys. One of the observation cameras happened to be pointed straight at her. In the video, you see her lying in the sun, looking innocent, while the last human leaves for the night. She waits two minutes, then spits a researcher's keys out of her mouth and heads straight for the door to open it. The others follow.

How'd she get the keys?

When you're in the enclosure, they constantly groom you. Given all that touching, picking your pocket is easy.

Frankie asked, When they get out, are they dangerous?

He snorted, They wander around the Foundation, staring at the gorillas and orangutans and eating marigolds out of the flower beds. Adele heads to the basketball court by the parking lot, does free throws for hours. The family that raised her used to play basketball with her. Goliath goes to the kitchen. He drinks dishwashing soap so he can burp bubbles. The female bonobos love that, but it gives the vets conniptions.

He said, With the locks now, we're using speech recognition

combined with scanning the person's BodyWare. You need to check in with the office later to make sure your ID is in the security system.

He said, Ok Door, open.

He turned to her and added, The bonobos can't talk. Not yet.

The screen flashed green, the lock clicked and Stotts swung the door open.

Five

A month after her 11th birthday, Francine stayed home from school with an ache in her gut. She was surprised because she rarely got sick. Since her parents never complained of being ill, she'd had the impression that health was partly a question of will.

Working from home that day, her mom checked regularly on her daughter, taking her temperature and making sure she was hydrated. Francine's childhood memories of her mom were of her always facing Francine, her eyes warm. She called Francine "the Marvel," for her love of Marvel comic-books and the fact that she'd been born at all. Although Francine's parents had tried a long time, they'd had no other children.

Through the morning, the ache gradually increased, began to radiate down Francine's left leg.

Midmorning she realized she had to pee, the need abruptly urgent. She stumbled to the bathroom and shoved down her pants. A person spends a life making the same actions each day. The actions seem simple but are made up of millions of complex biological processes—protein uptake, glucose levels, phagocyte function—walking down the stairs, picking up the newspaper, breathing. At some point, one of these processes goes wrong and the machine of the body stumbles.

As she clenched her bladder, she felt something tug that shouldn't, a fleshy pull, a sharp pain.

Yowww, she yelled.

Her mom moved fast down the hall to her, calling questions even before she got there.

When she stepped into the bathroom, she saw the blood on Francine's underwear. She stopped. Standing there.

Oh, said her mom looking. And for a moment her face held nothing at all. All humanity wiped from it. That distance appearing for the first time.

Oh, she said, It's that.

*

Inside the interaction area, behind the locked door, there was no more drywall or ceiling tile. Instead it was all durable cleanable surfaces: concrete, plexiglass and steel.

Along the hallway stood the woman who normally fed the bonobos. This woman, the keeper, was putting cleaning solutions away on a cart. She was faced away and had EarDrums pumping out music so loudly Frankie could hear the papery beat from a distance of several feet. Her short permed hair combined with her general thickness made her look a bit like a Ukrainian shot-putter, the power in her upper body waiting to be used.

To warn her of their approach, Stotts leaned forward and waved his hand where she could see it.

The keeper jerked around to face them. She turned not in a startled girlie way, but more like a gun turret. Her eyes wide and dilated, her expression fixed. Ready to battle. Her meaty hands held out.

Then she recognized Stotts. She blinked and rolled her cart to the side for them to pass.

Stotts nodded his thanks and wheeled Frankie forward.

Frankie raised a palm in greeting.

The keeper made no response, eyeing her.

Moving down the hall, Stotts said, She's deaf. Because of that she's been in some scary situations. Make sure never to sneak up on her.

Frankie said, Deaf? As in deaf-deaf?

Yes ma'am.

No hearing implant?

No.

Why not?

Never asked, he said, She copes by always playing music loud enough that strangers will realize she can't hear them. Her version of a blind man's stick.

Frankie considered this, looking back at the keeper. She asked, What did you mean by scary situations?

He said, When people want to warn you about danger they do it through sound. A car's honk, a fire alarm, someone yelling *Heads up*. People expect sound to be enough, especially these days. She's had some surprises.

She grunted, She was hired because she knows sign?

Yep, he said, Most of the staff know fewer than 30 signs. She's the only one who's bilingual. Also she's great with the apes. She doesn't take any guff, not even from the chimps.

Stopping in the kitchen, Stotts opened a cupboard and took some food out. He said, Ok Kitchen, I'm grabbing a banana and a bag of gummy bears.

The fridge beeped and said, Thanks David, I've logged those items.

Frankie asked, Bellows charges for food?

He answered, Everything I use, including electricity, is taken out of my budget.

She said, Electricity?

Stotts said, It's a big cost these days and he tries to be innovative. You don't have to worry; your budget's ample.

She listened for resentment around this statement, but he simply moved her down the hall to the next door and said, Ok Door, open.

The door clicked open and he pushed her chair inside. He said, Technically the bonobos are allowed anywhere in this locked interaction area, but mostly we keep them here within the research room.

The far side of the room had a large glass window into the enclosure. Light poured in, the nearest bonobos turning around to stare at them. Behind the bonobos was the cement hill and climbing structure, part of the pond visible. The hill lay between the tourists and researchers, blocking their vision of each other, allowing both groups to feel as though they were alone with the apes.

Stotts parked her in the corner of the room, next to the whiteboard.

Stay here, he said. Once Goliath enters the room, don't talk and don't get out of the chair. That's important.

At Stotts' words, the upper torso of the bonobo avatar appeared on the wall, next to the window. Her hands moved quickly and fluidly, translating his words into sign.

Stotts said, He will take awhile to get used to you. We don't want to alarm him.

Stotts' words flashed by under the avatar's face as she made each gesture. The speed so fast it was hard to match the word to the gesture. Still the gestures were hypnotic; the impulse was to watch as though the motions would soon make sense, as though a language could be broken with a few minutes of concentration.

Why not? Frankie asked.

The avatar-translator signed those two words as the text appeared below her chest. For the word *not*, she shook both her head and fist *No*. At least Frankie could translate this one word.

Whoever had designed the avatar hadn't spent a lot of money on it. The nose was a bit pointed and the hands small for a bonobo, the gestures brisk and the expression businesslike. The overall feel was of a human dressed up in a bonobo costume, some makeup applied.

He answered, First off, ma'am, that'd be cruel. Secondly, while he's a gentle soul, it's wise to remember he has the physical power to rip our faces off our skulls. Third, to do research here, we need the cooperation of the bonobos.

He suggested, Think of him as your colleague. We're introducing you. Try to act polite and give a good first impression. If you need to communicate anything, write it out on the whiteboard.

Ok, Door open, he said and opened the door into the enclosure. He called out, Goliath, you want to come visit?

Frankie stared surprised through the door into the enclosure, the sense of open space, the smell of manure and fruit and cleaning products. The visible bonobos glanced over, nothing between them and her.

Goliath, Stotts called.

A bonobo popped his head up over the edge of the hill, considering them.

Stotts said, That new researcher I told you about yesterday is here. You want to meet her?

The bonobo didn't move forward.

You told him about me? Frankie asked.

Of course, he said, We ask permission. He agreed when he heard you're a woman. All the bonobos prefer women.

He turned back to Goliath and called, I'll let you look through the new *People*.

Goliath began to knuckle toward them.

She asked confused, Look through the new people?

People Magazine.

Nooo . . .

Oh yes, said Stotts, Goliath has a crush on Jade Pitt, always looks for photos of her.

Jade who?

The actress from that L.A. medical show.

Really? How do you know?

Stotts stepped away from the open door to empty his bag of all edibles—gummy bears and a banana—into a desk drawer.

He closed and locked the drawer while he said, Ma'am, bonobo love is not subtle.

She blinked to get rid of the image in her head.

Goliath was moving leisurely toward them, pausing occasionally to examine a milk crate or some food debris. His wandering path reminded her of the way a cat will approach to be petted, moseying along indirect enough not to lose self-respect.

She asked, How much English does he understand?

The avatar repeated her words in sign, her brow raised to signal a question.

Stotts looked to make sure Goliath was too far away to hear. He said, Hard to know. Goliath was raised pretty much as a human child in an American family. Had his own bed, wore clothes and drank tea. Raised with spoken English and sign. Then he grew up—got strong and, well, sexual—and the family gave their child to us.

Frankie looked at him, waiting for a better answer to her question.

He said, The language researchers don't want our anecdotes. They want randomized trials using sentences the bonobos have probably never heard before, no potential communication through gesture or glance. So they perform tests where they wear masks, sit motionless and ask in spoken English for the bonobos to put the ball in the microwave or the rock on the shoe.

And . . .

Stotts shrugged, If someone in a lab coat asks a human to do a task, the person will generally obey as well as they can. The bonobos, if they don't like the researcher or find the experiment boring, they'll walk away. I once saw a researcher ask Goliath to put a banana in his armpit and he just stared at her.

So what are the results?

Pre-school.

What?

He said, On average, for those like Goliath who were raised with English, their comprehension is roughly equivalent to a four-year-old's.

Frankie blinked at Stotts, then turned back to Goliath who was near the door. Compact as a gymnast, he ambled forward with a bear's rolling stride.

He said, And when they talk with us—using sign—their vocab is on par with that of a three-year-old.

Behind him, the avatar signed each of his words, her expression bland.

Goliath entered the room, all curious eyes and shiny black fur, a boy morphed with a Labrador.

Stotts put some equipment on the desk: a beat-up metal box, a thick rope and some large rocks. He asked, Can you shut the door please?

Goliath didn't glance at the avatar's translation, but closed the door and turned the knob to latch it. He climbed onto the desk next to Stotts (the comfort between them apparent) and stared with interest at Frankie. He rested his hands on his knees. They were huge and weathered, substantially bigger than a human's hands, the knuckles so clearly hinges.

She sat still in her chair. Sitting with a bonobo in the same room felt different from watching one through plexiglass. The lack of a barrier shifted everything.

Stotts took a banana out of the drawer, showed it to Goliath and placed it in the metal box.

At the sight of food, Goliath got an erection. His penis, the color of a pencil eraser, was so narrow and long that even when erect it drooped at the end. He looked Stotts in the eye while pouting, a hairy version of Marilyn Monroe's come-hither look.

Ma'am, Stotts explained, Bonobos reduce conflict through

sex. In captivity, the main source of conflict is food. After a while, the males get conditioned to react this way.

Frankie looked at the avatar, of course trying to pick out the gesture for *sex*, but the avatar signed too quickly.

He closed the metal box with the banana in it and began to tie the box shut with the thick rope.

Goliath's erection began to slump.

What about in the wild, Frankie asked.

Both Stotts and Goliath looked at her.

Stotts said, Perhaps I wasn't clear. Please don't talk around Goliath. He's not my pet. I can't control him.

He continued, To answer your question, in the wild, if they find a large fruit tree, they have sex before they eat. If they bump into a strange group of bonobos, both sides break large branches off trees and bellow, demonstrating how strong and tough they are. After that, the two groups mingle to have sex. Like with humans, sex calms everyone down, creates bonds.

Frankie had always believed in experimentation, checking each assumption to make sure it was true. Watching Goliath, she asked, Would he have sex with you?

At her speaking for the second time in front of him, Goliath's look became something more. Clear and piercing. His brow furrowed, he leaned forward, placing his huge hands on the edge of the desk.

She felt fear prickle up her spine. This might be a remarkably peaceful species, but that didn't mean it was without violence.

Stotts said almost under his breath, Goliath, she means no harm.

It was obvious he wasn't sure what Goliath would do. In spite of this, even though he could no more hold off Goliath than she could, he stepped into the space between them, placing his body in defense of hers.

He waited there, breathing, his hands loose at his sides.

Goliath looked from her to Stotts and back.

Frankie stayed very still.

There was a long moment. Then looking into Stotts' face, Goliath grunted and his expression eased. He took his hands off the edge of the desk.

Stotts absorbed the change before swiveling to her. He looked frankly baffled.

He said, Dr. Burk, if you speak again, I will escort you from the room; I will not allow you in here again.

He said sadly, I don't care if Bellows fires me.

He faced her like he'd faced Goliath, knowing that if it came to a fight, he was almost certain to lose, but facing her nonetheless.

She must admit he was growing on her.

He continued, I also want you to understand that you might be much smarter than me and an expert on many things I know nothing about, but in here, with him, until you get used to their rules, you're going to have to obey me. That clear?

She inclined her head, a subtle motion.

He studied her, then asked again, Are you sure?

She nodded more distinctly.

He looked at Goliath and then back at her.

He asked, Goliath, is it alright if she stays?

Goliath considered her for a long moment. His dark eyes narrowed, a bright pinprick of light in the back of each. Then he pumped one fist up and down. The avatar translated the sign into English, saying, Yes.

Stotts said, Thanks.

He said to her, Dr. Burk, I'm now going to talk a lot, so maybe I can answer your questions before you feel the need to ask them. To answer your earlier question, he'd have relations with anyone and anything, including this desk, if he got bored.

Goliath didn't watch the avatar's translation. The tension in his body had already evaporated, a personality who forgave. Now he just listened, letting his dark eyes move from Stotts' face to Frankie's and then back. Either he understood English perfectly or he wasn't that interested in what was being said. She tried to imagine how much a four-year-old would comprehend, a child almost ready to go to kindergarten.

Stotts finished tying the metal box shut. He glanced at her, checking she wasn't getting into more trouble, and said, My research here concerns the development of humanity, how we became what we are. Bonobos are similar to *Australopithecus*—body size, limb to torso ratio, and brain size. They even have lots of von Economo neurons, these neurons associated with higher order abilities like empathy, humor and self-recognition. Basically, they are as close as you can get to a living version of early humans.

She watched Goliath. His eyes were focused on the embroidered frog on her skirt. From his expression, she didn't think he liked her sense of fashion.

Stotts said, So I'm trying to teach him flint knapping.

She furrowed her brow in confusion.

He answered, Flint knapping—you know—making stone tools. By watching how Goliath masters the task, I hope to learn how the early humans might have done it.

With the box tied shut, he handed it to Goliath. Goliath tugged on the lid and then on the rope, a bit like a magician's assistant demonstrating the box couldn't be opened. Then, unlike the magician's assistant, he gnawed on the rope, his eyes half closed. After a moment he gave up, spat some rope fuzz out and wiped at his mouth.

Stotts said, Watch what I'm doing. If you can do it, you can cut the rope and get the treat.

For a moment, Frankie thought he was talking to her—the speed and intonation of his voice the same.

Goliath focused on Stotts' hands.

Stotts selected a rock from the desk, a smooth egg shape, a comfortable size for his hand. He said, This is my hammerstone. It's granite. A beauty. I found it in a riverbed near here.

She guessed this information was addressed to her.

The second rock he chose was bigger and uneven. He said, This rock is chert, a bit like glass. Easy to carve if you hit it right. Chert is what pre-humans used. There isn't a good supply around here, so I get most of my chert from Illinois.

Stotts sat down on the desk next to Goliath and slowly rotated the chert in his hands, examining it.

He said, Of course the big question is how the hominids found the right kind of rock to use, especially chert since it's fairly rare. We won't try to teach Goliath that part.

Goliath looked at the rocks and then at Frankie, perhaps checking what she thought of all this.

Stotts said, This will make a noise. Don't be startled.

She thought at this point he was probably talking to both of them.

Stotts balanced the chert on his thigh, then hit the edge of it with the egg-shaped stone, an easy motion of his arm. There was a *plink*, almost like pottery breaking, and a chunk fell off the bottom of the chert. Goliath's eyes narrowed.

The avatar said, *Yes.*

Frankie glanced at Goliath. He hadn't made any sign-language gesture. She didn't know why the avatar had spoken, what she was translating.

It's all in the angle, said Stotts.

He shifted the chert slightly, eyeing it, and then rebalanced it and hit it again. *Plink*, and another chunk cracked off and fell to the ground.

Even though Goliath still hadn't signed anything, the avatar repeated, *Yes.*

Watching the avatar speak made Frankie uneasy. Partly it was the image of a bonobo opening her lips to talk, but it was also the mouth and teeth. Whoever had designed this avatar had paid attention only to the outside, the shape and fur. Inside she was human. Each time she spoke, she parted her lips to reveal flat teeth inside a tiny human mouth.

Stotts rotated the rock and hit it again. He whittled it this way like wood, with ease. His hands moved confidently, shaping the chert. His body relaxed into this task, forgetting about her.

Meanwhile the avatar kept saying *Yes*.

Frankie realized the avatar must be translating his flint knapping motions into sign. Each time Stotts rocked his fist in the air before bringing the granite down onto the chert, she translated the fist-pump as *Yes*.

Yes, she said, *Yes, yes*. (Her intonation as flat as if she were on a call with her boss.)

The underlying mechanics of Stotts' hands and arms were very apparent—the working bones, the tendons pulling and muscles bunching, the fingertips pressed tight. The hands showcased in their capabilities. Frankie thought of a porpoise flashing through the water, of an ant carrying a pebble ten times its weight.

Like many modern humans, she didn't have any specialized skills with her hands. She felt the same mystified admiration as when she watched a person knit or play the piano or type (the way people used to before dictation got perfected), the hands shifting through their motions, filled with an eerie intelligence. Her own hands hung at the end of her arms, miraculous tools she'd never developed.

The image appeared to her of his hands holding his daughter's hand. She closed her eyes for a moment and, when she opened them, he was watching her.

He asked, You need anything?

She inhaled and shook her head no.

He watched her for another moment, then turned back to

the rocks, You're probably curious why I chose Goliath for this research. The female bonobos tend to refuse to work with a male researcher. So I started off with Petey, but after three months he couldn't get the hang of it. Now I've switched to Goliath. He's younger, smart and easy to work with. Right?

Goliath peeped his assent, his voice as high-pitched as a chipmunk's.

Stotts held up the final product, a sliver of a rock, an uneven but sharp shard. He cut the rope with three fast slices and pulled the banana from the box.

Ta-da, he said.

This time he put a few of the gummy bears into the box and began to tie the box shut. Goliath's interest was much greater at the sight of the sweets, his new erection a thumbs-up of gastronomic approval. He stared at where the gummy bears were even once they were hidden inside the box.

Stotts said to Goliath, If you can make a piece of rock sharp enough to cut the rope, you get the gummy bears. And if you just try for a while, I'll let you look through the magazine for Jade.

Goliath picked up the egg-shaped stone to use as a hammer. It sat so small in his hand he had to curl his fingers awkwardly to the side to get them out of the way.

Stotts took a bite of the banana, closing his eyes as he chewed. He said, Before Syria I never really appreciated fruit. Then I spent four years with prepackaged army meals—MREs. These days, they're 3-D-printed from soy or meat by-products, vitamins added. Since then, a banana . . . it seems like a miracle.

Goliath examined the selection of chert before choosing one, weighed it in his hand.

He didn't balance the chert on his thigh as Stotts had done, but held both chert and hammerstone out at the end of his arms, far from each other, before slamming them together straight-armed in front of him. The stones whacked together solidly, head on. The sound more of a *thunk* than a *plink*. No shards fell off. He narrowed his eyes, inhaled and tried again. He hit them together, harder each time. It must have hurt his palms to absorb each blow. In spite of his strength, only dust and tiny fragments came off.

The avatar translated this gesture each time as *Big. Big.*

Stotts said, You're getting a little better each day. Right?

Goliath peeped.

Stotts said to Frankie, He's working hard. No experience with tools or the applied physics of conchoidal fractures. It's possible there's some critical learning period when this can be mastered, the same as with language acquisition. If so, I'll try again with a juvenile.

She considered her question, stripped every extra word she could out of it and then jotted it on the whiteboard beside her for Stotts to see. At her movement, both Stotts and Goliath turned to watch, flat-eyed with suspicion.

How long he tried?

Her grammar like Tarzan's.

Stotts answered, A month.

Six

Bellows had given Frankie the only apartment on the Foundation's land—on the far side of the parking lot from the bonobos. The apartment had plain boxy furniture and there was a calendar pinned up behind the bathroom door showing shirtless women using wrenches for a variety of unlikely plumbing tasks. She assumed the last occupant was a janitor who'd been let go when the finances got tighter. With little notice before she'd moved in, the rooms smelled of new paint, but they hadn't been able to repair everything. Two of the stove's burners wouldn't light, the E-musement system wouldn't turn off and one of the awning windows in the living room wouldn't close itself when asked to. It only made a sad grinding noise, unable to shut that last half-inch.

In the early evening, through that window, she could hear the different species of apes calling or fighting in their enclosures, all those mysterious coughs and screams. She didn't know how to tell the species apart through their sounds, except that, among the full-throated barks and roars of the other species, the bonobos sounded like Chihuahuas.

Long before dawn, on the fourth morning she was there, the scream of some ape woke her. Maybe a chimpanzee.

Knowing she wouldn't be able to sleep anymore, she got out of bed, brushed her teeth and headed toward the bonobo building, pushing the wheelchair, walking so much more easily than even yesterday. The surgeon had liberally applied nanogels to each incision inside her to accelerate the healing.

When she got tired, she sat in the wheelchair and rolled herself along. Above, the stars glittered.

Her BodyWare ID had been entered into the security system so any door would unlock so long as she was within three feet of it when she said, Ok Door, open.

She moved through the building, all the way back to the room that contained the bonobos' sleeping chamber. The lights were in night-mode so they didn't click on at her entrance. She waited silently in her wheelchair, several feet back, staring through the metal bars. As her eyes acclimatized, she saw the cotton hammocks heavy with sleeping bodies, a few nests of hay and blankets on the floor. The smell was of straw and pee and musky bonobo. She became aware of the raspy slow breathing, some of them half-snoring. She sat there content, waiting for them to stir.

Maybe three minutes later, she felt the sneeze coming on.

Shit, she whispered and grabbed for her crotch, just enough warning to jam her fingers in under her skirt and underwear, as close as she could get to the incision.

Normally what is a sneeze? Nothing. A fast muscular movement of the guts, over in a second. Since the operation, it had become something different. She held on with both hands, braced into her hold as she would into a car crash.

She sneezed. Saw black with a sparkling of lights. The sensation of a slammed door.

She exhaled slowly, the air trickling out between her teeth. She'd been to all the pain clinics, knew the techniques. Her body cavity, she imagined, empty and peaceful, her internal organs back on 107th St., comfy on her bed, watching a video. She made the image vivid, then slowly drifted back from the scene, lowering the sound on the video, closing the door to the room.

Only as her vision cleared and focused did she notice two shiny points of light inside the cage. Eyes. One of the bonobos staring at her over the edge of a hammock, startled by the sneeze.

Looking more carefully now, she spotted several other motionless faces, watching her.

She let go of her crotch and sat up straighter, staring back.

This felt different from being in the research room with Stotts and Goliath, for in that case, with more humans than bonobos, the balance was shifted toward a human perspective. Here she was alone with the group of them, breathing the same air, only bars in the way. They considered her solemnly, their eyes bright.

After a few minutes, their attention began to drift. They groomed themselves or cuddled. One of the hammocks near her began to move. There were at least two bonobos in it. In the dark she couldn't tell which ones they were, but they began to French-kiss, tongue and lips engaged. The hammock swayed.

Soon after they were done, she heard a new movement. She searched through the darkness for the next couple having sex, then realized the sound came from behind her. Turning, she saw the keeper moving up the hallway, pushing a cart full of food. Through the windows, the sky was beginning to lighten.

The keeper stepped into the kitchen to rummage around for a while, the clatter of metal and pottery, the sink squealing on. Inside the chamber, Mama moved to the door, waiting. After a few minutes, the keeper stepped into the sleep chamber with a cup of coffee and a bottle of milk. She said, Ok Lights, on.

When the lights clicked on, she spotted Frankie and paused. She didn't look pleased. Perhaps this was the peaceful part of her day.

Frankie said, Morning.

The woman's only response was to say, Ok EarDrums, music on.

The music clicked on loud enough that the beat was audible from a few feet, her Bindi blinking, informing anyone looking she might not be able to hear them. Anyone would know to step into her line of vision, wave and speak where she could see the mouth—communicating the way she needed.

The keeper stepped past Frankie to unlock the door to the sleeping chamber.

Mama stood up and looked the keeper in the face. Not like a dog would greet its caretaker, all wiggling obeisance. Nor like a cat, tail up and demanding. No, Mama just stood there for a moment and looked, her eyes warm. On her shoulder sat Tooch, whining with hunger.

The keeper grunted and handed the bottle of milk to Tooch. He started nursing, businesslike as a machine.

In thanks, Mama rested her fingertips on the keeper's arm for a moment.

The keeper gave the cup of coffee to Mama, then closed the door and left the room. Mama sat down and took a slurp, her eyes closed. Concentrating on her coffee, bald and grey and scrawny, she resembled a female Gollum, ready to mutter about her precious ring.

Meanwhile the keeper wheeled a cart full of food into the enclosure. Her movements echoing off the plexiglass and cement, she began hiding fruit around the enclosure for the bonobos to try to find. She tucked bananas into crannies in the climbing structure, hid the mangos under the milk crates. Half the battle of keeping smart animals healthy in captivity was having them stay busy and interested in life. Through the metal door to the enclosure, the bonobos couldn't see where she was placing the food. They listened, heads cocked, eyes closed, clearly imagining each hiding spot. Mama was the only relaxed one, cradling her coffee.

When the food was all hidden, the keeper wheeled the cart back inside and cranked open the main door to the enclosure, giving the apes access to the food. All the bonobos stared into the sunlight, longing in their faces, but none of them moved. They turned instead toward Mama, watching her. The silence absolute.

Mama tilted back her cup, draining the last sip, then scratched her belly. Tooch climbed onto her back, looking outside.

Id, the youngest baby, dared to whine, breaking the silence.

The two grown females in the hammock next to Mama swiveled, giving the baby a piercing stare, their lips tight. Houdina hurriedly pulled Id to her breast to nurse her, hoping to keep her quiet.

Frankie guessed these two were Marge and Adele—the two who'd been having sex in the hammock earlier—although she couldn't tell which was which. Both were in their early thirties and powerfully built. In the file Frankie had on the bonobos, beneath the photos of these two was scrawled the phrase, *The Terrible Two*. Their eyes never wavered from Houdina and Id.

Houdina stayed very still, trying to look small, while Id nursed.

After a moment, once it was clear that everyone was obeying, Mama sauntered out into the enclosure, Tooch on her back. They watched her go. After a pause, Marge and Adele followed, checking over their shoulders to make sure no one else had moved—bank robbers leaving the scene.

The rest waited a good 20 seconds and then one by one they knuckled outside, letting time pass between each—first the eldest females, then the juveniles. Throughout the process, they watched the Terrible Two and Mama through the door, ready to freeze at the slightest disapproval.

By the time the adult males were allowed to leave the sleeping chamber, most of the biggest caches of fruit had been claimed.

*

Around the time Francine was 13, she'd begun to attract attention. She saw other girls and women walk along the street—taller and she thought much better looking—cutting through the crowds of people, utterly ignored. Instead it was to her that the men began to turn, toward her body as though it were waving at them, calling out some information. Something must have seemed different, something in the way she moved or held her face. Some days this signal seemed loud enough to carry across the street. Was it a statement, a question? It cut through whatever the males were in the midst of. Their heads swiveled, their eyes narrowed. Not all of them, but still a disturbing number.

Her body's message was understood in different ways by different men. If the man were white, most often he became still, his expression frozen. Whatever her body was saying, he seemed to hear it as an insult or perhaps a challenge. Most of these men didn't speak to her. She hurried by, head down. She was only 13 and they were grown men. She was accustomed to adults ignoring her, addressing her only to tell her the rules, where she could play or to not yell in the halls. The way these men looked at her now it was as though she'd done something—or was about to do something—very wrong.

Black men were less disturbing in general. For them, her body's call seemed more like a friend waving hi. They tended to examine her with appreciation, to call out in her wake, as if she'd given them a gift. She wasn't ready for any of this, wanted instead to play Parcheesi with her friends or read, but at least the black men's reactions were less upsetting. Perhaps her first thought along the lines of evolutionary strategies was that their actions were less likely to scare women off.

However, in her neighborhood, most of the men were white. She began to feel as though she were a passenger in her body, a fairly unwilling one, along for its ride.

Every year, her period got a little worse, the sensation she felt. At school, she spent time in the bathroom, leaning against the wall of a cubicle, her mouth slack. In class, her hearing at times receded, so the teacher had to call out her name repeatedly. Between classes, she walked tenderly, limping slightly, sliding her right foot forward like she was on ice. She watched the other girls in her class but never noticed them walking this way.

Her parents were getting divorced during this time, constantly rushing off to appointments with lawyers, accountants and mediators, leaving her alone. Divorce was not an outcome they'd ever imagined for themselves. Their locked-down expressions were tighter than ever, their movements nearly robotic.

Three times she tried asking her mother questions about her experience: was it normal, what strategies or products could she use? She never considered talking to her dad about it. Each time, her mother reacted the same way, her face hardening into a mask as her eyes skittered away from Francine's. Anger? Disgust? Guilt? It was hard to say.

Her mom clipped out the words—Take ibuprofen—and then she left the room.

The only fact Francine knew about her mom's reproductive experience was that right after giving birth, she'd had her uterus removed.

Francine never considered taking a sick day because she'd have to explain to her parents in what way she was sick and it was clear this subject was not to be discussed. Increasingly she was left wondering if there was something different about her body; if this was what the men on the street were sensing. She reasoned if total strangers could see it, then everyone at school must be able to also. During those adolescent years with her heightened social antennae, this idea terrified her.

When her friends asked her why she spent so much time in

the bathroom or why she walked so slowly, she tried to change the subject. If they persisted, she'd panic. She'd find herself yelling, saying it was none of their business. In Manhattan, she'd lost her polite Canadian voice. It sloughed off like a skin she'd outgrown. Still three of her friends were loyal, best friends since second grade. Instead of alienating them, the yelling made them more concerned.

So by the time she was 16, she'd had to master two new capabilities: a cold confident voice and an instinctive sense of what to say to make each person go away and leave her alone. The ability to see the secret weakness each person held: the lesbian sister; the father's likely affair; the tender dimpling of cellulite along the thighs. With her three ex-friends, she learned how to find this type of button and jab it hard, in public when necessary.

It became a strength she could use at any moment.

DAY 5

Seven

At nine A.M., she was lying down on the couch in Stotts' office, eyes closed, resting after a morning of watching the bonobos.

When Stotts walked in, he was talking to his Wrist-able. He said, Remind me to pick up Tess's meds on the way home.

At his entrance, the lights automatically clicked on. She cupped her hand over her eyes.

The Wrist-able's voice responded (the standard female voice, such an organized tone), On the way home, I will remind you to get Tess's meds.

Thanks, he replied to the device—his decency that ingrained—and then noticed Frankie in the room.

She jerked her chin toward the Wrist-able and asked, You a Philistine?

The Philistines were in the news a lot these days, individuals who believed technology had gone too far. The spectrum ran from those who turned off their access to the Quark for a few minutes on Sunday to diehards who refused body implantations and demanded paper notifications.

No, Stotts replied, I'm just cheap.

She asked, Who's Tess?

My daughter, he said.

The four-year-old? She's sick?

Asthma.

She took her hand away from her eyes, How bad?

With more floods and droughts, the levels of fungus, dust

and pollen were higher. Asthma had become a more serious diagnosis. About five years ago, there'd been that first "asthma storm" (a freak spring thunderstorm in Dallas followed by a westerly wind blowing pollen through the city); people who didn't even know they were allergic had difficulty breathing. Now the weather report commonly included recommended levels of pre-emptive medication, while fleets of freelance ambulances converged on the worst situations.

He said, There have been a few scares.

(Saying this, his voice was flat, less expressive than the Wrist-able's voice.)

Turning away to the closet, he began packing rocks into a bag. He said, Time for more flint knapping. You coming?

She said, It must be hard to see a kid sick.

He seemed to hear this. He paused for a moment, studying the rock in his hand.

He said to the rock, It's the worst. This morning . . .

He waved his hand in the air, cutting himself off and said again, You coming?

Yep, she said and got slowly to her feet.

He asked, You promise this time you won't talk in front of Goliath?

Yes. How'd you learn to flint knapp?

He said, It was a research project I designed as a postdoc. I spent a year in Tanzania, in the Olduvai Gorge, with two Fulbright scholars. We taught ourselves how to knapp.

She said, That's a long way to go to learn to slap rocks together.

He opened the door for her and took hold of her upper arm for the walk down the hall, his grip warm and no-nonsense.

He said, Tanzania was where humans first learned how to use tools. We wanted to master the same skills in the same landscape in order to explore how it might have happened.

He matched his step to her shuffle, pacing along as cere-

moniously as in a wedding. She was moving faster than yesterday. She remembered a cartoon she'd once seen of a snail riding on the back of a turtle, calling out *Wheeee!*

He said, Many fields hypothesize about why humans have
managed to monopolize so many of the planet's resources. You
evolutionists concentrate on the body: opposable thumbs,
bipedal stance.

In an attempt to move at her speed, he tried adding a pause
to his step, his right foot catching in mid air, a slow-motion
limp. He said, I concentrate on tools.

She eyed the goal of the locked door at the end of the hall
and said, Chimps use tools. Are they human?

Ma'am, chimps haven't progressed past sticks and stones in
a million years. Humans have technology that ratchets upward.
We've moved from the cordless phone to implants in a few
decades. I specialize in how we began to learn to do that.

He said, With Goliath, I want to find out if bonobos can
master the first tools and if they have the precursor skills for
ratcheting.

Her incision was radiating heat upward. Information
about pain was transmitted along the same type of neurons as
heat; this was why pain frequently was confused with temperature: the cold slice of a knife or the burning of a wound.
The chemical compound in chili peppers activated the pain
sensors, making the tongue burn, not a flavor at all. Simplify,
simplify was the body's motto, each structure serving many
purposes.

She said, You got a big grant for this one, huh?

He grunted, Only way I can pay for my share of the food
costs.

Frankie had her head down as she walked, breathing
through her mouth. His hand round her arm was a comfort,
solid as a railing. She asked, So what happened in Tanzania?

Her need to think hard, to distract herself, was part of the reason for her success. Other researchers spent time watching TV or laughing with friends. She hunched over her work, taking notes, fingering her bottles of pills.

He said, The two Fulbrights and I, we learned to knapp stone knives and then used the knives to butcher scavenged meat, trying to figure out how pre-humans did it.

Scavenged meat?

Research shows pre-humans didn't so much bring down prey as fight for access to a kill long enough to slice off some meat and run.

Wait a sec, she said, They weren't hunter and gatherers, but vultures and gatherers?

It's the current theory.

Her eyes flicked from left to right. Her mind beginning to tick. She asked, What about the gathering part, finding tubers and berries. Some Tanzanian tribesman teach you?

He shook his head, We couldn't find any tribesman who knew enough anymore. The local tribes specialize in the tourist trade now or they live in government housing. So we learned from books, researching which plants were edible. In terms of scavenging, we practiced our butchering on the carcasses we found, mostly impalas and gazelles.

He added, And one elephant.

Serious? she asked.

It had been shot by poachers a few days earlier.

She asked, A few days in the hot sun?

She imagined the rotting elephant, Fulbright scholars running up to it holding sharp rocks.

Yes ma'am, he said. It took us two days to figure out how to cut through the hide. Like trying to slice through a tire.

Can you describe the smell?

He glanced at her, There were maggots.

She said, The research get published?

Scientific American. It won a Goetner, launched my career.

I think the clincher was that we finished the year off with a re-enactment, a week of scavenging and gathering.

She was no longer thinking about how she felt, You *ate* the maggoty elephant?

Oh no. Too many potential diseases and parasites. Also we legally weren't allowed to since most of the species were endangered. We simply weighed what we were able to hack off within 90 seconds—the average amount of time scavengers have at a kill. We calculated the caloric intake, balancing that against our output in searching for the meat.

She tucked her chin in. Thinking this hard, she walked more easily. She said, You were trying to get an accurate energy assessment of the lifestyle without allowing for the costs of parasites and disease?

He said, This was years ago. At the time those calculations had not—

Did you have guns?

Of course, he said.

She said, Then you would have been able to head directly toward what you were interested in, instead of sneaking up on it. No need to be watchful or sprint for safety. That would save a lot of—

Impatient with the speed of her words, she interrupted herself, For that matter, do you know how well their senses functioned? If they had, say, a better sense of smell and worse vision, the food they headed for would have been different from what you headed for. That food would be at a different distance, containing a different amount of calories.

In the years since his study had been published, he'd heard all these objections, but never so quickly and all from one person.

She stopped, waiting for his response.

Her gaze reminded him of one specific moment in Tanzania. Before dawn, he'd stumbled out of bed to walk the

20 feet from his tent to the poop-tent, scrubbing his face, when a lioness stepped out on the path in front of him—300 pounds of muscled predator heading home after a night of hunting, panting in the early morning heat. She jerked her head toward him, startled by the sight of a man in his boxers. By the time he could register what he was seeing, she'd shifted to a stop.

This was the moment he thought of, this eternal moment, their eyes locked, while they stood there, considering the distinct possibilities of the next instant.

Then she snorted out her nose and walked off, curving through the underbrush.

Frankie regarded him like the lioness had—not a predatory look, for the lion had not stalked him. A simple look of surprise at how foolish he'd been.

That whole year in Africa, he'd felt so alive, aware of his surroundings and his body's physical struggles. He thought about those days a lot. They felt so much simpler than now (this morning his daughter had struggled to breathe, the medication's speed measured in inhalations, his wife's fear turning to fury and him cradling his own helpless hands).

He answered Frankie with honesty, We did not control for those variables.

She paused, then asked, Given that, what conclusion do you feel you can draw from your research?

He could have used archaeological jargon to make the findings sound more precise or impressive, could have mentioned how many times the study had been referenced in other researchers' papers. Instead he stated in three simple words what he knew was true, the concept that the year of striving in the heat and sun had ironed into his body, an understanding deeper than any fact he had learned in school.

He said, Pre-humans were tough.

She blinked and went very still. Her expression internal.

She said, Laughter can rip my stitches.

He studied her, her complexion and stance. She'd managed the hallway more easily than yesterday. He'd never had a chance to threaten the lion.

He said, Ma'am, you disobey me again while we are with Goliath, I'll make you guffaw.

Her eyes sharpened with attention.

Ok Door, open, he said and helped her into the interaction area.

Eight

Each time Frankie opened the door to her Foundation apartment, the E-musement system clicked on along with the lights. The system still cued to the past tenant's preferences, her EarDrums broadcast the avatar's voice at a volume loud enough to make her jump.

The broadcast itself was on the living room wall, a face the size of a platter addressing her in a concerned tone while lines of text scrolled along the bottom in different directions, shimmering and insistent: the stock market, local promotional offers, breaking news.

Luckily the avatar that the past tenant had selected was not like his bathroom calendar of shirtless women with wrenches. Instead, she was in her 40s, fully clothed and had kind eyes.

Frankie's own media preferences didn't load, perhaps some basic incompatibility. Judging from the general repair of the apartment, this home system might be a bootleg. Or maybe the problem was with her implant, which was well over six months old and beginning to have version-incompatibility problems with devices outside of her BodyWare.

Those first few days, she kept asking her Bindi to turn the E-musement off. Each time there'd be a pause, then her EarDrums would announce the system wasn't responding. By the third day, the broadcast was bothering her so much she spent time searching for a physical override switch somewhere in the apartment—as though any system had such a switch anymore.

So, instead she turned the sound off on her EarDrums. The avatar continued to mouth important information, but soundlessly now. From the visuals it was apparent most of the stories concerned extreme weather events and cyberattacks. Perhaps these reflected the past tenant's searches, or maybe they were actually the major news of the day. Frankie studied the scrolling ads and product placements to see if they were individualized or not. If they were, then the janitor had been interested in weight loss, dietary fiber and local massage parlors. The avatar was shown drinking from a Metamucil cup and holding a Weight Watchers pen.

Each morning, as soon as Frankie snuck her feet out of bed to place them on the floor, the avatar appeared, soundlessly saying good morning and then starting on her roundup of news. Her jaw chewed on the words, high-def images flashing behind her. The only way Frankie could turn the screen off was to take her feet off the floor and curl back up in bed.

In the end, her solution was to turn away from the wall as much as she could, keeping her back to the giant kindly woman who mouthed muted words of warning about extreme rainfall and widespread cyber-breaches. Sometimes when there was a large movement, Frankie glanced over involuntarily to catch the image of a palm tree bowing sideways in the wind or the swirling logo of Duke Energy with the word *Blackout* just below it.

*

Resting on the couch in Stotts' office, there wasn't much to look at. The room was empty except for the necessary. His jacket hung up, all clutter put away, the chair pushed into the desk, the result nearly as impersonal as a hotel room. Perhaps he'd learned this sort of order in the Reserves.

One of the only clues that this was Stotts' office was the Moments™ cube on the desk. The cube was bright and changing. In the dark office, Frankie's eyes were drawn to it. Each

Moment was a photograph that shifted to video for an instant, just enough time to show the flicker of water, the start of a gesture. The simple trick of a photo starting to laugh was endlessly effective—as if by staring hard enough, any scene could be brought to life.

Stotts' wife was good looking, honeyed hair and a long neck. Even if Stotts hadn't mentioned she was British, Frankie thought she might have guessed—eyebrows raised, mouth pursed, that BBC look of mild dismay. The Moments showed a typical plot: a few vacation photos of the young couple followed by an image of Stotts kissing the bride; the now-wife grinning sideways showing off her swollen belly, then Stotts cupping the newborn closer in his arms. In every shot with the daughter, as she grew from baby to toddler to child, she stole the scene. Tess had big eyes and she stared out of the image deadpan. Her only motion was her mouth working on her binky.

In Stotts' office, Frankie rested, staring at the Moments of Tess. Since these images were probably taken using the Lenses of her parents, through their eyes, Frankie could see exactly how Tess looked at her parents.

From inside the image, Tess stared that way at her.

*

Moving down the hall, Frankie asked Stotts, Have wild bonobos been observed to use tools?

He answered, Nope.

She asked, But wild chimps have?

Yup.

Then how come you aren't doing this research with chimps?

Stotts answered, Two reasons, ma'am. First off, chimps have killed people. I really wouldn't enjoy sitting next to them, teaching them how to make knives.

She grunted. Each day she walked more easily, but still appreciated his hand round her arm.

He added, Second, I need a species that's likely to cooperate with each other.

She asked, Chimps don't cooperate?

He asked, You know the classic experiment in cooperation?

She tilted her head.

He said, A big pile of food is put on a tray in front of a cage with two animals in it. The tray's too far away to grab, but there's a rope looped through the tray's handles. Both ends of the rope are placed within reach. The rope isn't tied to the tray, so if only one animal pulls, it will snake free. To get the food, they have to pull together. Elephants and gorillas master it quickly, as well as four-year-old children.

She asked, And chimps?

Stotts reached the locked door to the interaction area. He said, Ok Door, open.

Ushering her through the door, he answered, The stronger chimp fights the other chimp away from the rope in order to yank on it on his own. When the rope comes free, the stronger chimp screams in frustration and starts beating on the weaker chimp.

Every time?

After a few trials, they begin to understand. Given the choice of a teammate, some of them will pick one who'll help. However even then, as soon as the food is pulled close enough to reach, both chimps drop the rope to grab the food, racing to eat more than the other.

What about the bonobos?

First they have sex, then they cooperate. Every time. It doesn't matter who the partners are: younger and older, more powerful and less, male and female. Once the food is within reach, there's no grabbing. The videos are great. A juvenile can actually reach into an adult's mouth for a piece of fruit and the adult will keep its mouth open, waiting for the juvenile to figure out which piece it wants.

Stotts opened the door to the research room. The lights clicked on and the bonobo avatar appeared on the wall. Frankie shuffled forward, needing to sit, her legs trembling.

Stotts said, The results are so consistent, that one set of researchers actually tried to get the bonobos *not* to cooperate.

Behind him, the avatar translated, her face impassive, the words flashing by just below her face.

Frankie lowered herself into the seat. Although she worked hard not to show any weakness, Stotts didn't let go until she was seated.

She asked, How?

Stotts said, They put one bonobo in a cage and another in a second cage, both cages connected to a common room. They piled the food up in the common room, then opened the door to the room for only one of the bonobos.

Frankie watched the avatar, trying to pick out individual gestures. The sheer speed blended it all together into one blurred motion, the visual equivalent of street Spanish. At this point, the only gestures she could recognize were *Yes*, *No*, *Big* and *Bottle*.

Stotts opened the door to the enclosure and called out, Hey Goliath, want to come down? I downloaded the new issue of *Vogue*.

From high in the climbing structure, Goliath began to descend.

Frankie asked, And what happened?

Stotts said, Well, the first bonobo would move toward the food, excited. Then the second bonobo—the one who was still locked in—would squeal and the first would knuckle right past the pile of food, to open the door for the second, without snagging even one piece of fruit on the way.

She imagined the scene Stotts was describing. She pictured the bonobo hurrying over to open the door: a bonobo version of Jeeves, or maybe Jesus. She pictured Miss Manners in a hairy sexual form.

She asked, Ok, so what does cooperation have to do with flint knapping?

He stood by the door, watching Goliath wander closer. He said, Deposits of rocks that you can use for flint knapping are rare, yet archaeologists have found the stone tools everywhere. To travel that far, the tools or rocks must have been traded many times between different groups.

He looked back at her and said, Chimps would never trade. If they met a new group, they would attack it.

She asked, And bonobos?

They'd have sex with the new group and then give the tools away.

Goliath knuckled in.

Stotts said to Frankie, Alright, time to be quiet.

She nodded.

Goliath climbed onto the desk, greeting Stotts with a happy peep. With Frankie, he just looked at her, a level considering gaze.

Stotts asked, You ready to try?

Goliath pumped his fist in the air.

The avatar translated, Yes.

Stotts sat down beside Goliath and demonstrated the correct knapping technique. Holding a slab of chert on his thigh, he struck it with the hammerstone. *Plink* and a chunk of rock dropped off, as easily as if it had been only glued in place. The glassy inside of the chert was revealed. He turned the slab and hit it again, carving it, his blows as relaxed as a blacksmith's.

Although Goliath watched the knapping (flinching a little at each *plink*), he also at times studied Stotts and Frankie and the box with the banana in it.

Once the shard was carved, Stotts used it to cut the rope and open the box.

When Stotts started to eat the banana, Goliath held out his palm and flexed his fingers in a give-me gesture.

No, said Stotts. This is my treat, Goliath. You know that. I earned it. You can get a treat too, but only if you carve a rock like I did.

Goliath studied Stotts' expression. Bonobo society wasn't based on individual ownership or the ethic of hard work. There was no bonobo meme for scientific testing, no framework to understand why Stotts would want to withhold the food.

Goliath flexed his fingers again, holding out his hand.

No, said Stotts, busy shaking his head.

In response, Goliath moved his eyes. It was a stagey eye movement, the kind used in silent movies—the hero widening his eyes and pointing them to the closet where the villain hid. Goliath looked not at the banana, but at the rock shard and then back to Stotts' eyes.

Nope, repeated Stotts, My banana.

Perhaps Frankie noticed Goliath's eye movement and Stotts didn't because she wasn't allowed to talk, wasn't distracted by speech.

She grunted to get Stotts' attention and then pointed. Pointing is a gesture that first appears in humans at 12 months old, a developmental milestone: the baby straightening the index finger and aiming it, curling the other fingers and thumb in, as instinctive a gesture as it was for a hunting dog to freeze its whole body into a point, one paw to its chest, shivering in its focus.

While Stotts hadn't understood Goliath's eye flick, he comprehended Frankie pointing at the shard.

What, Stotts asked, He wants the . . . ? Ohh. Goliath, no, you can't have the shard. You have to make your own. You know that.

Goliath considered this statement, then leaned forward

to try to pull open the drawer that contained the rest of the food.

Stotts blocked the drawer with his hip. He said, No, Goliath.

Goliath stared back, baffled.

It was possible that—while Stotts was attempting to teach Goliath how to bang rocks together—Goliath was wondering why humans were rude.

Nine

It wasn't until 12th grade (the teacher drawing on the chalkboard the chemical structure of gibberellic acid, while Francine leaned forward to cough vomit onto the linoleum) that she was finally taken to see the school nurse.

The nurse, a kindly round woman named Mrs. McGonickle, took her temperature. When the thermometer beeped and showed no fever, she asked Francine if she'd eaten anything questionable today.

Francine shook her head and whispered she was going to vomit again. Mrs. McGonickle got a bucket and sat beside her, rubbing her back while Francine heaved. Her hand was warm and didn't pause at any of the sounds. Since Francine hadn't eaten for two days, the size of the bucket was a bit optimistic. Afterward Mrs. McGonickle handed her a wet paper towel and took the bucket away. Her actions said she'd seen this all before and that nothing in the world of illness bothered her. She returned, sitting there quietly for a moment before she asked, Sugar, what's wrong?

Francine looked at the woman's face and felt such a yearning to be a child again, to confess the problem and have an adult deal with it. The nurse was a medical person, perhaps talking to her would be allowed.

For once she tried to describe what she felt inside.

Color has a large and specific vocabulary, *blue, cobalt, topaz.* Using these words, a person can describe an exact wavelength of light with little effort or imagination, the listener able to glimpse the experience. Hearing, touch, taste and smell also have their own vivid descriptors. *Loud. Sandy. Sweet. Musky.* Pain, on the other hand—not considered one of the senses—has few words all its own. Like a beggar, it is forced to borrow concepts and phrases from the others; *sharp, white-hot* or *pressure.* In a way, this lack is understandable, since most people experience this sensation only rarely. However when pain does arrive, it feels so familiar. Time stops. Language melts away, the experience expressed through motion and sound: rocking, moaning and clutching. In the face of pain, each of us becomes a mute animal, suffering and alone.

Later in her life, Francine would learn to describe what she was feeling through comparing it to an event that resulted in a similar level of pain: *a paper cut* or *fractured bone* or *amputation.* She memorized the Stanford Pain Scale so she could select from its descriptors: *occasionally absorbing, normal lifestyle curtailed,* or *temporary personality disorders.*

However with the nurse, she had not yet developed such techniques. Her sentences sounded like a child's. She said, Sometimes my gut hurts, deep inside. Sometimes I vomit.

Mrs. McGonickle leaned forward, her face concerned. This close, Francine could feel warmth radiating off her like from the side of a horse. She wanted to rest against the thick side of this woman, let go her worries.

Aww Sugar, said Mrs. McGonickle, How often does this happen?

Once a month, admitted Francine.

The woman's eyes refocused. She asked cautiously, From your period?

Yes.

And McGonickle sat back.

Francine found herself leaning into the space the nurse had left.

McGonickle sucked her teeth, focusing out the window.

She asked, Do the women in your family make a big deal about their periods?

Francine answered, I think my mom had a hard time with them.

McGonickle said, Pain is something that can be suggested. You can make it bigger or smaller with your mind. Try to think about your period in a different way. Expect it won't be so painful and you'll find the pain will diminish.

Her expression was kind, but her concern had left. She had the answer and was no longer worried.

At her words, Francine closed her eyes. She managed to ask, Isn't there something else I can do?

If it really bothers you, said McGonickle, You could alternate ibuprofen and aspirin every two hours. But you don't need that. It's all just suggestion.

The nurse added, Wait til you try giving birth. And she barked out a short laugh.

From this point on, Frankie considered Caesarean section the only civilized answer to labor.

However, thinking about the nurse's words afterward, she realized she'd been offered a potential solution. She got several books on the power of suggestion and read them with her whole heart. Each night before sleep, she chanted to herself that she would feel less pain. She imagined herself in specific detailed scenes, the slight cramp her gut would feel, the sensation only in her lower pelvis. She fell asleep each night holding the details in her head. She had, it must be said, real hope.

But right on schedule, her period arrived and she woke in mid stride halfway down the hall, running for the bathroom. The burning was back, filling most of her torso. On the toilet, she clenched her bladder and something inside disengaged, a frozen heat billowing outward.

She learned always to carry ibuprofen and aspirin in her

bag. During her periods, she drank as little liquid as possible so she wouldn't have to pee. She reached for items with her left hand so she wouldn't feel that strange tugging along the right side of her ribs.

Ten

One of the Moments in the cube on Stotts' desk was of his daughter being read a book—paper books mostly reserved these days for children before their first implant. Tess was about three years old, a stuffed animal over her shoulder, her eyes big and thinking. This was the kind of image Frankie forced herself to look at, examining the child, memorizing details, checking her own emotions.

(People tended to assume that Frankie, a woman in her thirties, would yearn to hold any nearby baby. They'd plop their infants into her arms, saying, Isn't he the cutest. Once, handed the baby while the mom ran to the bathroom, Frankie pinched the cheek hard. When the mom came back, Frankie handed the screaming baby back, holding her palms up as though confused.)

In the photo of Tess, there was no sign of asthma except her mouth was open, the pacifier clamped between her teeth like a cigarette.

The next Moment was a more recent one of Tess and her parents by a lake. Tess was standing while her parents crouched down on either side of her, posing. She was staring upward at something—a bird? A kite? Her mother looked at Tess, Stotts stared at his wife.

Frankie heard someone in the hall and rolled over on the couch, turning away from the images.

*

Frankie continued to sit outside for much of each day in the tourist area, observing the bonobos through the plexiglass.

Each time they were fed, she took notes on who mated with whom. Anytime more than one bonobo wandered behind the concrete hill out of sight, she used her Lenses to call up the video of the far side of the hill. She didn't want to miss even one mating. Within a few weeks she'd be able to assess if the bonobos really were random in their mating choices.

However, every once in awhile, the video from the far side of the hill went dark for a few seconds. She didn't know if this was a difficulty with the cameras, the power or feed, but she sent a sharp note to Bellows to find and fix whatever was going wrong. This wasn't the only problem at the Foundation. The longer she was here, the more she noticed the disrepair and outdated equipment—the flickering lights in the back hallways, the slow speed of data, the broken vehicles parked behind the building. Multiple coats of paint attempted to camouflage a clear lack of funding.

Perhaps these problems were specific to the Foundation or maybe this was typical of the whole Midwest. The cars outdated, the people heavier. Used to Manhattan, she examined this foreign land.

Meanwhile she did the best she could at her work, spending the whole day watching the bonobos, absorbing everything she could. By this point she'd learned their names as well as where each stood in the group hierarchy. The females ranged from Mama down to Houdina. Below the females came the juveniles and then the males. Houdina was the newest member of the group right now and was low enough in the strata that sometimes she appeared on par with the males.

One of the best ways to see the hierarchy was to observe who got groomed. Mama was groomed so often that Frankie began to suspect this was at least partly the reason for her baldness, others constantly tugging on what little hair remained. Houdina, on the other hand, was furry and even though she spent considerable time grooming others, she didn't get groomed often in return.

The hierarchy was demonstrated also in how treats were passed around. The biggest treat was the book of honey, hidden somewhere in the enclosure each morning, a few of its pages painted with honey. (The Foundation had received a truckload of books from the local library when it closed.) The daily book kept them busy and alleviated boredom. No matter which bonobo found it, under the attentive gaze of the Terrible Two, that bonobo would soon offer the book to Mama. The others would sit nearby waiting while Mama peeled apart the sticky pages, then ran the back of her knuckle across the honey and sucked on her finger. If Mama at any point felt the interest of another bonobo—especially one of the males—was too high, she would rest her eyes on the offender and Marge and Adele would turn to look. The offender would freeze, a nervous grin on his face, until Mama and the Terrible Two looked away and then he'd creep backward.

Frankie had begun to think of bonobo society like a group of high-school cheerleaders and bashful wallflowers locked together in a room for years. Yes, physical violence was unlikely and everyone had good manners, but status was still wielded like a stick.

After Mama had finished with the book and walked off, Marge and Adele took their turns scraping off honey, followed by the other females, then the juveniles. The males were left with the tattered remains.

Today Frankie noticed Mama taking an especially long time with the book, which was bigger than the books they normally got. Even after Mama had consumed as much honey as she wanted, she continued wiping off the pages, then scrubbing her knuckle clean on the ground. Once she had a page clean, she swiveled the book around to study the page one way and then another. From where Frankie sat, she could see there were photos on the pages, but not what the photos showed.

When Mama finished examining a page, she'd peel open the next one and scrub its honey off on the ground. The other bonobos watched, not making a sound.

At one point, as Mama angled the book, Frankie saw the title along the spine: *Hairstyles of the Last Century.* She watched Mama consider the photo, her eyes narrowed.

Then someone flicked the back of Frankie's head. She turned to look at the teenager next to her—so absorbed in whatever was displayed on his Lenses, he didn't realize he'd hit her. He had his hand up where his Bindi could see it and was flicking his index finger repeatedly to the right, paging through different files or sites. Frankie could only assume he'd Quarked the word *bonobo.* His finger froze as he found something interesting. His eyes focused up and to the right as he breathed through his mouth. He didn't glance at the species in front of him.

Of course with people constantly gesturing and talking this way, from a distance it could be hard to discern who was on a business call and who was delusional. This was partly why Bindis had been invented (the other reason was of course to allow corporate logos to be displayed even as technology disappeared into the body). Now, late at night, if a strange man was walking toward Frankie on the street talking to himself and gesturing, she could look for a blinking Bindi or a speck of light in the upper right corner of his eyes to know whether or not she should cross to the other side of the street.

From a few feet away, especially in the dark, the tiny screen on the Lenses made a person's eyes appear to have a strange luster. *Bright-eyed* used to mean a person was interested in the world. Now it was slang to mean the person was texting.

Behind the teenager were a lot of younger children slapping buttons on the sign-language kiosk.

From repeated use, some of the kiosk buttons didn't work anymore. This—along with the fact that most of the children could only reach the first two rows—meant the bonobo avatar said the same words over and over. *Stick. Human. Banana.* Perhaps the verbs were higher up.

The bonobos kept their eyes away, ignoring the avatar's apparent Tourette's.

There were kiosks scattered around the Foundation. Some were sign-language translators for the chimps, gorillas and orangutans. Other played short educational videos narrated by thoughtful voices. None of these videos, however, were allowed to play more than a second or two before a passing child would slap a different button, starting a new video. The children weren't interested in the education, only in control of the device. One of the kiosks near the Snack Shack had been broken by repetitive use. Every time Frankie walked by, even late at night when the Foundation was closed, it was lecturing the park bench in front of it about the geographic range that orangutans used to have when they lived in the wild.

Mostly only young children played with the kiosks since those over eight tended to have implants. These older children stood apart instead, their Bindis blinking as they gestured, playing an invisible guitar or gunning down unseen terrorists.

*

During the bonobos' pre-lunch orgy, while the tourists fled, Frankie moved back and forth in front of the glass, getting up on her tiptoes or lowering herself down to the ground, doing her best to see what all the genitals were doing. She kept a breathless running commentary for her Bindi to note down. However there were so many different acts, all occurring so quickly and in such a variety of positions, it was difficult to be certain which bonobo was connected with which set of genitals, much less if the interaction was traditional enough to potentially result in pregnancy.

Afterward she stood there just as breathless as they were, except while they were satiated, she was irritated. It was likely she'd missed important information.

She cocked her head, looking them over. She was wasting time and hated that feeling.

With so much action happening at the same time, she needed to focus her attention. In terms of what she cared about, the only copulations that mattered were those that could result in pregnancy.

A male and a female.

Actually, she could get more specific than that. She needed some way to figure out which females were ovulating.

Lucy knuckled by her, her sexual swelling wobbling behind her. This pink flesh advertised to the males that she could be ovulating, however the swelling was inflated for a majority of each month—like any good advertising, not entirely false, just exaggerating the truth. Frankie needed to figure out how to pinpoint the actual ovulation, then she could narrow in on which females to pay attention to each day.

For the rest of that afternoon, she found herself staring at the females' swellings. When the females sat down, the swollen balloon of skin would puff out like a pillow beneath them. She regarded this tight cushion, wondering how to see past it.

*

A little after lunch, the tourist area mostly deserted, a six-year-old sat on the ground near Frankie, his forehead against the glass, plumes of his breath appearing on the surface. He sat there quietly, staring into the enclosure, one hand on the glass, his mother on the bench behind him, talking on a business call, flipping through information on her Lenses.

In the enclosure, the one-year-old Id began to ease her way toward the child.

Although the boy and Id were only a few feet from Frankie, they ignored her. She tended to sit still enough that sometimes people tried to step in front of her as though she were just a concrete stanchion.

The bonobos seemed to treat her a bit like a stanchion too. If they knuckled up anywhere close to the glass, it was likely to be in front of her. Probably since she moved so little and had been here for days, she didn't make them as nervous as the other humans who called and rapped on the glass, trying to attract attention. Or maybe it was because, instead of staring mostly at her Lenses, she actually watched them.

Occasionally she caught one bonobo or another studying her. They felt no compulsion to turn away, looking as long as they wanted, their dark eyes concentrated.

Id edged closer to the boy, Houdina whining nervously in the background. The boy stayed seated, his hand on the glass. Id knuckled closer and then closer until she rose to her feet in front of him, peering into his face. Both the child and Id barely breathing.

Id examined the tourist area for danger, then extended one hand up to flatten it against the boy's, a single pane of plexi between their fingers.

There was a pause for sheer pleasure on both sides of the glass.

After a moment, the boy moved his other hand onto the plexi.

Id considered this, then flattened her hand against his.

A slow second passed with the two staring into each other's eyes.

The boy removed his hands. Id copied him.

Gravely they began the game of patty-cake.

Meanwhile the boy's mother flicked through the documents on her Lenses, discussing the pricing of different fonts.

DAY 8

Eleven

At 5 A.M., Frankie sat at the table in the apartment and opened a box of saltines by the flickering light of the muted broadcast. For over a decade, she hadn't been allowed food with gluten or salt. The operation she'd had removed all symptoms permanently, an average of 85 times out of 100. Before this, statistics had been against her, the doctors stating the probabilities in a serious voice, as though she gave a damn about those 99 other patients.

Placing a cracker in her mouth, she closed her eyes, inhaling through her nose. Her joy crisp and salty on her tongue. Behind her, the avatar on the wall mouthed her silent words.

Reaching for another cracker, she fumbled the box slightly and it fell to the ground. She eased herself off the chair to retrieve it. While she was on her knees, the avatar's wall suddenly went bright. She glanced up, assuming a malfunction.

It took her a moment to realize she was looking at a field. The field had furrows, in the background a wire fence, a single tricycle on its side and a sun-beaten house. The confusing detail was the color of the soil, close to the light beige she associated with hotel hallways.

Gattonville read the title.

Gattonville could be in so many different states. A lot of the south, as well as California, had declared federal emergencies because of the drought. Any broadcast in a restaurant or bar (the audience too large to conform to everyone's preferences) had to revert to actual news and within a few minutes would play some story about the drought. These stories so pervasive, she'd wondered at times if they might be subsidized by agribusiness in hopes of justifying the constantly rising price of food.

She had a basic dislike of E-musement broadcasts since with her work she spent so many hours staring at a digital display of some kind or another. Other people seemed different. Even while they were working on their Lenses, muttering and gesturing, they directed their eyes toward the broadcast on the wall, seeking out as much digital information as possible, as though it fed them in some way.

She picked up the box of crackers. On the wall, the scene had shifted to what looked like a New England forest, a man in a lab coat scooping up some soil and then holding it out for a close-up, the earth a rich brown color. His hand squeezed the soil into a moist clump, then rolled it between his fingers, letting chunks fall. A lab report showing the percent of moisture in the soil and the Latin names of unicellular life scrolled across the screen too fast to read.

She threw her arm over the seat of a chair and levered herself up. So many different muscles were needed to get to her feet. Even with minimally invasive surgery, so much inside had been what the doctors called *insulted*. Breathing hard, she found her eyes on the broadcast.

A hand was now scooping up some of the beige-colored dirt. The fingers squeezed, then let go. The dirt did not clump. The analysis began to scroll across the screen, the moisture content at zero and the Latin names crossed out.

The hand loosened, letting the contents dribble out between the fingers. Instead of falling in chunks like soil or funneling straight down like sand, much of this substance drifted sideways through the air, the broken flakes of plants and animals from time immemorial.

The broadcast now showed the avatar. Frankie was surprised

at how an avatar's voice would sometimes get emotional while discussing a story—about a product failure or famine—as though the avatar was being personally affected.

This delivery was so different from the way her doctors talked to her, a few sentences stated quietly to the person who would endure the result. This, she felt, was News.

In her chair again, she saw the screen had gone white.

The field again, a time-lapse video, in the corner a counter ticking off the days. The wind blew sideways, creating crests and hollows in the dust, the shape of waves. As the days sped up, the waves began to move, to roll like water across the screen, splashing up against any object in the way: the Hot Wheels bike, then the fence and the home, lapping higher and then cresting over everything, erasing all things human from view.

She forced her eyes from the screen. She shifted in her seat so she was facing away and returned to eating her crackers.

*

A tourist was studying a map of the Foundation. Nearby a toddler clutched her crotch and whined. The keeper walked by, pushing a wheelbarrow full of food. The tourist called out at the keeper's back, Which way's the bathroom?

The deaf keeper didn't pause.

Jerk, muttered the tourist and turned back to the map.

*

Mama was running her fingers through the hair of Adele, not the fur on her body, just the hair on the top of her head. Mama used her fingers to comb it upward.

Frankie wondered if this was some sort of vermin-finding technique, but Mama never paused to examine the skin underneath to search for bugs. Instead every once in awhile she shuffled back to examine Adele, eyes narrowed, before continuing to comb. She seemed intent.

The grooming appeared different also in that Adele

winced occasionally at how hard Mama tugged her hair upward.

After a few minutes, Frankie looked away, distracted by Stella requesting the mango pit that Houdina was chewing on. Powerful Stella held her hand out, palm up, the beggar's gesture transformed. Houdina handed the pit over, grinning nervously.

Then Frankie turned back to Mama and saw the pattern. Mama was combing Adele's hair into a clear ridge at the top of the head: a Mohawk.

Frankie looked around the enclosure for the hairstyles book that Mama had been staring at yesterday. The keeper must have thrown it away.

When Mama was finished, she knuckled slowly around Adele, pleased with the result, then noticed Frankie staring. She moved over to sit down three feet away, only plexiglass between them, examining Frankie, her head to the side.

Frankie tried to watch the other bonobos, but found her eyes kept sliding back. Once she'd traveled to Tokyo for a conference—long before the current Asian travel advisory had extended to everything within a thousand miles of North Korea. In Tokyo, there seemed to be no stricture against staring, at least at a Caucasian. Any person could stop right in front of her and gawk, no interest in any discomfort she might feel. Mama's dark gaze was similar.

When she finally lost interest and knuckled away, Frankie exhaled.

*

Goliath tried flint knapping again. He didn't do it the way Stotts did, but instead held both rocks in his hands to slap them together in front of him like cymbals. Each day it took longer to persuade him to do the flint knapping and when he did, he slammed the rocks together with force—the bonobo version of huffy.

At the end of his arms, the rocks hit with a dull *thunk*. A few chips splintered off, little puffs of dust. Encouraged, he pulled his arms back and slammed the rocks together harder, gritting his teeth. Dust and chips again.

Each time, there was a loud *thunk* but no big pieces broke off.

After a while, he put the rocks down and sucked on his right palm which was scraped and lightly bleeding. Frankie realized what she'd taken as uneven pigmentation on his palms was actually bruises from the last few days of this work. Sucking on the scrape, he eyed Stotts.

Twelve

Late that afternoon, Id approached Goliath. Frankie didn't know how much time most bonobo babies spent investigating the world, but Id seemed continuously in motion—big eyes, skinny limbs, unending curiosity. Goliath sitting there was a mountain of slow-breathing muscle in comparison. Id grabbed hold of the hair on his back and began to scramble upward. Houdina peeped in alarm and knuckled forward quickly to take her baby back, but froze when Goliath looked at her.

The baby reached the top of his head and began hopping around up there. Goliath weighed 10 times what Id did, his huge hands as long as her body. His mouth began to tighten.

Frankie felt a rising fear.

Freshman year, she'd seen an award-winning documentary about male infanticide in the animal kingdom. In many species, infanticide was routine when a new male wrested control over a group, his first act to kill every juvenile, all of whom were offspring of the last alpha male. The documentary had close-up footage of a male lion leaning down to bite systematically into mewling cub after cub, the mother making slashing feints from the side in defense. The deaths put the females into estrus sooner than if the babies were allowed to reach maturity, allowing the male to breed faster, increasing the number of offspring he could sire during his tenure. In another scene, a muscular silverback rushed a female, who screamed and kicked but was half his size. He yanked her offspring out of her arms as fast as if she'd handed it to him and then swung it by one foot toward the nearest tree limb. The camera lingered on the baby flailing just before its skull hit. The audience shifted uncomfortably.

In the next clip, the silverback was mating with the mother, holding her tight, his hips pumping. Francine had gone to the movie with her roommate, a women's studies major. Susan hissed through her teeth at this scene, assuming rape.

Francine had viewed the scene in a very different light. She was halfway through a seminar in Sociobiology, her introduction to evolution. After each two-hour class, she had a headache from how deeply the concepts made her think, her brain reconfiguring as she walked around campus, examining the actions of the nearby students. Organisms are programmed to feel desire for whatever had increased the chances of survival and reproduction in the previous generations. These instincts are surprisingly unfussy when it comes to contemporary details, able to ignore trivia in favor of function: a bag of Doritos = food; a popular brand of jacket = social status; the football quarterback with bilateral facial symmetry = potential reproduction of athletic and attractive offspring. The amount of desire the person experienced proportional to the size of the potential evolutionary benefits.

In college, she had finally found the courage to visit Student Health Services to state what she hadn't been able to tell anyone else. Health Services consisted of two very clean and white exam rooms with no one ever in the waiting room, the staff accustomed to asking only for enough information to figure out if they should hand out ibuprofen, antibiotics, the Pill or condoms.

She'd done her research beforehand, finding several multiple-choice questionnaires about pain, picking out the listed descriptors that seemed most appropriate. In the exam room with this first doctor, she looked him in the eye and stated the adjectives clearly, words such as *grinding* and *stabbing*. Watching his reaction, she wasn't sure he'd grasped the full import of the information she was relaying, so she added a few similes: *scalding water* and *ripping flesh*. Meanwhile his eyes wandered over her, searching for some proof of what she was saying. There were no visible marks, no bruises, no blood, no splintered bone. She was slender and lightly muscled.

Physical pain, like depression, is not pleasant to imagine. It's much more comfortable to assume hyperbole.

The first step, he announced, was to rule out the possibility of a persistent urinary tract infection, an illness he saw a fair amount of in Health Services. He put her on antibiotics. When she came back a month later, the pain undiminished, he gave her a different antibiotic because there were so many resistant strains. By the third visit, Francine had begun to feel a bit like a con artist, talking fast and trying to sound plausible. She stated that whatever she had, it absolutely positively wasn't a urinary tract infection and if he wasn't going to fix it, then the very least he could do was give her strong painkillers. He noted the request in her file. On campus there was a lot of recreational drug use. From then on, Health Services wouldn't give her anything more powerful than ibuprofen.

So Francine began to make appointments with specialists in the city. In the exam room, she would take off her clothes to put on the johnnie. Her identity stripped away. Like a prisoner, she sat there, waiting to be given her sentence. Each specialist had a favorite to be used with symptoms such as hers, so many diseases it could be. Inflammatory bowel disease. Ovarian cysts. Pelvic inflammatory disease. Adenomyosis. Each sentence pronounced in a firm voice by a person in a white lab coat, the costume of the medical judge. Different regimes of pills or procedures followed. A few helped, most didn't; all had side effects. Years later—once she could finally examine photos of the endometriosis nestled in her guts, once she knew its name—she found out it took an average of six years for an accurate diagnosis. Six years of fumbling with pharmaceuticals and scalpels.

Meanwhile, back during freshman year and for a long time afterward, the paramount thing she desired was to appear healthy, to pass as normal in front of the other students. By this point, in an attempt to do so, she'd learned to cultivate the appearance of a laid-back personality, the kind of person who didn't care about playing sports or arriving on time for class. She walked at a sedate pace, her right arm never swinging. There were days when she didn't leave her room, not going to class or answering her cell. She told those who asked that it was good to schedule downtime.

A few weeks before watching this infanticide documentary, she'd been in her Sociobiology class, listening while her professor explained Evolutionarily Stable Strategies. He had asked them as a thought experiment to consider the potential advantage to giraffes of having longer necks. He assigned some random values to how much a one-foot-longer neck might help (ability to reach leaves = +2) and how much it might hinder (increased tendency to sprain the neck = -1) and then solved the formula. The straightforward clarity of math. Next he asked would a giraffe born with a two-foot-longer neck be better off (more leaves = +3, many more neck injuries = -3), solved the calculation and compared the results.

The professor stepped back and said, Given the clarity of this sort of calculation, it's sometimes hard to understand why, assuming these numbers were real, every giraffe wouldn't have a neck that was one foot longer, all of them genetic clones of the one perfect being—basically a superhero—designed to answer the question of survival.

He paused, surveying the class. She was leaning forward. Her life, she knew, was spent impersonating this perfect being.

The professor said, Because the question of survival changes—a blizzard hits, a disease, a new predator, a meteor strike. Change can happen in a single day, a single moment. Evolution has to have different superheroes just in case, some of whom are definitely not designed for the current situation. A superhero of extreme cold. A superhero of starvation. A superhero of influenza. In what we currently consider normal conditions, these alternatives might do badly, might appear evolutionarily unsound, might faint in the summer heat or have a tendency to put on a few pounds.

He poked himself in the gut. Two of the students in the back were whispering, heads close together.

Glancing at them, he said a little louder, Evolution doesn't care about any one of us: superhero or not. It doesn't even care about our species as a whole. The only thing that matters is the continued existence of life. The random reshuffling of the surviving cards in the genetic deck is the method most likely to create a wide diversity of answers, perpetuating life. This means for every successful superhero, there are many more combinations that don't work under the current conditions, and others that simply don't work at all.

He added, A superhero with the ability to fly, but not to land.

Perhaps her reaction was audible—a cough expelled from her lips—for the boy to her left glanced over.

The clarity of this image. Herself as a superhero circling round and round the planet, whistling through space, all alone.

Strangely enough, instead of anger or sadness, she felt the fiercest joy. Finally some understanding of *why*. She was a necessary experiment in genetic diversity. From this day forth, each time she saw an albino, or someone seven feet tall, or a cleft-palate child with the shy grin of a rabbit, she felt the urge to smile at the person as she passed, a friendly greeting from one human satellite to another.

This moment of understanding was so intense, the reper-
cussions rippling out across her life, that she began to think
about her professor at different times: what his viewpoint
might be on a situation, what advice he might give, what his
life was like. She found she looked forward to class, not just
to listen to him, but to watch him; he appeared somehow
more interesting, his face better lit, his gestures graceful.
Outside of class, she turned with surprise toward anyone who
resembled him.

It took two weeks for her to understand—one Monday
morning at nine as he placed in her hand her midterm—that
she had fallen in love with him, this balding man with the
apologetic slouch, an encyclopedic knowledge and the unfor-
tunate first name of Hyman. Around him, she felt understood,
her pain accorded some purpose.

From the perspective of evolution, her choice of this man—
while perhaps not ideal—did make sense. Although he was sig-
nificantly older, he was a high-status male able to allocate
resources toward any offspring he might sire.

She, a young female with an attractive hip-to-waist ratio,
began to linger after class, asking questions about altruism,
reciprocity and W.D. Hamilton, engaging in such prolonged
eye contact that it took her an additional week to notice his
wedding ring.

She had never fallen in love before, was astonished by the
power, how she behaved as though taken over by an alien.
Previously an emotionally stable person, in his presence she
emitted high-pitched squeals of laughter, away from him she
swung violently from mania to depression. She no longer
seemed to require sleep or food, while her mind was unable to
stop from fanatically fine-tuning imaginary conversations with
him. Years later, researching what was known about the chemistry of love, she learned the names for the hormonal explo-
sives that had been dropped into her personality. Her neuronal

circuits hopped up on serotonin, dopamine and adrenaline. Her grey matter currently indistinguishable from that of an obsessive-compulsive on cocaine.

College was when she first learned to fear her ability to fall in love (what Hyman called her reproductive drive).

Perhaps the word *fear* wasn't accurate. Perhaps the more appropriate word was *awe* (as in the way people used that word with God), an inescapable force before which she would bow, a power that reduced her to a subservient if emotional ant, her only comfort from understanding that the force was well intentioned if not necessarily considerate in the details.

When she'd watched the male-infanticide documentary, she was in the midst of this emotional tumult. She watched the mating scene of the silverback and the mother in a very different way from her roommate (who, during the movie, whispered to her deadpan that next time they should see something more cheerful, perhaps a domestic-violence film).

A newborn nursing at the breast releases oxytocin in the mother's brain, that all-powerful hormone of attachment. Add some cuddling and staring into the baby's oversized eyes and a mammalian mother will almost always fall in love with her offspring with a biological *thunk* that drives her—no matter how exhausted, hungry or bored—to do all she can to help the baby thrive.

Now imagine the baby killed.

The mother's genes have just lost reproductive time and many hard-earned calories. As important as it was before for her to fall in love with the newborn, it was now even more critical to avoid such a disastrous loss again. The most effective way was to mate with the strongest male around, so he would use his strength to protect her next offspring as his own.

Watching the scene of the silverback and the mother mating, Francine found herself thinking of her professor. Unlike her roommate, she considered this scene solidly in the genre of romance films—not an American romance where all worked out in the end, but a European one where there were no guarantees at all. In love herself, she found it easy to empathize, to assume that for the female gorilla this was by far the greatest sex of her life and that it did not in any way negate the fact that her heart was still breaking.

A week later, lying entangled after that first time with her professor in his car, her muscles turned to serene jelly, staring up at the sliver of night sky visible through the back window, her fingers had idly pried from the seat's crevice the object her shoulder had been thumping into a few moments before.

A baby's pacifier.

Cupping this new information in her hand, she closed her eyes to check her reaction. Or perhaps, it was more she closed her eyes to hide from the sickening certainty she could already feel rising inside—that this would make not the slightest difference.

*

Id was still jumping on Goliath's head. The baby slipped and, catching herself, yanked on his hair.

Frankie turned her head away a bit, now watching from the corner of her eyes, unwilling to witness what might come next.

But Goliath only flinched. Carefully he pried Id off, put her on the ground and patted her butt to get her away from him.

Frankie stared. On her Lenses, she called up the information she had on Id. Name, date of birth, gender, mother, vaccinations. Nothing about paternity. She pulled up the info for the other bonobos, scanning each record, seeing the maternal name listed every time, but never the paternal.

In the last 24 hours, she'd watched Houdina mate with any male who was willing: Goliath, Ralph and Mr. Mister. Probably none of them knew which one of them was the father of Id or the other juveniles. The males had to treat all the babies as their own.

Promiscuity defeating infanticide.

This work to reduce infanticide might be why a female bonobo advertised her fertility for so much of each month, her pink sexual swelling lasting for week after week, hiding the timing of her ovulation so all the males might feel they were the father of the next baby.

Having no infanticide would be a huge win for the females. However if even one female became slightly picky about whom she mated with—selecting for instance a male with faster reactions or a stronger immune system—she might have children who survived longer to have more offspring. Being utterly unchoosey was antithetical to evolution.

A few minutes later, the keeper stepped out onto the balcony with her buckets of fruit. All the males stood up and the females reached for them. Frankie held her breath, intent on the ensuing melee, the pink female swellings bouncing with the motion.

She needed some way to see through the females' charade of fertility to figure out if—when it really counted—they were secretly being selective.

DAY 9

Thirteen

S totts stopped by where Frankie sat in her folding chair in front of the bonobo enclosure.

Ma'am, he said.

There was a pause.

She asked, When exactly are they ovulating?

He was looking at the tourists. His eyes froze and he ventured, The bonobos . . . ?

She looked at him, Of course.

He said relieved, I've no idea.

Behind him, she saw a tourist studying him, a brunette, her head tilted.

Well, Frankie asked, Who does?

From the woman's concentration, Frankie assumed she must have met him at some point, be trying to place him.

No one, he answered.

Surprised Frankie repeated, No one?

Then she saw the woman's gaze flick down his body.

He was faced away, oblivious. He said, The exact timing of their ovulation is concealed.

Frankie scanned the crowd, looking the men over, then returning to Stotts. He was tall and had a runner's build. Although she wasn't a fan of the buzzcut, it did showcase his blue eyes and bone structure.

At her expression he said, What? It's the same as with humans.

She felt an illogical jolt of pride. She got to work with him.

He said, The point of it being concealed is to have it be secret.

It suddenly felt awkward to be sitting down talking to him. She rose to her feet, standing next to him. If she were honest she would admit she stood perhaps an inch closer than she would have otherwise.

Glancing over, she saw the brunette had turned away, speaking to the young girl whose hand she held.

Frankie said, I need to un-conceal it. Most copulations don't matter. But those during ovulation, that's different.

Stotts paused, absorbing what she'd said. In the past she'd noted this male unwillingness to think of sex as having any other purpose than, well . . . sex. It seemed to her this reluctance was probably an adaption as impactful on human development as opposable thumbs. So far, however, she hadn't come up with a way to test the theory.

She said, To figure out when humans are ovulating, you get them to pee in a cup or you take blood.

And this was when the woman glanced back, her eyes landing on Frankie for the first time—her bony limbs outlined by stretchy fabric, her posture hunched.

The woman's expression shifted to pity.

Frankie blinked.

Watching the bonobos Stotts said, Good luck with that.

*

Frankie sat at the living room table, reading about bonobos' menstrual cycle and reproduction. The way she attacked a difficult question was through a process a bit like digestion. The first stage involved research, taking great bites of the material, chewing actively on the problem from every angle, until she'd swallowed all she could about the field.

If an answer didn't come to her during this learning phase, she let the subject settle inside her. She no longer thought about it consciously, allowing instead some dark and muscled lobe of her brain to take over. The issue was broken down into components and absorbed, images from the material occasionally appearing in her thoughts like neuronal burps. Every once in awhile she'd flip through her notes, having no expectations but going through the ritual in order to goose her brain along. After her mind had worked on the problem like this for long enough—a few days, a month, maybe a whole year—the answer would suddenly hit her. The solution glittering and fully realized, as obvious as though someone much smarter had handed it to her, frustrated with how long she was taking.

What was known about the fertility of female bonobos sounded remarkably similar to that of female humans: the length of the menstrual cycle (33 days), pregnancy (eight months), sexual maturity (nine years) and menopause (late 40s). Beyond this very general information, scientific knowledge was limited to what could be gleaned from fewer than 100 individuals in captivity. Data about the species in the wild was limited, at first because of the nearly constant wars in the area, then more recently because no researcher had been able to find any remaining living subjects. Overall, the lack of information was stunning—this species so closely related to humans. Much more was known about reproduction in caribou or naked mole rats.

Although she was trying to concentrate, the movement and color shifts of the E-musement on the wall kept dragging her eyes away. Words a foot tall twirled and twinkled: *Cyberattack*. This were followed by *Chicago Stock Exchange* materializing from left to right, 3-D and glittering.

Like any animal, humans turn toward movement. All screens was geared to this weakness, objects constantly swirling and shimmering. Everything displayed on the screen was high-def and color-heightened. The avatar was especially vivid. Her complexion was perfect, her clothing luxurious and crisp, her motions graceful, her diction perfect.

An uber-human, she sat there, a little taller and healthier than anyone living.

Frankie had wondered for years if humans had gotten impatient with biological evolution and thus invented avatars. Now, everyone could stare all day long at the screen, admiring this preferred version of their successors.

The detail that Frankie focused on was the avatar's spine. Even lounging in her chair, her neck and back were gracefully arched, suggesting years of yoga. From Frankie's disease and all those internal adhesions, her own posture was closer to that of a half-evolved human. She thought of the brunette's look of pity, then got up to retrieve an old towel rod she'd spotted in the closet. She positioned the rod across the small of her back, like a banister she was leaning against, and hooked her arms over the far side to hold it in place. The pressure arched her back. The surgeon had removed every adhesion he could find; nanogels healing it all rapidly. Stretching now would stop the scars from tightening into a knot. Using her elbows, she rolled the rod up her back, attempting to iron her back out, bit by bit.

The avatar watched this, continuing to talk, taking no offense that her voice was muted. She could easily be typecast as the supportive mom in any sitcom, the worried foil for all her comedic kids.

Frankie rolled the rod higher, while focused on reading the research on her Lenses. The stretching wasn't getting very far, something tugging on her left side. The point was not to push it so far she ripped any stitches. She leaned into the pain like into a wind, balancing against it. She had only two more studies on bonobos to read. After that she would review ovulation among the other great apes including *Homo sapiens*. Since they were all so closely related, the information might be pertinent to bonobos too.

When she looked over next, the avatar was interviewing an

executive on a split screen about the cyberattack. Across his chest floated the text: *Tyler Shank, CEO Chicago Stock Exchange*. Although well dressed and coiffed, he was clearly not an avatar: heavy, his hair thinning, his skin moist. Frankie could guess what he was saying even with the volume off; his expression telegraphing it all. He was admitting a mistake had been made and professing sorrow. Now his voice was becoming deeper and more confident as he explained a solution had been found. Greater vigilance was promised, customer trust implicitly expected.

Text dissolved onto the screen, the man's chest labeled *Poly-roach*. For an instant Frankie thought the news site had resorted to name calling, until the man's image dissolved to show a different human. *Poly-roach* must have been the intro to the next scene.

If avatars over the years had become longer and lankier, like greyhounds or gazelles, then humans (the ones who couldn't afford genetic or surgical augmentation) had begun to resemble groundhogs—a certain meaty compression, a tendency to breathe through the mouth. This was certainly true of the next person being interviewed. He sat at his desk, wearing an old Linux T-shirt, a large screen behind his head displaying computer code, the poly-roach expert.

For more than a decade, computer viruses had been polymorphic: able to change themselves to avoid detection, rewriting their own code to appear part of the program they'd infiltrated. The viruses had become better at this morphing over time—able to shapeshift endlessly, making it difficult to verify if a program was ever virus free. However that ability alone hadn't caused the scope of the current problem. That had come a decade ago when hackers gave viruses the ability to learn.

Since then, every experience made them smarter. With each program they touched, each antivirus they survived, they amassed more knowledge and skills, able to recognize and resist antiviruses they'd never seen, figuring out the weak spot in every code.

People began to call the new type of viruses "cockroaches," since they'd evolved to the point where they couldn't be exterminated no matter what products were applied. Antiviruses got rebranded as roach-spray. Because of the speed with which the polymorphic roaches learned, these sprays had to be updated daily, then hourly. Still the poly-roaches chewed on the edge of the digital world: causing childish pranks or stealing information or disabling critical infrastructure. The grid or Quark could go offline at any time, devices acting haywire, for minutes or even hours at a time, until the situation could be sprayed down. Poly-roaches and the weather had become the kind of difficulty that strangers chatted about while in an elevator.

This groundhog of a man was talking rapidly. He gestured with his hands like an Italian, his expression intent, his entire body working to communicate with the viewer.

Shown on a split screen, the avatar looked concerned. The segment seemed long, just the two of them talking. A surprising lack of graphics or product placement.

Frankie realized she was staring at the screen like some aimless teenager. Tired and still physically recovering, she was easily distracted.

She moved her chair so she wasn't facing that way. Sitting there, rolling the towel rod up her spine, she focused on the information on her Lenses.

*

Mama was styling Goliath's hair, brushing it back from his forehead and curling the hair out below his ears. She appeared to be attempting a Jackie-Kennedy bouffant.

After several minutes of work, Mama leaned back to examine the overall effect. She frowned and patted at the hair on his neck, trying to flatten it. When it wouldn't flatten, she grabbed a hank of it and yanked it out. Goliath yipped and clapped a hand to his neck. She wiped the hair off her palm and then grabbed some more hair. After the third chunk, she gave up, discouraged.

She wandered off while Goliath sat there, whining, his hand cupping the back of his neck.

*

The keeper noticed Stotts' face was pointed at her, his mouth moving. She stepped forward and placed two fingertips to the side of his trachea to feel the vibration of his voice, looking at his mouth to see the shape of his words. This combination let her read lips most accurately.

Two years ago, when the Foundation's minimal insurance finally started paying for kinetic implants, she'd gotten one. The implant was inserted under the surface of her tongue, an area dense with neurons that could be retrained.

The implant translated sound into movement and pressure, her mouth transformed into an ear. Sharp sounds felt sharp, soft sounds soft, the direction of a noise implied through location on her tongue. A loud echo would bounce from one side of her mouth to the other.

In the beginning the implant only told her that sound was occurring and that she already knew. Mostly the constant sensation was annoying. She found herself moving her tongue around like a horse playing with a bit, scratching noise away on the edges of her teeth.

But synesthesia can be trained. The nerves rewired. One day her brain figured the code out. One moment she was walking through a door and her tongue was simply itchy; the next she *heard* through her tongue the metallic snick of the door behind her.

A bird called and she turned to face the sound.

Over the next few days, she tasted sound constantly, the

crackle of glass breaking in her mouth, a cow's vibrant moo, the rumble of a car. All in all, it wasn't what she remembered or thought she remembered from childhood, before she'd woken up one morning with the flu to find she was abruptly stone deaf. Her memory of sound was of only one noise at a time: her mother talking, a bell ringing, her father's laugh.

Now as an adult, hearing again after decades, she learned sound happened everywhere, interrupting itself, ubiquitous and tiring. Perhaps because her brain had to work so hard translating her tongue's input into sound, it didn't have capacity left to edit out the background noise. All of it delivered with just as much import: the rustle of air through her lungs, the gurgle of her gut, a person talking to her, the wind overhead. Used to so many years of silence, her mind jittered at this constant input. She felt as though she stood on a noisy fairground, carnival barkers yelling on all sides for her attention.

Exhausted by this, she turned the implant off earlier each night and turned it on a little later each morning, until one day she stopped turning it on at all. She returned instead to listening with her eyes and, when she could, with her fingers.

She waited, her fingers on Stotts' neck and watched his mouth.

Knowing that her touching his neck helped her lip-read, he didn't step back. He simply repeated his words, In the enclosure, there's some diarrhea. I don't know which bonobo is sick.

She said, It's Stella. She's not sick. She eats too many mangos.

With each word, she worked on enunciation, reconstructing the feel of it from memory, making sure her lips or tongue didn't drag.

She paused then, wondering if what she'd said was enough, was clear.

Talkative people gave her a headache, making her concentrate just to comprehend chitchat. Stotts, she didn't mind as much. He was succinct and allowed her to rest her fingers on his neck. Perhaps in Syria, holding a rifle, walking down a street toward what might be an I.E.D., he'd learned not to be bothered by the small stuff.

In general, the Midwest was a bad place for deaf people: stoic expressions, hands motionless, personal space large. Most people didn't allow her to touch them, forcing her to read their lips. She wished instead she'd been born somewhere in the Mediterranean, where people touched one another easily and stood close, where they emoted with hands and eyes and shoulders, where everyone employed some type of sign language.

She could see from his expression he'd understood her words.

She turned away, having conveyed what was necessary.

Fourteen

Frankie sat down in Stotts' chair wanting to see the Moments up close. After a minute of watching the images, she realized this side of the cube (the side only Stotts normally saw) showed all the images she'd seen from the other side as well as two more private ones.

The Moment of Tess, maybe two years old, wearing Winnie-the-Pooh footie pajamas, her face yellowish and gasping. She was struggling with the oxygen mask, shoving it away with both hands, terrified of anything blocking her mouth and nose.

The Moment of his wife holding a sleeping Tess, rocking her, staring at the viewer. She was tired and at bay and very very angry.

Frankie didn't know why Stotts had chosen to have these Moments on his desk where he could see them each day, what he was working to understand or remember. When she heard someone in the hall walking her way, she moved back fast to her spot on the couch.

*

That afternoon there was no video at all from the cameras on the far side of the enclosure. Every time more than one bonobo moved behind the cement hill, Frankie would call up the video on her Lenses, but see just static. She sent another sharp text to Bellows telling him to get the cameras fixed, now.

She was frustrated. She hadn't figured out a way yet to determine which females were ovulating. Now she couldn't even see all the matings. Until she could manage both, she wouldn't be able to get enough information to come up with a hypothesis, much less start to test the theory. She was wasting time.

Her EarDrums beeped within three minutes. The note from Bellows rolled across her Lenses; he had four people working on it. He apologized deeply, would keep her up to date as the issue developed and he urged her to inform him of anything else he could do to facilitate her work.

*

At some point during college, Francine began to lose faith in medicine, at least in its ability to fix her problem. Instead she began to visit clinics or ERs where she no longer tried to describe the pain in her gut, but used words such as *migraine*, *back spasm* and *gut pain*. In response the doctors sometimes used words like *codeine*, *Vicodin* or *Neocontin*.

Checking into these medical facilities, she gave her name as Frankie Burk. Changing her first name like this wasn't an attempt to hide her identity, because the name Francine was clearly printed on her insurance card. More she was trying to assume a role, take on the kind of persona who could lie to a doctor. She considered the words she said not as mirrors of reality, but instead as the words necessary to convey the truth of her pain and get an appropriate response from the medical community.

It wasn't until the end of senior year that she finally learned the name of her disease. Long before this, during sex, she felt with each casual slam of the hips that her internal organs were made of the most delicate silk.

Her professor, Hyman, told her the pain came from her conflicted emotions about having sex with a married man. Women, he said, rolling his eyes, And guilt.

But Frankie wanted sex, had long detailed dreams of it where Hyman had miraculously developed telekinetic powers so precise he could look at her and she would feel pleasure roll up her spine. She woke from these dreams too scared to even masturbate.

Given this, she preferred kissing and petting. Hyman got angry, said she was an immature tease. Did she know what he was risking to be with her? His career, his marriage, his child? Could she have some perspective?

Then on March 14th, that year when she was 21, his four-year-old son went into convulsions from pneumonia, was taken by ambulance to the hospital. His wife stayed that night with the boy. Hyman was supposed to get a good night's sleep, so he could be by his son's side the whole next day. Instead he brought Francine to his home. She didn't know how bad the pneumonia was or what the doctors had said, but Hyman was jittery and tense, pacing back and forth for hours, unable to settle down until late that night. He wanted her presence, but hardly spoke a word. A part of her watched him, clinically interested in how he showed his distress. He appeared physically healthy and yet no one, hearing his story, would doubt his pain.

In the middle of the night, he woke her to demand sex. She didn't feel under the circumstances she could deny him. Assuming the doggy position so at least the weight of his body wouldn't press on her gut, she tried to turn the pain into a loud train chugging away from her, receding into the distance. Chug, she thought, chug chug. Although he wanted this, his erection at times flagged, the sex dragging on, until he began to pound into her, punctuating each stroke with a grunt close to a sob.

In this moment, trying hard to breathe, she heard the voice speak to her for the first time.

(In the years after this, she heard the voice twice more, each time during an extreme situation when in the heat and bustle of life she'd missed some critical detail. Each time, the voice didn't sound like voices in her dreams, which floated fuzzy and unanchored in her skull. No, this one had a physical location in space, about two inches from her right ear. She could hear the wetness of the mouth, the raspiness of the throat—an older woman, definitely a smoker, the kind who referred to all strangers as *Honey*. Although the information this voice relayed was always helpful, the tone wasn't what might be expected. There was no feeling of affection, alarm or even interest. It sounded more like a crossing guard's voice, impersonal and factual, paid for by the hour.)

The voice said, *He's not a good guy.*

Then she felt something tear—a bit like soggy linen ripping—there was a piercing pain and she blacked out.

*

Her next memory was of standing in the brightly lit hall in front of her open apartment door, her roommate staring at her. She had no idea how she'd gotten there.

(Afterward she decided Hyman must not have panicked at this unconscious naked student in his bed. Instead she imagined him understanding this was an emergency and picking her up in his arms to carry her clear across campus, not caring who saw them. She visualized him opening the front door to her dorm and riding the elevator up to her floor. She pictured him propping her up dazed in front of her door, ringing the bell and then retreating a few feet to hide around the corner while inside their apartment her roommate Tina closed the image of her newest science fiction book on her Lenses to walk across the room and open the door.

Frankie believed this is how it must have happened, because she couldn't imagine any other way she could have made it across campus when she was barely conscious, naked and with blood dripping down her legs.)

In the E.R., for the next three hours, Tina sat with her, chewing methodically through a pack of Juicy Fruit, moving from the waiting room to the exam room to the hallway before pre-op, never displaying impatience, even when she finished the first book and had to search for a second.

During the surgery, endometriosis was found throughout Francine's body cavity: small chunks of uterine lining that had implanted where they shouldn't. The implantations thickened with blood until the end of the month, when each attempted to forcibly shed the blood, small chunks of flesh torn off her abdominal wall, her liver and other organs, over time the scars webbing together, delicate strands that tightened into ropes. Sex with Hyman had torn a hole in her bladder.

In the recovery ward, she got to know her roommate much better. Before this she'd purposefully stayed distant, keeping her door closed when Tina was home, scared if she engaged in idle chitchat, the secret of her professor might slip out.

Hyman didn't try to contact her in the hospital, nor at any time after that. So far as she knew, he never found out if she was all right.

Tina had spent the summer of her junior year being a Mormon missionary in Mexico. She visited Francine each day, delivering a banana smoothie from a nearby café (nutritious food so rare in the hospital) and five prunes (so Francine wouldn't have to clench her surgically traumatized gut to poop). At the start of each visit, Tina made a small pyramid of the prunes on a napkin on the bedside table and placed the smoothie beside them.

Francine was hypnotized by the kindness of the prunes.

Hyman had used the word *love* repeatedly with her, although of course never within anyone else's hearing. Tina—who did not love Francine at all but was in the habit of helping people—didn't use many words at all, just plopped herself down in the chair beside the bed to read.

Francine, staring at that pyramid of prunes, realized she would not contact Hyman again. It made sense to her that the only way she could have left him was to have him torn from her guts, blood welling from the wound.

For Tina, there seemed to be nothing about hospitals she didn't know. Big family, she said dismissively, A lot of older relatives. She folded another slice of Juicy Fruit into her mouth and said nothing more.

Once Francine had finished the prunes and sipped as much as she could of the smoothie, Tina cleaned away the garbage to replace it with the nurse's call button and a bottle of water with a bendable straw.

Watching her roommate position these essential objects within easy reach, Francine remembered the way Hyman had pronounced the word *love*, extending the *v* into a slight fricative, so it sounded more like *luff*. She pictured a sail in the wind luffing, the material unable to catch the wind appropriately.

On the third day, when a doctor finally appeared by her bed, Tina was away at class. The man introduced himself, not with his name, but just as the surgeon who had performed the operation. His name was written across his shirt pocket, but a banana peel drooping out of that pocket obscured most of the letters. The word started with a *ch* and ended with a *b*, perhaps four letters in between. He looked only a few years older than her.

He glanced up and to the right to examine the display on his Lenses. At this point Lenses weren't universal, so it wasn't until he flicked his finger to page through the display that she was sure he wasn't staring at a bug on the ceiling. She'd learned enough from the nurses to know the disease he'd found in her guts matched her symptoms. She'd been waiting to talk to him, assuming now that she had a real diagnosis, modern medicine would finally cure her.

He flicked through her file, describing what he'd found during surgery. He used precise medical terminology she did not know, mixed in with vivid phrases such as *extensive scarring* and *stage four*.

The more he talked, the harder she found it to hear what he was saying.

Bright-eyed, he stared at the photos of her adhesions, explaining how the granulation tissue webbed her organs together, how every time she reached upward, the scarring must have tugged on her liver.

Some distant part of her brain began to busy itself with the options for the four missing letters of his name—*Chaffob, Cheralb*—her mind a hamster on a wheel, spinning nowhere, making noise.

When it didn't seem as though he would ever pause, she interrupted, How will you fix it?

This, to her, was the point of the conversation.

He blinked and focused on her, seeming to remember he wasn't talking to another surgeon. His eyes bounced away to the wall.

Well, he admitted, Endometriosis is hard to treat.

She grew very still.

He said, Mostly we just try to control it.

Chriseb, Cheebob.

It was to the wall that he confessed, Unless you choose to get a hysterectomy. That frequently works.

She asked, A what?

(Of course she knew what the word meant. Her question was more a way of saying, You gotta be kidding.)

He didn't seem to comprehend this subtlety. Instead he defined the word, adding that he would recommend removing her ovaries too.

They stared at each other, as baffled by each other's responses as if they spoke different languages. The only reply she could think of was, I'm 21.

In response he offered, The treatments for surgical menopause have radically improved.

She blinked, unable to process this statement. She said, But if you took out my . . . —she didn't speak this word for utter-ing it would make this situation more real. Instead she simply paused, leaving an empty spot in the sentence for the name of the organ he wanted to edit from her body— . . . how would I have children?

Later on, the fact that she asked this question mortified her. However the enormity of this concept, like a mountain, needed to be climbed in stages.

When the surgeon spoke again, it was more slowly, using words with few syllables, Do you want kids?

I'm not . . . I don't . . . , she said. At 21, when she thought of the word *home*, she still pictured her mother's apartment. She was years away from figuring out if she wanted to become a parent herself.

The doctor spoke with less interest. Clearly this part of the conversation was outside of his purview, like a plumber being asked to consider paint colors. He asked, When would you want the kids? Three years from now? Five years?

She pictured her naked body standing in the hallway in front of her apartment door and closed her eyes, unable to answer.

After a moment he offered one more word she had never considered associating with her life, offering it in the same tone with which he might suggest a more convenient restaurant. He said, Adopt.

Her eyes snapped open, for in a way this word did take away her pain, at least for the moment. She heard herself speak, deep and gravelly, every consonant sharp.

She said, You seem confused about your function here. It is to offer medical solutions for my disease. If you cannot, you pass me on to a more competent doctor.

She listened to these words, as surprised as he was.

This deep voice lied without effort, saying, My Lenses have recorded this whole conversation.

(She did not even own Lenses.)

Her mouth said, If you and this hospital don't start finding solutions very quickly, I will call a news conference from this bed and I will replay this conversation where, in under 97 seconds, you moved from informing a college-age woman of her disease to suggesting she adopt.

He was staring at her now and she realized with an internal lurch her professor would probably never look at her again, certainly not with such attention. Her eyes began to well and her voice said, You will find I can look quite distraught.

From this day forth, this voice appeared whenever she needed it to, rising raspy from the scars inside her. She lied, she threatened, she said whatever she needed to get help. From this point on, she introduced herself as Frankie.

The hospital arranged the medical appointments for her, so she could try out the potential treatments. These new doctors treated her as a fundamentally different patient than the one she'd been before her operation. Their fingers flicked through her medical records, the file filled with precise vocabulary and color photos. These doctors informed her she was in terrible pain.

Fifteen

At 5:15 A.M. she tried walking across the Foundation, wanting to see how far she could manage. Young, with the adhesions surgically removed, she was healing quickly. As she walked, she windmilled her arms round and round, looking a bit like a slow motion video of a person attacked by bees. She was trying to stretch out her muscles and tendons, to break the adhesions inside.

Stepping off the path, she'd wandered past three flower beds and around a large hedge. Walking here, outside of the area visible to the public, the lawn felt rougher, rustling under her feet. After 10 yards, the grass simply dead-ended, the line precise. Examining the edge, she saw this part of the lawn was actually a carpet, a plastic green skirt. Past the carpet, the bare earth continued for 100 yards all the way down to the highway, devoid of detail except for two dead trees and a desiccated patch of grass. On the far side of the highway was an irrigated field lush with some type of pink flower, the field placed precisely in the bare landscape, its corners as exact as a box. Water so expensive these days.

She made a slow circuit of the lawn carpet around the Foundation, stretching her arms, staring out at the dry landscape, then headed back to her kitchen, hungry. She finally wanted something more than a spoonful of mayonnaise or some crackers, something better than the chips or rubbery hot dogs from the Snack Shack near the Visitors' Center. In her apartment's cupboards, the only food was a few dusty jars of marinated olives. Either olives were the previous tenant's favorite type of food or he hated them so much he hadn't bothered to pack them when he left. Even hungry, she didn't consider opening them. After years of dietary restrictions, she was only going to eat what she truly desired.

So she sat down at the counter and said, Ok Bindi, make a list.

Each item she named appeared in a small window on her Lenses: bulleted, spelled correctly and with all pertinent trademarks. She ended the shopping list with, Ok Done.

Since *ok* had become the vocab that activated so many devices, the word had fallen out of use in normal human conversation, for fear a nearby oven might click on or a garage door shut.

On the wall, the E-musement broadcast was currently showing some flooded street—people wading past submerged cars with children on their shoulders. Probably Miami or St. Louis, those cities seemed to be flooded every few weeks. The video was shot from 10 feet above the water; the person who shot it must have been leaning out a window. E-musement used a lot of amateur videos. Since everyone had Lenses, the videos were uploaded to a news site long before any professional reporter could get to the scene.

The current video zoomed in on a three-year-old, holding tight to her mom, her other arm wrapped around a teddy bear. One side of her face was discolored, a birthmark or bruise. The Lenses were zooming in closer.

Frankie jerked her eyes away and got to her feet to search through the apartment, checking every closet and drawer, until she'd found a box of garbage bags and some nails. The crowd-sourced scenes had a tendency to linger on the sad and horrific, images a professional crew might have avoided. These amateur videos were given more leeway given the hypnotic intimacy of looking at an emergency literally through the eyes of someone involved. The videos drove ratings up.

Frankie had no need for gratuitous pain and so stopped watching E-musement years ago. The little information she got about current events came through Public Broadcasting: calm avatars explaining context, divergent opinions aired, warnings delivered before any disturbing visual in case children were watching. All of this created a certain emotional distance.

Since she couldn't find a hammer in the apartment, she grabbed a frying pan instead and climbed onto a chair in front of the E-musement wall. Using the pan as a hammer, she nailed a garbage bag flat across part of the image, then got down off the chair to take a look. The upper right quadrant of the newscast was now projected onto the surface of the dark bag—the visuals much harder to see.

Satisfied, she started to step forward to hammer the next garbage bag in place when the camera—still showing scenes of that flooded city—panned past a half submerged subway entrance. The water lapping at a sign for the 1, 2 and 3 lines and those familiar green railings.

Frankie froze for a moment. Manhattan.

Glittering text twirled onto the screen: *Poly-roach Attack.*

The visuals now showed three engineers in some sort of control room working at their screens, speaking commands quickly, intent.

An official in a suit stepped in front, holding his hands up, blocking the view of the engineers. He addressed the camera, groomed and calm. The text at the bottom of the screen said, *Jack Santos, NYC Water Department Communications Director.*

The poly-roaches had been hitting a lot of infrastructure recently: the grid in Texas, satellite radio, the navigation of self-driving cars.

A roach must have gotten into the water department's computers. She'd heard of this happening in Singapore. The roach made the software think the water pressure in the main pipes was falling. In response the system cranked the pressure up higher and higher, trying to compensate, until pipes started exploding across the city and a human stepped in to shut the system down.

The scene now showed the poly-roach expert who'd been interviewed yesterday, the one who looked a bit like a ground-hog. He was speaking intently into the camera.

She bustled into motion, nailing the second bag in place below the first and stepping back to see the effect.

The right half of the video was now projected on the two bags. Against the dark plastic, only a shimmer of reflected light was visible, a sense of flickering movement, of something alive and struggling.

The left half of the broadcast however was still clear. The visual had changed from the programmer's face to an animation of a poly-roach: the roach constructed out of computer code, thousands of lines of text scrolling across its wings and legs.

The roach scuttled forward, its wings morphing into all sorts of weapons—wood spears and stone axes and arrows—charging directly at something moving on the garbage-bag side of the screen. Whatever the thing was, it was sprinting just as quickly at the roach.

The two hit, the strength of the collision spinning both of them for a moment onto the left side of the screen.

It was another roach, the same size.

Of course. The roaches were everywhere and tried to infiltrate anything made of code. Sooner or later, sheer probability decreed that two roaches would attack each other.

These two were struggling, shifting, their wings morphing into crossbows and battering rams and catapults. Learning new tricks from one another, they increased the rate of their own innovations—Colt 45s and sticks of dynamite and missiles—each innovation spurring on the next, the increase in speed not linear but geometric, almost faster than the eye could see. Both of them pressed in, hungry for the kill, their limbs a blur of evolving power—mushroom clouds and drones—erasing all space between them, until . . . they simply absorbed each other. Merged into a single roach.

That roach stood there, motionless but breathing.

Bigger than before. More powerful. Now opalescent.

Its eyes opened. Data shimmered across its pupils. These eyes focused on the viewer.

The scene cut back to the human expert. He was talking into the camera, his hands extended as though he wanted to grab hold of the viewer, shake the person into understanding.

Frankie looked down at her hands holding the other two garbage bags and then back up at the screen. E-musement used fear to get people hooked.

She hammered in the other two garbage bags, covering up the rest of the broadcast.

*

For several months, the Foundation had been a finalist for a large grant from the National Science Foundation—their proposed program to increase public understanding in Kansas City of the basic principles of evolution. As soon as Frankie had agreed to work at the Foundation, Bellows had sent a note to the NSF committee informing them she'd joined his team. He included her resume and a press packet.

Today Bellows sent an announcement to all Foundation staff that they'd won the grant. He added that the award notification had included a personal note from the chair of the committee mentioning he was a fan of Frankie's work. The grant was big enough to keep operations going for two years without additional lay-offs and without selling any of the apes.

Throughout the morning, different Foundation employees kept walking up to Frankie. Each person told her thank you, grabbing her hand and pumping it up and down, as grateful as if Frankie had written the grant request herself. Some woman who worked with the orangutans pulled her into an emotional hug, rocking her back and forth, while whispering, Thank you Thank you. Frankie extricated herself as quickly as she could.

In response, she texted Bellows saying he'd better fix the cameras in the enclosure or she'd notify the NSF committee she was leaving. An hour later, Frankie spotted a repair crew hustling toward the office of the Foundation.

Bellows had a large bouquet of flowers delivered to her apartment door. She didn't bother to unwrap it, so the plastic-wrapped bundle sat on the table where she'd dropped it, wilting in size over the next few days.

*

Recovering, Frankie was able to sleep more deeply now, even when she napped on the uncomfortable couch in Stotts' office. One morning she woke to find Tess sitting at the desk, busy drawing. Her face was lit by the Moments cube, as though she'd been summoned by the images of herself. In comparison to the vivid hi-res photos, she looked small and somewhat faded.

Frankie inhaled and began the process of sitting up, first rolling onto her side, then getting her hands under her.

Tess looked up, watching. She asked, You sick?

Frankie paused. She'd thought she was doing well enough by now to appear just tired. She said yes, then pushed herself up into a sitting position.

Tess clambered down from the chair. There was the small thump of her feet on the floor, then she stepped out around the corner of the desk. She had a preschooler's tippie-toe walk, the law of gravity not yet applicable. Her eyes serious.

She asked, Is it a booboo?

From the Moments, her face was so familiar yet unknown, like meeting a famous person.

Frankie answered, No.

Tess stepped in close, no sense of personal space. She rested her hand on Frankie's knee and asked, Is it azz-ma?

She pronounced the word with concentration, almost two separate words.

No, said Frankie. (Here was one small thing to be grateful for, that by the time her disease started, she was old enough to pronounce its name.) The girl's hand was warm.

Tess spotted the embroidered gecko on Frankie's sleeve and pressed her stomach against Frankie's leg to reach it, running her fingers over the smooth threads, her breath audible through her mouth, a tiny machine. Each motion of her fingers considered and precise.

Tess said, I don't like azz-ma. It hurts.

Frankie held her breath, very still, as though a bird had landed on her knee. She said, I have a different type of boo-boo.

Tess looked from the gecko to Frankie.

Frankie said, It's like asthma in that it hurts inside and slows me down.

At these words, Tess's hand stopped. The two of them stared into each other's faces.

They could hear Stotts now walking back up the hall from the bathroom.

Frankie found herself speaking low and serious, looking into the girl's eyes. She said, Whenever you have problems breathing, imagine me standing in front of you. Take your pain and put it in my arms.

Tess listened.

Frankie said, I have big arms and know how to hold it tight. I'm used to it. I'll take it all away. You won't feel it anymore.

Tess listened with her whole body.

Frankie whispered, When you have problems, imagine me. Watch me carry the pain away. I'll help.

Then Stotts stepped in and they moved back from each other, instinctively keeping this secret. He eyed them, suspicious.

*

The self-driving car pulled up in front of her to drive her to the supermarket. Frankie had been in college when self-driving cars became widely available—the lack of steering wheel and brake startling, no physical mechanism with which to control the vehicle, only a dashboard with a gleaming display showing miles-per-gallon and estimated arrival time. Such implicit trust. The ads however pointed out the spacious interior, how it was possible to work or nap instead of steering, how blind people and children could finally chauffeur themselves. Also the car could hurtle along at 90 miles per hour while the windshield played movies or displayed the passing cobblestone streets of ancient Rome or the arching trees of a national forest, hiding all unpleasant scenery.

As soon as the selfer's door clicked open for her, Frankie heard the broadcast blaring: paid content discussing the absorption rates of different paper towels.

Stepping into the car she said, Ok Selfer, take me to the nearest supermarket and turn off the E-musement.

The car's voice repeated the destination, closed and locked the doors before smoothly accelerating, but the broadcast stayed on, now playing a show's theme music.

Ok Car, she repeated, Turn *off* the E-musement.

The audio stayed on. The music finished and the host welcomed the listeners back to his show. The rich baritone of his voice and the enjoyment with which he rolled his words made it obvious he didn't have a strict allegiance to journalistic integrity. At least there was no visual on the windshield.

Frankie tried her own device, Ok Bindi, turn off the selfer's audio.

The host said he was taking calls about the recent stories of Ruminant Flu being spread via Chinese take-out.

Her Bindi responded with soothing authority, Unable to turn off the audio.

The host said, Let's welcome our first caller. Sarah from North Adams, you're on the air.

Frankie asked, Why not?

Her Bindi answered, Unable to determine that.

Sarah said, Last week I got real sick after eating at the Lucky Noodle.

Frankie asked, Version incompatibility?

Her Bindi responded, Unable to determine that.

Frankie put music on her EarDrums but could still hear the show in the background. She really needed to replace her implant so it was more up to date. These incompatibilities were happening more frequently.

The selfer pulled up in front of the supermarket, automatically deducting payment from her Bindi. The transaction completed in a millisecond, the selfer and her EarDrums beeping in accord. At least in terms of payment, the manufacturers made sure there was never any difficulty with version differences. It was only the actual applications that gradually became impossible to control.

For the slower comprehension of the human, the car's speakers repeated the payment in English, the voice as condescending as a preschool teacher's. Frankie got out of the vehicle and closed the door. It hummed as it drove itself away, the audio still blaring.

DAY 11

Sixteen

Frankie woke in the middle of the night. The dream still floating in front of her, the vision: a pink inflated female balloon, steaming with fecundity.

Hot, she said.

The resting temperature of the female body increased during ovulation, the temperature of the reproductive area going up the most—at least a degree Fahrenheit in most primates.

Pleased with her idea, she slept soundly until seven. During breakfast, she found a thermal app and downloaded it onto her Lenses. When she turned the app on, she could see temperature rather than light. Heat was visible as brilliant oranges and yellows, cold as deep blues and purples. A psychedelic kaleidoscope of temperature. Lucy in the Sky with a Thermometer. In the center of her vision were crosshairs. Next to the crosshairs, the temperature of that object was displayed in Fahrenheit.

Looking down at her hand, she could see her palm was two degrees warmer than the fingertips.

She grunted with satisfaction.

However, once she got to the viewing area in front of the enclosure, she found the app couldn't see through the plexiglass. The surface became a mirror that reflected the warmth of the objects near it. The glass showed herself scowling, an orange monster with purple hair.

She turned off the thermal app and examined the enclosure, searching for some spot where she could watch the bonobos without glass between her and them. After a moment, she moved into the building and headed for the balcony, the one that the keeper fed the bonobos from.

Unfortunately as soon as she stepped onto the balcony, the bonobos turned to face her, curious. This meant of course she couldn't see their sexual swellings to get a temperature reading. Even when the bonobos saw she had no food, they still took a seat, waiting for her to entertain them. She figured they'd get up and wander around soon, but as the minutes passed, they just sat, watching, moving only to scratch a shoulder or cuddle in against one another.

So she sat down as well and leaned back against the wall, turning the thermal app off—its psychedelic colors disorienting.

Each time a female bonobo stood up, Frankie would say, Ok Bindi, thermal app on.

At her voice, the bonobo would sit right back down. They were patient creatures, the perfect audience, waiting for such long periods of time that inevitably she'd turn the app off again and they'd chirp to one another in appreciation of the show.

After an hour of this, she noticed that whenever she turned the app back on, a single percent sign appeared in the lower corner of her screen. Off to the side, away from the other readouts of temperature, distance and emissivity, this percent sign flickered on and off. She wondered what it signaled.

The tourists arrived at nine A.M. Each time a group—a family or a couple or a crowd of students—walked into the viewing area, it was obvious when any of them spotted Frankie inside the enclosure. The person's head would jump and he or she would point her out to other people in the group, sometimes even to strangers. All of them standing there, ignoring the bonobos to stare at her.

About 10 A.M., the keeper stepped out into the enclosure through the door below the balcony, to pick up the food the bonobos hadn't eaten for breakfast. There seemed to be a lot remaining, lying on the ground everywhere.

Frankie was tired of waiting. She leaned over the balcony and waved her arms at the keeper, calling out, Helloooo.

The woman had her head down shoveling the uneaten fruit into a bag, so Frankie had to keep calling until Mama caught the keeper's eye and flicked her gaze up toward Frankie.

The keeper turned to look, then paused, absorbing Frankie sitting up there.

Frankie said, How do I get them to turn around?

The keeper squinted, watching her mouth.

Frankie tried to make her mouth movements distinct, I need to see the sexual swellings. To do that, I need to get the females to stand up and turn around. How do I do that?

The keeper snorted and answered, Your problem.

The keeper turned away, then paused and looked back. Her expression this time was calculating. She said, I'll get them to turn around for you, but it'll cost you 15 pounds of mangos.

At the word *mangos*, several bonobos peeped, looking from the keeper to Frankie and back.

The keeper said, You get the mangos delivered to the kitchen by 7 A.M. tomorrow.

The bonobos rustled and looked to Frankie for her response, focusing the way kids will when parents discuss the possibility of dessert.

Frankie examined the fruit lying in the sun. She asked, Why? They aren't even eating the food they have.

The keeper said, It's not real fruit. It's printed.

What?

3-D printed.

Nooooo.

The keeper said, The price jumped again. Bellows thinks they'll get used to it. It has all their vitamins injected. He says it's better for them.

What about that NSF grant? He can afford real fruit.

Check hasn't arrived yet. Can you buy the mangos?

The bonobos *chirped* back and forth.

Frankie eyed the keeper and said, Of course. The food will be here tomorrow. Can you help me now?

The keeper said, There's a pineapple cut up on the kitchen counter. Grab it. I'll get them to do what you want.

At these words, the bonobos reached for each other and the orgy started. Down in the kitchen, Frankie found the pineapple slices and scooped them into a bowl, the sweet scent of fruit. Turning away, she spotted on the other counter a plate of mango slices and was reaching for that too when she noticed that each slice was identical: same size, color and shape. Picking one up, Frankie sniffed it. Instead of the sweet scent of mango, there were only the overtones of printer cartridge. The piece of fruit sat in her hand as bland and practical as an eraser. She put it down and backed away.

By the time Frankie had returned to the balcony, the bonobos were cuddled together, happy. They looked from the fruit in Frankie's hand to the keeper.

The keeper grunted at Mama and made a series of signs. Her hands moved with confidence, tiny cheerleaders bouncing through their routine, occasionally slapping into one another.

The avatar appeared on the plexiglass to translate, Turn around so the woman sees your butt. Then she will give you fruit.

Mama looked from the keeper to Frankie. Her brows raised with surprise, she signed, Fruit fruit?

The keeper nodded.

Mama turned around immediately to show Frankie her butt.

Frankie read the temperature of her sexual swelling—98.3°—and threw her a slice of pineapple.

The rest of them gaped at this, then copied eagerly, twisting around to wiggle their butts back and forth, the males included.

Frankie read the temperature of the females, one by one—98.5°, 98.2°, 98.3°—throwing each a slice as she got their temperature. Stella's temperature was 99.4°, a degree higher than the average.

Frankie said, Jackpot.

Just before she turned off the thermal app, she noticed the percent sign was still there in the corner, pulsing.

*

Back when Frankie had been starting her Ph.D., evolutionary psychologists were focused on female mating choices, trying to figure out the reason for what appeared to be some of the more illogical preferences.

For instance, human females around the world preferred a mate with a strong jawline: the jutting chin of Dick Tracy. Researchers spent years studying this aesthetic caprice, searching for its benefit, before learning a bulging male jawline was associated with a high level of testosterone during adolescence. Elevated testosterone was hard on the body (only a teenage male in good health could tolerate it), but the increased level led to higher sperm counts as an adult. Thus, for a woman, a man's lantern jaw meant there was more of a chance of many children, all of whom were healthy.

Or take peacocks. Male peacocks with the weight and length of their heavy tail feathers could barely get airborne, had a hard time escaping predators. Logically it seemed a female should want a male with a smaller tail so any male offspring she had would be less likely to get snagged by a leopard. However researchers found, in the jungle, a more certain threat than a leopard was parasites. Cecal worms, trichomoniasis, tapeworms—they sapped calories and health. Since protozoans, as well as worms of all kinds, had shorter lifespans than peacocks, they had the advantage of being able to innovate genetically faster than their hosts. In order to maximize her chance of having offspring capable of living long enough to reproduce, a female had to find a male with some proven ability at deterring these parasites.

It turned out the most certain way to determine which peacocks had few parasites—aside from expensive medical tests—was to examine their tail feathers. Freeloading worms of different kinds sapped the calories and chemistry necessary to grow long and vibrant feathers. The longer and more colorful the peacock's tail, the better that peacock was at deterrence.

The first step in any male's courtship was to stand his tail straight up and fan it out to display every inch of it, hoping his tail might pass inspection.

For two decades, evolutionary psychologists had continued in this manner, obsessively cataloging the practical reasons behind female mating preferences.

Frankie, for her Ph.D. dissertation, had decided instead to examine the whimsy, the mating preferences with no logical reason at all.

The feathery top hats she glued on the heads of a few randomly selected male finches obviously showed nothing about their genetic abilities. From a strictly evolutionary viewpoint, the females shouldn't care about the hats.

However, it turned out the females craved them. They wanted the hatted males so much that—although normally they required their males be monogamous and share the childcare—if a male had a hat, he could philander to his heart's content and not help one whit with the offspring.

The red stockings Frankie painted onto some of the male finch legs were also not related to genetics. However, again the females had a strong opinion, hating the stockings. These red-stocking males were lucky if they managed to find a mate at all and if they did, they got stuck with most of the childcare.

In her thesis, having shown that females could have strong

aesthetic preferences utterly unrelated to evolutionary survival, she ventured the theory that females who shared a similar ideal of male beauty (no matter how capricious) would outcompete those who didn't. Using the analogy of fashion trends, as well as some elegant math, she pointed out it didn't matter what the desired style was—high hems or low hems, top hats or red stockings—only that the majority of available and healthy females wanted it. In this case, the males with the trait had their choice of many females. They were able to mate more often and could select the very best females, thus creating more and healthier offspring. The male offspring were more likely to have the desired trait, the females to want it. The trait replicated.

Certain aspects of male beauty, in other words, became the equivalent of the platform heel, demonstrating primarily the exuberance of life.

She called her paper *The Whimsy of Desire*.

The men in her department were confounded by her study, kept asking about it. They seemed to have a hard time putting the words *male* and *beauty* in the same sentence, or *female* and *desire*. In no way is science immune to the surrounding culture. Just a decade earlier in the field, one of the research topics had been if females of other species experienced orgasms and, if so, what possible function that experience could fulfill.

One of the men in her department who seemed most bewildered by her study had a girlfriend who worked at *Bust Magazine*. The girlfriend ended up writing a story about Frankie, asking which famous men might be so desirable that simply looking at them made strong women ignore their principles. Frankie answered these questions while thinking of her old college professor, how when he spoke about evolution her mind lit up, making her utterly forget about his wife.

Two years before, she'd learned that red meat, chocolate

and wine accelerated endometriosis. Since then she'd been surviving off what she termed rabbit food. She had developed a visceral hatred of the watery scent of salad bars, as well as the earnest smiles of waitresses at vegan cafes. She dreamed each night of slicing flesh off the shoulder of a sleeping cow, the cutlery made of pure chocolate, each mouthful bloody and sweet. She would startle awake, her pillow wet with drool.

In the magazine photo, she looked lanky, her hair gleaming.

A local entertainment-show host saw her photo and brought her on for a five-minute segment on a slow news day (avatars in those days were only on national sites). He questioned her about women's preferences and what she in particular wanted in a man. She kept trying to bring the conversation back to zebra finches and statistically significant correlations. For this morning show, the two of them were seated at a kitchen counter on stools, facing the cameras and studio lights. Perched on the uncomfortable stool, she worked to sit perfectly still, her right arm cradled protectively over her gut. She imagined her pain locked away in a bank vault on 54th Street. The interviewer sat very close, saying the cameras needed to frame them. He leaned in closer. Three minutes into the interview, he asked her if the research showed older men were the most attractive. Under the kitchen counter, he pushed his knees hard enough against hers that she had to shift slightly. The bank vault opened. She said in her gravelly voice, Not if they're like you. The station got a fair number of calls.

For two weeks she became popular on different shows. Although she tried to keep the conversation on the principles of evolution and her study of finches, the interviewers kept asking about the attractiveness of different male movie stars, as well as the details of her personal life. She explained she was not a zebra finch and expressed caution about extrapolating results across an entire phylum without additional testing. At the time, she had difficulty with patience. She was on

50 milligrams of codeine a day and, because of the internal adhesions, she hadn't been able—with her legs straight—to reach her shins for two years. No matter what she said, the interviewers continued to ask her to draw sweeping conclusions. She responded by telling one interviewer if he had paid more attention during tenth-grade Bio, maybe he wouldn't have to wear pancake makeup to work each day. She informed another if he learned not to interrupt then maybe his wife would have sex with him more often. Clips from her interviews went viral. In the city, for a short time, teenagers used her last name like a verb, the word meaning to be sharply insulted, as in *He was Burked*. She began to get mail calling her an angry lesbian or asking her if she was busy Friday night. She refused to go on any more shows.

In the field of evolutionary psychology, her study caused a lot of angry rebuttals. In a country where a large percentage of the population still expressed skepticism about Darwin's theories, no evolutionist liked the word *whimsy* connected with the field, especially not in a public way.

She received her degree and managed to secure an adjunct position at Barnard, but had difficulty getting funding for further research. Every foundation she applied to denied her application. Unable to afford even finches, she searched for an animal she could get access to in the middle of the City.

Logically enough, she began studying the mating criteria of humans.

By that point she'd started dating JayJay, a 28-year-old waiter who moonlighted in a local funk band. She did a literature review on what details were correlated with lasting relationships. One of the strongest correlations was that the man needed to smell good to the woman. JayJay, an affectionate and good-looking man, smelled as attractive to her as Styrofoam. Her physically soft and older professor, on the other hand, had a sort of malted salty scent, like some combination of warm

Guinness and fresh sperm. She used to cuddle in against him, her nose pressed into the center of his chest, her arm over his belly, dozing, content as a cat.

What might smell signal? Limited in terms of funds, she began an experiment with T-shirts and cardboard boxes, using students at the school as her subjects.

DAY 13

Seventeen

First thing in the morning, the keeper stepped into the enclosure to hide the food.

That new researcher, she saw, was sitting up on the balcony watching. She was skinny as a plucked turkey, wearing what looked like kids' clothes. She always seemed to be near the enclosure, her posture clenched as a fist, watching the apes.

Once the keeper had hidden all the fruit, she let the bonobos into the enclosure and they spread out, searching. When any of them found one of the few slices of real fruit, they'd peep with happiness, calling the others over to share it. When they found printed fruit, they'd sniff it, then drop it to the ground and continue searching.

Later in the morning the keeper stepped back into the enclosure to clean up after the meal.

On the climbing structure several feet away, Tooch opened his mouth in what looked like a squeal and jumped onto her shoulder. He was her favorite. She was the one who had named him Touch for her favorite sense, but she hadn't pronounced it clearly enough, so now everyone called him Tooch. Perhaps they thought Tooch was a family name for her—short for Tucciano or Tucciato.

With Tooch holding on, she systematically searched for feces or uneaten fruit, using her shovel to scoop all of it up and drop it into a trash bag.

She spotted a piece of printed fruit up on a beam on the climbing structure. She grunted at Goliath and gestured to the fruit.

Get, she signed.

He shook his fist *No.*

She made the sign for *please*, right hand moving in a small circle over her heart.

He looked at her with his dark eyes, then knuckled over to the printed peach and dropped it down in her bag.

Frankie, sitting in the balcony, watched this interaction, listening as the avatar on the wall translated the exchange. She was surprised by the gesture, *Please.* The meaning of *please* was hard to teach. It wasn't a word that signified a physical object—like *ball* or *stick*—an object could be held out each time that word was used. Nor did it mean any clear action—like *come* or *sit*—actions that could be repeated until the meaning was understood. *Please* was more complicated and harder to convey. It could modify any verb and roughly meant, *If you do that action, it would make me happy.*

If a dog didn't do the action you wanted, most people would never use *please* with it. If they did, the dog would just continue to stare, its ears perked. No, a person would only use *please* with someone who could really understand language, someone who also had choice, someone who also did not have to obey.

Frankie watched the keeper scrubbing the enclosure down, a small efficient tank of a woman. Stotts had mentioned she'd worked here for seven years, one of the only people who went inside the enclosure every day. As the keeper walked by Mama, Mama reached her hand out so her fingertips just brushed her calf, a casual gesture of affection.

*

At 8:15 A.M., Stella stood up on two legs to walk behind the small concrete hill. Goliath watched, then knuckled after her. Both of them disappeared behind the hill.

The temperature of Stella's sexual swelling was still elevated. She was likely to be ovulating.

Frankie tried to call up the video feed from the cameras on that side of the hill, but got only static.

She rushed downstairs and ran through the building to look through the windows in the interaction area. By the time she got there, Stella was sitting in Goliath's lap, her head on his chest. She didn't know if they'd just mated or not.

She watched through the windows for several minutes, until Stella got up and wandered back around the hill. Frankie hurried back upstairs to the balcony, counting one Mississippi two Mississippi, her maximum speed a half trot. It was a big building. It took her 21 seconds to get down the long hallway, climb the stairs to the balcony, unlock the door and step out. By the time she'd arrived, Stella was now sitting in Sweetie's lap, her arms around him.

Frankie leaned over, pressing one hand to her side and huffing. She was abruptly angry. She needed a way to see both sides of the hill. Given the general disrepair at the Foundation, she couldn't depend on the video feed.

She let her eyes roam around the enclosure. They came to rest on the climbing structure. It was built on top of the hill. If she sat on its first level, just seven feet off the ground, she'd be able to see everything that happened anywhere inside the enclosure. There wasn't another viewpoint that would allow her to do that.

So she walked downstairs to the door to the enclosure, the one inside the research room, and said, Ok Door, unlock.

Opening the door, she took a step inside, waiting to see what the bonobos would do. Other people stepped into the enclosure without a problem: the keeper, Stotts and a few others.

Every bonobo in sight turned to stare at her: furrowed brow, rigid stare, tight mouth. When she didn't step back immediately, they started to scream. The screams, however, sounded like enraged parakeets.

She took a second step forward, further into the enclosure.

Parakeets didn't weigh 70 pounds.

The Terrible Two—Marge and Adele—charged at her, two hairy bullets, shrieking Dobermans with huge hands. Mama right behind them.

The muscular grace, an inhuman speed, an unearthly keening.

Frankie jumped back out of the enclosure and slammed the door. She was standing there double-checking that the door was locked, when the keeper barreled into the room.

The keeper yelled, Don't *ever* step in there without permission.

Frankie turned, incredulous. This woman was wearing coveralls smeared with dung. Permission, she asked, From you?

No, the keeper said. She pointed to Mama on the other side of the plexiglass and said, From her.

DAY 14

Eighteen

In the morning Frankie set out looking for the keeper. She found her and Bellows on the path near the Snack Shack, having some sort of disagreement. The keeper was leaning into her words, her chin jutted forward while Bellows stood there looking offended, then glanced down at his wrist. Frankie noticed he actually wore a watch, the wind-up analog kind, perhaps a real antique. Watches had come back in style lately, demonstrating wealth, and giving the owner a gesture with which to signal impatience.

As Frankie approached Bellows interrupted the keeper to say, It'll be *fine*. They'll get used to it. Give them a few more days.

Clearly expecting Frankie to want to talk to him, he turned to her and spoke in a very different voice, Dr. Burk, how may I help?

However Frankie instead addressed the keeper, I don't think we've been properly introduced. I'm Frankie. What's your name?

The keeper—powerful as a plow horse—answered, Daisy.

Frankie blinked. Unable to associate that word with this woman, she immediately discarded it, never using it either in speech or in her mind. She asked, How do I say, *Can I enter*, in sign language?

The keeper watched her lips, concentrating. She didn't seem surprised at the question. She spoke the word for each sign, her actions graceful and exact.

She said, *Me*, while she thumped herself in the chest with her fist, thumb-first.

For the word *enter*, she scooped one hand under the other, as though her hand was sliding under a wall. She raised her eyebrows to signify a question.

Frankie repeated the gestures as best she could, unsure about the exact position of her thumb or the angle of her wrist, performing the visual analogue of mumbling.

The keeper demonstrated again, her movements as crisp as a voice on the BBC. Frankie tried again.

The keeper grasped Frankie's hand and adjusted the curve of it for the word *enter*.

Frankie repeated the two gestures again. *Me enter?*

The keeper nodded.

And Frankie simply turned away, without saying thank you. The whole interaction nearly silent. On the way back to the enclosure, she kept repeating the gestures to herself to memorize them.

Behind her, there was a pause, then Bellows and the keeper continued their disagreement.

*

Frankie sat in her chair in the visitors' area, waiting. The next time Mama knuckle-walked by, just two or three feet away, Frankie got out of her chair to sit on the ground in front of Mama, only the plexiglass between them. She found by this point she could pull her legs into something approximating a cross-legged position.

Mama glanced at her, curious. It was just after lunch, only two tourists in the area. At Frankie taking a seat on the cement, they both looked over.

Frankie directed a bonobo pout at Mama, her lower lip pushed out as far as possible. A pout was used by inferiors when requesting a favor from a superior. She flicked her eyes to the spot just in front of her, then back at Mama, still pouting. In order to be clear, she repeated the eye gesture.

Mama tilted her head. Her lack of surprise reminiscent of

the keeper's. She sat down in front of Frankie, Tooch draped across her back like a cape that snored. Frankie had begun to think of Mama as Queen Elizabeth I—something about her high forehead and the regal tilt of her chin. All she needed was a red wig and a dress with a tall collar.

Looking into her eyes, Frankie thumped herself in the chest with the thumb side of her fist. Then her right hand scooped under the bridge of her left hand. She raised her eyebrows and waited.

Mama stared at her, thinking it over.

In case her gestures had been unclear, Frankie repeated the question. She flicked her eyes into the enclosure to be specific about what she wanted to enter, and then added the word *please* for good measure, her palm tracing a circle over her heart. She hoped she got all the gestures right. She remembered once in Spanish class trying to say she was embarrassed—making a guess at the right word—and being told instead she'd declared herself pregnant.

Tooch woke, smacking his lips. Leaning forward, he jabbed a curious finger as far as he could up Mama's nostril. She backhanded his finger away with a clear *thwap*, not taking her eyes away from Frankie.

Then Mama shook her fist, *No*. Briskly and decisively.

*

October now, the days were getting shorter and colder, long Vs of ducks and geese migrating overhead, honking. Other smaller birds migrated also.

A little after 2 P.M., a tiny songbird hit the plexiglass with a startling thwack and tumbled to the ground inside the enclosure. All the bonobos looked over, surprised.

It lay on the cement, unmoving, its beak open. Frankie couldn't see if it was breathing or not.

Mama knuckled over to pick it up, turning the tiny body over. She lay it on her palm and unfolded one wing ever so gently, then folded it shut. Repeating the action with one wing, then the other.

She looked up at the plexiglass where the bird's imprint was still visible, as she softly stroked her thumb over its bright yellow head.

Still holding the bird in her hand, Mama rose on two feet and walked over to the climbing structure. The structure was made of rebar and metal I-beams. Using just two feet and one hand, she climbed the structure as easily as Frankie could ascend stairs. At the top she sat for a moment, scratching her armpit and sniffing the wind, before looking down at the bird in her hand.

Then she drew back her arm and flung the bird into the air, returning it to its element.

The body arced over the enclosure wall, rolling through the air like a tiny feathered ball. At no point did it start flying. Instead it hit the ground outside with a small bounce, motionless.

Mama stared at the body, wondering what she'd done wrong.

Frankie watched, her mouth open.

*

That afternoon, Stotts asked, When you met Tess in my office, what'd you say to her?

They were walking down the hall to flint knapp with Goliath. Frankie asked, Why do you ask?

He said, She keeps asking about you.

She glanced at him, pleased, and said, Nice kid.

What'd you talk about?

Politics.

She was feeling so much better than when she first arrived: eating real meals, no pain, able to trot for short distances. Whenever she was around Stotts, she'd remember the brunette's look of pity and work to stand up straighter.

She asked, How's Tess doing?

He said, Good. Heading to England to try gene therapy.

Gene therapy?

Thymulin analog, he said, sixty per cent chance of a permanent reduction in the remodeling of the airways.

Frankie remembered parroting doctors' statements like that, fearful but hoping, an incantation that answered anyone's questions, a medical novena. She asked, Your insurance paying?

He blew air out his lips, You kidding? That's why she needs to go to England. Cause Ava's British, Tess can get free health care.

She looked to the right, trying to remember who Ava was, then realized this must be the name of his wife. Frankie nodded, I hope it works.

He exhaled, Wish it wasn't so far.

You're not going?

He glanced at her from the side of his eyes and she felt bad about her question. Airplane travel so expensive these days, it was amazing they'd been able to pay for Tess and Ava.

She waved away her question with her hand and said, Sorry. Let's change the subject. Are the bonobos much smarter than the other apes?

He said, Last year a researcher tested the I.Q. of every ape here using a puzzle with a prize inside. The bonobos figured out the puzzle fastest, but it was mostly three bonobos who skewed the results. Mama, Sweetie and Houdina.

Sweetie? Is he smart? Frankie asked. She hadn't paid much attention to him because he spent most of his time grooming others and sleeping in the sun.

Stotts said, Maybe. It's possible these three are geniuses of the bonobo world. Or it might be all the bonobos are just as intelligent and these are the three who happen to love gummy bears the most.

She asked, Aren't gummy bears bad for their teeth?

Stotts held open the door to the interaction area for her. He said, That's nothing. The chimps work for a vape pen.

Nooo, she said.

He glanced over at the pleasure in her voice, used to her sounding tired. She had more color in her face today. He said, The Trust got the chimps from this lab studying addiction.

Whenever she needed to stand up now, he still helped her, but not by clasping her upper arms to heft her upright. Instead he just held onto her hands and pulled gently upward, waiting until he was sure she had her balance.

He said, When the chimps smoke, they look a bit like Winston Churchill. They get this very internal expression.

He made a gesture like he was pinching a cigarette away from his lips while he tried to stick out his gut to imitate an older heavier man. Since he didn't have much of a gut, mostly he just jutted forward his ribs and hips. Rather than appear heavy, he looked like an athlete stretching.

She looked away. She didn't like noticing his body. The healthier she felt, the more being around this man made her feel tired.

She opened the door to the research room and asked, You ever feel weird about them being in a cage?

He said, Where the bonobos come from they are sometimes killed for food. If we sent the Foundation bonobos back there and released them, they'd run right up to the first human they found, expecting to be handed a peeled mango.

They stepped into the room, both standing there for a moment, blinking in the sunlight from the window.

He said, Or if we released them here, let them wander off Foundation property, a policeman or farmer would gun them down inside of an hour.

Tooch and Id were rolling on the ground nearby, tickling each other.

He said, Most people think of the enclosure as a method to keep them in captivity. It's more of a restraint for humans, to stop us from killing them. It says, *Don't shoot; private property.*

Ok Door, unlock, he said and opening the door called into the enclosure, Hey Goliath, I've got a new issue of *Glamour.* Want to come in and visit for a few minutes?

Goliath was getting groomed by Mr. Mister. He looked over at them and didn't move. Every day he seemed more reluctant to do the flint knapping, discouraged by his lack of progress.

Stotts had to call a few more times, before Goliath wandered inside to take his seat on the desk.

Stotts began to flint knapp. His hands moved without doubt, so precise and competent. Every time he snapped the hammerstone into the chert, there was a porcelain *clink* and a splinter of rock would slide off the chert. The shard began to take shape, a glassy edge appearing, the spine becoming longer and straighter as he worked. Having watched this process repeatedly, Frankie thought about rock differently now, as something mutable and fragile. With each glancing hit, the edge didn't shatter, but just shed another flake of rock, the blade becoming sharper.

Although Stotts always knapped with his hands out so Goliath could see every step, he was enough of an expert that he had no perspective about what the difficult points were for a learner. He hummed to himself as he worked. Frankie didn't know how hard this task was to master. Was it like drumming where you just had to copy the general motions and then gradually perfect the beat? Or was it more like trying to play a Chopin étude by plonking your fingers down on the keyboard?

At one point, he scrubbed the hammerstone across the edge of the blade in a side-to-side motion.

Why you doing that, Frankie wrote on the whiteboard. Although Goliath no longer got tense if she moved, she hadn't yet tried to talk in his presence.

Stotts was so absorbed, she had to clear her throat to get his attention and tap her marker on the board.

After reading the note, he frowned down at his hands. He asked, Sorry, why am I doing what?

She made a rubbing motion with her hands.

He said, Ahh, abrading the chert helps reduce splits.

At this statement, she glanced over at Goliath and saw he didn't understand that any more than she did.

When Stotts finished knapping the shard, he used it to cut the rope and open the box, pulling out the banana. He then put some gummy bears inside the box and tied it back up, settling into his seat and eating his banana while Goliath picked up two rocks.

As usual Goliath simply slammed the rocks together at the end of his arms, their centers hitting rather than their edges. *Thunk*, said the rocks and only dust sprinkled off. He pulled his arms back further and did it again harder. *Thunk*.

Watching him so imprecisely mimic Stotts' action, he didn't look all that smart, certainly not smart enough to comprehend language. However Frankie didn't know how hard it was to figure out how to knapp.

She leaned forward to examine the unused rocks left on the desk. When she picked a hammerstone and a chunk of chert, both males turned to look at her.

She set the hammerstone down and turned the chert around in her hands. She had no idea what criteria Stotts used when deciding which side to carve, so she just placed the flatter side down on her thigh so she could balance it there with one hand. The hammerstone was big for her hand. Holding it, she drew her arm back and hit the edge of the chert hard. The hammerstone bounced off with a dull *bonk* and she nearly dropped it. Not even dust came off the rock.

Stotts said, A MacArthur, huh?

Goliath, on the other hand, was watching.

Her next strike was sloppy, too close to the center. The hammerstone again bounced off like a ball.

She focused, picking out the exact spot she wanted to hit, then swung hard. This time she hit the right spot, but nothing happened. Like Goliath, she hadn't spent a lot of time using handheld tools. The hammerstone was heavy enough it was difficult for her to aim. She kept trying, narrowing her eyes and holding her breath before each hit. After three minutes, she hadn't chipped a single piece off the rock.

She flicked her eyes up at Stotts. He was enjoying this.

She gritted her teeth, saying nothing, but continued to concentrate, experimenting with her grip and the length of the strike. Her arm was already aching, as well as her hand. Her thigh (which absorbed the blows through the chert) felt bruised. After each strike, she paused to examine what had happened.

She wasn't playing Chopin; she was trying to pick her way through a few notes of Chopsticks.

Goliath studied every motion she made.

DAY 18

Nineteen

S taring at the Moments cube, one picture of Stotts' wife stood out. She was younger, late twenties, wearing waders in a stream, fishing, the water twinkling around her. She was turning to look at whoever was taking the photo.

Images were supposed to be about what was in the frame, the people, the action and setting, but Frankie had always considered a Moment also a description of the person who framed it. She could learn so much about that person from what was included and what wasn't, from which moment was selected and from the emotion on the faces of the people as they looked at the photographer.

In the image, Stotts' wife's smile was open, her eyes soft.

Curious now, Frankie searched for a picture of Stotts where he had that softness in his eyes. There was that one in the hospital when he held the newborn Tess, staring down into her face, but none where he looked at his wife that way. Of course, who would select such an image to look at repeatedly? Each person would instead select images of the spouse's love.

In these earliest photos, his face was different. He wasn't just younger, but seemed untroubled.

*

Every morning on the balcony, Frankie read the temperature of each female's sexual swelling. The first few days she had to hold up the mango to get the females to turn around. Once she'd gotten the temperature readings, she'd toss the chunks of food down.

However with each day that passed, getting the readings took less time because the bonobos had begun to treat her differently. Perhaps this change had been going on for a while and she'd only begun to notice it. Before they'd sometimes stared at her, eyebrows raised and waiting, like at a magician hired to entertain them. Now, when they turned to her, it was more to check her reaction. For instance when Tooch, hanging off the climbing structure by two fingers, slipped and landed on Sweetie's head, several would glance over, to see if she was amused also.

And they'd begun to respond to her in other ways. To get a female to turn around, rather than hold up a slice of fruit, she could now simply call out the name of the female and make the gesture for *turn around*. If she added, *please*, the female would most often comply.

And she'd changed how she dealt with them too, for after she'd gotten all the readings, she'd lob down to the bonobos one by one every piece of fresh fruit she had, throwing fruit even to the males, making sure each of the apes got at least one piece. She enjoyed watching them snatch the fruit out of the air, then sit down, peeling the skin off, chirping with happiness. After the food was eaten, some of them would look at her and tap their pinched fingertips together, the gesture for *more*. Others—such as Petey, Lucy and Stella—preferred the bonobo begging gesture, holding their palms upward and flexing their fingers. She assumed these bonobos hadn't been raised with sign.

Each morning, after they'd finished eating, she'd call out Mama's name and ask with gestures if she could enter the enclosure—thumping her fist into her chest, then swooping one hand under the other.

Mama would consider her—searching her face for who knows what—then look away, not even bothering to respond.

Frankie didn't like having all the tourists stare at her on the balcony, so before the gates to the Foundation opened each day, she'd return to her normal viewing spot in front of the enclosure. Taking a seat in her folding chair, she noticed that, even with the thermal app off, that percent sign was still visible, pulsing in the corner of her Lenses' screen.

Probably this was another sign of incompatibility. She really needed a new BodyWare implant. Getting the new implant would just take a fast visit to an app store. A nurse practitioner would inject it, explain the potential adverse reactions and bill her Bindi. Frankie had been putting this visit off for months, along with a visit to the dentist, filing her taxes and other such chores, because she'd been sick. Now she needed to get to these tasks.

*

In front of the bonobos, some of the tourists answered mail while they waited for their children. They talked to themselves in a continuous muttered undertone, gesturing, their eyes fixed on something only they could see, like toddlers whispering to imaginary friends. The main difference was they specified punctuation, saying, Thought you'd be interested. Period. Send.

Meanwhile Adele jumped from one side of the climbing structure to the other, flying 15 feet through the air to catch hold of a metal beam with one hand. Only a few of the adults glanced up at the athleticism of her loop-de-loop.

The parents who watched videos were less unnerving. They didn't talk to themselves, but just stood there quietly staring up and to the right, their mouths slightly ajar, their Bindis lit, as motionless as if they were asleep standing up. From a few feet away the cumulative audio of a crowd of EarDrums sounded like the sea or distant traffic.

Two men wearing Kansas City Royals shirts yelled and pumped their fists at the same time.

Alrighty, one called looking up and to the right.

The other yelled, *That's* the way.

The nearby children turned to stare. They'd been watching Adele fly back and forth.

Frankie, like the children, watched the bonobos. Not having yet reached a point where she'd begun to develop a theory, she mostly sat in her foldout chair observing and thinking, while eating as much as she could.

Frankie's disease, endo, was made worse by gluten, wheat products and dairy. Bread with butter had been a forbidden food for her for a decade. Post-operation, she was ready to experiment. This morning she'd defrosted readymade pizza dough and cut into small bread rolls. She'd let the dough rise until the rolls were plump balls of gluten, then cooked them in the lunchroom toaster oven.

Watching Adele, she pulled one of the still hot rolls out of her bag and tore it open to drop in a generous chunk of butter. Waiting for it to melt, she held the roll beneath her nose and inhaled the scent.

With her first bite, she closed her eyes. The crunch of the warm crust, the rich butter. As soon as she finished the first roll, she started on the second.

When she'd gone to the supermarket a few days ago, she'd selected anything she desired, tending toward the organic, artisanal or imported options, piling it all into her cart. The Foundation was located half an hour outside of Kansas City. In the Midwest over the last decade, the rains had become less predictable, the summer temperatures soaring, the crops failing year after year. Locally there were few jobs left. Most factory workers had been replaced by high-tech machinery, administrative assistants by apps. Lately big data had taken the jobs of many doctors and lawyers. As she pushed her heaping cart up to the self-check-out, several customers had turned to stare.

She was eating her ninth roll when a loud bang made her jump.

A few feet to her left, a teenager—maybe 18 or 19—had kicked the plexiglass. He was with another boy. Both wore camouflage jackets decorated with safety pins and spray paint. The older one had a tattoo of a spider on his neck.

The bonobos, used to humans slapping the plexi to get their attention, glanced at the boys and then turned their backs.

Seeking a bigger reaction, the boys began to kick the glass rhythmically with their leather boots. *Bam-ta bam, bam-ta bam.* The level of noise reverberated. Inside the enclosure, it must be louder. The juveniles jumped and Mama's baby, Tooch, startled awake and began to wail.

Mama looked at the boys: furrowed brow, intense stare, rigid mouth.

The teenagers kicked harder, encouraged.

The humans considered the boys and then looked away, wanting someone else to deal with them.

The teenagers continued to kick the glass. *Bam-ta bam, bam-ta bam.*

Mama panned her eyes across the assembled people, looking for help. Spotting Frankie, she paused, staring directly into her eyes. Once she was sure she had her attention, she flicked her gaze to the teenagers and then back.

Frankie stared back, surprised.

Mama raised her eyebrows at Frankie's slowness and repeated the eye flick for clarity.

Irritated at her attitude, Frankie did nothing. For a moment there was a standoff.

Then the teenagers' kicking escalated and Tooch threw his head back to scream louder, flailing with fear.

So Frankie turned to the boys. Unlike the other adults here, she'd lived in Manhattan for most of her life and had a sense of which strangers were dangerous and which just dressed the part.

She called, Cut it out.

The rhythm of their kicking didn't change. Perhaps they hadn't heard her.

Mama waited, her eyebrows raised.

Frankie inhaled and boomed out in the gravelly voice she normally saved for medical staff, You dicks touch that glass one more time and I'll call security.

The teenagers paused mid-kick to assess if she meant it.

Over the years, she'd learned how to be the loudest patient, how to make doctors obey. The ability to lie was a muscle; it grew with exercise. She said, Head of security here is Roger Craig. He was a Navy Seal. Want me to call?

They looked at each other.

Ok Bindi, she said, Call Roger.

Quickly they backed up, walking away down the path. They couldn't hear her EarDrums say, Roger who?

Mama grunted to herself and then sat back down. She didn't glance again at Frankie, not even to acknowledge her help.

*

During grad school, Frankie wouldn't consider a hysterectomy. This wasn't an intellectual thought; it was more a demand of her body. The urgency reminded her of the time she'd tried scuba in college. Scuba had attracted her because she'd assumed it would be a languid swim where life was weightless, a sport she could manage. However during her second scuba dive, 20 feet down into the water, the instructor had snuck up behind her to yank the respirator from her mouth, tugging it back over her shoulder where she couldn't easily reach it. The teacher had been doing the same to different students, forcing them to practice retrieving the respirator with a slow roll of the arm. This way if the respirator ever came out of the mouth when in deep water, the person would be able to get it back.

However when the respirator was pulled from her own

mouth, Frankie forgot what she was supposed to do. Watching her lifeline air dart out of sight, she forgot everything. All conscious thought disappeared. The only thing that remained was the emptiness of her mouth, the lack in her lungs. She kicked toward the surface.

Her reaction to a hysterectomy was at the same biological level, an unthinking physical flight.

So instead, she scheduled laparoscopic surgery to burn away all visible endometrial adhesions, as well as to cut through the scar tissue that tied her diaphragm to her liver and her uterus to her bladder, freeing her innards from their webbing. Waking in the recovery ward, the first thing she was conscious of was how easy it was to breathe, her gut moving freely for the first time in years. With that simple difference, the pain she was in seemed negligible. Recuperation was effortless. She had hope.

She went on the Pill to minimize her menstruation, decreasing the speed with which new adhesions would develop. Within two weeks, her legs straight, she could reach down as far as her ankles. She discovered, without adhesions, she had a walk that bounced. Everything seemed doable. Her laugh returned, bubbling up at the slightest excuse. She hardly needed sleep, having spent so much of the last few years in bed. She wrote her dissertation in three weeks, her EarDrums blaring Shakira, her concentration laser sharp.

Within a month, she'd met JayJay in a Tribeca rooftop bar, the bar decorated with plastic lit-up skeletons, the night air smelling of vinegar from the artisanal pickle plant around the corner (forever afterward JayJay called her his little cornichon). He fell in love with her over a plate of onion rings while she grinned at the bright skeletons.

At first their time together was effortless. He was a happy-go-lucky soul who played tambourine in a band called Eat a Peach. He worked at a restaurant and had a large collection of Japanese erasers in the shape of food products. Once on a lark, he took her trash-picking with some Freegans he knew. He clambered right into the supermarket dumpster, up to his knees in trash, yodeling with delight when he found some steaks past their due date, encased in plastic and still cold from the fridge.

Everything was different from how it had been with the professor. She could be with JayJay whenever she wanted, holding hands and calling him Baby in front of others, sleeping with him in the same bed at night.

There was an ease to being with him, a nice guy who got along with everyone and made her laugh, but who under no circumstances could make her lungs ache with loss. The few times they argued, she engaged without fear or limits, feeling the high-wire exhilaration of knowing she could walk away right now. Inevitably, he gave in. Afterward they'd have sex and she'd rock hard against him, grunting with surprise.

They moved into a beat-up Victorian on Staten Island, a group house with 12 other people (a combination of landscape-design students, would-be recording artists and anarchists). Lines of carpenter ants bustled across the floor and walls, doing their best to transform the building into sawdust. The living room chandelier was made of coat hangers strung with slices of pizza that at some point had been carbonized by mistake in the oven to the airy perfection of graphite. The slices glittered in the sun, twisting gently. The house pet was a wild spider that scuttered about on its own shelf over the kitchen table. The housemates left offerings for it of the dead ants they found on the floor. The spider grew rapidly, glandular and misshapen, an inflated glove with beady eyeballs. Frankie hadn't realized spiders could get fat. When she stepped toward the shelf, cupping the comma of a dead ant in her palm, the spider would edge into sight around the corner of the books it hid behind. It waited there, motionless as a rock, until her hand retreated. Then it would pounce upon the dead prey.

JayJay and Frankie were the last couple to move into the house. There were no rooms left so they chose the knee-wall closet on the top floor. The door to their closet was only four feet tall so they had to get on their hands and knees to enter. Inside, the ceiling slanted down at a 45° angle to the edge of the roof. In cross-section their room was an isosceles triangle 10 feet wide at the base. JayJay said they were living the Pythagorean dream. The most they could jam inside this space were two boxes of clothes, a lamp and their mattress. All of this, of course on the taller side of the room.

There was no insulation in the roof between them and the outside. In the morning, the pigeons would land on the shingles—so little between her and them that it sounded as though they were landing on her back. On summer afternoons, the closet was blisteringly hot. In the winter, Frankie and JayJay had to bundle up in quilts and spoon one another for warmth.

Still the rent for the space was affordable, even considering their low incomes (an adjunct teacher and a waiter). Near the City, this type of living wasn't unusual; especially since the war in Syria had begun to drive up oil prices, increasing costs on almost everything. JayJay's best friend lived in a Village apartment with a warm-bunk schedule. It took 10 of them to pay the rent on the small apartment, so each roommate was given a scheduled time to sleep, the blankets still warm from the last person.

Frankie didn't mind. She was in her twenties and without pain. Life at this point seemed a stage play that she had no need to take seriously, neither the scenery nor the role. Their attic garret was a set, a child's hideaway, the pigeons cooing like the audible purr of her heart.

And she really needed the cheap rent, because a majority of her income went to her health insurance and medical expenses.

Ever so gradually over the next few years, the pain began to creep back. One day a month, two days, then more, gradually becoming worse than it had been during college. Each morning she spent a little longer in her knee-wall room, lying on her side, staring at the underside of the roof while she mustered energy to move. She thought of the dead ants she found everywhere in the house, stiffened into that final contortion. In her mind, she listed all the tasks she needed to accomplish before she could lie down again, calculating the shortest distance between each. Although life remained a stage play for JayJay, for her it returned to reality. She did whatever she needed to cope.

She found a second job—an easy one with access to strong painkillers—as a part-time employee in a compounding pharmacy. She told her manager she couldn't start her shift until 11 A.M. When he asked why, she answered flatly the mornings were when she had her chemo.

At this, her manager's eyes went wide, then flicked away. As though he'd glimpsed her nude. He didn't ask follow-up questions.

Most people had no association with endo, no idea of its scope or implications, whereas they did know about cancer. By giving him the wrong disease, she communicated more about the truth of her experience.

She had a shuffling walk already, so now each day before work she simply tied a scarf over her head to cover her hair. She stole from the pharmacy whatever pain medications she needed. Although she knew others probably saw or suspected the thefts, no one said a thing. Instead each day they asked in a voice close to a whisper how she was feeling.

She answered honestly, Not great.

Even with health insurance, her medical bills piled up, all the items that somehow weren't covered—lab tests, pathology reports, deductibles on medicines, the referrals to specialists. Her credit card bill grew larger every month. She could barely manage the interest, much less pay down the debt.

DAY 19

Twenty

I n the morning, when she turned on the thermal app, she noticed an ampersand had joined the single percent sign in the corner of the screen, both of them pulsing.

Once she'd read the temperatures of the females' sexual swellings—Marge's temp now the highest—Frankie asked Mama if she could enter the enclosure.

Mama considered her, her brown eyes focused. Only after a moment did she shake her fist no.

This, Frankie figured, was an improvement.

She took her seat in front of the enclosure. This morning in her circuit of the Foundation, she'd managed to maintain the speed of a shuffle-jog, the whole time thinking about what she would eat for breakfast. Now she unwrapped this food, a pork sandwich with lots of mayonnaise. Holding the sandwich up under her nose, she inhaled the scent, feeling her mouth water.

Goliath was sitting near her nibbling on a piece of printed fruit, his nose wrinkled. She pulled the sandwich away from her mouth long enough to tell her Bindi to increase her daily order of mangos to 20 pounds and to add five pounds of papaya.

Then she bit into her sandwich, feeling the hunger deep in her bones.

For years, her diet had been restricted in an attempt to control her symptoms and pain. She understood pain was necessary in the world, a sense as critical as sight or hearing. It functioned to keep people safe, a very persuasive stop sign. In a way it was the mother to us all, slapping us back from the hot stove, forcing us to put down the sharp knife, teaching us self-preservation, training care into our bones. Pain was the reason we were alive. It was why as children we didn't toss ourselves down the staircase for the thrill of the ride, didn't stop eating just to bother our parents, didn't nibble off our fingertips to examine our insides. Pain made our existence in this world possible, opened life up to us.

And pain was not only about damage. In smaller doses, it could be a sign of improvement and increasing strength: the ache of muscles growing, the gasp of lungs strengthening, a soul learning to endure in order to fulfill its desires. Pain could be the sign of achievement.

However all these benefits were predicated on the pain being able to be avoided—on the assumption that if the knife were removed, the agony would go away; that once the muscles were stronger, the ache would stop. A lesson learned, an adjustment made, the hurt circumvented in the future.

Unstoppable pain was different. The sensation in this case was not a mother. It was an abuser. It taught nothing. Instead it wrapped itself around the ribs, settled on the shoulders, a weight to be borne, making it hard to breathe or talk. During college, it had pressed Frankie down into a smaller person.

Pain like this did not open up the world; it erased it bit by bit. Over time, it erased her love of yard sales, of eating, of the simple act of laughing. By the middle of graduate school, it took away her good temper, as well as her desire to spend time with friends. Then one by one, it erased the last of her college friends. She survived through drugs like Vicodin and Riophine and through learning to focus on problems she found very very interesting, difficult problems with many variables.

*

In the research room, Goliath studied her attempts at flint knapping. Her fumbling motions were much slower than

Stotts' and she practiced each strike in the air a few times before attempting it. Watching her, Goliath stopped slamming the rocks together in front of him at the end of his arms. Instead he began to imperfectly copy her attempts, raising one stone to slam it down onto the other. Sometimes he slapped the chert into the hammerstone, other times the hammerstone into the chert. Both of them paused at times to eye each other's progress.

At one point, she heard a loud *clang* and looked up startled. Goliath had propped the end of the carved rock on the desk to hold it steady and was hitting the rock with the hammerstone. The metal desk now had a divot in it.

She propped her carved rock on the other corner of the desk and began to hammer at it that way too.

Ma'am, said Stotts, shaking his head.

Both she and Goliath shot him an annoyed look and continued.

Mostly Stotts was alright with her experimenting with flint knapping in front of Goliath. He said it was possible the two of them learning from each other might be a closer analogue to the way pre-humans had mastered the skill. After all it was unlikely there had been one pre-human genius who figured out knapping in a single generation. Instead there'd probably been a group of them who, through innumerable experiments over many generations, taught each other what they needed to know.

She could feel Stotts at times studying her as she slammed the hammerstone into the chert, her strikes weak and without skill. Still she worked at it, willing to take pointers from an ape. She was not the person he had expected.

After a few minutes Goliath and she found that hitting the chert while it was on the desk tended to shatter the rock into small chunks as useless as gravel. They returned to balancing the rock on one thigh when hitting it.

*

Living in the attic with JayJay, in spite of her illness, she continued her research into the smell of love. She persuaded 20 male students to help her, gave each an identical white T-shirt. Each slept in his T-shirt for a single night, then returned it to her. She folded each into a cardboard box with a hole cut into the box (not a hole big enough to see through, just big enough to smell through) and placed all the T-shirt boxes on a table. Each research subject—always a young woman who was ovulating that day—was brought into the room to pick up box after box, hold each to her nose and inhale.

Which box, Frankie asked, smells the most attractive?

She did not tell the woman what was inside (held to Frankie's own nose, she couldn't discern body odor, but only the sweet scent of cardboard). Whichever box the woman chose, Frankie noted it down: Female Subject A selected the box from Male Subject 14, Female E selected Male 7's box, etc. Sometimes the woman wouldn't want to put the box down once she chose it, lingering over it, inhaling, then saying, God, what's in here?

The most obvious initial finding was that attraction based on a person's scent was not like attraction based on looks. There seemed to be no universal criteria that would allow most women, eyes closed, to point to the man in the room with the most attractive scent. Instead, Frankie found, each of the men's shirts had its own fan club of ovulating females.

She had every male and female subject also take IQ and personality tests, fill in a questionnaire about lifestyle and eating habits, and give a saliva sample for genetic analysis. She ended up with a thick book of data on each person. For this first iteration of her research, she sifted through these books, searching for clues about what Female A might have comprehended with a single sniff, why she selected Male 14's cardboard box.

Meanwhile, Frankie's new doctor suggested, if she wasn't going to get a hysterectomy, the best treatment was for her to get pregnant, now. Pregnancy had been shown to frequently reset the endometriosis to an earlier stage and in any case, it would stop her from menstruating for nine months. He suggested this treatment in the same way he might have suggested she take ibuprofen—a dry logical voice. As though this particular type of medicine wouldn't need to be diapered, clothed and loved. At the moment, she didn't have enough money to take care of a hamster, much less a child.

JayJay had no interest in children, but he did pressure her to have sex more often. He wanted the kind of sex she used to have with him, the kind where she laughed and rocked hard. She wanted that too, but at this point even leaning over to get off her underwear hurt. So instead they tried reading erotica aloud together, lying on their bed in their knee-wall room. He would rub his penis; she would rub her temples.

Get a hysterectomy, said the specialist, Or pregnant. (His voice mildly aggrieved.)

Years later, stepping up to the microphone after her MacArthur Award was announced, she looked across the audience and spotted three different colleagues she believed would score higher on intelligence tests or have a more comprehensive understanding of their fields. Standing there, wondering why she was on this stage instead of them, the only difference she could think of was the way her disease had taught her mind to focus. Like a snapping turtle, once her brain had clamped its jaws on a specific problem it would not let go, not unless someone sawed through her scrawny neck. During the day, everything reminded her of her research into love: a couple holding hands, her mother sitting alone in the kitchen, the smell of JayJay's dirty laundry which she couldn't believe anyone would find attractive. And at night, her work infiltrated her dreams: her dental

174 - AUDREY SCHULMAN

hygienist leaning over to floss Frankie's teeth while reciting data from Male Subject 3; her mother wandering naked through the house tattooed with a chart of monthly estrogen levels.

In the end, she again chose a treatment her doctor had not recommended, taking Promisium in order to go into a pseudo-pregnancy, stopping her period entirely. The medicine worked well; if not to erase all pain, at least to decrease it. The reprieve glorious. She ballooned out in weight, appearing gravid and spotlit with joy. Plump, she developed breasts like a lactating Madonna. She felt a kinship with the pet spider that lived on the kitchen shelf, waddling around in its inflated body. Taking her Promisium pills each day, she felt she was swallowing stolen time.

It was during this respite that she grasped the pattern running through her research results: the differences in the genetic encoding of immunoglobulins. Each woman who selected the smell of a T-shirt box was choosing a man with immunities that she lacked. Like some sci-fi bloodhound, each woman was sniffing into the future, following the trail of children who had not been conceived yet but who were likely to be more disease resistant than either parent. True love for a woman was at least partly based on the tantalizing scent of healthy offspring.

Frankie published these findings to some interest in the field—tenured staff in her department now stopping to talk to her in the hallway, asking her what she would work on next and even suggesting she apply for the tenure-track position that she ultimately got. However, it was how she followed up on this paper that earned her the media attention. With the recommendation of her department head, she secured a Putnam Grant to take what she considered the next logical step. Based on genetic differences in immunoglobulins, could she predict who would fall in love with whom?

She advertised for research subjects on several Manhattan meet-up sites for singles, collecting the subjects' blood samples as well as the slept-in T-shirts from 200 men between 25 and 35 years old, and the blood samples from 57 women of the same age. From each blood sample, she classified the immunoglobulin type and subclass. Then she began to match-make. For each woman, she selected the 20 men with the most radically different immunities. She scheduled the test for when the woman was ovulating, lining up the selected men's T-shirt boxes on a table for a sniff test.

Soon afterward, the woman would be sent on two dinner dates: one with the man whose box she had selected, the other with a second male subject, randomly chosen. The woman was not told at any point what had been in the boxes, nor what the boxes had to do with the two men she went on dates with.

When the experiment worked, it was a life-changing event. Female Subject T sent Frankie a Sim-mail at 3:47 A.M. on the night of her date, divulging in one long run-on sentence how his face had seemed more and more interesting, his words more pertinent until at one point the bowling alley tightened and shifted and she'd sat down plop on the floor with the weight of all that had changed. Subjects G, N and AA arrived the next morning to tell her about their dates, but as they talked they kept back from her, their eyes big. She wasn't sure what they were imagining might happen if they got too close—that, with a wave of her hands, she might erase this emotion they felt, or might make them feel even more of it.

Before she'd finished the experiment, three women had moved in with the men whose T-shirts they'd chosen. One was engaged. As the word spread, there began to be a line out her door of men and women asking to be in her study. However, these new subjects acted differently; now they had demands.

Some women wanted only to sniff the boxes of men who were Jewish or had a full-time job, or at least were guaranteed not to have a criminal record. The men began to request their sniffers all be younger than them, or brunette, or have a low B.M.I. Several already enrolled subjects, who had not yet gone on their dates, abruptly pulled out of the study saying they weren't ready for this level of commitment.

Even before her research was published, an online dating company contacted her (one of the company's marketing staff happened to have been in the study). The company paid her $163,000 cash for the rights to her research. At the time, this seemed a miraculous deal to her, pulling her out of credit card debt and putting money in the bank for whatever medical intervention she might need next.

However, within six months, this company released their product based on her research. They called it the Love Bank, charging $5,000 for a chance at true love. Not only did the price ensure a hefty profit, it also suggested the applicants might be of a certain economic class (which in turn increased sign-ups). For a short while—before all the lawsuits hit: the baby born with Tay-Sachs, the polygamous husband, that battered wife—men lined up in droves to deposit their T-shirts, and women lined up to sniff them. The Love Bank opened up branches across the country, became a staple in Hollywood and the Hamptons. A popular movie star was introduced to a hedge-fund manager, the wedding a whirlwind three weeks later. Two reality shows were filmed at the Bank, as well as one sitcom.

Much of the publicity revolved around the CEO of the Love Bank, filming him driving around Manhattan in his Bugatti with his supermodel girlfriend. Public broadcasting of course preferred to talk to the researcher behind the science. Ari Shapiro asking about Frankie's earliest memory of smell, Science Friday posing its nasal questions about the possibility of synthesizing individualized perfumes to keep a couple together.

Marketplace Money on the other hand never called. Instead for the week after the Love Bank had its first public offering of stock, the low price of $163,000 was the punchline to every joke.

By that point though she didn't care. The Promisium wasn't working anymore, and the pain had returned.

Twenty One

After the keeper rolled up the gate to the enclosure, the bonobos exited their sleeping chamber. Certain that all the fruit hidden around the enclosure was 3-D printed, they didn't bother to look for it. Instead they just sat in front of Frankie on the balcony.

Even after she'd thrown all the real fruit and they'd finished eating it, they continued to sit there for a while, hoping for more. Only after she held up her empty hands and then the empty bucket did they begin to knuckle around the enclosure, searching for the printed food.

A minute later, Lucy peeped with surprise, scooping up a scrap of real mango where it had fallen into a crevice. Petey, next to her, snatched it out of her hand and cantered away.

At a male daring to steal food from a female, every female reacted as one, bolting after him, screaming, all teeth and ferocity.

Although Petey weighed 10 pounds more than any one of them, chased by this crowd of fury, he dropped the mango chunk and backed into a corner, crouching and covering his head, while the females *waa*-barked and whacked branches onto the ground near him. Finally, they wandered off to nap in the sun, exhausted.

The hunger was getting to all of them.

Frankie watched this, then said, Ok Bindi, double my order of fruit for tomorrow.

Her EarDrums said, Doubling your order of fruit for

tomorrow to 40 pounds mangos and 10 pounds papaya. The total, with delivery, is $653.87.

She paused for a moment at this number, then said, Ok, buy.

Her BodyWare seemed strangely slow. The cursor on her Lenses spun for two whole seconds while it processed the order. Watching it, she noticed the percent sign and ampersand in the corner pulsing.

Ok Bindi, she asked, How far is the nearest App Store?

Her Bindi responded, 63 minutes away under present traffic conditions.

Frankie said, Jeez.

Her Bindi asked, Would you like me to schedule a car?

Frankie inhaled, considering. She looked at Adele, whose temperature was currently elevated, then answered, Not yet.

*

Stotts and Frankie were both at the table in the kitchen, eating lunch and working on their Lenses. Both gestured in the air, flicking from one page to the next and talking to their devices. He was eating a peanut butter and jelly sandwich. She was dipping pork rinds into a bowl of warm caramel and then swinging them into her mouth. She savored the sweet greasy crunch. There was not a single ingredient here she would have been able to eat before: sugar, meat, lard. Meanwhile, on her Lenses, she charted her data of bonobo copulations, wanting to see if any of the pairs were mating with one another more frequently.

He asked, Why do you study mating?

For a moment she assumed he was on a call. Glancing around the 3-D histogram on her Lenses, she noticed he was looking at her.

She wiped a spot of caramel off her chin and replied, Secret to evolution, right?

He said, It's something more than that to you.

She spread her fingers to increase the size of the histogram and spun it gently. It showed the pair who mated the most were Marge and Adele. Two females mating were not going to have the evolutionary impact she was looking for.

She said, Relationships are a mystery to me. Maybe if I can figure out how other animals manage, it'll help me.

He answered with doubt, Maybe.

What do you mean?

He said, You are a trifle . . . direct.

She looked at him. In that single word, so much was compressed.

He didn't speak as Kansas-polite around her anymore. She didn't speak as Manhattan-rude around him. They were instead developing a common language. Lately she'd noticed him sometimes watching her, his head to one side, like the bonobos, trying to figure her out.

And she was curious about him too. She imagined he had the life that she did not—at night when he went home, a child running to him, a spouse smiling.

She admitted with only the greatest reluctance when he was right.

*

Mama was leaning back against a tree, a child's book in her lap that she was scraping the honey off of and eating. She used her nails to pry the next two pages apart.

For a single moment she stared at the pages, clearly gobsmacked with surprise.

Her scream of terror was piercing.

She dropped the book and, in a display of raw athleticism, flew to the top of the climbing structure. Up there, unable to get any further away, she leaned over the side, shrieking down at the book where it lay on the ground, the little hair she had left standing up on her arms and back. All the bonobos bolted up after her, terrified. At the top, they spun around confused, searching for danger. Only after a moment did they spot the book. Squealing down at it, their voices were truly hysterical, probably partly because they didn't understand.

In front of the enclosure, Frankie got up and stepped closer, one hand on the glass. The bonobos stood on the metal bar at the very top of the structure, holding on with their toes. Sweetie tried to climb Mr. Mister's back, wanting to get further away. Id clung to Houdina, terrified.

Then Frankie spotted Goliath. He was howling with fear and eyeing the top of the plexiglass wall, bobbing his head up and down, judging the distance. If he attempted the jump and missed, he would fall 30 feet to the cement.

So Frankie bolted around the building and down the hall, moving faster than she'd moved in years. She opened the research-room door and stepped inside the enclosure. The level of noise was physical. Above her, Goliath was taking half steps from one side to the other, trying to find the best spot to jump from.

None of the bonobos, at the moment, cared she was in here. She ran to the book.

Above her, their voices changed, trying to warn her of the danger, Goliath looking down at her.

Picking the book up, she saw it was a normal preschool book. *A is for Armadillos* said the first page. *B is for Bird* said the next. Then she turned the page to see, *C is for Chimp*. A photo of a chimp grinned out at the viewer, many teeth visible.

Above her, spotting the photo, the bonobos began to wail with an entirely new level of terror.

Mama was looking at her, making the same gesture again and again, a gesture where her hand moved rapidly from her mouth down. The avatar translated. Frankie couldn't hear what she said, but the text underneath read, *Bad. Bad.*

Mama's hands were shaking. She made a new gesture: her right thumb heading for her eye as though she wanted to gouge it out, the motion stopped by her left fist. She made the gesture several times.

The text under the avatar read, *Danger. Danger.*

Frankie closed the book to hide the chimp. She said, It's alright. It's fine. Just a picture.

None of them could hear her so she used one of the only signs she knew, shaking her fist *No no.*

Her motion however shook the book and they shrieked louder.

So Frankie opened the book and ripped out the page with the chimp.

There was a shocked silence, then more wailing.

She held out the page and tore the image of the chimp in half and then into smaller pieces, using large gestures so they could see what she was doing. Their screams changed, but did not quiet down. Cupping the pieces and the rest of the book in her hands, she carried all of it out of the enclosure. As soon as she started moving, the bonobos all scurried away, as though she carried an armful of flying snakes that might launch themselves into the air at any moment.

She dumped the book and pieces of paper inside the building, then stepped back into the enclosure, holding out her empty hands for them to see. She walked over to where the book had been and patted the ground.

All gone, she said, All gone. It's alright.

Since they couldn't hear her, she made the sign for *no* and then for *danger*, imitating as best as she could Mama's gesture.

Their voices now held a note of confusion—either her gesture was garbled or they weren't sure now if they should be scared.

On the way out, she stopped to pick up one last scrap of paper, a tiny curl of blue background. She took it with her, closing the door behind her. Through the window, she could see the bonobos still crying, sniffing the air and searching for any sign of the book or photo.

She walked back around the building to her normal spot in the tourist area. The bonobos stayed up on the structure, holding each other and rocking, their cries quieting. Now that she was outside of the plexiglass, she could hear the apes in the other enclosures bellowing at all the commotion.

It took her a moment to separate out the sound of the chimps, behind her and to her right. A chaotic roar, deep voiced and primal.

The bonobos held each other tight, sobbing with frustration at a world with chimps in it.

The keeper came running up the path. She yelled, What happened?

Frankie said, One of the books had a picture of a chimp in it.

The keeper stepped closer, staring at her mouth and said, Speak slowly.

Frankie said, Chimp. Mama saw a photo of a chimp.

The keeper looked at the bonobos, then back at Frankie, How?

It was in the honey book.

Damn.

Frankie asked, Why is she so scared of chimps?

Mama came from the same lab as the chimps. They hate her.

What? Why?

The keeper shrugged, Something happened.

Since Frankie had been buying fruit for the bonobos, the keeper had been treating her better, more willing to answer her questions.

The keeper added, They know she's here.

Frankie asked, Why does she like you so much?

The keeper paused, confused at the sudden subject change.

Frankie said, She trusts you.

The keeper looked at Mama who was clinging to Marge on

top of the climbing structure. She said, Her breasts don't produce much milk. She had two babies before Tooch. Both starved to death.

Ohh, breathed Frankie.

The keeper said, With Tooch, I taught her how to feed him with a bottle. She's grateful.

For several days after this, every bonobo gave a wide berth to the spot on the ground where the book had been.

Twenty Two

Frankie slept in. She'd been sleeping much deeper as her gut healed and for some reason this morning her Bindi didn't wake her up at the right time. When she opened her eyes, the sun was streaming in the window. Turning on her Lenses for the time, she saw the percent sign and ampersand had been joined by a dollar sign in the corner of the screen.

She shuffle-jogged around the Foundation, then ate breakfast, before heading to the enclosure. By this point, the tourists were already entering the gates. Since she'd arrived at the Foundation, she'd been working with less intensity than normal, giving herself time to recoup—to cook and eat, talk with Stotts and knapp with Goliath. At night she'd even started reading a novel. Soon, she was sure, she'd start working at her normal pace again.

Setting her chair up in front of the enclosure and sitting down on it, she waited for Mama to walk by. Looking into Mama's face, she asked in sign language, *Me enter?* The gestures came to her more naturally now and she ended the question with the sign for *please*.

Mama considered her for a moment, then made her decision. She flicked her eyes to a spot just beside her, inside the enclosure. She did it just once. The minimum needed to communicate.

Surprised, Frankie stared back.

Mama's eyebrows rose at Frankie's slowness.

Obediently, Frankie hustled around the building and down

the hall to the interaction area. The keeper was nowhere in sight.

At the door to the enclosure, Frankie said, Ok Door, unlock.

She opened the door and took a tentative step into the enclosure, checking Mama's reaction.

Mama glanced at her and then away. The other bonobos, seeing this, simply watched, their eyes big.

For a full minute, Frankie fussed around near the door, coughing and scuffing her feet and clearing her throat, watching their reactions, before she let the door shut behind her and began to walk up the hill. Every movement she made echoed off the plexiglass as though she were in an aquarium. She felt like an audience member who, searching for the bathroom, had wandered by mistake onto the wrong side of the stage lights.

Once she was visible over the hill, there was a swell of noise from the tourists, the surprise on their faces.

She stopped beneath the climbing structure, looking it over. She needed to be at least seven feet up on it. From there, she'd be able to see every mating that occurred in the enclosure, no matter where. Since the bonobos made scaling this look so easy, she hadn't considered how she'd do it. Even baby Id could scoot up the structure at a run. There were handholds— metal rungs that crossed the posts at irregular intervals—but the lowest of these was a foot above Frankie's head.

She grabbed hold of this rung and tried to do a chin-up on it, but only managed two inches before she coughed out air and dropped back down.

The bonobos stared.

Next she attempted wrapping her hands and thighs around a post to shimmy upward, but—grunting and heaving—succeeded only in looking like an angry pole dancer.

She didn't glance toward the tourists, but could hear their attentive silence.

So she stepped onto the tire swing, standing up, holding on to its rope. The weight of her feet canted the tire away from her, making her twirl about in a somewhat horizontal position, a human piñata. With effort, she kicked first one thigh, then the other, onto the top of the tire and pulled herself up into a sitting position.

Spinning slowly, she saw the tourists staring motionless, hands on the glass. This day was turning out so much better than they'd imagined.

She moved her hands up the rope, then clambered to her feet on top of the tire. From this new height, she was able to grab a post and lurch over onto the structure.

Taking a seat there on the metal beam, her back against a post, she glanced over at the bonobos. At first, she thought something medical had happened. They'd fallen on their sides, writhing, breathing hard.

Laughter. She'd seen them laugh before, but through the plexiglass hadn't heard it. It sounded like they were half huffing, half grunting, the chuckling of asthmatic piglets. Mama had her arms round her ribs, her face in pain. Marge and Adele were clinging to each other. Goliath seemed particularly hard hit, spread-eagle, waving a hand in front of his face as though brushing away the memory of her climb.

She sat there with as much dignity as she could muster.

After the bonobos had recovered, they climbed into the structure to cluster around her, ready for her next miraculously entertaining action. She sat still, assuming soon they'd get bored and return to their normal behavior. Then she could become the unobserved scientist, taking notes with her Bindi.

However, nothing this exciting had happened in the enclosure for years and the bonobos had patience. When Frankie refused to move, they began exploring her hair, picking at the insides of her ears and tugging at her clothes to see if they came off. She slapped at their hands.

The tourists continued to crowd in, five deep, then 10, staring. At one point she spotted one of the Foundation staff pushing through the crowd to find out what was going on. When he spotted her, he froze, absorbing the scene. He recovered and nodded at her, doing his best to act as though of course she should be sitting inside the enclosure.

*

After three hours, the attention of both the bonobos and tourists exhausted Frankie, so she climbed down and went to take a nap on Stotts' couch. When she woke, Stotts was sitting at his desk working.

He was relaxed around her now, didn't stand at attention anymore or address her as ma'am—perhaps because Frankie was so bad at knapping or maybe because she rested each day on the couch in his office, looking rumpled and tired.

Or maybe, simply, like horses, they'd become physically accustomed to each other.

She wasn't the kind of person who talked when it wasn't necessary, so whenever he was working in the room she continued to lie there, her head pillowed on her arm. There were long silences. He coughed and opened drawers, jotted items down and muttered to himself. Occasionally he spoke, saying whatever was on his mind.

He said, Tessie's learning how to play checkers, she beat me yesterday.

Frankie responded, Can't be that hard.

He looked at her. Instead of being amused, his eyes were sad. He said, She's leaving today for London with Ava. First appointment with the gene-therapist is Wednesday.

You worried?

He raised his brows and inhaled.

He talked about Tess much more than he talked about his wife. To Frankie, this was understandable, a focus of attention built into the genes. The desire for romantic love was strong, yet a person could fall in love with any number of people—the resulting relationships broken sometimes for the smallest of complaints: he didn't do the dishes, her friends weren't fun.

The parent-child bond was different. Even though the relationship started off with the parents in the role of the lowest sort of slaves (wiping the master's butt, responsible for every meal, being screamed at for mysterious infractions in the middle of the night), what parents divorced their newborn? No, instead hopped up on hormones, they gasped with joy at any moment devoid of physical pain, filled with love for their incontinent tyrant.

The more essential and difficult an action was, the larger the desire for it. The chemical messengers released, the physical need pumping through the body. The greatest joy in life found in meeting the biggest challenges.

When Frankie considered the word *bliss*, the image that came to her mind was of wildebeests leaping into a river, migrating, thousands of them, their heavy bodies arcing through the air. She felt jealous of this moment—even though a second later when they hit the water, the powerful current shoved them sideways, others crashing onto them, a few drowned bodies twirling downriver—because this moment, the moment of the leap, their hearts were filled with exhilaration at this action they'd been born to do.

On the other hand, she had had to deny all she most desired. A juicy hamburger, a strong cup of coffee, the ability to inhale without pain.

Stotts got up and began to fill a bag with chert. He said, I'll try to use the time while they're away. Get stuff done around the house. Go biking off-road this weekend.

He closed the bag and said, Wakey wakey, time to flint knapp.

She grunted.

He said, My bike's a beaut. You should see it. Made of stainless steel.

On the couch, she pushed herself up into a sitting position, moving almost smoothly, her daily stretches beginning to have an effect. She asked, Stainless steel?

Yep.

Can you cook with it?

He smiled—superior in his biking know-how—and answered, It means the bike presses down into the road, gets better traction.

Cause it's heavier? Doesn't that mean it's harder to bike?

Makes me exercise harder.

She asked, Why don't you pop the wheels off then? *That* would make it hard.

He blinked at her. The longer she was around him, the more she noticed his eyes. They were a color that seemed so right for him, the most transparent blue, like clear water. The color felt very Midwestern, untroubled and straightforward. She felt if she stood close enough and the light was right, she could peer through his eyes straight into his brain. Everything in there would be just where it should be, clean and well cared for, nothing to hide. This decent man.

Her own eyes were dark brown, her brain shaded, twisted and dark, some gears whining and straining with speed, some areas utterly blocked off.

She waved her comment away with her hand, feeling slightly ashamed.

It was time for her to stand up. Automatically he helped her. By this point in her recovery, he held out just one palm. The solidity of his hand always surprised her, like a bookshelf in its lack of give. Inside her jumped the shimmer of gratitude, a fish in the air—the fear of her body's weakness still coiled there.

He waited, holding onto her fingers, until he was sure she

had her balance. She imagined him as a child, his mother training him, ingraining the requirement to help. The gallantry of strong men, she realized, must break the hearts of old women.

Today, she was wearing what she thought of as her Milky-Way outfit. The matching shirt and stretchy pants had a pattern of yellow stars against a dark pink sky. The material shiny and clearly flammable. He considered the grinning asteroid on her shoulder for a beat too long. She was a puzzle he hadn't figured out.

He asked, Have you started dreaming about them yet?

What? she said.

He seemed surprised he'd asked this.

He answered, Dreaming about the bonobos. Everyone who works with any of the apes dreams about them. The chimps, the orangutans, the gorillas. Not of them in the enclosure, but them outside, on a Sim-call or driving to work or ordering food at a Denny's.

He shouldered his bag of chert and held the door open. She stepped forward, the ease of her stride still surprising to her. For breakfast, she'd eaten 12 pieces of crispy bacon soaked in maple syrup. Crunching through the grease, she'd kept her eyes closed. The fatty rinds she'd held in her mouth for a moment, sucking on them like candy.

She asked, What do you dream?

His eyes considered her. For a moment she thought of the way Mama had eyed her when the boys were kicking the plexiglass, wondering if Frankie could help.

She didn't speak. She was curious, but felt no real investment in whether he answered or not.

Perhaps her silence was reassuring, for he offered, They phone me. I answer and can tell instantly it's a bonobo. They're chirping the way they normally do, but this time I understand the chirping as words. I even recognize the voice. Normally it's Mama, but sometimes it's Goliath or Sweetie.

The voice is always urgent and fast, relaying something critical. I can speak passable Spanish; from Tanzania I know some Swahili; from Syria I have a few phrases of Arabic. Whatever language this is, I can't identify it.

He glanced at her, It isn't a quiet dream. It's a nightmare. I wake up in a sweat every time.

He didn't smile to erase the edge in his statement. After a moment he looked away.

They were quiet for the rest of the walk to the research room.

With flint knapping, she was now better than Goliath. She didn't have as much strength, and her hands were half his size, but she could fairly consistently apply the blow at the correct angle, flicking her wrist at the last second to increase the impact, that glassy *clink* followed by a piece of rock sliding off. Now that she could do this reliably, she concentrated on learning how to shape the rock.

Goliath watched, trying to copy her technique, but could still only chip off small divots. He couldn't seem to master the timing of the wrist flick. Instead of swiveling smoothly in one fluid motion with his arm, his wrist would click mechanically into the swing, too soon or too late. After a while he got frustrated and gave up, playing instead with a metal cart that had been left in the room. Standing, he pushed the cart around the room, rolling it left and right, marveling at the miracle of its wheels—looking like a hairy naked shopper.

For the first time, the chert she was knapping began to look a bit like a blade. Even though the edge of the shard zig-zagged and wasn't that much sharper than the end of a screwdriver, she was excited and pushed herself to improve it, her arms aching and fingers beginning to tremble.

Then she missed.

She had enough time to think *Oops* before the full force of the hammerstone—a pound of granite—slammed down onto the tip of her thumb.

For a single instant it was as though the blow had hit her temple instead of her hand. It smacked away her vision and hearing, left only a vacuum where time was whistling.

When she returned, she saw there was a bleeding divot where her nail used to be. The nail was now standing upright like a car's open hood, connected by a thin strand of flesh to the nail bed. She knew what had to be done. Before the pain of the injury could truly arrive, she bit the corner of the car's hood and yanked it free.

She spat her nail onto the floor and slid her thumb into her mouth like a baby.

Both males stared. At no point had she whimpered or even exhaled.

What? she asked.

The sensation was starting to heat up her thumb, the hum of it rising, a choir searching for its pitch. The pain from small wounds—paper cuts and bonked noses—struck fast as lightning, no pause for worry. The agony from a larger injury took its sweet time, the anticipation terrible, like hearing an earthquake approach through the motion-alarms of cars, the wave of mechanical screaming rushing closer, heralding all that was about to occur.

She listened to her thumb's scream with something close to professional interest.

Jesus, said Stotts. You alright?

Well no, she answered, I need a Band-Aid.

Yes, said Stotts, I'll grab the first aid kit.

He hustled from the room, leaving her for the first time alone with Goliath.

Like guests at a party where the host had stepped out, the two of them looked at each other, wondering where the conversation would go.

Goliath was hunched forward, his shoulders pulled in, his expression pinched. He was, she understood, mirroring the pain she should be showing. If someone stepped into the room now, the person would assume he was the one who was hurt.

He held out his hand, palm cupped upward, arm extended and flicked his eyes to her thumb.

Curious, she popped her thumb out of her mouth and held it toward him.

He shuffled a few inches closer on the desk. She lowered her hand into his. His palm was warm, the skin solid and burnished smooth. Once on vacation in Maine, buying lobsters in the harbor, she'd touched the hand of an old fisherman to give him the money. His skin had felt like this, solid as a tight leather glove.

With her hand in his, she realized any fear of his greater strength had disappeared at some point during the days of sitting beside him on this desk.

Although he weighed less than her, his hand was huge, the palm elongated. Framed in his, her hand looked like a child's— tiny soft fingers, someone who had not yet lived but somehow been hurt. He cupped his fingers round her hand and rotated it ever so gently to see the wound better. A drop of her blood hit the desk with an audible splat. He grunted deep in his chest.

Then they heard Stotts in the hall saying, Ok Door, unlock.

Goliath and she both jerked away from each other as though caught cheating on a test. She slid her thumb back in her mouth, the damaged baby.

Stotts stepped into the room with the first aid kit. He put the kit down on the desk and held out his hand to her. Palm upward, arm extended.

Almost hypnotized by this repeated moment, she lowered her hand into his. Here, her hand looked different, like a painting in a new frame. Her hand and Stotts' were much closer to the same size, same color and hairlessness, the skin just as soft. Held in his, her hand didn't look so childish or unformed. Perspective, perspective.

However his touch was just as gentle as Goliath's as he patted the blood away with some gauze and then began to bandage her thumb, first smearing the inside of the bandage with antibiotic cream so he wouldn't have to touch the wound more than necessary.

The throbbing of her thumb was rising in volume. With her other hand, she rummaged through the kit for ibuprofen. Awkwardly she ripped open the paper envelope with her teeth and shook the two pills into her throat. She dry swallowed them with the ease of long practice.

Pain could be amplified dramatically by the mind. When worried about an injury, a person attended to the sensation, wondering why there was a sharp pain with every blink, was the retina getting lacerated? Was it getting worse? Was it irreparable? Before modern pharmacology and the specialization of pain clinics, an old treatment for unendurable chronic agony had been a lobotomy. A fast side-to-side motion up the nose with a scalpel and the person instantly became a Zen master, able to endure physical torture without it ruining their good mood.

There were many pain receptors packed in the nail bed of her thumb, but the wound signaled nothing permanent about her future, so she let the heat of it wash over her. Gratitude is all about comparisons.

She kept her eyes away from her thumb, looking through the window into the enclosure. Stella and Adele hung by their hands from the climbing structure, having sex, legs wrapped around each other, pelvises grinding.

Frankie said, You know I think I've figured out how to tell when they're ovulating. I've been using a thermal app to see when their sexual swellings heat up.

Stotts grunted, busy taping down the bandage.

She added, Of course, I'm going to need to confirm the method through urine or blood samples.

Stella and Adele orgasmed nearly simultaneously, lips curling back as they squealed with pleasure. They dropped to the ground and knuckled away, the pink inflated balloons of their nether regions wobbling behind them.

Irritated at their easy joy Frankie added, If they don't want to give blood, can I tranq them?

At that word, Goliath's face jerked toward her.

Stotts went very still. He said, A lot of them came from labs. *Never* use that word around them. *Never.*

She ignored him because she was staring into Goliath's eyes.

His eyes filled with horror.

She spoke quickly, I won't do it. I won't.

The first time she'd addressed Goliath in English.

She touched his hand and said, I'm so sorry. I wasn't thinking. Please excuse me.

DAY 22

Twenty Three

Each morning as soon as she opened the door to the enclosure, the bonobos turned to her, delighted. At her first step in the direction of the climbing structure, their panting laugh would begin to rise. Their taste in humor clearly ran toward the slapstick. By the time she'd laboriously climbed the tire swing, Tooch and Id would be gasping for breath so hard their mothers would pull them close to their chests, protecting them from seeing more.

Once she'd taken her seat, they'd swing up into the structure to cluster around her, staring, waiting for her next trick. While she tried to sit still, they began to play with her clothing and hair, tugging and sniffing.

As the tourists entered the Foundation at nine, filing down the path into the viewing area, they focused on her also, as though she were the species they'd never seen before. They crowded into the area in front of the enclosure, pointing and calling, rapping their knuckles on the plexiglass, working to attract her attention, framing her with their fingers as they asked their Bindis to take video. She sat there, attempting to be the very embodiment of boring, only moving to slap away the hands of the bonobos if they got too personal.

She reminded herself scientists couldn't always afford dignity. She thought of Darwin during his study of earthworms, yelling loudly at a bowl full of worms to test if they could hear.

When she talked, it was to her BodyWare, having turned on its transcription feature before she stepped into the enclosure.

Each time she spoke, the bonobos looked at her, assuming she was addressing them. However she would only state the temperature of a female's sexual swellings and then the female's name. They'd listen, their brows raised.

Today she added, Adele's in estrus.

The tourists watched her talk to herself inside an exhibit of apes.

Later on she said, Adele mating with Rupert. No penile entry. 9:13 A.M.

The bonobos turned to her, considering her words gravely.

Each time she spoke, the cursor on her Lenses spun for a second or two, thinking. Her BodyWare seemed slower each day. The ampersand and other characters collecting in the corner of the screen like dust bunnies.

Around 10 A.M., she checked over the transcript of her words on her Lenses. It looked at first like gobbledygook. *Adele's in estrus today* had been recorded as *A Dell in S-trust today.*

Adele mating with Rupert had become *A Dell may ding with rude perp.*

So she called for an appointment at the App Store. She waited, watching her cursor spin. In the end she got the earliest appointment possible, in four days. Her Bindi put it on her calendar. For the next few days, she'd just hand correct the notes.

Id climbed onto Frankie's shoulder and experimented with how far she could jam her index finger into Frankie's ear canal, especially if she wiggled it from side to side and pushed hard. When Frankie clapped her hands over her ears to stop her, Id began tugging on her hair—so much longer and easier to grab hold of than bonobo hair. She seemed to be trying to figure out how the stuff was attached. At first hesitant, she quickly became systematic, pulling and twisting like a product-tester checking for tear resistance.

Frankie blinked, leaning into the tugging, doing her best to concentrate on Adele.

About 10 A.M., she let her eyes wander across the viewing area and there was Stotts standing still in the crowd, several boxes on a dolly in front of him. Staring at her.

Marge and Mr. Mister were having sex beside her. Mr. Mister's butt sometimes bumped into Frankie's back with the sheer exuberance of their act.

After a moment, Stotts raised his hand and waved hi with two fingers.

*

After lunch, while most of the bonobos napped, Sweetie sat in the pool, squirting water out of his mouth. Adele waded in to stand near him. Frankie watched.

Up to their waists in the dark water, Sweetie began to groom her diligently, starting with the middle of her back and moving upward. After a few minutes, he'd reached the top of her head. He glanced around, all the other bonobos dozing. He pressed his body in close against her back.

In a species known for its loud and public sex, a secretive coupling could not be imagined. As he caressed her head, they spooned together—their hips moving slightly in the dark water. Anything that happened below their waists was invisible.

Adele opened her mouth, her orgasm for once silent.

Instead it was Frankie who made the noise. *Aha!* she said.

*

With JayJay, Frankie hadn't suspected the affair. She only learned about it by returning home on a Thursday half an hour earlier than normal. JayJay was standing in the front hall, closing the door to one of the other bedrooms in the home they shared. Jerking around at her step, his eyes were caught by her gaze, his expression stricken.

As she stepped forward, he eased backward, moving away from the door as though from a snake. Curious about why he was reacting this way, she grasped the still warm doorknob in her hand and stepped inside. A naked housemate, Nanette, lay on the bed dozing, a blue sheet tossed across her crotch. She and her boyfriend had moved into the house six months ago.

Frankie needed a moment to absorb this, so she sat down on the bed, grunting a little from the endo pulling inside her, feeling better once her weight was settled firmly on the mattress. There was the musky odor of fresh sex. She looked at her housemate in a new way, considering her from JayJay's perspective. The woman's armpit caught her eye, the wispy hair in that soft pocket of flesh.

She said, Nanette, wake up.

This was the moment when Nanette understood the person sitting beside her was not JayJay. She bolted upward, clutching the sheet to her chest.

Frankie asked, Why? Why JayJay?

Nanette looked around her room like she'd never seen it before, amazed at where she'd ended up. After a moment, she answered in a small voice, It hurts when I look away from him.

Frankie inhaled. After six years with JayJay, this was when she stopped sleeping with him. Not sleeping with him as in sex (the last time they'd managed intercourse had been at least a year before), but sleeping with him as in dozing next to him in the same bed, the rhythm of their breathing deep and slow, their bodies intimate and exposed.

She looked at him standing in the doorway, hunched with grief. For a second, she felt the full impact of what she'd lost, this easy-going attractive man who truly loved her. If only, she thought, if only her research had discovered some way to pick who she fell in love with, some genetically engineered scent to rub on him, some pill for her to take, she'd scrub the scent all over him, she'd take a full bottle of his pills; he'd be the man she'd choose.

Without that feeling though, without it . . . she remembered the way her professor used to say that he *luffed* her. Each time he said this, she'd looked into his face, so hungry for this statement that she'd ignore the fact that he wasn't looking at her, but over her shoulder to make sure no one else could hear.

She gathered her strength, then rocked forward twice, the bedsprings squeaking—the only way she made bedsprings squeak these days—in order to get to her feet and walk away.

She kicked JayJay out of their knee-wall closet and he began to sleep on the couch in the second floor hallway until Nanette broke up with her boyfriend so JayJay could move in with her, with the woman who could be at work 40 hours a week and so could afford a real room all on her own, not just a closet, who could wake up and stretch without pain, could have sex and give a big belly laugh, could do so much more than simply lie on her side for a while each morning concentrating on the task of breathing.

Still, each time JayJay and Frankie bumped into each other in the hallway, heading to the bathroom or on their separate ways to bed, he watched her with those sad eyes. She realized that while she knew Nanette loved him, it was unclear if he reciprocated. Of the three of them, she considered him the most injured.

Her own regrets, she began to purposefully funnel into a fascination with infidelity. After this, her second experience with it—albeit from different perspectives—she investigated the subject with all her strength. Working late at the library allowed her to avoid bumping into JayJay and it helped pass the time until she was able to sleep again.

She learned many studies had tried to figure out the extent of the phenomenon through interviews or anonymous questionnaires, but she didn't trust the answers people gave when asked how often they cheated on their partners.

Genetic testing was a way to get at least one solid data point. These tests showed 10% of newborns were not genetically related to the ostensible father who grinned down at them. There was some variation in this result, ranging from as low as 3% to as high as 30% depending on the particular society and the study's methods, but worldwide the average was 10%. The researchers compared this rate to a variety of other "monogamous" species—red-winged blackbirds, warblers and golden-cheeked gibbons—and didn't find it terribly noteworthy.

Frankie however did find it noteworthy, very noteworthy, because of course red-winged blackbirds did not have access to contraceptives or abortion. One in ten pregnancies, she discovered, were terminated during marriage by abortion. How many of these occurred because the wife was terrified her husband would take one look at the baby and know?

She wanted to figure out how much infidelity there was in the human population in order to learn if her experience was in the realm of normal. 10% was clearly the lowest possible percentage. The question was how much higher that percentage might be if not for condoms and Planned Parenthood.

Almost as soon as she started looking into this question, she came upon the startling fact that a woman with a lover felt an increased desire for him (rather than for her husband) when she was ovulating and, in her desperate passion, was less likely to insist on contraceptives.

When Frankie read this fact (*The American Journal of Human Biology*, Vol. 36, pg. 384) she was in the library in her normal position, stretched out on the floor under her favorite table, her knapsack pillowed beneath her head. In this position, she could endure reading for several hours. She blinked at the sentence and reread it twice to make sure she hadn't misunderstood, then flicked shut the journal on her Lenses and looked away, across the library at the forest of legs, both table legs and human legs, the human legs in all shapes and sizes, the feet propped up on chairs or crossed over knees. Nestled away behind these protective legs, hidden away under skirts or pants, were all those crotches with their mysterious goals.

She knew she'd spend the next few years investigating why a woman would desire her lover more when fertile. For a woman, reproductive instincts during ovulation were evolution's final exam. Any mistakes at that point could wipe her genetics right off the chalkboard. An increased desire for the lover when ovulating strongly suggested there was a benefit in having the lover's baby rather than the husband's—that conceiving a bastard helped in the long run.

At first glance this seemed unlikely. For millennia in most human societies, getting caught being unfaithful, much less conceiving a child through the affair, carried many potential dangers to the wife, as well as to the conceived baby and to any pre-existing children. Historically, the woman could be put to death. In contemporary times, there was the risk of divorce. In the U.S.—a country where it was relatively easy for a woman to earn an income—the average divorced mom had an income below the poverty level, impacting her children's health, food and life expectancy.

How could the evolutionary benefit of conceiving a lover's child be so large that it outweighed these risks?

Of course there were many situations where humans were programmed to put themselves into calculated peril. Young men, for instance, had a well-known difficulty with personal risk assessment, especially in front of their peers. *Watch this* were the famous last words of many a lad. They were programmed to run this risk because the small possibility of death or injury was worth the more likely prize of catching a woman's eye long enough to reproduce.

A young man's programmed stupidity however endangered only himself, not his progeny. Ten years later, that same man would be tightly gripping his minivan's steering wheel because his children were in the back seat.

If a woman conceived a child during an affair—especially if she already had children—she was risking much more than any young buck hamming it up along the edge of a cliff.

Frankie had difficulty sleeping because of the pinching pain of breathing, so she began to watch movies each night on her Lenses, lying on her side waiting for her exhaustion to become so desperate that it took priority. At that point, she wouldn't slide into sleep so much as click into unconsciousness, like a power cord was yanked. Three or four hours later she would snap awake. The only ways she knew time had passed were from the drool dried on the side of her face and that the movie was over, her BodyWare silent as it waited for her next command.

Each night she'd watch two or three shows—movies, documentaries or miniseries—whatever she could find that portrayed infidelity. She was surprised by how little there was. War (another human tendency) had many more shows and movies, whole cable stations seemingly devoted to examining and re-examining the Civil War alone. Why, she wondered, were cable stations and the film industry much less interested in infidelity, an experience so common that every tenth person was the product of it? The basic story was of love and betrayal—surely rich movie-making material.

Once she could no longer find any more shows on the subject, either narrative or documentary, she branched out into the genre of simple romance: the kind involving only one man and woman, no broken promises. Night after night she examined humanity's portrayal of what female desire looked like. The movies from around the world: American, French, Indian, Cambodian, Nigerian. In a way, the movies with subtitles were more informative. She would be so exhausted the flickering words wouldn't register, only the actions of the man and the woman, their movements on the screen. The similarity in these actions began to strike her, movie after movie showing the assertive and more sexually experienced actor leaning toward the actress who looked down and away, hesitant. The man stepping forward, the woman stepping back. As predictable as a waltz where the man knew the steps already and the woman wasn't even sure she wanted to dance.

During the day, Frankie read scientific reports on what was known about human sexuality. She learned the average heterosexual man reported having seven sexual partners in his lifetime.

For a heterosexual woman, that average was four.

The researchers of these studies generally reported these two numbers without commentary, didn't discuss the inescapable problem in logic. Who exactly were all these hetero men having sex with if it wasn't women?

At night, watching the movies, Frankie considered this problem. She began to wonder if these movie directors (virtually all of them male) might be sketching cinematically the mathematically impossible world that the average hetero man lived in; if the directors were coloring in this wished-for world, giving it emotional weight, running through variation after variation of the scenes until the myth felt like truth. These movies becoming something similar to propaganda, as thorough and vivid as Mao's monolithic portrait in every public square, the kind smile on his lips lit by a saintly halo. The researchers plugging their ears, the directors humming a lovely tune, everyone scrunching their eyes tightly shut.

Logically there were only three possible reasons for the numerical difference between the men's and women's answers, that gap between seven and four:

These hetero men were having sex with each other.

The vast majority of them were going to prostitutes (and the prostitutes weren't getting asked by academic researchers to fill out questionnaires concerning their lifetime number of partners. Of course if this were true, it would mean no gender gap in the average number of sexual partners, but only that the distribution curve for women was highly skewed.)

One or both genders were out-and-out lying and the entire culture nodding yes to this lie whenever they went to the movies.

Frankie became fascinated by the culture's unquestioning acceptance of this obvious numerical impossibility. During class, she handed out to her students a questionnaire with two simple questions on one side of the paper:

> *How many sexual partners on average do you think an exclusively heterosexual man has in his lifetime?*
> *How many sexual partners on average do you think an exclusively heterosexual woman has in her lifetime?*
> *(When finished, please turn page over.)*

On the backside of the paper was the final question.

If your two previous answers are different from one another, please explain the reason for that difference.

She watched the students as they read the two questions on the front. Their lips pursed, they hesitated only a second before they jotted down their answers. Then these young researchers—budding scientists at an Ivy-League university—flipped the paper over to read that final sentence. There was the longest pause. There came the rising sound of them flipping the paper back and forth from one side to the other. The rustling was the literal sound of their confusion, them shifting back and forth between their grasp of the mathematical incongruity and their deep societal belief in this essential difference between the genders. In the end, each student chose to write on one side of the paper or another. Only a few chose the first page, adjusting their original estimates so that the two numbers matched. Most spent their time on the second side of the sheet, justifying their answers with frantic theory-making.

This difficulty of smart people understanding such a simple concept reminded her of the way young men tended to stomp their feet on accelerators, unable to believe they might get hurt. Research showed that although an individual man could accurately assess the danger to other men in the same situation, he was unable do so for himself, always classifying his own skills as above average, his chances of getting hurt as nearly nil. This basic inability to comprehend was hardwired into his brain in the same way that every newly hatched turtle staring across the glittering sand to the ocean was certain it could reach the safety of the waves before the gulls got it.

So Frankie created a theory with three simple postulates:

1. Under the right circumstances, women *substantially* benefited evolutionarily by breaking the taboo against infidelity to conceive children with their lovers.

2. This benefit helped the species as a whole.

3. In response to the dangerous dilemma of needing regularly to break an important taboo, humanity had evolved a basic inability to assess the possibility that a wife might have a lover, or even to comprehend the blatantly obvious fact that heterosexual women had as much sex as heterosexual men.

The question now became how to test her theory.

Twenty Four

Leaving the enclosure that afternoon, she bumped into Stotts.

She noticed with surprise he was wearing a Bindi. It glittered in the center of his forehead, its logo one of the less expensive Asian knock-offs.

She asked, Hey, what happened? You got a Bindi.

Oh, he said and raised his hand to touch it, Yes, I finally broke down and got one since Tess is away. This way I can Sim-call her through Ava's eyes. I've never been separated from her this long before.

She added, You got the works installed? Lenses, EarDrums and implant?

Yes.

Good color choice, it brings out your eyes.

His expression showed a flicker of discomfort. He said, Let's move to a different subject. I was looking for you. Have you been assigned a bus yet?

Bus?

To leave on.

Leave?

Cause of Mavis.

Mavis?

He tilted his head and considered the conversation, then said, You don't listen to the news?

No.

Mavis is all they've been talking about for days. It's a dust storm heading this way. You'll have to leave with the rest of the personnel. You need to choose a bus.

Dust storm, she said.

He said, Maybe I should slow down. Mavis—the dust storm—is heading this way.

She nodded.

You ever been in a dust storm?

She snorted and shook her head.

Seen them on the news?

Well, yeh.

Around here, the last few years, they've gotten big. It's like during the Dust Bowl in the 1930s. Sometimes people die: from breathing problems or the static zaps them or they stumble into a farm combine in the zero visibility. In general, you want to avoid the storms.

She waited, conceding this point.

This one's big enough that the Governor issued an evacuation order for several counties. The Foundation will close. All non-critical personnel will leave. We'll crank shut the roofs on the enclosures and turn on the recirculation vents, so dust doesn't get inside. After the storm is over, we'll vacuum every square foot of the grounds, before reopening.

How many days?

The vacuuming?

How many days would I be gone?

Well, you'd leave tomorrow or the next day, be back next week sometime, maybe early the following week. Once the roads are clear.

Frankie looked back into the enclosure at Adele and Sweetie. She'd already lost so much time because of the broken cameras, as well as her recuperation. She might have just started figuring things out.

She said, I don't want to go.

He answered, Tough patooties.

DAY 23

Twenty Five

She woke early, around five in the morning, to the generalized feeling of fear.

She lay there, blinking, wondering what was wrong, then realized this was the day that her period would have started. It took her a moment to muster the courage to cautiously stretch, a little at first and then more, in the end leaning into her stretch and arching her back. No pain.

As dawn began, she shuffle-jogged around the foundation, pushing herself, thinking the whole time about how to celebrate. Back in her apartment, she made a pot of coffee twice as strong as the coffeemaker's voice recommended, heaping the coffee to the top of the filter. While it brewed, she pulled out some ground lamb, a package of chocolate chips and a tube of wasabi paste. She melted the chocolate in a double boiler. When the coffee was ready, she added cream and two spoonfuls of sugar, tasted it, then added another spoonful. Drinking, she let her eyelids flutter shut. There were a few grains floating that she chewed on thoughtfully.

From years of watching others eat what she couldn't, she'd learned how to appreciate food without putting it in her mouth. Stirring the melting chocolate, she inhaled the smell, admiring the spoon's wake, the thick folds that engulfed one another like some hidden biological process.

By this point in her recuperation, she'd put on enough weight that her clothing was beginning to fit differently, her limbs less insect-like, her face less pasty. Opening the package of lamb, she pulled a chunk off to roll it into a perfect bite-sized sphere, a ball of ground meat. She tapped the sphere delicately into the wasabi paste, then swirled it through the chocolate to coat it on all sides and pop it into her mouth. Spicy sweet meat.

After taste-testing different quantities of the three ingredients, she stirred some finely diced Vidalia onions into the meat to add texture, then prepped and ate 20 or so of the chocolate balls, sucking her teeth after each. She made more for lunch, setting the balls of chocolate on wax paper to harden. They were round and shiny as homemade bonbons.

*

In the enclosure that morning, Goliath sat beside her, holding her hand. Each time anything of interest happened nearby, he turned to her with his large silent-movie eyes to learn what she thought of it.

With no other toys, Id groomed her as though she were an oversized Barbie. The grooming started with a methodical search through her hair and clothes for vermin, then shifted to Frankie's face. She worked to scrub away anything that might be dirt.

Houdina didn't like it when Id was near Frankie. However she wasn't as tough a mother as Mama. She sat as close as she dared—three or four feet away—but didn't touch either Id or Frankie. She rocked back and forth on her heels, whining. The whine got louder whenever Id stepped into Frankie's lap.

Frankie's freckles were irritating Id. She huffed her hot baby breath on Frankie as she leaned in, concentrating. Her eyes focused. She licked her thumb and swabbed at the freckles, then, frustrated, tried digging them out with her nail.

Oww, said Frankie. She picked Id up from her lap.

At this, both Id and Houdina squealed in outrage.

Frankie placed Id on the beam next to her and patted her on the butt to scoot her away.

Id stalked off, limbs stiff with hurt pride, to the farthest end of the climbing structure. She sat down there, her back turned loudly to Frankie.

Frankie muttered, Pain in my ass.

Her Lenses transcribed this as *Paying MIS*.

Her BodyWare was taking longer to respond to any of her commands, as though distracted by some other more interesting conversation. Or perhaps evolving backward toward the abacus. Whatever the problem was, the transcriptions were developing a strong preference for business vocab.

She began reading the text right after she spoke, becoming accustomed bit by bit to its mistakes. A Dell = Adele, Suite E = Sweetie, It = Id, etc. By the end of the day, she was becoming competent at translating the BodyWare's transcription into what she'd actually said.

From her spot up in the structure, Frankie kept an eye on Lucy who was now ovulating, watching to see if she got near Sweetie or any other male. From this vantage point, she could also watch the Foundation prepare for the dust storm. Staff rushed about, pushing wheelbarrows of equipment or food. Kiosks and other outdoor equipment were covered up. Anything portable outside was removed. Beyond the trees, she could see the highway. One side was filled with cars speeding North, crammed with people and luggage. The other side was deserted.

Still there were a few tourists wandering around. Perhaps they couldn't leave until later today and had brought their kids to the Foundation as a distraction. Or maybe they wanted their kids tired so they'd sleep during the drive. Each time new people entered the viewing area, it was clear the exact moment when they spotted her. Their eyes would open with surprise, their mouths pursing around an exclamation like *Hey* or *Wow*. Then, as predictable as a dog sprinting after a ball, they would point and step in close to the plexiglass, all of them seeming to forget there were other great apes in the same enclosure.

And whenever she turned to look at the tourists, she'd absentmindedly try to figure out which were the mating couples and which were their offspring.

At one point, she spotted Bellows in the back of the crowd, staring at her with an open expression on his face. Then a Foundation employee with a wheelbarrow called to him and Bellows turned away with relief to deal with that more pressing situation.

*

When she turned 28, the endo reached a new level and she minimized her life accordingly.

She moved out of the group house on Staten Island, cutting herself like a cancer out of JayJay's life. She started living in her office to reduce expenses and so she could wake up and be at work, no need to muster the energy to walk to the subway. By this point in her career she actually had an office, even if it was rather unluxurious—off-campus on 107th Street, in a non-air-conditioned space on the fourth floor of a brownstone. Still she owned nearly nothing: her mattress and sleeping bag, some clothes and bathroom stuff, a plate and spork, a knife and mug. She kept all this in the office's curtain.

The only activity she engaged in, aside from doctors' visits and her work and occasional Sim-calls with her parents, was swimming. Exercise reduced pain while swimming was known to even out fluctuating hormones, so every day she swam half a mile in the university's pool. Dog-paddling was the only stroke that didn't pull too hard on the adhesions inside. With a snorkel and mask, she could rest her face in the water and paddle along, no energy wasted in lifting her head to breathe. The other swimmers raced past, their arms cutting through the water like synchronized scissors, forcing her into the lane for the elderly. Facedown, sucking hard on her snorkel, she struggled forward foot after foot.

Pain releases endorphins into the brain, chemicals similar

to morphine. The kindness of endorphins was why—right after extreme danger or a serious wound—a pure exhilaration sometimes coursed through the veins, the moment slowed down and transfigured with beauty.

Dog-paddling up and down the pool, distinctly high, she watched through her mask the semi-naked bodies in bright nylon kick past her, rowing their way through different stages of life and strength and health. She felt only gratitude that she got to swim on.

Outside of the pool, her heart was not nearly so generous. Once a week she would randomly choose an acquaintance to treat to lunch at the nearby Happy Burger. With great attention she watched the person eat, while crunching through her own spinach salad. Watching was the closest she could get to sinking her teeth into the juicy meat. Watching filled her stomach up more than her salad. She would try to be satisfied, but by the end of lunch, when the other person ordered a brownie or ice cream, the rage would begin to rise, the need to speak and hurt. Saying something cruel helped clean the taste of spinach out of her mouth.

One spring day, she felt better than she had in months and looked for someone to go to lunch with, but when she asked around she found there was no one left who would willingly have a meal with her, even if she paid. On her own, she stared out at the sky, which was a tender blue.

She realized this person sitting here, admiring the sky, wasn't a person she recognized anymore. She didn't know who she was without pain.

*

Without much else in her life, Frankie continued to work on her theory about the benefits of the lover's child.

Historically, a woman didn't have much choice in her mate. She was married to whomever in the tribe had enough resources to support her and her future children. Although this system increased the likelihood her offspring would get enough to eat, it didn't optimize the genetic diversity. Evolution could never allow this to be the only way to reproduce.

Thus, it was possible at some point during her life, the now-married woman would fall in love with someone from another group, falling for him because of his smell, the scent of a different immune system, the odor of future healthy offspring. Any baby that resulted from this love, if camouflaged successfully as the husband's baby, could continue to utilize his social status, food and protection. This child would then have the twin benefits of more resources and a stronger immune system, benefits that could result in a strong advantage.

However, the ability of the child to capitalize on this advantage depended on the secret not being revealed. This secret remaining a secret helped one out of every 10 children, along with their half siblings (since otherwise they could be tossed out along with the mom). Over generations, the need to keep this widespread secret had an impact. Her students flipped their questionnaire from one side to the other, unable to understand a simple concept, programmed to assume woman were sexually hesitant, no matter how many aberrations they knew personally.

For her research, Frankie used a national study from the 1970s that examined blood types in different populations. Through the sheer size of the study, it was possible to locate in the data 439 children who could not be their fathers', since the combination of the fathers' blood type with the mother's could not create the child's. With the help of three grad students, she began laboriously to track down as many of these children as possible, along with their "legitimate" siblings, in order to compare outcomes.

*

She was sitting in the lunchroom, finishing off the last few chocolate balls of raw lamb when Stotts walked in.

He asked, So what bus you leaving on?

Before she could answer, he spotted the food—what looked like chocolate bonbons—and tossed one into his mouth, saying Yum.

She watched, her eyebrows raised, giving no warning.

He chewed once before his expression got internal. A beat of time. Optimistically his jaws tried once more before he spat the food into his hand.

What the . . . he said.

His eyes were watering. Occasionally there was a larger chunk of wasabi.

He stared down at the ball of chocolate and raw meat, then at her. His tongue searching his mouth. He held out his hand and asked, What is *this*?

My new recipe, she said. Chocolate lamb tartare.

He absorbed that phrase, then moved straight to the sink to rinse his mouth out and drop the ball of food into it. He said, Jesus.

She asked, What bus are you on?

He gargled and spat before answering, A few people stay to help the keeper care for the apes. I'm one of them.

She narrowed her eyes, Some people are allowed to stay?

He said, Getting paid time and a half. It's great timing. I have to help pay for those tickets to England and this Bindi.

*

Three days after that restaurant meal where she'd stared happily at the sky, she went in for her regularly scheduled appointment at the pain clinic to update her prescription. She was handed the normal survey. There were many multiple-choice questions about pain intensity and timing and location. If she filled this questionnaire out, concentrating on her suffering, she would feel more conscious of it for days.

At the moment she had a bad cold. Each time she coughed, her ribs and gut convulsed, making everything inside of her twist, ripping at the adhesions. On the way to the clinic, she'd started coughing and sat down fast on the sidewalk, scared she might faint. A teenager Simming on his Lenses stumbled over her, his knee clonking her in the ear.

In the clinic, after glancing at the pain survey, she put it down on the table and said, No.

The doctor, a Nordic-looking expert in analgesics, was scanning her medical records. Staring up and to the right, his eyes shimmied back and forth as they read, as though he were dreaming with his eyelids open. He asked, No?

She said, I won't fill this out.

He flicked a finger to move to the next page and said, The survey? Oh no, you have to.

She asked, Why?

His eyes stilled for a moment, staring at what might be a photo or graph. Perhaps, because he was concentrating on something else, he was honest. He said, The insurance company needs it before I can get paid.

Into Frankie's mind flashed an image of her mattress on the floor of the closet of her office, her spork and hot pot sitting on the shelf above. During office hours, she kept the door to the closet shut. She asked, Do you think I care if you have to pick up chicken tonight instead of steak?

The doctor blinked and glanced at her, his distraction evaporating. His eyebrows were so blond they were nearly invisible, making him look a little like a newborn. She wondered how much personal experience he had with pain.

He said, If you want me to update your prescription, you're going to have to fill out the survey.

His attempt at coercion so unimaginative.

Through her years of being a patient, Frankie had earned the equivalent of a doctorate in how to make the medical system meet her needs. She knew why a shark would bite, tired of the grinding of its belly.

She said, If you ever use that word, *survey*, in my presence again, I will call 911 to say I suspect widespread drug abuse by the personnel in this clinic.

The doctor's gaze changed in some essential way. Instead of just looking in her direction, he focused on her, registering her for the first time as a separate human soul.

Frankie had reached the stage in her disease where she felt violence inside her, just beneath the skin, a savagery that pulsed in her throat and behind her eyes. She knew if it would decrease her pain even a fraction, she would stave this man's skull in with a rock. What she felt shone in her face.

She said, I've read 15% of medical personnel are addicted to the drugs they have access to. If I make that call, every employee here will have to take a urine test. What are the chances this clinic will be locked down for months while the situation's addressed?

In her years of pain, she'd developed her ability to find the soft spot in anyone, her instinct unerring.

She said quietly, every consonant enunciated, Write out my prescription *now*.

And he did.

*

A few days later there was a heat wave in Manhattan, accompanied by a rolling brownout as every AC in the city struggled to cope. The temperature on the sidewalk hovered at 112°, the entire grid strained. Rotating brownouts were mandatory any time the temperature exceeded 105°—all discretionary power turned off in the affected area, including Sim towers and elevators in buildings under six stories. A neighborhood's brownout lasted two hours before it was automatically rotated to a new area. The affected area visible from blocks away, hundreds of people lined up along the perimeter where they could get a signal, engaged in urgent conversations on their EarDrums. Once the brownout was over, the human perimeter dispersed.

Without the elevator working, she had to walk up three stories to her office. Her cold had gotten worse, the coughing yanked on her adhesions. Each step an effort.

Halfway up the third set of stairs, she fainted. With her last thought, she tucked forward, so she slammed onto her shoulder rather than capsize backward headfirst down the concrete stairs. Long illness can train anyone into an acrobat's roll.

Unconscious, her cheek pillowed on concrete, she had a dream or perhaps something more powerful: a hallucination. A vision. She saw her womb walking around a room, separate from her, people talking to it. Fleshy and panting, it stomped about on its clumsy ovary feet, barking orders out its cervix, its flesh surgically mangled, a creature from the black lagoon, scarred and imperfect. It moved forward only with effort and, as it got closer, she saw this difficulty came from having to drag her limp body along behind.

Within a week of this vision, she made her main doctor put her on Monopherix, the drug shoving her into an artificial menopause. She experienced hot flashes mixed with an adolescent's temper tantrums, but the drug stopped menstruation, decreasing her pain. A year before she'd started shaving her hair short as a nun's and wearing bright toddler clothes, stretchy and comfortable.

In her costume of a child nun, she meditated constantly on relationships and procreation and babies—not in terms of herself, but in terms of her research—as though she were an extraterrestrial studying the human species. She finally found herself able to look at babies without pain, somewhat in the same way she might examine zoo animals, curious creatures she wouldn't encounter in normal life. She began to relate to men as though they were taller women who were less likely to confide.

Without pain, she crunched through her statistical analysis in under a month on all the data she'd pulled together on the families from the 1970s blood-bank study. She told the families she was doing a long-term follow-up on the blood-bank study.

The questionnaire, along with follow-up research, showed on average the "extra-marital" children did better than their half siblings. Their stronger immune systems resulted in fewer urgent-care visits, as well as fewer chronic or genetic diseases. Perhaps because of their improved health, they grew three-quarters of an inch taller and a double-blind test graded their faces in their high-school photos more attractive.

Some combination of fewer sick days and a winning smile created a slightly higher grade point average, which was what probably led to an average of six months more schooling. These taller better-looking more-educated adults secured jobs with a higher salary and had an average of 0.7 more children per person.

She published her paper in *Science* magazine, calling it "The Secret Benefits of Bastards." She concluded the evolutionary duty of each mother was to secure the best genetics and resources for her offspring, and logically of course these benefits might not be found within the same man.

She was 33 years old and $73,000 in debt when this research got published. The uproar was intense, not only in the field, but also in the popular press. *Study Calls the Wealthy: Bastards*, ran the *Wall St. Journal* headline. *Women Designed to be Unfaithful*, said the *Times*. She didn't care, because a few days before this her pain doctor had finally figured out a way to get back at her.

He'd never stopped hating her in a restrained Nordic way. At this appointment he pointed out that the Monopherix was no longer working, not surprising since it normally was effective for only six months.

She nodded, having realized this weeks ago.

Since that time she'd threatened him, he was very attentive to her, never letting his eyes drift away—in a strange way acting like the ideal doctor.

He said, Well, perhaps you didn't know this part. Considering all the pain you've experienced, even if you got a hysterectomy today and had all the endo cut out of your body, your nerves might have become so habituated to reporting pain, they could continue—like the way amputees sometimes feel pain in their missing limbs.

He said, If this happens, you'll have pain for the rest of your life, no matter what you do.

*

The next day in the swimming pool's changing rooms, Frankie saw a very pregnant woman. Watching the woman waddle toward the showers, Frankie felt nothing at all.

Instead, staring after the woman, she heard that voice again, speaking in her ear, that raspy crossing-guard voice that she heard during moments of extreme duress.

The voice stated flat and factual, Honey, it's time.

Three weeks later, her cell phone rang. A man's voice introduced himself as the Director of the MacArthur Fellowship Program and asked to speak to Dr. Francine Burk.

The day she stepped off the stage with her prize money, the money everyone assumed would further her research, was the day she booked the surgery.

Twenty Six

As Frankie made breakfast in the morning, she noticed her fridge's voice was slow, sounding a bit like a computer's impression of a drunk person.

When she asked what was wrong, the fridge said, Processing, and then took so long to answer, she told it to forget her question. She wondered if she had a roach in her BodyWare and it had moved into her appliances.

Walking to the enclosure, she saw both sides of the highway were now heading in the same direction, the autos as tightly packed as ball bearings rolling North, away from the storm.

Then Bellows came striding up the path, head down and muttering to himself in the light of dawn, a large trash bag clutched to his chest. She'd never spotted him at work before nine.

He stopped short when he saw her. Ahh, he said, Dr. Burk, ready to leave?

No.

He paused, then tried again, Perhaps I can assist you? Help you pack? We'll be back in 10 days. We always are.

I'm not going. I'm finally making progress with my work.

He examined her. She stood there in her overalls covered with smiling robots, her hair still wet from the shower. He was dressed in a pressed shirt and pants—the only difference from his normal attire was he wore no tie.

He said, It's a mandatory evacuation.

She watched him with interest.

He added hopefully, Ordered by the governor.

The trash bag he held was full of stuff. From the bumps and outlines in the plastic, it seemed to be mostly papers and folders. These days, only important documents were printed: property titles and business contracts. He probably had to bring these along each time he evacuated. The corners of the folders had torn the bag in a few places and the rips were stretching wider.

She stated, If you try to make me leave, I won't come back.

He paused. She knew what her face looked like when she'd made up her mind.

She added, And I'll send a note to my NSF admirer who's giving you all the grant money. I'll tell him I've left.

One of the rips in the bag was big enough that some of the papers were close to spilling out. He cradled the bag closer to his chest, then glanced toward the parking lot where he'd been headed.

He exhaled then and drew himself up to say, Ok Bindi, record. Dr. Francine Burk, please note I have informed you the dust storm Mavis is coming and that the governor of the state has issued a mandatory evacuation. I have informed you that you must leave the premises of the Foundation until the evacuation is over. If you choose to stay, it is without the permission of the Foundation and the state. Is this true?

She nodded.

He blinked and added, Please answer for the recording.

She said, This is Dr. Francine Burk and I confirm you've informed me and I am staying at the Foundation without permission.

Ok, he said, Bindi, time and date stamp. Stop recording.

Then he jumped slightly—probably an incoming Sim-call— and looked past her to the car, Ok Bindi, tell her to hold her horses. I'll be there in a second.

He became less official, his voice rushed as he addressed

Frankie, Well, if you're staying then maybe you can help the keeper care for the bonobos. They're very sensitive to respiratory problems. Breathing the dust would be bad for them.

She nodded.

Do you have enough food for yourself?

She said, Yep, my kitchen's stocked. I'll be fine.

He paused and seemed ready to ask more questions, but then startled instead and touched his ear, saying, Ok Bindi, tell her to take it easy.

He waved and hurried away, calling back over his shoulder, Have fun.

*

During her hysterectomy, she was given just a local and thus felt a distant tugging and prodding throughout the operation. The instruments were inserted through two small incisions on her lower belly. Carbon dioxide was pumped in to inflate her body cavity, allowing the instruments enough room to work. With her gut puffed up like this, she looked pregnant.

Early on during the procedure, the surgeon figured out she was *that* Dr. Frankie Burk and began questioning her about her research and ideas. At no point did he look her in the face, but asked his questions while looking up and to the right on his Lenses, his empty hands gesturing, controlling the laparoscopic instruments that worked inside her. The conversation roughly followed the format of the newspaper interview she'd given the day before, only in this case the interviewer was busy slicing her uterus up and tugging the pieces out her vagina, a birth process of a very perverse kind. Her surgical menopause at the age of 33, the delivery of herself into what she'd decided to think of as a third sex.

Occasionally while she talked, the surgeon made a *tch*-ing noise with his tongue. She thought at first he disapproved of what she was saying, then realized he was instead contemplating his next cut.

After he'd removed her uterus, he searched through her now less cluttered abdomen, cutting away all the endometrial adhesions he could find. Cleaning up, he called it, as though her body cavity was a kitchen after a meal. As the last step, he searched methodically for any capillaries still bleeding, using a hot needle to cauterize them. He said inside of a month she wouldn't even know she'd had the surgery.

The machine that the needle was connected to sat beside her right hip. It made a busy humming noise each time it was used and at one point, she got a whiff of what smelled like pork chops.

A button-sized implant—that she'd agreed to more for health reasons than for social ones—was inserted under the skin of her right shoulder, to keep her hormonal levels within a preset range.

In the recovery room afterward, she and the other women lay bloated with carbon dioxide, beached on their beds like seals, their crotches singing out musical notes, their bellies gradually deflating. Sometimes these noises sounded like low sighs of relief; other times like a dog barking or a tuba warming up. At one point, her vagina exhaled a thoughtful *hmm*, as though it was ready finally to tell its story.

*

The Foundation grounds were deserted by 10 A.M. except for the keeper, Stotts and two other staff: a guy with a beard who Frankie had seen around the chimp enclosure and the skinny young woman who worked with the orangutans. From her spot up in the climbing structure, she watched them bustling up and down the paths carrying boxes or pushing dollies.

About 11 A.M., Stotts stepped into the enclosure to call for Goliath. He spotted her in the climbing structure and asked, You managed to stay?

Yes, she said.

You're in for some work, you know.

She nodded, Yep, that's why I'm staying.

He considered her, his eyebrows raised. Alrighty, he said, You want to come down for some knapping? I only have a few minutes but I thought I'd get in one last bit of research before the storm.

No, she said, Lucy is ovulating. I'll watch her instead.

Alright, he said and then called, Goliath, you coming?

They both turned to look for Goliath. They spotted him high in the climbing structure, faced away, chewing on a mango pit.

Stotts added, Goliath, I've got a *People* and a *Glamour.*

Goliath didn't turn around.

Stotts added, The *Glamour* has a photo spread on fur coats. Pretty women in fur. Your favorite.

Goliath put the pit down, but continued to face away.

Stotts put his hands on his hips, staring upward. He said, He's tired of not succeeding. It's your fault. You try.

Me? asked Frankie.

You've hurt his ego by getting better at the knapping. You call him.

He won't come to me.

Look, bonobos obey women more than men. They're just born that way. And Goliath, he likes you.

He what?

Stotts turned, examining her.

She saw she'd missed something obvious.

Embarrassed she called out, Goliath.

High in the climbing structure, he looked over his shoulder at her.

She paused at this.

See, Stotts whispered.

She refused to be distracted, didn't look away from Goliath's eyes.

Hey, she said lifting her hand in the begging gesture and making a bonobo pout, Come on down.

Goliath watched her for a moment, considering the request. She added the sign-language gesture for *please*.

He climbed down to where she was and they swung out of the structure onto the ground. He stood up on his feet to slide his hand into hers and she decided she could take a few minutes away from watching Lucy.

Walking to the research room, she studied him from the corner of her eyes. Next to her, he moved with pride, this short and hairy male.

They took their seats on the desk and each picked their rocks. Unlike him, she'd grown to enjoy the knapping. She found it absorbing and rather meditative, like washing the dishes. It seemed appropriate that today every hit she made was perfect, as clean as if she'd been knapping for years. It took her only 15 minutes to sculpt a sharp edge three inches long. A shard. A Stone-Age knife.

She held it in her hand for a moment, turning it from side to side, the rippled glass of the rock's secret interior. Its beauty gave her great satisfaction. She tested the point against the metal of the desk and there was a high-pitched screech. Goliath and Stotts turned to look.

Stepping over to the box that held the treats, she began slicing through the rope that tied it shut. The other two never looked away. When the last fiber was cut, it broke with an audible snap. Opening the box, she pulled out the gummy bears. She handed half of them to Goliath, sharing as a bonobo would. He took them with ceremonial care, his fingers grazing hers, the burnished leather of his skin.

She was already hungry again or perhaps had never stopped being hungry. Sitting down beside him on the desk, she tossed all her gummy bears into her mouth.

Goliath delicately started chewing on a single gummy,

bouncing around with happiness like a child. In his excitement, one of the gummy bears slipped from his fingers and tumbled to the floor. He knuckled down to get it. She watched him move, on all fours, his wrists locked and weight-bearing.

Her jaw stopped and she focused on his wrists, thinking.

Stotts meanwhile sat in the chair, filling in some form on his Lenses about the day's events. Not used to the Lenses, his eyes narrowed as he tried to click the checkboxes with his finger. He looked unhappy. This wasn't how he'd imagined his prized project going.

When Goliath returned, sitting down beside her, she picked up one of his hands. He chewed, his expression internal with pleasure. His hand was heavy with muscle and bone.

She grasped his forearm and the back of his hand to swivel his wrist through its entire range of motion. Something inside made a grinding noise.

She said, You know what? I bet bonobo wrists are different.

Stotts looked up.

She said, They're engineered for strength, for knuckle-walking and climbing trees. Not for flexibility and speed.

Stotts paused. She thought he'd understand this point instantly and congratulate her on the insight, but instead he responded in a quiet voice, We don't discuss expectations in front of the subject.

Goliath didn't seem particularly interested in the conversation. He'd finished eating the last gummy and was looking around for more.

She stood up to put more gummy bears in the metal box so he could try to earn the treat. She clarified, I'm not talking IQ. I'm talking physical capabilities.

Stotts said, Stop.

From the corner of her eye, she saw Goliath turn to look at Stotts' tone.

I'm telling you, she said tying the rope around the box, His wrist can't flick fast enough to knapp.

Stotts inhaled and said, Ma'am, it's time to leave the room.

She looked. Distracted by how smart she felt, she hadn't paid attention to Stotts. His expression serious.

Stotts stepped forward to place his hand on her arm, ready to march her from the room. However, as he touched her, Goliath stood up.

He seemed strangely bigger than before, his hair rising like a dog's, transforming him into a creature she didn't know. He weaved from side to side in warning, his face rigid, staring at Stotts.

The two humans went very still.

She said, Goliath, are you . . . are you protecting me?

He looked from Stotts to her. The expression in his brown eyes changed.

Oh my God, she said, That's so sweet.

Stotts shot her a glance.

She added, Hey, but it's alright. I'm fine.

Goliath studied her.

Really, she said, I want to go. I'll be back in a minute.

Goliath stayed still.

I'm going to take Stotts with me. That alright with you?

Goliath glanced at Stotts, then back to her, his face less rigid.

So she took Stotts' hand and eased him backward while opening the door. Stotts moved through it as smoothly as water and she followed, closing the door after her, leaving Goliath inside the room.

Wow, she said. Did you see that?

Stotts turned to her, You *cannot* discuss your expectations in front of them. Ever. It contaminates the research. Goliath *understands* English.

Frankie was amazed by what had happened. She said, Hey, talk nice to me. Remember, my boyfriend's in there.

Perhaps Stotts was worried about the dust storm or about his family being so far away. He continued in a tone she hadn't heard from him before, And manipulating his wrist is not proof.

She said, Oh, come on. You know he's smart and strong enough to knapp. There has to be something stopping him.

He said, That's your *assumption*. Science isn't about assumptions.

She ignored him, thinking through the issue, You know, it makes me wonder if early humans managed to evolve large brains simply because our wrists could flick.

He coughed out, What?

She said, Come on. Our wrists must have given us a serious advantage. We could chuck rocks hard at other animals to chase them away from their own kill, then use the stone knives we'd made to slice off a really big chunk of meat. Getting access to all that food might have been how we managed to afford our calorie-hungry brains.

She looked in through the small window in the door. Goliath was sitting on the desk, very still, his eyes focused off into space. It looked almost as though he were wearing Lenses and watching a video.

Stotts said, Armchair theorizing is not science. The idea is you have to prove things.

Goliath sat there, hunched and intent, his brow furrowed.

She said, Perhaps instead of *Homo sapiens*, we should be called *Nimblo wristus*.

Nimblo . . . Stotts stuttered, Nimblo . . .

His tone was much worse. Only now did she turn and really look at Stotts. His face was tight and a little flushed. Startled, she remembered this was his prized study, that it must have taken him at least a year to raise the funding. She was suggesting the study had never had a chance of working.

Her stomach lurched and she changed the subject, Where do the bonobos stay?

Excuse me?

During the storm. Where do the bonobos stay?

He jerked his chin toward the enclosure and said, In there. Look, nimble wrists are not . . .

Where?

In the enclosure, like normal.

She said, I thought the dust was bad for them.

We shut the roof to the enclosure. Close the outside vents.

Is there enough food for them?

He waved his hand toward the kitchen, We've got lots of the 3-D food cartridges. Stop trying to distract . . .

Am I going to be in danger?

What? No.

What work do we have to do?

Care for them. That's why I . . .

There was an explosive *bang* from inside the room.

Stotts and Frankie jerked around to look through the window in the door. Goliath was no longer on the desk, no longer visible. They scrambled to open the door, running into the room.

Damn, said Frankie.

Goliath had pulled the carpet back from the corner of the room, revealing the cement floor underneath. This cement now had a large impact mark on it, fragments of the shattered chert scattered all around. He must have hurled the chert at the cement.

Frankie asked, What is he . . .

Goliath was ambling around from one fragment to the next, picking each up to try the edges against his lip. His gait close to a swagger.

She stared, understanding, Holy crap.

The third shard was sharp enough that he pulled it back fast from his lip, a small bead of blood welling. He threw a meaningful look at the two of them, then knuckled over to the metal box. Using this shard, he began to saw through the rope.

She repeated, Holy *crap*. He . . . He . . . .

No, said Stotts. Goliath, you can't . . .

Goliath ignored them, half-grunting/half-humming to himself while he sawed, like a man on a quiet Sunday morning cooking breakfast. He was the only relaxed one in the room.

Stotts said, No. That's . . . that's *cheating*.

Goliath hummed, Hmm hmm.

Perhaps all the tension set Frankie off. A honk burst from her lips, the noise surprising. A second honk followed. She worked to smother the rising laughter and ended up snorting out her nose, a violently biological sound.

Stotts turned to stare at her.

The rope broke, and Goliath opened the box, pulling out the gummy bears. He sang a lilting two-tone chirp—the bonobo version of *ta-da!*

Feeling terrible for Stotts, she tried to stop, clamping her throat tight and stuffing her fist into her mouth. This seemed only to make the noise louder—grinding muscular sounds. She couldn't remember the last time she'd laughed. Over time the need built up. Leaning against the wall, she slid down until she sat on the ground.

Goliath placed half the gummy bears in her other hand and rolled her fingers shut round the treats. He sat beside her, patting her head like a parent trying to quiet a child.

Frankie cradled the treats to her chest, grunting and honking in the most unattractive manner, her eyes watering and alarmed. There was the distinct possibility she might wet her pants. Goliath put the first gummy bear in his mouth and, closing his eyes, began to chew.

Stotts surveyed the room—the rock shards, the pulled-back rug, Goliath humming to himself, her snorting and rocking. He let his eyes rise to the enclosure window. Mama stood there, looking in, probably drawn over by the *bang* of the rock hitting the cement. A hairless skinny homunculus with a regal posture, she locked eyes with him.

Staring into her eyes, he forced himself to exhale, letting go of the air trapped inside of him. He leaned back against the wall and slid down it until he was sitting on the ground next to Frankie. With his head resting against the wall, he gave up.

With nothing else to offer him, Frankie held out a single gummy bear.

He took it, half whispering, My beautiful research.

Twenty Seven

By the time the afternoon rolled around, everyone was moving a lot faster, everyone that is but Frankie. She sat in the enclosure, observing the bonobos and occasionally turning to watch the keeper, Stotts and the two other staff people half-jogging along the paths pushing handcarts full of supplies. Every once in awhile, one of them drove by in a forklift. The dust storm would hit late tonight.

The Foundation was closed, the highway empty enough now that every time a car drove by, Frankie looked up. Each one speeding along.

The bonobos seemed uneasy at all the changes. They peeped sadly to themselves and sniffed the air, standing up to look around.

Meanwhile Frankie concentrated on Lucy, whose temperature had been elevated for a day. In the morning she had mated only with females. After lunch, while the others napped in the sun, she moved to the top of the climbing structure. Sweetie climbed after her, pausing occasionally to pick his teeth and look around at the others, checking they were sleeping. Lucy's sexual swelling was large and pink. When he reached her, he began grooming her, running his hands over her, while she cuddled in close and then closer, staring into his eyes, then sitting in his lap. The mating itself was so fast that if Frankie had looked away for a few seconds she'd have missed it.

Lucy, who normally orgasmed with a high-pitched *Ahuh*

huh huh, this time pressed her lips closed, making not a sound beyond the noise of her breath. Right afterward, she swiveled around fast to look at the other bonobos, the way a kid glances toward the mom to check if she heard the *clink* of the cookie jar.

Frankie stared. When Adele was ovulating, she'd also chosen Sweetie as the one to have silent sex with. Up until now Frankie hadn't paid attention to him because he seemed to blend into the background, spending his time grooming the others or napping. She didn't know what characteristics a bonobo female might find attractive. He was young and healthy and gentle. Physically, he didn't appear that different from the others except his head and especially his eyes seemed one size too big for his body, as though a caricature artist had sketched him.

Above them, there was a click and then a slow *whirr*. The roof began sliding shut, glass panels clicking one by one into place, closing off the enclosure in preparation for the storm.

As the last panel slid into position, the ventilation clicked on with a soft *whoosh*, the warm re-circulated air pumping in. She figured she'd enjoy this storm, no tourists here to stare at her. She would sit inside the enclosure warm and happy, observing the bonobos, especially Sweetie, while the dust storm howled outside.

If she found the females mated with different males when ovulating, she could extend her work to the two remaining groups of captive bonobos: one in the San Diego Zoo and the other in Brussels. It would be a huge coup if she revealed a secret mating strategy of one of humanity's closest relatives.

The keeper opened the door to the enclosure and beckoned to her.

What, asked Frankie.

The keeper said, Come.

I'm working here, said Frankie.

The keeper said, Come. You need to help.

The bonobos all turned to see why Frankie wasn't obeying.

Hello, she said, I'm busy.

Mama's mouth began to tighten. Marge and Adele sat up straighter at this sign of displeasure.

The keeper beckoned impatiently and Marge and Adele got to their feet, their hair beginning to rise.

So Frankie climbed down and followed the keeper. She couldn't afford right now to have Mama bar her from the enclosure.

The keeper held the door for her and then marched off down the hall, leading the way. Frankie got a little ahead of her and walked backward so the keeper could read her lips as she said, Look, I do research here. It's important.

The keeper raised her brows, not slowing down at all.

Frankie said, I'm studying how they *evolve.*

The keeper answered, If they don't have food and water, they won't *survive.* You need to help.

Frankie tilted her head, trying to figure out how to argue with that. In the end, she stopped walking backward and just followed the keeper outside and over to the orangutans' building.

The man who cared for the chimps was just backing up a forklift, having dumped many bales of hay and some pumpkins across the ground beside the side entrance. The forklift drove off down the path, while the keeper grabbed a nearby wheelbarrow and rolled it over to the pile.

While she heaved the first bale into her wheelbarrow, she jerked her chin at the other wheelbarrow. She said, Come on. We have to get these inside where the dust won't bury them.

Frankie looked at the bales and pumpkins and said, They need all this?

She had to wave her arms to catch the keeper's attention and then repeat her statement.

The keeper watched her lips and answered, Eight adults, eight pounds of food each a day. Three bales of hay a night for sleeping in. 10 days til people return after the storm. Help out.

She said, I'm not strong.

You know how to use a forklift?

No.

Then this is the best you can do. Get moving. We have to finish before dark. We have three other enclosures.

Frankie considered the pile in front of her, then the enclosure. She caught a glimpse of one of the orangutans shifting deeper into the trees—red hair and a knuckled hand. She retrieved the wheelbarrow.

By this point in her recovery, she was allowed to lift anything she normally could—the recuperative magic of modern nanogels—but physical labor was not something she'd ever spent much time doing. She figured the bales of hay might be lighter so she reached down to pick one up. Hefting, she grunted with surprise, then let go of it and selected a small pumpkin instead.

After loading her wheelbarrow half full of pumpkins, she tried rolling it forward. It wobbled from side to side. She followed the keeper, concentrating, bumping the wheelbarrow over the threshold and down the hall to dump the contents into the office designated as a temporary storage area. Twice over the next few minutes, attempting the turn into the office, she lost control and the wheelbarrow tumbled, spilling all the pumpkins. The keeper glanced at her as she weaved her much more heavily loaded wheelbarrow smoothly past Frankie's mess.

As they were finishing up, the keeper rolled one last load into the orangutans' sleeping chamber. Frankie set her empty wheelbarrow down and followed behind, curious, pausing in the doorway. With a fast twist of her arms, the keeper dumped her load of pumpkins across the floor. The pumpkins thudded onto the ground and spun away from each other among the hammocks and piles of straw. The keeper stepped out, clanked shut the metal door to the chamber and pressed the button to roll open the gate to the enclosure so the orangutans could enter.

Frankie stared out into the enclosure.

From somewhere out there, one of the orangutans made a noise between a fake laugh and the sound of wood creaking. She could see nothing move.

The keeper walked away, saying, They won't enter until you're left. Come on. The chimps are next.

With a backward glance, Frankie followed, pushing her empty wheelbarrow.

Next to the chimps' enclosure, Frankie rolled her wheelbarrow up to the pile of hay and pumpkins and paused there for a moment, one hand to the small of her back. At first glance through the plexiglass, the chimps seemed so familiar—their size and movements and the color of their hair. Part of the reason that bonobos hadn't been discovered for so long was everyone just assumed they were chimps. Located in the same region of central Africa with only a river between the two species, for decades any differences had been attributed to individual personalities.

She continued picking up only the lightest pumpkins, putting them into her barrow one at a time, using her legs to heft as much as she could. Wheeling the pumpkins into the building, Frankie found the hallway smelled of the chimps, musky with sweat, the odor of a locker room crossed with a kennel. Because their diet included meat, there were overtones of human sewage.

Once they'd moved everything inside, Frankie followed the keeper out of the building. She eyed a male sitting in the enclosure, his back to her. He could have been a disheveled and more muscular Goliath. Feeling her looking at him, he turned.

242 · AUDREY SCHULMAN

It was like mistaking a stranger in a crowd for a friend.

Or perhaps it was more like visiting the friend in an institution—the body there, but the friend gone. His eyes were small beneath his brow; they glittered.

The keeper strode on ahead of her, heading down the path toward the gorillas. Frankie followed as quickly as she could, away from the chimps.

The gorillas were impressive. Even though she'd been at the Foundation for weeks now, she hadn't taken time to really look at any of the other apes. Each gorilla sat there with the presence of a giant, of a mountain, most of them chomping through something that looked like celery, grinding through it like a horse. They watched the women approach without comment, until the keeper reached down to pick the first pumpkin up and drop it into the wheelbarrow. Then they grunted with excitement and knuckled over to the closed gate that led to the sleeping chamber, waiting to be let in.

By this point, Frankie's arms were trembling and even when empty, her wheelbarrow wobbled from side to side. The scent of this building was of hay and sweet manure, like a stable.

When Frankie and the keeper finished carting in the supplies, the keeper dumped her final load of pumpkins into the sleeping chamber. On the other side of the gate, the gorillas sniffed and snorted air in loud gusts. They pressed in against the bars until the gate clanked in its frame. Frankie stayed back a few feet, while the keeper stepped out of the sleeping chamber, clanged shut the door behind her and pressed the button to roll up the gate.

They knuckled in, grey and large and huffing with happiness. A sense of inertia, heat and weight.

Each scooped up as many pumpkins as possible, piling them up in their arms and then walking upright, carrying them away from the others to eat. A young female picked up two large pumpkins and then, not satisfied, stuck a third between her knees and waddled away, her legs swiveling around the pumpkin, like a heavy woman in too tight a skirt. A few feet away from the others, she put her prizes down, rumbling happily in her chest. She palmed a pumpkin with ease and tapped it on the ground, cracking it open like an egg, then began spooning out the fibers and seeds with her fingers, slurping it all in like spaghetti.

The silverback, after he'd scooped clean one half of a pumpkin, turned the shell over in his hands, investigating it. He lifted it, then fit it carefully over the top of his head, like a hat, like a wig.

Transformed into a redhead, he turned to look deadpan at each of his wives.

They snorted at him, then looked away. The amusement of long married couples.

Frankie followed the keeper back to the bonobo building. She'd kept a running count of the apes she'd seen so far—eight gorillas, 12 chimps, no idea how many orangutans. All this, plus the 14 bonobos. If each orangutan consumed eight pounds of food a day, each gorilla must eat at least 10. She remembered once seeing a hippo in a zoo wade into what looked like a small sea of hay and take its first bite with the efficient grace of a marathoner. Feeding all these great apes must require several hundred pounds of food a day. She understood why Bellows would choose to 3-D print as much food as possible.

They now ferried pumpkins into the bonobo building, dumping them in one of the offices. After her last load, she paused by the kitchen. The 3-D printer was busy extruding a gleaming papaya, stacked beneath were maybe 20 food cartridges. She didn't see other food cartridges on the shelves nearby, instead just plates and pans and human food. She stepped forward to open the fridge. The fridge hummed, its shelves filled with hamburger and milk and salad.

When the keeper walked by, she asked, Where's all the bonobo food?

The keeper said, Pantry.

She walked to the pantry. Inside were shelving units, packed with food cartridges, the logo of 3M repeated endlessly. She took two steps inside—far enough to see the next set of shelves filled with them also—and then backed out, reassured.

Twenty Eight

By the time the keeper dismissed her at the end of the evening—the Foundation ready for the storm—Frankie was wobbling slightly as she carried the stuff she needed, clothes and food, into the bonobo building. She'd sleep here until the storm was over, since the dust would make it difficult to get from her apartment to the building.

Inside, she found Stotts had already set up a cot for her in one of the offices in the building. She pulled off her shoes and sweater, lay down and fell asleep.

In the middle of the night, she woke—her bladder full—and remembered the storm. After visiting the bathroom, she headed toward the enclosure, to see if the storm had arrived. The rasping snore of one of the bonobos echoed down the hall. It sounded like Mr. Mister.

In the research room, she stopped in front of the door to the enclosure and said, Ok Door, open.

The door unlocked and she stepped out into the empty space. The overhead lights snapped on, blinding, so she said, Ok Lights, off.

With a metallic clunk, the lights turned off. In the darkness, the enclosure felt spooky, a deserted auditorium at night. With the glass roof closed, the echo was perfect, the rustle of her clothes, the rasp of her breath. She sniffed the air and looked up. Of course there was nothing to smell, aside from the normal fragrance of fruit, manure and cleaning products. Above, the stars were clear and bright.

She sat down, leaning back against the wall, hoping to stay awake until the dust storm arrived. The image in her mind was of howling winds and groaning walls, small objects flying about.

Sitting there, she half-dozed, images in her head of endless piles of pumpkins and wheelbarrows. At one point, she startled up, unsure of what had woken her or how much time had passed.

The quiet complete. Profound. The silence of a dream.

No traffic, no voices, no wind. Nothing except the breath in her throat. Above her, half the stars were gone.

She blinked up at the sky. At first she assumed the object between her and the stars was a cloud, then noticed how clean the line was, like a giant piece of paper creeping majestically forward across the night sky.

She looked over at the tourists' viewing area. One by one the lights along the path blurred, then disappeared, wiped from view, from existence. This silent darkness sliding forward along the path, erasing object after object, until only the enclosure remained—this building the last in all the world.

The storm arrived in this way, not with noise or fury, but instead like fog, a creeping absence of sound and light and vision. Like death or anesthesia, an inching thief.

Staring upward, she imagined all that dirt, that dust, hanging in the air above her, thousands of feet of it, higher than she could see or imagine, the sheer weight of it all. For a moment she felt how truly tiny she was, how utterly insignificant.

Then she stood up and shook herself. Heading off to bed, she concentrated instead on the fact that she was inside, the lights and heat on, the fridge full, the sink working—that cozy sense of comfort that came from being warm and safe during a storm, that sense of being privileged and smart.

STORM: DAY 1

Twenty Nine

In the morning, when she woke, every muscle in her body was stiff with exhaustion. With some effort, she rolled over.

Turning on her Lenses she found the number of percent signs and other stray characters littering her Lenses had proliferated overnight into a pile that obscured the bottom 20% of her vision. She peered over this pile as though over bifocals, then turned her Lenses off.

Without Lenses, the world looked bare—no readouts, ads or cursors—but at least she could see.

Shuffling down the hall and through the locked door into the interaction area, she found Stotts in the kitchen. His hair was still wet from the shower, while she hadn't yet brushed her teeth. The feeling was jarring, like going to the office in her jammies. They both minimized eye contact for the first minute. These days of the storm, she realized, would be a bit intimate.

He was prepping the food for the bonobos, cutting up the printed papaya into smaller slices. Perhaps he was trying to make the identical globs of printed food appear more like hand-cut real fruit.

The printer beside him hummed busily, its head zipping back and forth extruding fruit.

Stotts jerked his chin toward the printer, Can you load that up with more cartridges?

Reaching down to grab some cartridges from the shelf under the printer, she had to stretch into the stiffness of her muscles. The cartridges were wrapped in mylar with symbols declaring the contents vegan and kosher.

As her fingers touched the mylar wrapping, she felt a sharp pain.

Ow, she said and looked at her fingers.

Stotts said, Yeh, watch out for static. One of the problems of dust storms.

Static?

He said, All that dust above us, rubbing against itself. It's like . . . well, like millions of tiny feet scuffing around on a giant shag rug.

She ripped the mylar off, revealing the cartridge which had pictograms on it showing how to load it. With so many companies being international, pictograms had become their own language, an attempt to reunite Babel or at least to reduce the costs of printing directions. These pictograms made the two steps look simple, however when Frankie turned to the printer it didn't look like the pictogram.

He said, During the 1930s Dust Bowl, in order to drive during a storm, people had to hangs chains off the bumper to ground the car. Otherwise the first person to step out could get defibrillated.

She gave him a confused look.

He said, You know, the car has these pistons pumping, building up static and it's driving on rubber wheels so the static can't discharge. First person to step out—*kzat*.

Ahh, she said and stepped to the other end of the printer to examine it from that angle.

Using the knife, he scraped the slices of papaya off the cutting board into a bucket on the floor.

This end of the printer also looked wrong. Pictograms just as capable as words of bungling communication.

Seeing her confusion, Stotts reached over with one hand and clicked open that end of the printer for her. Now it looked like the pictogram.

He said, You can tell the storm is big. The shocks are already bad.

She loaded the cartridge and lined up more in the feeder basket.

He pointed his chin toward the cup of coffee and baby bottle sitting on the counter, Can you bring Mama's coffee and Tooch's milk to them, then start hiding fruit around the enclosure?

Picking up the warm cup of coffee, she inhaled its scent. She asked, Will you pour me a cup?

He said, Daisy worked you hard, huh?

For a moment she couldn't imagine who this was, then remembered the keeper's name. She grunted.

She walked down the hall to the sleeping chamber where the bonobos chirped greetings to her from their hammocks. Tooch took the bottle from her, rolling onto his back and nursing from it with enthusiasm. Mama took her first sip of coffee, exhaled and settled back.

Lugging the bucket of fruit, Frankie stepped into the enclosure. The lights clicked on at her entrance. She stopped, assuming at first she'd opened the wrong door because she stood in a large room with beige walls.

The dust pressed against the glass—the color of paint selected by hotels averse to making any statement at all. The only difference was this paint swirled subtly. On the roof, the dust had built up, turning the glass a dark brown. At seven A.M., it was as dark as dusk inside the enclosure.

She hid the fruit in the nooks and crannies of the enclosure. When she was done, she pressed the button to open the gate to the sleeping chamber. The bonobos stepped out one by one, Mama first, all of them subdued. They looked around at the erased world and then began to search for the food, staying a few feet from the walls as though uneasy about what might be on the other side.

When they found the printed fruit, they turned it over in their hands, then ate it, their expressions similar to hers during her years of endo, when she chewed through piles of spinach and lentils, wishing for steak and ice cream.

Hungry, she returned to the kitchen to drink her coffee and cook herself a burger for breakfast. Not having brought any buns from her apartment, she sandwiched the burger between two chocolate bars, the heat of the meat making the chocolate sag as though tired. She had to eat quickly because her fingers kept poking holes through the melting bars. She thought this might be the best burger she'd ever eaten.

Stotts drank his coffee, watching her. He missed no detail of the grease and chocolate that dribbled down her arms, his face a study in politeness. Afterward she sucked the mess off of each finger, then cleaned herself up as best as she could and headed back into the enclosure.

*

The static got worse. Inside the enclosure, the cement floor and metal climbing structure were grounded. However when Frankie climbed onto the tire, she dawdled for a second, looking at the swirling dust outside, before she reached from the ungrounded tire to the climbing structure. The zap of static was strong enough that she yanked her hand back and hissed through her teeth. When she reached again, she got a second shock almost as big, but this time she held on and pulled herself into the structure.

She turned her Lenses on in order to read the temperatures of the females' sexual swellings. To see over the debris littering the bottom of her screen, she had to tuck her chin in and peer out the top of her eyes. As soon as she'd figured out Marge's temperature was the highest, although only by half a degree, she turned the Lenses off again. Even though Marge probably wouldn't ovulate for a day or so, she settled down to watch her.

30 minutes later, while Mr. Mister and Marge mated, she said, Ok Bindi, transcribe. Time and date stamp. Mr. Mister and Marge mating. Penile entry.

Since she couldn't read the transcription with her Lenses off, she said, Ok Bindi, read back transcription.

Her EarDrums started speaking, her BodyWare's voice garbled and sing-song as though drunk, the consonants mushy. It said, Tine an date stamp. Missed her. Missed her, and margin may ding.

Ok, stop, she said.

She spoke her notes slower this time for transcription, then played them back. The result, if anything, was more indecipherable.

She tried transcribing twice more, enunciating as though for someone just learning English. When that didn't work, she rebooted out of frustration—pressing her Bindi for the count of three while saying, Ok Bindi, power off.

There was a small beep, a mechanical click from somewhere near her nose and the silence in her ears got deeper.

Impatiently she counted out 10 seconds, then turned her BodyWare back on. Her EarDrums began to make that background fizzy start-up sound. The last time she could remember rebooting—after getting a new implant—the initialization sequence had finished within a few seconds. This time, after two minutes, her EarDrums were still fizzing and had yet to give the trademark Road Runner *meep-meep* that signaled the system was online. Frustrated, she powered down again, waiting longer before powering back up. After trying this a few more times, she just left her BodyWare off. She'd take written notes instead. Perhaps the static shocks she'd gotten had worsened whatever problem her system had.

She couldn't remember the last time she'd left her BodyWare off. She surveyed the unenhanced world, knowing nothing more than what her senses told her and her memory recalled. The sensation was a bit like skinny-dipping, a vulnerability that heightened all sensation.

She needed pen and paper to take notes and so she lowered herself from the climbing structure and dropped to the ground. Reaching the door, she grabbed its knob and said, Ok Door, open. She took a half step forward at the same time and plowed into the door when it remained locked.

Behind her, she heard the bonobos explode into breathy laughter. She glanced at them with dignity and they huffed harder.

She turned her BodyWare back on. Even though her system wouldn't finish booting up, after a few moments, the door recognized her as human and unlocked at her command. She retrieved a notepad and pen, returned to the enclosure and powered off her BodyWare again.

Goliath and Lucy were still giggling. They sat down next to her, patting her head.

To stop the bonobos from running off with either notepad or pen, she tucked them into her bra whenever she wasn't writing. Seeing her hide these interesting toys, the bonobos kept trying to sneak their hands down her shirt. She slapped them away.

Each time any of them climbed onto the ungrounded tire swing, their hair would begin to stand up from the electricity. As soon as they touched anything other than the tire, there would be an audible *kzat* and the bonobo would yip in pain. Soon none of them would climb anywhere near the swing.

Thirty

The first sign of trouble came midmorning.

The lights in the enclosure began clicking off, then turning back on, then dimming down, then turning all the way up. Shifting through every possible level. Frankie looked up at the lights, wondering what Stotts was doing.

The avatar appeared on the wall. 10:48 A.M., she announced, The pencil terrifies the hand.

Frankie blinked then glanced around, but none of the bonobos were signing anything. She looked out to the tourist area to see if anyone was pressing the keys on the kiosk, but of course there was nothing there but swirling dust, the tourists long gone.

The avatar spoke calmly, her hands signing each word, the volume high. She stated with great confidence, 10:48 A.M. Avocados are morphed with lichen.

Frankie stared.

The avatar paused, her eyes bright and friendly. She opened her bonobo lips to reveal her flat human teeth. She asked, 10:48 A.M. Can a pinched cat climb the coal?

Above, the lights clicked on and off.

The avatar said, 10:48 A.M. After a tongue moans, the flute reverts.

Her sign-language gestures were confident, her voice serious. The effect was unsettling, like a well-dressed lunatic.

The bonobos turned away so at least they could lower the visual volume. This was the way they reacted when children slapped willy-nilly at the buttons on the kiosk.

254 · AUDREY SCHULMAN

Meanwhile Stotts opened the door. He yelled, You playing with the building controls?

No, she said, What's going on?

He gestured her inside. She lowered herself from the structure and dropped, careful not to touch the swing. As she neared the door, the bonobos watched with interest. Stotts, however, held the door open for her so she stepped through easily.

The lights inside clicked on and off. The avatar inside the room was talking.

Frankie repeated, What's going on?

He waved his arms for the occupancy sensor and shouted, The lights are acting crazy.

I know. Why you yelling?

He bellowed as though he hadn't heard her, The toilet keeps flushing, the oven turning on.

The avatar on the wall nodded at his wisdom and added, 10:48 A.M. Observing the continuum permits another exercise.

At the avatar's gestures, Stotts looked over—trained to face the person talking, to listen and consider.

Frankie waved her hands to get Stotts' attention, overemphasizing her mouth movements so he could read her lips, WHY . . . YOU . . . YELLING?

He jerked his thumb at his ears and shouted, My system's playing how-to videos really loud.

The avatar commented, Retail accidents listen to the Pope.

He froze, his eyes flicking back and forth, watching something only he could see flash across his Lenses. Jesus, that's my bank account.

The lights above clicked on and off.

Must be the static, he yelled, Frying the controls.

She said, Turn off your BodyWare.

He shouted, What?

She grabbed the back of his neck to hold him still, while she pressed his Bindi for three seconds.

Understanding he shouted, Ok Bindi, power off.

Then he blinked and focused on her again, his face no longer tight from the audio assault.

Frankie asked, This happen before? During one of the earlier storms?

No, he answered.

The avatar added, Is surprise what generates the silk?

She jerked her thumb, Can you shut her up?

He pushed open a small panel in the wall near them, looked inside and turned a dial. The avatar continued to talk, but silently.

In the new quiet, both of them heard some noise from the enclosure, a faint repetitive sound.

Stotts said, What is . . .

She looked through the window and said, Marge is coughing. What?

She forgot about her BodyWare being off and reached for the door, starting to say, Ok D . . . . However she didn't even have to finish the statement; the knob turned easily. She paused long enough to twist the knob back and forth, the bolt sliding in and out.

She whispered to him, The door's unlocked.

Crap, he said and stopped by the door to play with the knob.

In the enclosure, Marge was sitting on the ground, hacking, her shoulders working with the violence of her cough.

In here, the avatar's volume was still on. She said, Humans hold the stick.

Frankie moved toward Marge, You alright?

Crouching down beside Marge, she touched her fingers to the ground, felt grit on the cement.

The avatar said, Bonobos stick the hand.

A fine dust lay across the ground, Marge in the center of it. Frankie looked around for where it was coming from, examining the walls, searching for some hole or gap. Gradually she looked up. She saw what seemed to be steam coming from the vents at the top of the wall, the steam floating gently downward.

The vents to outside had opened, dust drifting in.

Behind her, Stotts saw it also. Shit, he said and bolted back into the building.

She took Marge's hand and led her, coughing, away from the vent to the center of the enclosure.

The avatar's vocabulary seemed to be de-evolving. It asked, Why do sticks stick?

Next to Marge, Frankie patted her back until she stopped coughing. Meanwhile she watched the dust drift down, examining the bonobos for any effect.

A few minutes later, Stotts opened the door again and asked, Vents closed?

No.

He disappeared again.

The avatar said, Hand the hand.

The next time he came back, he was huffing. He asked, That work?

No.

Damn, he said and closed the door.

Meanwhile the avatar latched onto these last two words as though onto a life raft. Damn, she said, No no no no.

Frankie waited, the dust drifting in. The lights above were flashing on and off, fast as the lights on an ambulance.

No, said the avatar, Damn damn damn damn.

Sweetie was the next to start coughing, then Mr. Mister, then Houdina. Frankie called them one by one out of the climbing structure and away from the plexiglass, promising them gummy bears, moving them further and further from the walls, until they were all clustered next to the door to the research room. By this point, most of them were coughing on and off. They were much more sensitive to the dust than she was. She could only smell a certain mustiness in the air. When even Id began to hack, her tiny shoulders working, Frankie opened the door and called them all into the research room. Mr. Mister was coughing so hard, she had to lead him by the hand.

By this point the avatar in the research room was palsied, unable to speak or sign at all. Her shoulders and hands twitched and twitched, as though she were struggling to wake from a bad dream.

Inside, with the door closed, the air was clear. Frankie moved anxiously from bonobo to bonobo, touching their backs and waiting for them to stop, their coughing gradually easing. The lights strobed on and off.

Stotts opened the door at a half run, expecting the room to be empty. He almost tripped over Houdina and came to a hard stop, staring at all the bonobos sitting inside.

She asked, You fix it?

No. I tried everything. Why are they here?

They were coughing.

Why not the sleeping chamber?

That room just has a gate. It wouldn't protect them from the dust.

But we can't have them . . .

He started to pick his way through them toward the door to the enclosure—probably wanting to see how dusty it was in there. Behind him, Houdina reached up, turned the unlocked doorknob and stepped out into the hall.

Frankie called, Stotts.

He turned and said, Christ.

He moved fast out the door, calling, Houdina, come back here.

Meanwhile Id scooted out just behind him. When he lunged forward to make a grab for her, Adele slipped out, followed by Sweetie. They made happy peeping noises at this new area to explore.

No no no, said Frankie, weaving her way through the bonobos to the door to stop them. The rest of the bonobos, figuring everyone was heading that way, trailed along.

In the hall, Houdina was knuckling straight for the door that led out of the interaction area and into the offices. Stotts ran ahead of her to shove a table in front of the door.

Frankie asked, You have keys? We could lock it by hand.

Keys, he said, as though she'd asked for a slide rule.

Meanwhile the bonobos spread out in every direction, exploring the interaction area. Id disappeared into the kitchen. The lights flickering overhead gave a stop-action quality to everything, as though this was a silent movie showing action taken long ago, no possible way to stop it.

Grab Id, said Stotts, Don't let her find the knives.

Got it, said Frankie.

Something crashed in the bathroom and Stotts headed that way.

In the kitchen, Frankie grabbed Id, but by then Goliath arrived and Marge, so she put Id down and, uncertain of what to do, held her palms up in a let's-not-be-too-hasty gesture. None of them even looked at her. Goliath grabbed the bottle of Dawn dish soap and began to suckle from its nozzle as though from a baby bottle. Id jumped onto the counter and opened the first cabinet—filled with glasses—while Marge slid open the cutlery drawer. Frankie hip-checked the drawer, pinching Marge's fingers hard enough that she squealed and dropped the forks, offended. On the counter, the blender danced around, its motor whirring out of control.

Frankie yelled, Out out out. All of you, out of here.

She could have been the avatar for all the attention they paid her.

Id dropped the first glass into the sink where it shattered with a satisfying *ker-ash*. Marge tried to open the cutlery drawer again. Frankie jerked the whole drawer out of the cabinet—the sound of wood cracking—and holding it up above their heads, kicked open the walk-in freezer to shove the drawer inside on a shelf. The bonobos peered with interest into the freezer, so she slammed the door shut. Behind her, two more glasses shattered in the sink and Id hooted with excitement. Keeping a foot on the freezer door, Frankie tugged the next two glasses from Id's hands, threw them in the trash and picking the trash up, swept all the glasses off the shelf into it. Beside her, Goliath made glugging noises, swallowing the dish soap.

Meanwhile more bonobos pressed into the room, cooing as they opened cabinets and drawers and pressed buttons, while Frankie unplugged the toaster and tugged steak knives out of their hands and yanked away the glass coffee pot. Marge touched one of the now-lit burners and screamed, clutched her hand to her chest and bolted off down the hall.

Goliath stepped into the center of the room, still cradling the dish soap to his chest, to take a big breath. With a concentrated expression, he let go an enormous burp. A stream of bubbles floated out of his mouth. The females squealed and began bouncing high in the air with joy at the beauty of this day.

Through the wall, she could hear crashes and thuds and the hand-dryer whirring insanely and Stotts calling, No, no. Hey! No.

Her back against the freezer, she yelled, What do we do?

Stotts bellowed back through the wall, No idea.

Goliath burped again. The females shrieked like teenage girls. One large bubble floated in Frankie's direction.

She shouted louder, I need a plan.

He yelled, Stella, put that *down*.

There was the thud of something hitting the bathroom floor hard. Whatever it was, it shattered.

The bubble burst on the cabinet next to her and she got a distinct waft of Goliath's fruity bonobo breath.

Goliath knuckled out into the hall to show off his burps. The others followed.

Stotts called, We make the rooms safe enough that we have time to figure out how to get the vents shut.

She called back, Then we get them back in the enclosure.

Agreed, he called.

Eyeing the room for danger, she started by blocking off the walk-in freezer. She leaned her shoulder into the free-standing fridge and grunted. It didn't move. So she wedged herself between the wall and the fridge and shoved with her legs until the fridge juddered backward into place, blocking the freezer's door. Next, she stuffed everything dangerous she could find into the fridge, going systematically through the drawers and cabinets, stopping occasionally to jerk an object away from one of the bonobos who'd wandered in. When she was done, she taped the fridge closed with yards of duct tape.

Overhead the lights flashed, frantic.

Of course if the bonobos wanted to open the fridge or freezer, they still could; it would just take some work. She could only hope, with so much else to explore and play with, they wouldn't bother.

Once she finished, she stepped out into the hall. Four bonobos were in the janitor's closet, the crash and thud of things dropping. Shattered jars on the ground. Mothballs scattered everywhere. Ralph had cut one of his hands and was sitting on his butt, sucking on the wound. Two others, next to him, chirped sympathetically and tugged on his wrist, trying to pull his hand out of his mouth so they could see all the blood. Sweetie was drumming on a tin of turpentine—luckily still shut—making a sloshing *ker-plash ker-plish* sound. He began to hit it harder. She tugged it away from him and pushed all of them out of the closet. They knuckled toward Goliath who lay on his back, burping long strings of shiny bubbles up toward the ceiling. Five bonobos near him were laughing hard, leaning against the wall for balance, Mama gasping the hardest. When Goliath let go a particularly resonant ribbon of bubbles, Mama's laughing got worse. She clutched at her crotch and began to tinkle all over the carpet.

Frankie swept all dangerous items out of the closet and into a garbage bag. On the third shelf down, she came upon a small toolbox and paused, looking in at the tools.

She glanced at the closet's doorknob; two small screws at its base held the knob in place on its metal neck.

With a screwdriver and a bit of concentration, she loosened these screws and then wiggled the knob off so only the bare neck was left. Grabbing the remaining doorknob on the far side, she yanked it and the bolt entirely out of the door. Now there was just a face-plate with an empty hole.

She stared at the faceplate for a moment, then slid the bolt and its attached knob into the hole like a key. She turned the knob easily, opening and closing the door a few times with this bolt-key, pleased.

She stuffed everything dangerous nearby into the closet— including the turpentine tin—and slammed the door shut, removing the bolt-key and tucking it into her pocket.

Sweetie, she called, Could you open this door for me?

Sweetie knuckled over and looked at the door and then at her. He tried to jam his finger into the empty faceplate hole but it wouldn't fit. He scraped at that area with his nails for a second, trying to get purchase, then attempted to wedge his fingers under the bottom of the door. After a moment, he lost interest and headed off in the direction of the bathroom instead.

So she unscrewed and removed all the doorknobs and bolts in the interaction area. Until the bonobos started battering doors in or found some tool that could work the latch mechanism, they were now restrained to the kitchen, bathroom, office and research room.

When Stotts saw what she'd done, he grabbed her by the ears and planted a kiss hard on her forehead.

Brilliant, he said.

She was pressed for a moment against his sternum, a sense of warm muscle and ribs. She inhaled once, then stepped back, blinking.

She handed him one of the doorknob bolts and said, You go find what's wrong and fix it. I'll stay here to make sure they're alright. Hurry.

Using his bolt as a key, he opened the door and left.

Frankie bustled about removing whatever struck her as dangerous. Each time she filled a garbage bag, she opened the door to the office part of the building and tossed the bag unceremoniously down the hall, slamming the door so she only heard the crash.

Meanwhile every motorized Quark-enabled device whirred louder and louder—the blender, the coffee grinder and the hand dryer in the bathroom—until it burned out, going silent, its LEDs continuing to blink a silent SOS. The smell of burning plastic in the air.

Perhaps 20 minutes after that, the lights clicked off, not even flickering anymore. Everything went dark. She stood in the unlit hall, her eyes struggling to adjust. After that she had to stumble up and down the hall toward any thumps or crashes, trying to protect the bonobos.

Soon she was using garbage bags to get rid of the occasional poop she discovered in the dark—her sneaker landing in it and skidding slightly, her body struggling for balance.

Without a working clock and with little light from the storm outside, it was hard to judge how much time went by. All she knew was by the point Stotts finally returned, she'd begun to worry about him.

She didn't hear him open the door, but saw the bright beam of light striding down the hall toward her, the light about six feet up. He stopped in front of her and angled the headlamp up toward the ceiling so she could see him.

She asked hopefully, The vents closed?

He shook his head no, the beam of light tracing an arc back and forth across the ceiling.

You fix the problem?

The beam of light traced its arc back and forth again.

Any idea what's causing it?

He said, Static? Dust inside some server somewhere? This is not my field of expertise.

Anything like this happened before during a dust storm?

Not that I've heard of. I've only been here for two storms.

He handed her a second headlamp. She turned it over. It must be at least five years old, from before the night-vision app came installed on all Lenses.

With all the devices burned out, the only sound left was the toilet, evidently on a different power source because it continued to flush endlessly.

She added, The system will figure out the problem soon and fix it, right?

He grunted in a somewhat positive but inconclusive way and said, Meanwhile we keep the bonobos in here.

She pulled the headlamp's elastic band over her head, positioning the light in the front, and turned it on.

Goliath squealed with pain from the bathroom and they both moved that way. He'd cut his hand on a piece of glass from a shattered light fixture. She plucked the piece of glass out, while Stotts began to sweep up the shards.

Thirty One

Sometime late that afternoon Stotts and Frankie remembered the bonobos' lunch. Stepping into the kitchen, they saw the 3-D printer head had secreted a shiny ball of goo around itself, like an insect preparing to pupate. Frankie touched the glob with her fingertips. It was hard and she couldn't feel any vibration inside. The motor had burned itself out.

She and Stotts turned to look at the bin next to the printer. It was only half-filled with printed fruit.

They stared into the bin, waiting for the facts to change. There was a slow silence.

We still have the pumpkins, said Frankie.

Stotts asked, How many?

They moved fast down the hall into the office area to check, slamming the door behind them to stop the bonobos from following.

In the light from the headlamps, the 12 medium-sized pumpkins lay scattered across the floor. They'd been intended primarily as a garnish for the few days of the storm, a tasty tidbit mixed in with the printed fruit to encourage the bonobos to eat. Yesterday in the wheelbarrow, this had seemed like a large number of pumpkins. Now it looked paltry.

That's what, asked Frankie, Three meals?

It's alright. There's emergency fruit in the walk-in freezer.

Let's see how much.

He caught her arm, No, the power's off. We need to keep

the contents cold as long as possible. We need it to last until the cleanup crews arrive.

How much food is in there?

It's enough. Gropius buys the fruit in bulk whenever it's cheap. Anytime the price spiked, he'd make us feed them defrosted fruit. They hate it. All squishy.

Then he got the printer?

Yep.

So we're fine? It'll be ok?

They won't be happy, but they won't starve.

She exhaled, the fear subsiding. She looked at him, filled with gratitude for his presence. She said, Can I ask something? If Tess was in town, what would you do?

He answered, Her asthma, in a dust storm? I'd have to be with her.

They paused, imagining this.

She said, Good thing she's in England.

Hell yes. Help me carry a few of these in. We need to prep their lunch.

Back in the pantry, Frankie and Stotts chopped up three of the pumpkins, as well as some of the printed fruit, while the bonobos sat outside and peeped with hunger. When the food was ready, Stotts opened the pantry door and piled it up in the hall for the bonobos.

Seeing the food, the bonobos reached for each other, starting their normal pre-food ritual. Somehow in a hallway with furniture, their actions looked different, the movements of their hands and hips. Goliath sat in a chair with Stella straddling his lap, the chair squeaking with their motion. For the first time Frankie felt uncomfortable and turned away. Stotts, she found, was already back in the kitchen.

Eating, the bonobos loved the pumpkin seeds, sucking on them one at a time, clucking at each other at the taste and texture—happy hedonists.

For their own lunch, Frankie and Stotts rummaged through the pantry. They found an institutional-sized box of granola bars and sat down in the hallway to eat enough to keep going. Both too tired to say a word.

*

Frankie needed to pee. She glanced into the bathroom but Ralph and Houdina were in there, playing with the faucet, cranking the water on and off, on and off, endlessly amused by this magic.

She had no interest in pulling down her pants in front of the curious bonobos, so she told Stotts, Back in a second. I'm going to . . .

She paused, strangely shy. In the end she just jerked her head toward the office area.

He nodded, his face expressionless, as though he himself had never had to use the facilities.

The whole time she sat on the toilet, it flushed itself again and again, as though horrified at being used in this way.

*

Without the ventilator pumping heat in, the temperature began to drop. 65 degrees, 60. The bonobos, tropical animals, began to shiver, especially Mama, bald and skinny.

So Stotts explored the office area and came back carrying all the clothing he could find. Staff coveralls, a few suit jackets, a raincoat, three down vests, shirts and two sweatshirts. Some of this clothing was probably his own. Over his shoulder he carried her duffle bag, the one she'd packed for her few days in the bonobo building.

He handed the bag to her, Can you check through this to see what you can give them?

He scattered the other clothes across the ground for the bonobos, while Frankie put her bag down and unzipped it. Unfortunately Mama caught a glimpse of the red pants on the top and grabbed them, squealing. Some of Frankie's T-shirts were tugged out along with the pants and Sweetie and Houdina snatched at these. Frankie tried to grab what remained, but the bonobos moved faster. She ended up holding just three socks and a pair of undies.

From the bonobos' reaction to the clothing, it was obvious which had grown up in human families and which had grown up in labs or zoos. Half of them pulled on the clothing, peeping to themselves with excitement, like shoppers at a midnight sale. The others watched, puzzled.

It took a while for Mama to tug on Frankie's stretchy pants, but when she stood up on two feet—wearing them and an oversized sweatshirt from the Foundation ("*Great Ape Trust— Studying the Ape in All of Us*")—she looked as though she should be carrying a latte and checking her mail.

Houdina pulled on layer after layer of clothing until she was dressed like a homeless person, patting her sides and burbling happily. Goliath picked out some coveralls, a pink turtleneck and a baseball cap.

Mr. Mister managed to tug on a pair of Frankie's underwear, bright yellow chicks marching across his butt. Stotts glanced at him, then closed his eyes, looking genuinely in pain.

The lab-raised bonobos attempted to copy the others, but had difficulty. While Adele pulled on a T-shirt and skirt, Marge sat beside her, trying to jam both her legs into a ski hat.

After this there were two different groups of bonobos. In the coveralls and suit jackets, the human-raised bonobos were mostly dressed for work, while the lab-raised apes managed only to wrap a few shirts or pants round their necks, looking essentially like chilly nudists.

Eying this difference, Frankie wondered if she'd chosen her favorites—Goliath and Mama—partly because they'd grown up in human families, the continuous interaction making them smarter, since the brain like any muscle grows with use. Or maybe all of them were just as smart, but she most appreciated those who were socialized to communicate with her, bypassing the immigrants with strong accents to talk with those who were native-born.

*

As the afternoon passed, it became clear that the bonobos would comply more with Frankie's requests than with Stotts'—because they were used to obeying females and she'd spent more time in the enclosure with them. So Stotts concentrated on childproofing the area while Frankie rushed from room to room like a frazzled preschool teacher, trying to keep them out of trouble.

Stotts duct-taped cellophane over the vents to make sure the dust didn't sneak inside the building. Then he removed anything that was sharp or made of glass. He carried his tools tucked inside his shirt, where the bonobos couldn't get them. As the afternoon passed, the number of tools increased so he began to look almost pregnant and clanked audibly as he walked.

Working, he yanked and pulled and hit, the sound of metal squealing or wood breaking. As the afternoon progressed, he wielded the pry bar at times with more energy than might be required. Gropius was not going to be happy with all the damage they were doing.

The bonobos cocked their heads, watching the humans. Their expressions held some of the same surprise that cats might feel, lying in the sun, watching ants bustle everywhere on their frantic little errands.

In the growing dark, even with headlamps, Frankie and Stotts kept bumping into the chairs and tables the bonobos had knocked over. So they started removing the furniture also.

Late that afternoon, she caught Marge and Bernie swinging from an exposed pipe in the bathroom, the pipe groaning. Frankie rushed toward them but, exhausted, stumbled slightly and bumped her shoulder into the wall.

Marge and Bernie pant-laughed at this so hard they fell off the pipe.

When they recovered enough to eye the pipe again, she took two steps toward them, saying, *No no*, then performed her first ever pratfall, landing on her knees.

Their reaction this time was even bigger, pounding the ground and covering their eyes. This was the species you'd invite to any party, always having a good time.

From then on, she performed this type of slapstick when she needed to distract them.

*

The bonobos who'd grown up wearing clothing must have been used to diapers, because each time they needed to pee or poop, they just did it, right inside their clothing.

After the first few accidents like this, Frankie tugged the clothes off the bottom half of all of them—the pants, the underwear and skirts.

They became a type of centaur. On the top, they were dressed and ready for work. On the bottom, they were naked and furry with obvious sex organs.

*

Slowly the static from the storm built up so that touching flesh or metal delivered a painful shock: an audible *tzit*, the blue spark visible in the dark. When shocked like this, a bonobo would scream and writhe in a ball, then hold out the affected hand for others to inspect. Stoic, they were not.

Whenever Stotts was shocked, he'd inhale and shake his hand, then stick it in his armpit.

When Frankie got shocked, she'd go very still, listening to the electricity shimmer up her arm.

*

Every once in awhile, Stotts tried turning on his BodyWare. Each time it came on, he'd flinch and grimace at the assault of sound and visuals, then press his Bindi to turn it off again.

That evening he tried again and this time he stood there motionless, his head cocked, looking off to the side.

What, she asked.

Nothing, he said.

What?

Nothing, he said, There's nothing there.

She turned her system on too and for a few minutes they talked to their BodyWare, saying Ok Bindi, Ok Lenses, Ok EarDrums. No response except a distant static. They spoke the commands louder and louder, as though with someone who was hard of hearing.

Her eyes fell on Tooch cuddled up inside Mama's sweatshirt, his fluffy head sticking out. Frankie felt the first flicker of real fear.

Both she and Stotts turned off their BodyWare after a few minutes. They were careful not to look at each other, busying themselves with the bonobos.

*

Without any way to tell time, they waited for the bonobos to start whining again before they began prepping a second meal of pumpkin and printed fruit. After they were done, there were only four pumpkins left and no printed fruit at all.

The bonobos had already eaten this meal once today. They picked through it. Afterward, they turned to the humans and tapped their fingertips together, signing, *More, more.*

*

That night it got very dark outside, the kind of perfect darkness Frankie hadn't seen often. Not a single light visible through the dust.

The bright cone of light from her headlamp made everything on either side pitch black. Frankie tried turning her lamp off, but the darkness looked solid. Unnerved, she turned her light back on.

Id was the one to figure out the humans didn't have good night vision. She jumped onto Frankie's shoulder from behind, grabbing for balance. Frankie felt something heavy hit her in the dark, something hairy clutch at her face. She half-screamed.

After that, Id occasionally dropped onto her from above. When the other bonobos saw Frankie's reaction, they began to sneak up next to her to squeal in her ear or run a wet tongue across the back of her neck.

They did the same to Stotts. Each time he made a sort of strangled inhalation that was, if anything, more amusing to them.

*

To make sure none of the bonobos snuck out into the storm during the night, Frankie slept in front of the door to the enclosure, while Stotts made his bed up in front of the door to the offices.

Frankie lugged her bedding in from the office area, the covers and pillow clamped between the mattress and her arm, the end dragged along behind her. The bonobos watched her walk past, then followed, chirping, a parade of hominids in the dark. She kept her headlamp pointed at the ground to check she wasn't dragging her mattress through poop.

As soon as she put the mattress down, Goliath jumped on it, bouncing up and down. Adele scooped up Frankie's pillow and pressed it to her face, chirping. Frankie shooed them away, but when she turned back, Mama was sitting on the mattress, Tooch in her arms, the covers pulled up to their chins.

Go on, get out, Frankie said. When she touched Mama's shoulder, she could feel her trembling, hunched and grey in her clothes. The temperature was probably 55° by now.

As Frankie paused, Stella and Marge knuckled onto the bed, Lucy and Sweetie following. She tried to shoo them away, but they just moved around her. In the end, she had to struggle for a spot under the covers. All of them piling in and on top of each other on the twin-sized mattress. It became difficult to move. From the weight of the bodies, Frankie thought it possible that Stotts was sleeping alone. Such a straightforwardly sexist species.

The blankets kept getting tugged in different directions, but at least the warm pile of bodies made up for it. One of them—she didn't know which—patted her hair rhythmically, soothing her. The bonobos fell asleep as fast as children, Marge snoring, wheezy and regular in her ear.

Staring into the darkness, having a hard time falling asleep, Frankie realized she'd officially lost her scientific distance. She lay there, snuggled up with her research subjects, worrying about feeding them tomorrow.

*

In the middle of the night she woke with a start, from the deepest sleep. She woke at the thought that her hormone implant, the one inserted after her hysterectomy, might be a device.

By this point, her legs had been pushed off the mattress, her head resting on the belly of one of the bonobos. She lay there, blinking at the dark.

The implant was buried under the skin of her shoulder. She wiggled her hand under the sleeping bodies, to pinch the implant and roll it slightly from side to side. It felt smooth as a stone, no discernable bumps of wires or circuits. Thinking of all the documents she'd signed before the procedure, she couldn't remember any concerning permission for remote access. However, she'd read only the title of most of the documents before scanning down past all the tiny print to find where to sign.

If there were electronics inside, had they gone haywire, no longer dissolving estrogen into her blood? Or was the capsule even now crumbling like a cookie, dumping the whole year's allotment in a single day? She imagined herself lactating or beginning to grow a beard.

In order to get back to sleep, she had to visualize the pill as a simple bolus of hormones encased in a time-release coating, no electronics at all.

As she began to drift off, she realized the silence was perfect. The toilet's sensor had run out of power.

Thirty Two

When she woke in the morning, it was from Marge and Adele having their early morning sex, Marge's butt thumping into her head.

Every muscle in her body sore from all the work yesterday, she didn't bother to walk as far as the bathroom in the office area, but used the bathroom in the interaction area. Several bonobos followed along, curious. They surrounded her, watching with great interest, as she pulled down her pants and sat. Mama tugged on the waist of her pants, playing with the elastic, while Goliath tried to pull up her shirt to see more. Frankie slapped at his hand and finished peeing as fast as she could.

She stepped away from the toilet, before remembering the sensor wasn't working anymore. The bonobos were already clustered around the bowl, looking in and sniffing. She had to fill up a bucket with water from the sink and shoo them away in order to flush the toilet by pouring water into the bowl.

She ran the hot water in the sink but the water never got hot. Goliath, Mama and Petey sat there, watching as she scrubbed a very cold soapy washcloth in her armpits, then rinsed and applied some deodorant. In the mirror she could see her hair was all lumpy from sleep so she patted it down half-heartedly.

A few minutes later Stotts returned from the bathroom in the office area. He appeared clean, even his hair wet and neatly brushed. From the color of his lips, she guessed he'd taken a shower in the cold water.

For the bonobo breakfast, they cut up the last of the pumpkins and placed the pieces in the hall.

The bonobos looked at the pile of pumpkin and then at the humans, the way a cat will when offered the same type of food once too often—equal measures of surprise and incomprehension, as though a brick had been placed on the plate.

After 20 minutes none of them had taken even a bite of the pumpkin, so Stotts shoved the fridge out of the way to get food from the walk-in freezer. Stepping around him, Frankie realized something was wrong as soon as she touched the handle. It was hot. Cracking open the door, the inside exhaled the moist heat of a mouth, the scent of juice and rot. She froze, then opened the door wider and stepped inside. The thermometer hanging from a shelf registered 116°, the boxes dripping what looked like jam all over the floor.

They both stood still, absorbing this information.

Stotts' voice when he spoke was quiet, The heat pump ran backwards.

Marge stuck her head in between their legs, snorted at the stink and wheeled away. Frankie and Stotts called a few other bonobos over, but once they got a whiff of the freezer they backed up, coughing and jerking their heads away. Frankie and Stotts opened some of the boxes but the contents were partly putrefied and sticky and got all over their shoes.

So they closed the door and shoved the fridge back to block access to the freezer, then peeled the duct tape off the fridge to see what might still be edible. The fridge wasn't hot, but it exhaled room-temperature air—the device transformed into a shiny styrofoam box. Inside were two gallons of milk, some orange juice, hamburger meat, cheese, some sliced luncheon meats, condiments and salad dressing. In the drawers, some fruits and vegetables were visible—a few apples and a head of lettuce on top. Standing here, she could smell the meat and milk beginning to turn. This was not going to feed 14 bonobos for the next few days.

She looked to Stotts to learn how to react. Her first impression was he appeared bored. Only after a moment did she realize his expression was locked down, all emotion removed. A soldier's face.

He swiveled and marched into the pantry. She followed. He picked up one of the 3-D printer food cartridges and slammed it on the edge of the metal shelf, breaking the cartridge's casing. Inside was what looked like grey silly putty. He attempted to pinch off a wad of the putty, but it stretched out rubbery, so he had to bite a section off with his teeth.

He chewed industriously.

She asked, What's it taste like?

Grinding it between his molars, he answered, A plastic bag.

She bit off a piece also. She chewed twice before spitting the chunk back into her hand. She said, Maybe the printing process changes it.

He spat out also and said, I sure hope so.

They stood there, eyeing the pantry shelves. There was a long silence. Packets of mac'n'cheese, hot chocolate mix and ramen noodles lined the shelves, almost everything dehydrated and meant to be microwaved, no fruit at all.

He said, I'll search the other buildings for food. You stay here and make sure they're alright.

He pulled on a pair of safety goggles from the janitor's closet and tied a scarf over his face as a dust mask, before heading outside. Frankie watched from the window, but through the dust could see nothing.

Meanwhile the bonobos kept whining. So one by one she handed out the vegetables and fruit in the fridge. A head of lettuce, three apples, a Spanish onion, half a tomato and some pears. They passed each around, taking little nibbles and cooing.

The Spanish onion made them huff in with surprise. Still they ate it. When all of the fruits and vegetables were gone, they looked to her for more. Meanwhile she poured the sour-smelling milk into a baby bottle and, with no way to heat it, simply handed it to Tooch for his breakfast. Frankie had seen him eat solid food, but not much. He took the bottle eagerly from her and rolled onto his back to nurse from it. At his first sip, he jerked his head away and coughed, spitting it out.

Mama sniffed the bottle's nipple and shot Frankie a piercing look.

Hey, said Frankie, I'm doing what I can.

She moved into the pantry, opening every cupboard and searching systematically now. She eyed the can of espresso but had no way to make the coffee for herself and Mama. In the end, she returned with the last of the granola bars, this being the least harmful item she could find. She unwrapped a bar and handed it to Mama. Mama turned it over in her hands, then raised it to her mouth to lever off the smallest bite. She chewed with an inward expression, then with more enthusiasm.

Frankie opened the rest of the bars and handed them out, then gave Tooch a bottle of orange juice.

When Stotts came back in the door an hour later, he pushed a dolly of dusty food: two large boxes labeled *Dried Fruit Medley*, a 30-pound sack of corn on the cob and a commercial-sized container of Fluff.

She asked, Where'd you get this?

Snack Shack, he said, The selection was somewhat limited.

They offered the dried fruit first, cutting open the individual bags and handing them out. It took the bonobos 30 minutes to eat it all. Then they looked to the humans for more, having finished the appetizer.

She walked around with a large bottle of water, letting each drink for a while, hoping the fruit in their bellies would expand enough to fill them up. Still they continued to tap their fingertips together in the sign for *More more*, so she and Stotts went into the pantry to shuck the corn.

Frankie asked, You checked on the keeper and the others?

Yep.

How they doing?

He said, The keeper, she's got the gorillas. She seems stressed. Martin's got the chimps and Rita's with the orangutans. They seemed less worried. No one has much food left for their apes. I reminded them about the Snack Shack.

And how are the other apes doing?

The gorillas and others aren't as sensitive to the dust as the bonobos, so they're in their normal sleeping chambers—bored and without a lot of room to move, but at least not roaming the hallways causing trouble.

She asked, Was there any milk at the Snack Shack for Tooch?

It's all gone bad, said Stotts, He's gonna get weaned fast.

Is he old enough?

We'll find out, he said.

*

With every hour, the static electricity got stronger.

Midmorning, Frankie slid her doorknob bolt into the door of the janitor's closet to open it. Tired, her fingers fumbled slightly so one finger brushed the metal of the faceplate. The electrical *zap* she got was strong enough that her hand quivered, an object she could not control. Strangely she tasted licorice on the back of her tongue.

Scared the bonobos might get hurt, she began baptizing them, carrying water around in a bucket and running her wet hands over their clothes, hands and heads, wiping away the electric charge. They reacted by nestling their faces into her hands, holding their chins up for her touch, their trust complete. She filled up the bucket every time she saw tendrils of their hair begin to rise into the air from the static.

Houdina was the only one who didn't want Frankie to touch her. Frankie had to plead with her to run her wet hands over her.

In reaction to the shocks, Stotts started wearing socks over his hands, decreasing the chance his flesh would touch anything conductive. He got shocked less often than the rest, but when he did, it was actually audible—the *kzat* of all that built-up static and his teeth clacking shut. He stepped away from them all, trying not to brush against anything, moving through the rooms and between the bonobos with the slow-breathing caution of an astronaut.

Not being the kind of person who touched others a lot, she found under these circumstances that touch was comforting. She walked around hand-in-hand with Goliath and tucked Id into her sweater to keep her warm. Midmorning when Mama patted the ground in front of her, she obediently sat down to be groomed.

Mama began to run her fingers through her hair, combing it upward, trying to style it. She worked, clucking to herself, her fingers warm and gentle. Frankie's eyes closed in enjoyment.

*

In the late morning, Id decided it was time to clean Frankie's nails properly. She picked up Frankie's hand, examining the nails one at a time, making a small tut-tut noise. Frankie sat there patiently, her nose an inch from the top of Id's head, the scent here somehow the richest, a mixture of heat and baby flesh and milk. Id ran her fingernail beneath Frankie's nails, trying to scrape out the dirt, then paused to examine the results. Dissatisfied, she placed each fingertip in her mouth and sucked with the rhythmic power of someone who still breastfed.

Throughout this, Houdina glared at Frankie. The more time Id spent with her, the more Houdina seemed to resent her. As soon as Id stepped away, Houdina threw a pumpkin chunk at Frankie, the chunk sailing past her head.

Mama turned to Houdina, displeased. Adele added an angry *waaa*-bark. Houdina whined and slunk away. However, from then on, she wouldn't let Frankie baptize her, not even for a granola bar, so Stotts had to do it. At least this decreased the static for both Stotts and Houdina.

With Stotts, Houdina cuddled into his lap, delivering sloppy kisses to his chin, hungry for attention.

*

For lunch, Frankie and Stotts shucked the corncobs and piled the corn in the hall. The bonobos eagerly scraped their teeth over the cobs. When they finished, they looked up at the humans, wanting more.

Stotts picked up one of the remaining pumpkin chunks and said, Hey, you can eat this too, you know.

To demonstrate, he bit into the pumpkin's raw flesh. He chewed—an audible crunching noise—and said, Yum-yum.

The bonobos turned to Frankie for her opinion. Having no choice, she picked up a chunk and put it in her mouth also. It smelled faintly of bonobo pee, but then everything smelled that way by now. To get her teeth through the pumpkin, she had to move the chunk to the side of her mouth. Chewing, her head bounced with the force of her jaws.

The bonobos did not pick up the pumpkin, but just watched, fascinated, their eyebrows high.

So she got the jar of Fluff from the pantry and spread some on her pumpkin slice.

What're you doing, asked Stotts.

Whatever I have to, she said.

Checking that the bonobos were watching, she took a bite of the Fluff-covered pumpkin. It still took work to get her teeth through the flesh, but once the sweetness hit her taste buds, she inhaled, chewing with more energy. She realized she hadn't eaten all that much since the storm had started.

The bonobos watched, attentive.

Still crunching through the pumpkin, she smeared a thin coat of Fluff on another piece and handed it to Mama. Mama sniffed the piece, then passed it to Adele who sniffed it and passed it on. In the end, Houdina was the only one brave enough—or hungry enough—to try it. She needed enough calories to breastfeed Id. She glared suspiciously at Frankie before licking the Fluff.

As the taste registered, her eyes went still—commercial sugar such a heightened version of the sweetness of fruit. Then she jammed the whole chunk in her mouth and began chewing.

The bonobos chirped excitedly, while Frankie and Stotts smeared Fluff across pumpkin and handed the food out.

If any of them tried sucking the Fluff off the pumpkin, Frankie and Stotts wouldn't give that bonobo any more until the slice was eaten. In this way, they cajoled the bonobos into eating their full meal, using the same mixture of threats and praise that a parent employed.

*

At times Frankie and Stotts forgot their BodyWare was turned off and addressed it out of habit, saying *Ok, Bin*—

Then they'd pause, remembering.

*

Each time Houdina breastfed Id, Tooch stared. He'd had no milk all day.

Bit by bit, he knuckled in closer, whining. Whenever he got within a foot, Houdina became uneasy, picked Id up and moved away.

*

Stepping into the bathroom, Frankie could see the cubicle was shut, bonobo legs underneath. Curious, she opened the door. Inside were Marge and Sweetie, having sex standing up. They turned to stare at her.

Sorry, she said and shut the door.

Then stood there for a moment, considering what had just happened. Marge, she remembered, had been the female whose temperature had started rising two days ago. Probably she was ovulating now. Each time a female ovulated, she selected Sweetie to have secret sex with.

For the rest of the day, Frankie watched Sweetie, considering him.

As soon as the dust storm was over, she'd order genetic tests on all the juveniles. She bet the results would show most of them had been sired by Sweetie.

*

Before dinner, Stotts put on his goggles and scarf again to get more food from the Snack Shack.

When he returned, he brought two boxes of ice cream bars, a pack of hot dogs, several bags of chips and many loaves of Wonder Bread.

That *really* isn't bonobo food, Frankie said.

He nodded, The question is what's the least bad for them.

They stared at the food options, considering, never having had to make a decision like this without being able to consult the Quark.

By this point, each time Frankie looked at Stotts, she felt a palpable relief, a little less worry in her veins. She wasn't the only human working to keep the bonobos alive and healthy. In the hallway, whenever one of the bonobos wandered by wearing anything close to the green of his sweater, she'd turn. Then realize her mistake.

She said, Someone once told me the amount of salt on a single potato chip can kill a cat.

That true?

I don't know.

Better safe than sorry.

She nodded, Alright, we eat the salty stuff. They get the non-salty.

Stotts picked up one of the boxes of ice-cream sandwiches. Noooo, she said.

They'll melt soon and we won't have these calories anymore. Might as well try it.

How come they're still frozen?

He said, There's a tiny fridge in Gropius's office, so old it wasn't Quark-enabled. These and the hot dogs were inside, on top of what was left of the ice.

He tore open the box and handed her a single ice-cream sandwich, Go for it, you trendsetter.

Frankie stepped out of the pantry and peeled the wrapper off the sandwich. Her audience watched. She bit a small bite off a corner. She wanted to eat as little as possible to save the food for the bonobos, but when the creamy sweetness hit her taste buds, she looked down at the bar and inhaled.

Mama reached out, asking for part.

Frankie handed the ice-cream sandwich over and Mama lipped a bite off, then took a second bigger bite, grunting in surprise.

While the bonobos began their normal orgy, Stotts and Frankie ripped the wrappers off the rest of the ice cream so none of them would choke on the paper. Frankie wondered how much this moment—social bonobos having orgasms and harried humans accomplishing tasks—illustrated the differences between the species.

The bonobos loved the ice-cream sandwich, eating not like thoughtful gourmets, but like hungry children, jamming most of a bar into the mouth in a single bite.

Unable to cook the hot dogs for themselves, Frankie and Stotts ate some American cheese and Wonder Bread. Sitting on the floor in the research room, they chewed mechanically and chugged water. They leaned back against the wall, so happy to be still, staring out a window at the storm. The dust swirled, shifting subtly.

Frankie said, Today I caught Marge and Sweetie in the bathroom having secret sex.

Stotts looked at her, *Secret* sex?

Yep. I've caught several of the females doing this when they're ovulating. They wait until the others are sleeping or distracted, then sneak off. When they climax, they're silent, just sort of huffing.

Stotts blinked, Silent?

Yep, she said, And every time so far it's with Sweetie. I believe it might be because he's got neoteny.

Neoteny?

Means looking like a baby even as an adult. It's genetically linked with domestication.

He cocked his head.

She said, Back in the 1950s, this Russian scientist—what was his name?— started experimenting with foxes. With each generation he let only the most peaceful foxes reproduce, the ones who wouldn't bite or freak out when handled. Within 20 generations, the foxes began to act like dogs. Social, playful, affectionate. Domesticated. They'd wag their tails and lick your fingers.

She continued, The interesting thing is even though these foxes were bred entirely from wild foxes, they looked different, a bit like, I don't know, a Japanese cartoon of a fox. Huge heads, tiny bodies, less muscle. Like a baby fox. Cute as all get-out.

He said, Sweetie's like that.

Yep, he's even got that little white tail tuft like a baby bonobo. Researchers have repeated this experiment with other species and found the same results. If you breed for lack of aggression, you end up with adults that look like babies. Neoteny.

He leaned his head back against the wall, Like domesticated pigs?

Yep, pigs are big soft babies compared to wild boars. The important thing to realize is the males in most species will breed with any female who stays still long enough. It's the females who are selective. What they desire has a huge effect. If all the female walruses got together one day to decide they wanted polka dots, within a few generations the males would have polka dots. The female's wish made physical on the male's body.

He said, But bonobo females aren't selective.

She answered, *Until* they're ovulating. At that point, it appears the only male they'll copulate with is Sweetie, a gentle male with baby-appeal.

He looked out at the storm and said, You believe the females are domesticating their own species? That they're breeding peaceful social bonobos?

Yep, a race of oversexed Gandhis. Of course it'll take a long time to get enough data to see if it's true.

He asked, And chimps are heading in the opposite direction?

She pictured the male who looked like Goliath in the chimp enclosure, his muscled body and tiny eyes.

She said, Could be. With chimps, I believe the alpha male gets the most mating opportunities. If that's true—and the females aren't able to sneak around him—then the aggressive brawny males are the ones who will pass on their genes.

What about humans?

Humans?

He looked away, Women. What do they find attractive?

It took her a moment. She said, Well, to generalize, women tend to marry the peaceful males, the guys who can sit still through school, who manage not to punch the boss. However when a woman ovulates, there is a somewhat increased desire for an aggressive man with a square jaw. This keeps a bit of the brute in our genotype.

Stotts said under his breath, Knew it.

Then he blinked, realizing he'd spoken out loud.

There was a pause while she considered his words.

You, she said, You had a problem with gals?

He was starting to formulate his response, when Petey and Rita bolted into the room, moving with such speed that they kicked up onto the wall and galloped along it sideways like acrobats, before running back out. The sugar high had hit.

Frankie and Stotts got to their feet and hurried after them.

*

Tooch hadn't had any milk all day. That evening, he approached Houdina again, whining. She started to get up to move away from him, but Mama grunted, a harsh demanding noise.

Marge and Adele looked over, every bonobo in the room staring at Houdina.

She froze.

Tooch cautiously climbed into her lap and began to nurse. Houdina stayed still, looking big-eyed at Marge and Adele.

Late that evening when Id nursed, she kept at it for a long time, whining with frustration, trying to get enough milk. Throughout it, Houdina held Id close, grimacing each time Id yanked.

*

That night, Frankie noticed the way the bonobos squinted into the light of her headlamp, holding a hand up to shade their eyes.

So she began turning her headlamp off whenever she could. Once she'd started this, switching the light on hurt her eyes. Soon she just kept the light off, finding her way through the rooms with one hand on the wall, her eyes adjusting.

A few minutes later, Stotts approached, his headlamp on.

She squinted into the beam the way the rest of them did, blinded.

Can you turn that off, she asked, We need to save the batteries.

He looked around at their faces, then switched off his light.

After that, they moved around mostly without the light. Even once their eyes adjusted, there was still a certain amount of bumping around in the dark. All of them becoming physically familiar with one another, like siblings in a family.

At one point she bumped into Stotts. Since he was crouched over cleaning something up, she assumed it was Goliath and patted him on the butt.

He said, Hey!

Her first reaction—before she realized she'd touched jeans instead of fur—was to think, of course they can talk.

Thirty Three

First thing in the morning, she started prepping the bonobos' breakfast—sandwiches of plain Fluff. She'd cleaned herself up again with just a hurried scrubbing of a washcloth. Stotts emerged from the office area a few minutes later, clean and shivering. When he spotted her, it took him some effort to drag his eyes away from whatever her hair was doing in the back of her head.

By this point, their discussions were shorter. Tired and hungry, their dialogue was winnowed down to a few words or a gesture. No need to say more. They knew what had to be accomplished and that there was no one else to do it.

Stotts said, It should end tomorrow.

She understood he meant the storm, Then help arrives?

Probably two days from now.

Will they have food the bonobos can eat?

Maybe.

Milk?

Maybe.

After they'd handed out the food, Frankie searched the pantry yet again for something other than potato chips to eat. On one of the top shelves, stacked in the back, she found a single sterno container, an item she'd ignored before. She picked it up, considering it. Then her eyes darted to the cans of espresso.

Briskly she searched for matches and a structure she could place over the sterno on which she could balance a pot of water. She could already feel how the coffee would taste, that jolt of caffeine, that warmth in her gut. She thought if she could have just one cup, even black and without sugar, she could deal with the day ahead.

In the kitchen she filled up a pot with water and then experimented with several setups. In the end, she settled on a metal colander placed upside-down over the lit sterno, the pot on top. Because the base of the colander was smaller than the bottom of the pot, as well as a trifle convex, the pot wobbled. She stood patiently in front of it, holding its handle while the water heated up. For coffee, she would have stood here for most of the morning without complaint. Her other hand, she scrubbed through her hair. In the back, she found something crunchy and matted. She worked at removing the object, trying not to guess what it might be.

Stotts made no comment. He stood nearby, watching, clearly not a coffee person.

The water was beginning to boil. Frankie continued to hold onto the pot's handle while, with her other hand, she tried to pry the metal lid off the coffee tin. She couldn't do this with one hand, so she let go of the handle. She popped the top off and was reaching for the handle, when Mama squealed with joy in the hall—at the smell of the coffee or the sound of the tin opening. At her squeal, Frankie turned slightly and her hand touched the handle.

The pot toppled, simple as that.

Boiling water spilling across her stomach.

So many Americans, raised in safety, don't have fast reactions. They turn to stare at the oncoming car, mouth open. Disbelief can kill.

Stotts—having been in Syria—punched his hand out, through the water and against the burning metal, to knock the pot away and into the sink.

Most of the water however had already poured out, running

down her legs, the sensation not of heat or pain, but of sudden clarity, a skip out of normal time.

He jerked his hand away from the metal, clamping his hurt fingers into his armpit. Oww, he said, Yow.

She, on the other hand, made no noise. She looked at her wet clothing, her flesh cooking. In one smooth motion, she shoved her pants and underwear down, then yanked her shirt off over her head.

He froze. She stood there, naked except her grimy jog bra, her pants and undies around her ankles like a child about to sit on the potty. The path the water had taken appearing on her skin.

Glancing at her calm expression, his reaction was fury. He slapped on the faucet, yanked the hand sprayer out to the end of its hose and shot cool water at her belly and legs.

He yelled, nothing soldierly or polite in his voice, just an enraged bellow, Why don't you care about yourself?

She stared, trying to parse the extent of this emotion.

And something bolted down the hall toward them.

Goliath. Barreling toward Stotts, fangs glittering, attacking anyone who dared to yell at Frankie.

Protecting Stotts, she stepped in the way. When Goliath hit her, she ricocheted into Stotts.

Goliath, his eyes shut, sank his canines into her shoulder.

She screamed, No!

He jerked open his eyes and, horrified, let go, backing up, whining.

However by now Marge and Adele and Mama were in the doorway, *waa*-barking. For the first time Frankie saw them truly enraged—a male yelling at a female! Standing up, their fur erect, a wall of fury, they began to hurl whatever objects were nearby—poop, a pan, the coffee tin—their aim bad enough that they hit Frankie as often as Stotts, their strength immense.

Knowing she was his best protection, she shrieked as loudly as she could and kept her body between them and Stotts. She grabbed a pan and slammed it against the oven, the metal clang loud as a bell.

Startled, Adele backed up a step. Mama paused uncertain.

Frankie banged the pot around more, bellowing out the most unnerving sounds she could think of—an Arabic ululation, a Tarzan call.

All of them stood there quietly, heads cocked, listening to Frankie's full-throated rendition of a Swiss yodel. Then, seeming to feel that summarized the matter, they backed away and disappeared down the hall.

She exhaled a ragged breath.

Silence.

Stotts was backed up against the fridge, as far as he could get from them. From her.

She stood there, splattered with poop, bleeding from Goliath's bite, her pants around her ankles, her belly and legs parboiled. Standing alone in the doorway, in the space between the bonobos and the human.

Thirty Four

After the fight in the kitchen so much changed between the triangle of them—Goliath, Stotts and Frankie. Frankie worried constantly now that the bonobos might attack Stotts. She didn't like leaving him in a room alone with any of them, so she followed after him like some scrawny guard dog. The only time she relaxed was when he was outside getting more food from the Snack Shack.

For his part, Goliath needed reassurance that she wasn't angry with him for biting her. Every hour or so, he would start to follow her, whining. It didn't matter what she said—if she told him it was alright, her shoulder was fine, that she still loved him—he would look more and more upset until she reached down to give him a hug and a kiss. Then he'd grin, forgiven and head off toward whatever looked interesting.

The whole routine made Stotts uneasy, the unease conveyed in an eloquent silence. And he tended to witness the routine, because he preferred also to be near her now, ready to step in if she held anything sharper than a pencil or went near the kitchen, as though she were a child unable to understand basic dangers. When she did something that worried him, he'd move within an arm's length, pretending to be busy with some other task, but wearing the slightly unfocused gaze that said he was ready to move quickly.

The change that really bothered her was the way he looked at her now, or rather, didn't. His expression would be normal, until his eyes got close to her. They'd jump over her, skip past, as though looking at her pained him. Probably he was embarrassed she'd protected him from the bonobos or every time he looked at her, he remembered seeing her naked. Probably, worried about his wife and child, he wished he was with them instead of her.

By this point, all of them looked different than they had before. Stotts had a large bruise on his cheek (from one of the pans Mama had thrown). Because of her scalded belly and legs, Frankie moved around with a stiff-hipped gait. The bonobos all wore soiled ripped clothing on the top half of their bodies. Several of them had developed persistent coughs from the dust, which seemed to sneak in no matter how many layers of plastic Stotts taped over the vents.

The physical contact at least helped. Through much of her adulthood, she'd gone without touch—not just sexual touch, but touch in any form at all, a hand on the shoulder, a hug, leaning in against a friend. Her gut in pain, she'd picked her way through life, trying not to get jostled. Around the bonobos, post-operation, that had changed. She was touched now all the time. Id investigating her clothing, Goliath wrapping his arm around her, Mama playing with her hair. She touched them back almost as much as they touched her. She tucked Id into her clothes to keep them both warm, held Mama's hand to her cheek, or leaned against Goliath's shoulder, exhausted.

*

A little bit before lunch, she was in the bathroom, getting water for more baptisms—the faucet all the way on, the water pouring into the bucket—when the faucet made a small rasping sound deep in its throat and ran dry. No more warning than that. She stared, trying to comprehend this betrayal.

She only had to say Stotts' name once before he was in the doorway, watching her twist the faucet on and off and on again. No water came out.

They walked fast to the kitchen sink. She put a pot beneath

the faucet to capture the slightest dribble and turned it on. The faucet sputtered out a cup or two, then hissed and stopped. All that remained was a regular click-click from somewhere in the wall.

The water pressure in the system had run out.

The room got very quiet.

Id was sitting on the counter watching. Frankie was struck with how truly small a bonobo baby was, almost birdlike, those spindly legs and arms, the oversized skull and dark eyes. That little belly was the only cushion.

Stotts was furious with himself. He thwapped his head with the flat of his hand as he marched to the pantry, saying, Fuck fuck fuck.

He stepped to the shelf with the drinks and counted them, his hand tapping each one. Thirteen gallon bottles and four half gallons: soda, apple juice and water.

His hand on the last one, he inhaled and said, The sodas for the vending machines are in the Snack Shack.

She said, The other apes and humans are going to need some of that too.

He said, It's enough. Rescue the day after tomorrow. It won't be long.

She was silent.

We'll go easy on the liquids, he said, Just in case.

He tried to sound confident, but a few minutes later he left to check on the others. When he came back he brought back four six-packs of Sprite from the Snack Shack.

From this point on, Frankie noticed he drank only a single measuring cup of liquid at each meal. He closed his eyes while he drank, throat moving. Frankie restricted herself to the same amount. She found herself becoming more conscious of drinking—the taste, her thirst, the cool drink running down her throat.

Still, Frankie had to baptize the apes because the air crackled with electricity; touching metal or flesh was dangerous. However she baptized them less often and used much less liquid, wiping tiny libations of Sprite across each bonobo, running her hands over their fur and fingers, a cleansing of sin and static.

Mama quickly figured out the sticky soda could be used as a hair mousse. She followed along after Frankie as a stylist. The curls dried hard. The bonobos knuckled around, the hair on their heads in bouffants, pomades and marcel curls.

With so few baptisms, the bonobos began to get shocked more often. From the pain they learned, not that they shouldn't touch, but that they should never let go. They hugged, clinging to one another. Locked inside, the food different and so little of it, the humans tense, the air stale and dusty, the bonobos became so loath to let go that if one of them wanted to move down the hall or into another room, they all followed, holding on—a long conga line of apes.

Twice, all of them climbed into each other's arms, a warm pile of bonobos, one big cuddle. There, their heads bowed on each other's shoulders, they sighed and closed their eyes. They looked small and tired.

Watching them, Frankie understood this as a way of saying, *We are one. I care for you. It will be fine.* Watching, she wanted to climb into that pile.

*

For several weeks now, Frankie had spent a majority of every day staring at the bonobos, their faces and movements and expressions.

Occasionally now, when Stotts stepped into her field of vision, she felt surprise. He loomed over the rest of them, weighing close to twice as much, his upright stance and startling eyes.

She'd turn to watch him, tracking him.

*

That afternoon, Frankie sat down on the ground, exhausted, leaning back against the wall, feeling the endless pull of gravity.

Goliath sat down next to her, gently grooming her hair. He made soft noises, concerned.

After a minute of this, he got an erection.

As he would with another bonobo, he stood up on two feet, his legs parted for her to appreciate his condition. His penis, bright pink, was skinny as a wobbly pencil.

He waggled his hips from side to side. He squealed and gyrated, spearing the air in front of her. It was clear he wanted her to touch it. He seemed determined.

She rested her head against the wall and ignored it. Goliath, in response, just wiggled his crotch closer to her face.

Stotts, nearby, was trying to clean up a poop with a shovel. Straightening up, he saw what Goliath was doing and went still.

Focusing past the bouncing metronome of Goliath's penis, she looked at Stotts and asked, Any advice?

Pay no attention. It'll go away.

You speaking from experience?

He took this the wrong way, looking shocked.

I didn't mean your . . . She trailed off.

Goliath continued to pump his penis in front of her, like an enthusiastic cheerleader with a very skinny pom-pom.

Criminy, she said and in an attempt to get Goliath out of the way, she patted his penis like she'd pat a dog. Two taps with the flat of her hand. It bounced, slightly rubbery.

She wasn't sure what she expected to happen, but Goliath stopped spearing the air. He grinned and sat back down. He did not orgasm and, except for the fact that an erect penis was involved, the touch seemed hardly sexual.

(She remembered a conference she'd attended years ago outside of Mumbai. One afternoon, tired of the workshops, she'd snuck out of the hotel for some fresh air, wearing a T-shirt and shorts. Each of the men she passed on the street reacted as though her clothing was pasties and a sequined G-string, when actually it was only a signal that the weather was over 90 and humid.)

She turned to Stotts, Did you see that?

His eyes were wide. He looked as shocked as if she'd bit the toe off a newborn.

(Perhaps Goliath had been trying to greet her, waving a bonobo version of a hand at her, wanting only some acknowledgement of his existence.)

She said to Stotts, I think that was him just saying hi.

Stotts didn't answer, but jerked his eyes away.

Abruptly she'd had enough: being tense, physically exhausted, thirsty, dirty and hungry. She said with her voice sharp, Stop it.

He nodded, impassive, a soldier's nod.

I mean it, she said truly angry, You've been acting weird all day. You're not talking much. You won't look at me.

Yes ma'am.

She got to her feet and stepped in close. He, the much bigger person, took half a step back, still not looking at her. She rose onto her toes to say into the side of his face, Look at me now or I will chant the word erection.

He made no response.

Erection, she said, Erection, erection.

He forced his eyes toward her, his gaze as impersonal as a cubicle.

No. She said, *Look* at me.

His expression changed not at all.

She hit each consonant as sharply as a BBC announcer, Ejaculate. Prick. Woodie. Hard-on.

He said, Ma'am, could you please stop?

She called up toward his face, singing the words with all the built-up tension of the last few days, A boner. A chubby. Throbbing gristle.

His face suddenly alive, he stared into her eyes and said, *Cut* it out.

Thank God, she said.

She added, I missed you.

His anger wiped away in a second.

She was the one now to break the look. All around her, the bonobos sat, uneasy, watching the interaction.

Thirty Five

L ate that afternoon, exhausted, Stotts left the interaction area so he could take a nap on the couch in his office without one of the bonobos clambering over him. He asked Frankie to wake him up in an hour. At this point, the concept of an hour had a loose definition. Although they had searched hard, they had found only one clock, in the back of a closet, dusty, no AAA batteries anywhere. Through the storm, the light from the day was faint at best and disappeared early. She sat with the bonobos watching that light disappear entirely until she felt an hour must have passed, then opened the door to the offices and walked down the hall to wake him up.

This, the human area, had reached a state that was, if anything, worse than the interaction area. Furniture piled up with garbage bags tossed on top, full of broken items they'd removed from the interaction area. In order to weave her way through it all, without stepping by mistake on a bag of feces, she turned on her headlamp. In the unforgiving beam of light, everything looked so tired and broken, like the scene of a long-ago crime. She picked her cautious way through it all to his office.

He lay on the couch, wheezing slightly in the dusty air, curled on his side, hands between his knees. She imagined this was the position he'd slept in since he was a baby. She could see him as a boy, blankets piled on top, breathing deeply. He would have been kind to his mom.

To wake him up, she turned off her lamp, not wanting to jar his eyes. However, standing there in the dark, listening to him wheeze, the two of them alone, she found herself unable to reach her hand out to touch him.

So she turned her light back on and then shook his shoulder. Her touch brusque. Accustomed to the bonobos, the solid mass of his shoulder was surprising.

His eyes opened, that transparent blue. Looking into her light, he occupied his face again, returning to the Stotts she knew. He stood up quickly, embarrassed.

Watching this metamorphosis, it was she who was abruptly exhausted, emotionally and physically. She sat down on the couch he'd vacated and asked him to wake her in half an hour. At the moment she couldn't even muster worry about him being alone with the bonobos.

Lying down, she did not fall into sleep, but more snapped into it, the way she used to when pain from the endometriosis had kept her awake for long stretches. Unlike with the endo, she dreamed.

The dreams were long and confusing and faded into one another. In one, she was walking through a crowded mall wearing a baby-sling. This was a dream she used to get a few times a year. A warm and solid weight lay inside the sling, moving against her chest, passersby smiling at the bundle.

In the past, this dream had always ended the same way. The passersby would lean forward, cooing, to open the sling and peek inside. This time, however—instead of her scarred uterus cradled there—Id popped out, hairy and grinning.

The mall dissolved and Houdina appeared, walking closer, pulling on some sort of jacket. She worked to button it up, concentrating, head down and serious. After the last button, she smoothed the material down. A white lab coat.

Stotts shook Frankie awake.

His hand on her shoulder, she realized he smelled like a bonobo from being around them so much: musky with sweat and urine and sex. Probably she did too.

He'd turned on his headlamp to touch her. She blinked into the bright light, unable to see his expression.

Then he turned and walked away.

*

For dinner, they fed the bonobos sandwiches made of Wonder Bread smeared with ketchup. Afterward, Stotts cooked the hot dogs for him and Frankie over the sterno, the ones he'd found yesterday frozen in Gropius's freezer.

He acted as though she were a child, wouldn't let her near the lit sterno. Out of an abundance of caution, he cooked the unrefrigerated hot dogs so thoroughly they withered in their skins. He forked the dogs onto two different plates and handed her portion to her. They'd used up all the ketchup and bread so the hot dogs were unadorned. Taking off his sock-mittens, he picked up one of the dogs and bit into it, chewing industriously, standing there, intent on the chore of calories.

She, on the other hand, sandwiched a hot dog between potato chips. Biting into it, she found the meat chewy from being cooked so long, but at least the chips gave it a bit of a salty crunch. Pleased, she placed her plate full of hot dogs and potato chips on the kitchen counter, hopped up beside it and began to eat.

Stotts watched her, still chewing that first rubbery bite. Swallowing with some difficulty, he took a seat beside her and sandwiched his next bite between potato chips also. Eating, their silence was peaceful.

The only problem was the lack of water. She could feel already the salty chips increasing her thirst.

After Stotts finished his food, he sat there for a moment breathing, his posture for once slightly slumped, before hopping down from the counter. As he did so, he reached with his bare hand for the fridge's metal handle, intending to use it for balance.

She had time to realize he must be very tired.

The electrical discharge was blue and cracked like a shot. Stotts was thrown back from the fridge. Hitting the floor, he bounced.

He lay there, face up, his mouth gasping like a fish's.

His eyes rolled to look at her—pleading.

CPR was a class she'd always meant to take. No way to Quark the information now. No hospital to rush him to, no doctors or medicine.

So she took her best guess. She jumped off the counter to sit astride him and pump the heel of her hands down onto his sternum, all her strength, elbows locked.

Ouch, he coughed and inhaled with a shudder. The wind only knocked out of him.

She stared at his face, at him breathing again. His face was all she recognized about the last few days, all that connected her to the planet. For her, he was the last human.

He wheezed, rubbing his sternum, You *really* hurt me.

She touched her fingers to his lips, needing to feel the air moving in and out of his mouth.

He jerked his face away, as though she'd given him another shock, pushed her off and got to his feet. Either embarrassed to be saved (men!) or feeling the touch inappropriate (Midwesterner!).

Standing up, she found she still wanted to touch him—his back or shoulder—to feel his ribs moving, his breath continuing, the warmth of his living body. To stop herself, she stuffed her hands in her pockets.

*

For the rest of the evening, each time she baptized the bonobos, she insisted on blessing Stotts too. He stood still for it, but she could feel his discomfort as her fingers brushed his face and hands. He must not be accustomed to being cared for.

Thirty Six

When Frankie woke, the room was so bright that for a moment she thought the lights must have turned back on. She was groggy. The only way she'd been able to sleep last night was on her side, with the pillow pressed tight to her belly, trying to protect her blisters from the bonobos brushing against them. From below her belly button to a few inches above her knees her skin was burned red in stripes.

Blinking, she saw the sun streaming in through the window. The storm gone. Peeping, the bonobos got up to knuckle over to the window and stare outside.

The air was clear, the sky blue.

She rose to stand beside them, looking out the window at this new world.

She called, Stotts, come check it out.

He appeared a moment later down the hall, drawn by the morning light.

She asked, It's over?

He stared out at the bright day. He said, The storm is over.

Ha! It's over!

The enclosure had an inch or so of dust on the ground, the roof dark from dust. Still, the area was recognizable and the bonobos stared out at it, whining. Stotts eased the door open. Keeping his leg in the way, he stuck his head out and inhaled, the air clear. Marge, excited, shoved hard past his leg and bolted outside. The rest followed in an eager stampede.

So happy to have space, they rocketed along in every direction, their speed and grace startling. Frankie watched Goliath gallop slightly sideways, one arm leading, reaching always for more speed, all four limbs kicking off the ground at the same moment with an effortless bounce, like a muscled pony cantering on soft hands.

Houdina headed for the pond. Breastfeeding, she was so much thirstier than the rest of them.

Frankie and Stotts followed her to find the pond empty, only a few muddy puddles left near its steel drain.

Houdina climbed down and lowered her face to one of the puddles. She spat out what she sampled, shaking her head and snorting, then tried again, straining the mud through her teeth. This time she coughed harder, spraying out what little she'd drank.

The other bonobos, curious about this new world, swung up into the climbing structure. At the top, they stood on two feet, looking around, peeping with surprise.

Curious, Frankie clambered up the tire swing after them, Stotts following. The world out there was newly beige, a lunar landscape covered with dust. With roads and lawns erased, the placement of buildings and fences appeared whimsical, toys dropped willy-nilly in a sandbox. The drifts were higher on the windward side of every obstacle, the busy sharp-edged world of humanity partially erased. No movement anywhere.

Stotts pressed his Bindi, holding it down, while he said, Ok BodyWare, on.

Surprised, she turned to him to see his Bindi light up, turning blue as it initialized.

Woohoo! she said and pressed her Bindi.

Following some unwritten social rule, they angled slightly away from each other while they waited for their technology to come online, giving each other privacy. She heard her EarDrums click and start fizzing, the low and distant sound of a living device. She thought about how the story of the last few days would be heard in Manhattan, her students imagining how hard it must have been—no showers, no Quark, locked in a room with large primates with sharp teeth—while she remembered the actual experience: Stotts and Goliath and Mama and Id.

Waiting, she let her eyes wander across the landscape. So strange to see nothing moving, no cars, no people. The seconds went by. No icons appeared on her Lenses, no date and time, no status update. She heard no eager Road Runner *meep-meep*, which would signal that her EarDrums were on-line. There weren't even stray characters along the bottom of her Lenses anymore—no asterisk or percent sign. Glancing over at Stotts, she saw from the stillness of his eyes that he was waiting too.

She asked, My light on?

He looked at her forehead, Yes.

Reassured, they both looked away from each other again waiting.

He said, Ah! I got a cursor in the lower left. It's blinking.

Is that how it normally boots up?

Don't know. I've only had this system a few days.

She asked, Your EarDrums on?

I can hear them, he said and added, Ok Bindi, camera on.

She waited. His eyes searched for any information on his Lenses.

She asked, Ok Bindi, what's the date?

Her EarDrums said nothing. Her Lenses blank.

They ran through every command they could think of, trying each one two or three times, a game of Marco Polo where Polo wasn't there.

Afterward they stood there silent for a long moment. His expression very internal. He hadn't been able to contact his family in days, to check in on Tess.

Could our BodyWare be fried from the static? she asked.

He looked in the direction of the road and said, When help gets here, the techies can figure it out.

She turned in that direction also, but found she wasn't sure anymore exactly where the road had been.

The hum of the EarDrums combined with the empty landscape began to make her uneasy. She powered her BodyWare off and climbed down. Along the way she noticed Mama was shivering, so she called her back inside. The rest followed gradually.

Stotts was the last one in. He closed the door after himself and said in a quiet voice, I'm going to go grab some more supplies from the Snack Shack.

I'll come along.

We shouldn't both leave. They could get in trouble.

She looked around the rooms, emptied of furniture, light fixtures and wall ornaments, and asked, How?

Well, they could break down the front door to follow us.

I'll tell them not to.

You think that will work?

She turned to Mama and said, I'm going with Stotts to get you something to drink and eat. Don't go outside. Don't let the others out. It's dangerous.

Mama's shiny eyes regarded her without expression.

Frankie imagined speaking these words to a four-year-old. She added the word, Chimps.

The focus of Mama's eyes changed.

Frankie found it easier these days to think like a bonobo. She said, That was a bad storm. The chimps could have broken loose. They could be outside. Stay inside. Please.

Mama glanced at the door and then back at Frankie. Perhaps she'd lost more weight than the others, or maybe it was because she was hairless, but the tendons in her neck were apparent. She wore a pink knit hat with a large pom-pom. Her jug ears stuck out. Tooch clung to the front of her sweatshirt.

Mama made the sign for *Danger*, and raised her eyebrows to indicate a question.

Yes, said Frankie nodding her fist, It could be dangerous outside. Stay inside. Keep the others inside. We'll be back soon.

Outside, their feet made no sound. Walking in the dust took energy, the air clear and still. Looking back, she could see a light haze kicked up by their movements.

The door to the Snack Shack was open, noise coming from inside. They peered in. The three other humans were already here, packing up drink and food. She stared for a moment, surprised by their hairless skin and upright stance. The Snack Shack also looked different. The door must have been left open during some of the storm—the shelves, food and appliances covered in a layer of dust. The commercial griddle transformed into an altar from some long-ago civilization.

Oh, said Frankie, Thank goodness you're alright.

The three people looked over, but didn't stop packing. Frankie blinked at this.

The keeper asked, The bonobos alright?

A little cold, but fine. Your apes all fine?

Yep, said the skinny woman—Rita—who took care of the orangutans. She was standing by the stacks of sodas for the vending machine, packing cans away. She kept her body between the Mountain Dew and the rest of them.

Frankie moved her eyes from Rita to the others, her head cocked.

Martin (the man with the beard who took care of the chimps) said, They're hungry.

And thirsty, added Rita.

Martin was filling his knapsack with bags of defrosted french fries. He asked, Your BodyWare working?

No, said Stotts. He stepped to the stacks of Orange Crush and began packing cans into his bag.

This was at this point that Frankie noticed how little food and soda remained on the shelves, how there were holes in the dust where supplies had been.

Stotts asked, Yours?

She saw every shelving unit in the middle of the room was either emptied of food and drink or claimed by someone who stood in front of it, packing away whatever remained. Each of them was responsible for caring for the group of apes they knew best. Each of them had watched these apes suffer the last few days. They packed the supplies away with determination.

Frankie moved to the back where she started opening the cupboards. The others turned slightly to track her, to see what she might find.

Martin said, No, it's weird. My BodyWare has power, but won't boot up.

Rita said, Me too.

Frankie asked, You think it's from the static?

The third cupboard was full of food. Excited, she began tucking it away into her duffle bag—mac'n'cheese packets and instant mashed potato mix—keeping her shoulders and the bag as much as she could in the way, claiming this.

Martin said, Yeh, that could be it.

Help should get here soon, said Rita.

How long does it normally take, asked Frankie.

Rescue folks will be here tomorrow, said Martin.

What, she asked, Five meals from now?

Maybe six.

They sped up their packing slightly. As soon as Frankie and Stotts had all they could carry, they hefted their bags and left the Snack Shack. Stotts lugged a large bag of sodas, breathing with the weight.

When they reached the bonobo building, Frankie put her bag down in the hallway and some of the boxes of mac'n'cheese spilled out.

Stotts stared down at the boxes.

What, she asked.

He said, Did you only grab mac'n'cheese?

She held up a bag of dehydrated potato flakes too.

He said, Cooked. That has to be *cooked*. We don't have more sterno.

She looked down at the mac'n'cheese in her hand and opened her mouth to respond, but nothing came out.

He said, I'll go back to the Snack Shack to see what else I can find. You stay. Give them a little soda. They're thirsty.

She let each bonobo drink a half a can of Orange Crush, holding the can to the lips so none of it spilled. As each drank, the large leather hands rested on her arms, eyes locked on hers.

When she pulled the can away, each bonobo would look surprised and sign, *drink* and *please*. The sign for *drink* was easy to understand since an imaginary drink was cupped in the hand and raised to the mouth. They would sign these words again and again and then frustrated they would try other signs she didn't know. She couldn't understand half of it. The ones who'd been raised in human families used so many signs, their hands weaving complicated symbols through the air.

She gave a whole soda to Houdina, since she had to breast-feed both Id and Tooch. Houdina stepped close enough to drink from the can, but as soon as she was done she stepped back, away from Frankie.

A moment later Stotts returned with several bags full of cans and jars. Corn, peaches, baked beans, some pickles. They used the can opener, pouring the contents into bowls they put on the ground for the bonobos. The bonobos ate every speck of food. Stotts saved a few cans for later in the day. After the food was gone, Houdina was the first one to try the pickle juice. With each sip, she shivered, contorting her mouth like a hairy Mick Jagger. Then she'd drink some more.

Frankie and Stotts allowed themselves only eight ounces

each to drink. They measured it carefully, looking at the bright orange soda.

She downed her drink in two fast gulps. He sipped his slowly, his eyes closed, holding the liquid in his mouth for a long time.

Thirty Seven

Twice, that morning they let the bonobos out to exercise, calling them back inside when they started shivering. Their combined body heat kept the air inside the rooms warmer than the enclosure.

Every once in awhile Frankie would turn her BodyWare back on and try a few commands, then switch it off fairly quickly. The unresponsive hum she found spooky.

Stotts continued to scout for more food and drink.

After the Snack Shack was emptied, he searched the other buildings. She stood at a window watching him move from one building to another. He always seemed to be in motion now, moving mechanically and tense. He'd lost some weight. It was likely he had never gone this long without talking to his family, without knowing Tess was ok.

Twice that morning, she caught him staring at her, an expression in his eyes somewhere between unhappiness and alarm. Probably he wished she was a veterinarian or Quark expert or at least someone who didn't parboil her crotch.

She spotted the keeper and others also out there searching. They didn't seem to be finding much since most times when they left a building they carried nothing.

*

Midmorning, Stotts returned carrying some lighter fluid and a hibachi, the heavy cast-iron kind that sat on the ground.

He said, Ta-da.

What, Frankie asked.

Now we can cook.

She stared for another second, then understood, My potato flakes?

She hugged him hard—so grateful he was fixing her mistake. Perhaps from being around the bonobos so much, she was losing some sense of personal space: how long to hug, how close. He stepped back from her a bit abruptly.

He said quickly, Along with teaching Goliath to knapp, as part of that grant I got, I'm supposed to teach them to cook.

She stared into his eyes, worried she'd offended him. She could still feel his chest against her cheek. She said, Cook?

It's another Stone-Age technology.

Early humans cooked?

Yes ma'am, he nodded.

She imagined Mama crouched by a fire, turning a mango on a spit. She asked, You want to teach the bonobos that?

My next bit of research. Probably get to it in the spring.

She looked at the hibachi and said, Well, no time like the present.

He paused.

She said, Right now, they're motivated to learn.

He looked over at Adele and Sweetie, the closest bonobos. Adele was giving Sweetie what appeared to be a dental exam.

Frankie jerked her thumb at them and said, Right now they wouldn't play with their toes or stare off at the sky or take a nap. If you told them food was coming, you'd have their attention.

At the word *food*, Adele and Sweetie turned around.

She said, It took you months to get Goliath to begin to knapp, right? And before that you worked with some other bonobo who wouldn't do it. Lack of success is not necessarily lack of smarts. It could be lack of motivation.

Adele knuckled closer, watching them.

Stotts looked down at the ground for a moment. She saw ambition flicker in his face.

She said, You'd never be allowed to keep them hungry like this normally.

He asked slowly, Could you keep them back from the fire?

Yep.

He turned to her, his eyes serious, I mean a good four feet back. They could get burned in a second. You understand that?

Let's try it with Mama. If she gets it, we can do it.

He said, They get too close, even once, we stop. Agreed?

Agreed.

They set the hibachi up in the enclosure so the smoke could disperse out the open vents. For wood, they broke up a small table from the office area. Kneeling beside the grill, it took them awhile to start the fire—the surprising difficulty of lighting a flammable object. They ended up using a lot of lighter fluid. She felt admiration for her ancestors rubbing sticks together.

Once the fire was crackling, she let Mama into the enclosure. Tooch was tucked into Mama's sweatshirt, his head sticking out, his eyes riveted on the fire. Standing between Mama and the hibachi, Frankie said, Dangerous. Don't touch. Hot hot. It can hurt you. It can hurt Tooch.

Frankie made the sign for *danger*—jabbing at her face with her thumb and blocking the motion with her other arm.

Mama stared at the flames flickering above the hibachi. She covered Tooch's head with her hand, backing away. It might have been because of Frankie's warning, or maybe, growing up with humans, Mama had at one point hurt herself on a gas stove.

Since Mama so clearly understood, they let the others in, one by one. Anytime one of them got too close to the hibachi, Mama would *waa*-bark at them, sharp and no nonsense. Once Marge and Adele caught on, they joined in on the barking. Soon they'd settled down several yards back from the fire, in a semi-circle, eyes big. They watched every move Stotts made.

Like a magician, he held up each of his props for them to see, making big gestures. Demonstrating the pot was empty, he poured in Orange Crush, then added the Crisco and set it on the fire. The bonobos considered his actions gravely, pressed in against each other for warmth. Frankie held onto Id just in case.

Once it was boiling, he took it off the hibachi and added the potato flakes, stirring. Frankie moved from bonobo to bonobo, giving each a precise allotment of soda, Id tucked into her sweater.

The mashed potatoes ended up tinged a light tangerine. Frankie spooned a small amount out, waiting until it was just warm to the touch. She offered the spoonful to the bonobos.

This time she didn't have to demonstrate the food was edible. Houdina leaned forward to lip off a tiny bit of food. She moved it around in her mouth, her eyes focused on the distance—the taste of Crisco and potatoes, mixed with the sweet soda—then took a bigger bite. Seeing her reaction, the rest of them held out their hands.

While the bonobos ate, Frankie fed Id tiny bits of mashed potato from her finger, hoping to make up for some of the breast milk Tooch was taking.

Frankie and Stotts saved their allotment of liquid to drink instead of using it to make the mashed potatoes. Earlier that day Stotts had told her an object held in the mouth could help fight the thirst. In Syria, in the desert, he used to suck on a pebble during the heat of the day. It made the salivary glands work, keeping some liquid in the mouth.

At the moment, they were each sucking on a raw macaroni noodle, moving it around in the mouth like a horse mouthing its bit. Over time the noodle softened enough to eat. They tried to concentrate on the fire, but could hear every sound of the bonobos eating.

Stotts said, I wouldn't be able to do this without you.

She turned to him, surprised by the surge of gratitude she felt.

The two of them didn't talk as much now, but at each decision point they looked to the other, partners on a high wire struggling for balance.

*

Later in the day, Stotts went outside again.

Frankie caught a glimpse of him through a window, turning slowly in a circle, surveying the sky. From inside, she couldn't figure out what he was searching for. After he came back inside, she stepped out the front door.

Out here, the depth of the silence was intense, as though the world was holding its breath. The few clouds seemed incomplete. She turned all the way around, staring upward, before she realized what was missing. No planes. No helicopters. Not even an emergency drone.

Just before dusk, Stotts clambered up the climbing structure again and stayed there a long time. He turned slowly. His gaze didn't pause once. She didn't need to climb up to know there was nothing there to see.

*

That evening they lit the hibachi again. Stotts hadn't said a word since dusk.

They opened the five cans of sweet corn remaining and forked the corn into bowls. Frankie had never liked canned corn, but she found her eyes focused on this food, as though it were talking to her in some way: the yellow so very bright, the niblets plump and gleaming. Even though there was so little corn, the bonobos enjoyed it enormously, tossing a single niblet into the mouth at a time and sucking on it like candy.

She forced her eyes away, biting instead through the piece of raw macaroni in her mouth. It made a loud crunching noise.

Meanwhile Stotts sautéed some macaroni in a little soda. In

the darkness, the bonobos watched with great seriousness when Stotts spooned the noodles into a bowl, then squeezed on a packet of cheese sauce.

Once Houdina—the taste-tester—tried a spoonful, the others picked up individual noodles to try. At the taste, some of them peeped and bounced on their haunches. Perhaps those who'd been raised in a human family remembered this food.

Stotts and she sat together, off to the side, sipping their allotment of soda She felt such gratitude for the concept of liquid. The fire heated her face, sparks popping and flying into the air.

She tried to drink as slowly as possible, to make it last, but when she was finished, her head still hurt. She began picking up the empty cans of corn, one at a time, and tilting them over her mouth to catch any drops that might remain.

They hadn't been talking much all day. Perhaps this was why she heard Stotts' words so clearly.

He asked, Is there any way I met you years ago? At a conference? Or earlier, when we were kids?

Doubt it, she said, I grew up on the East Coast. Why?

The last few days, you just . . . you seem familiar.

Holding a can in her hand, she turned to him. He waited, his expression intent.

Each important moment in life has about it a stillness, an extra beat, an awareness at the edges. Something inside her clicked. Some animal part of her brain.

For the third time in her life, she heard that raspy inner voice whispering in her ear. It stated flat and factual, *He's fallen for you, honey.*

The can dropped from her hand.

The clank of it hitting the ground echoed in her ears. Flustered she reached for it but her fingers seemed all rubbery and the can rolled. In the end she had to use both hands to pick it up.

Even in the gloom, every detail of the can appeared crystal clear. She stared at it, the bright image of yellow niblets and the red Del Monte logo. The thought crossed her mind that she might be experiencing something medical—a minor stroke or some pre-migraine ephemera.

Her eyes drifted, tugged back to him. He was lit up, luminous, by far the most interesting sight here. Her eyes unable to turn away.

He was saying something, probably teasing her about dropping the can. She couldn't hear his words for there was a high-pitched metallic *ping* at the limits of her hearing.

He felt right to some essential part of her—her gut, her skin, her toes—this, the most decent man she'd ever met.

Him, a married man with a child.

Thirty Eight

That night she was restless in her pile of bonobos, had difficulty falling asleep, kept jerking awake, filled with disbelief.

Even with this broken sleep, in the first light of dawn, she woke with a zing of energy.

Pushing her way out of the pile of sleeping bodies, she walked down the hall. She saw his mattress already put away for the day, as though he'd never slept here, as though he'd never existed.

She moved into the office area, a rising urgency, searching for him. Through one of the windows, she spotted him outside, looking upward.

When she stepped outside, he looked over. His gaze different, intent.

She walked closer.

She'd spent enough time around him that she could close her eyes and describe him so anyone could pick him out in a crowd—his eyes, height and buzzcut, the small scar in his right eyebrow, the attentive way he occupied his body.

At the moment, however, she stared at him like she would at a total stranger who'd stepped out of her bathroom.

Morning, she said.

Ma'am, he replied.

His eyes seemed different somehow, bigger than before or luminous. She stared into them, wanted to clamber inside, wander around, bring in a pup tent to live there in that shimmering space.

He dragged his gaze away to the sky.

He said, Help should arrive today.

Rescue meant all sorts of things now. She listened. The silence was perfect, the sky empty. With this knowledge, they looked at each other and then away.

They prepped mashed potatoes for the bonobos. Beside him, she forgot her thirst and hunger. They sat next to each other as they had before, but the space between them was different.

In her lungs, she could remember the pain she'd felt after she left her married professor—the emptiness, how hard it was to breathe.

She should concentrate on being relieved she could feel this way again. It had been so long. This was a sign of her health returning, like the way she was truly hungry again for food. She should simply enjoy this different type of hunger. Soon after the cleanup vehicles got here, the two of them would stop being together all day long. His family would return from England. Chores and people would separate them. This feeling would ease, the ache in her gut. She didn't need to take this seriously. She was just healthier.

He held out a few more pieces of raw macaroni for her. She scooped them from his hand, the feel of his palm on her fingers. She tossed the pasta into her mouth and sucked on the pieces, as though on the finest of chocolates, closing her eyes.

They sat there, waiting for help to arrive, for sand-plows, the National Guard and FEMA, all the people and noise and busy life to step between them.

*

After they'd fed the bonobos and brought them back inside, he pulled a knapsack on.

Where you going?

I'm just going to check the farmhouse down the road. See if I can find any supplies.

She looked out across the dust in the direction she thought he meant, then asked what she hadn't dared to until now, But rescue will get here today, right?

He wouldn't look at her when he said, Might as well get something for us to drink while we wait. You stay here and make sure the bonobos don't misbehave.

He headed off down the road toward the nearest house. She watched him get small in the distance.

He came back an hour and a half later, dragging a red plastic sled piled with Gatorade and Diet Coke, a full knapsack on his back. She caught sight of him through the window. He visited each of the other enclosures first, dropping off some of the liquid with the other humans, talking with them, standing in the doorway, pointing in the direction that he'd come from.

She met him in the doorway of the bonobo building. Before unloading the sled, he pulled out of his pocket a single Frappuccino in a bottle and handed it over, saying, For you.

She cupped it in her hand for a second. This jar of liquid glittered.

She said, Thank you.

Her emotions banging around inside her, like a child told to sit still for way too long.

He inclined his head.

Twisting the metal cap, the bottle made a satisfying *pop*. She held it under her nose, the scent of strong coffee.

She kept her eyes shut to savor it, drank two long gulps, then stopped herself and handed it to him. He considered the mouth of the bottle that she had drunk from, then raised it to his lips and drank also.

*

After Stotts' success, all the humans left the Foundation midmorning to search the nearby farmhouses for supplies. If they heard rescue vehicles, they would rush back.

Frankie was worried the very hungry and thirsty bonobos

would break out of the building if she was gone more than an hour, so before leaving she called them into the sleeping chamber, telling them there was fruit hidden in the piles of bedding. Once they were all inside, searching through the hay, she stepped out and locked the door. They turned to look at her, their eyes big with betrayal.

Sorry, she said, I just . . . We need to . . . Sorry.

Once she was outside, she heard for the first time the rising animal howl coming from one of the other buildings, an atonal song of distress, echoing and muffled. Turning, she tried to place the noise.

Stotts jerked his chin toward the gorilla building. He said, In the wild, the gorillas don't drink water, but eat juicy vegetation all day. Without food, they get dehydrated quickly.

She stared at the cement building, then back at him, How much do they eat?

40 pounds a day.

She paused, The whole group?

No, each one of them.

Startled, she looked at the building again, then back at the plastic child's sled they pulled. It wouldn't carry more than 40 pounds. If they made trips all day long, filling the sled completely each time, they wouldn't be able to lug back enough for even the gorillas.

She asked, What about the others?

They're doing better than the gorillas.

What do they think is going on?

He looked confused, so she added, The humans.

He said, Oh. I didn't talk that long with them. Martin, the chimp guy, seems pretty angry. He thinks the governor's incompetent.

What about Rita?

She reads a lot of sci-fi. She asked if I thought it could be a solar flare or an EMP.

And the keeper?

She's the one caring for the gorillas. She's just worried.

They headed out, moving quickly across the fields away from the Foundation. She could hear the gorillas when the wind blew in the right direction. So long as she was walking beside Stotts, it seemed easy to move with energy. She tried to remember when she'd last had a full meal.

Being from Manhattan, she was accustomed when outside to noise. This silence was deep and biological: the wind, the rustle of their clothes, their feet moving through the dust.

She said, Everyone's just *gone*.

Hope so, he said.

She looked at him, considering this remark.

He tried to distract her. You grew up in New York?

She explained her Canadian birth and how American manners had seemed so foreign when she first arrived. She asked about his childhood. For once, without the bonobos listening, they talked easily.

The distance was impressive, the endless field they walked through, then the field beyond that, most of the land filled with weeds and stunted bushes, out of production. He'd already emptied the closest house of food and drink. In the distance, a dog barked, a deep resonant baying, perhaps a large dog. They stayed away from that sound, finding instead another house about a half a mile further.

They walked across the wood porch, their steps echoing. *Edgars* was the name on the mailbox. The flower boxes held withered pansies poking out of the dust.

Stotts tried the doorbell first, but with no electricity, the button only made a small squeak. So he knocked, the rap of knuckles against wood. They stood there waiting as though this were a normal day.

He knocked a second time and called out.

With no movement from inside, he took the *Home Sweet*

Home plaque off the door and tapped its corner through the window. The sound of this violence was loud, the glass shattering and tinkling onto the floor inside. He dragged the plaque around the frame to clear it of glass, then reached in to turn the door handle. With the door open, they peered down the dark hall.

There was a thunk and a scramble and they both jumped back. A small grey cat rocketed out the door and off the porch. They ran down the stairs after it, calling and looking everywhere, but the cat just disappeared, under the porch or in the bushes, nowhere to be seen.

Inside, there was an easel set up in the living room, muddy portraits of lilies hanging on the wall, bottles of pills on the kitchen counter, the smells of cat litter and Lysol. Frankie opened the fridge a crack, but the stench of putrid meat made her slam it shut. In the pantry were stacks of Chef Boyardee and cat food cans, two 10-pound-bags of sweet potatoes only beginning to sprout, two tubs of margarine, two boxes of Cheerios and, most miraculous of all, 10 half gallons of seltzer and lemonade.

Unable to stop themselves, they each poured themselves a glass of lemonade. Holding the glass, she paused to watch Stotts drink, his head back and throat revealed, a tight undulation of cartilage. In this moment, she had a glimpse of him as an organism, a multicellular creature pumping liquids into his alimentary canal, an *animal* wrapped in clothes and balanced on his haunches. Civilization is based upon a charade, such careful theater. Each of us buttoning up our costumes, hiding our fur, living in carefully sculpted sets, while we pretend we've never pooped or had coitus. The illusion broken each time we tighten into death or squeeze a baby out our hoo-ha or fall in love.

She felt light-headed, looked away and drank the glass down. She asked, Of this food, what will the bonobos never eat?

Carrying food to the sled, he said over his shoulder, The cat food.

She rummaged through the cans until she found one labeled Purrfect Tuna, cracked it open and took a big forkful, looking out the window as she chewed, considering the taste. She hoped if she ate some food, she might feel a little more normal. When she turned back, he was standing in the doorway, staring.

It's just tuna, she said putting another forkful in her mouth, Tastes like casserole, but a little . . . mealy. I need to eat something in order to make the walk back.

That is revolting, he marveled.

She grunted and, spotting a mostly empty bottle of honey, squeezed it over the cat food, then scraped the can clean.

He weakened and grabbed a tin of Chef Boyardee for himself. When she raised her eyebrows, he said, They probably wouldn't eat this either.

You just don't want to eat cat food.

Damn right.

When they left, Stotts pulled the sled and carried two large bags over his shoulder. She wore a full knapsack, slogging forward through the dust.

She wasn't sure how long it took for them to return to the Foundation, but the sun was low in the sky.

By this point, denial was impossible. Rescue would not happen today.

They dropped off some of the supplies with the other humans. For the bonobos, they brought back the sweet potatoes and all the seltzer, as well as one tub of margarine.

As soon as they stepped into the building, they could hear the bonobos squealing. They'd been locked in the sleeping chamber now for most of the day, without food or drink. When Frankie unlocked the chamber, they exploded outward, running down the hall, squawking and throwing her hurt looks. She didn't think she'd be able to persuade them in there again.

She poured two gallons of seltzer into a large pan in the center of the hall and let them share it, while she held the pan to make sure it didn't get spilled. The bonobos each took a turn, stooping their heads for a long time, the sound of gulping. Houdina drank the longest, a desperate sort of gasp to her swallowing.

Meanwhile Stotts stepped into the enclosure. After they'd finished drinking, she followed him. He stood at the top of the climbing structure, staring at something on the horizon with attention.

She climbed fast. At the top, she searched in that direction for vehicles cleaning the roads, a phalanx of sand-plows, a line of dump trucks, life returning to normal.

The horizon was empty, the sun setting.

Still he continued to stare.

It took her a moment to spot the three tiny figures walking maybe half a mile away, humans, a smaller one in front of the other two. They either wore knapsacks or many layers of clothing, perhaps both. They walked in a straight line, heading west, until they disappeared behind a small hill.

She looked at Stotts. He didn't move. She asked, You don't want to chase them?

He said, Probably couldn't catch them. We don't know who they are. They might have guns.

He added quietly, They'd be more mouths to feed.

Thirty Nine

Frankie woke up late, the bed empty, the sun up, the bonobos and Stotts already in the enclosure. Sitting up, her headache started, her mouth dry. She moved her tongue around in her mouth like a sock, trying to find a comfortable spot. She thought back to her life before the storm and realized with disbelief that first thing, every morning of her life, she used to sit down over a gallon of clean drinking water to pee into it and then flush it away.

After the bonobos were fed, Frankie sat down with Mama. She knew she wouldn't be able to trick the bonobos into getting locked in their sleeping chamber again.

Mama, she said, I have to go outside for a while. There might be chimps outside. It's dangerous. While I'm gone, you need to keep everyone inside, alright?

Mama looked at her, her eyes focused and considering, the gaze of a shopper wondering if the scale was accurate or not.

Frankie said, I'll be gone a long time, probably most of the day. Don't go outside. Don't let the others outside. Alright?

Mama's stare didn't waver.

Frankie made the gesture for *danger danger* and added the gesture for *please*, circling her palm over her heart.

Mama nodded her fist once—the most she would concede.

Frankie didn't know if the fist pump meant *Yes, I will not go outside*, or if it meant *Yes, I don't trust you anymore*. Either way, she had no choice. Before leaving, she pulled Id out of her sweater and, since Id just grunted and continued sleeping, she

328 · AUDREY SCHULMAN

tucked her into some of the blankets to keep her warm. Id had been sleeping a lot the last day or so.

Outside Frankie and Stotts walked fast in a direction where the dust was untouched, none of the other humans having walked this way, the area slightly west of where they'd traveled yesterday.

At first they just marched straight across the fields, until they spotted a line of utility poles and followed those instead, figuring the poles would lead to houses. However, as the morning passed, the poles only led them to boarded-up buildings. So many farms had gone bankrupt.

As they walked, they talked about childhood, their research and the bonobos—pretty much anything but their situation. She found the closer to him she walked, the more energy she had. At one point her shoulder bumped into his and he flinched as though there was still static.

In the end, they gave up on the poles and instead headed in the direction of the dog that still bayed in the distance, its voice breaking with exhaustion. It turned out to be a young and skinny mutt, probably half beagle, chained up at the back of a small house. A metal dish was overturned on the ground and every blade of grass had been eaten within the circumference of the chain. Seeing them, the dog whined and backed away, the chain rattling after it. Stotts tried to call it, then simply to chase it down, but it kept bolting away, so in the end he stepped his feet along the chain, decreasing the dog's field of motion until it could do nothing more than lean backward, the collar riding up its neck. Stotts unclipped the chain and the dog ran away, yipping.

Frankie meanwhile broke into the house by lobbing a piece of firewood through the front door's window.

In the kitchen there wasn't much to drink, just two half gallons of Lipton's pre-sweetened iced tea. They stared at those two small jugs and didn't say a word. Then Stotts started packing the bottles and all the available food away into his bag.

Frankie grabbed a mug and walked to the bathroom where she opened the toilet tank and scooped out a cup of water to drink it straight down, one hand on the wall. When she'd finished, she wiped her lips and breathed for a moment, before finding some plastic bottles to fill up with this water. She emptied the upstairs toilet tank also and brought a cup of water back to Stotts. He must have heard the clatter of the porcelain tank and the clank of the mug. He eyed the water.

She said, It's from the tank, not the bowl. Perfectly clean.

Yuck, he answered and drank it down.

They opened a can of black olives and ate with shaking hands. After they'd packed up all the provisions they could find, they half-jogged back to the Foundation, approaching the bonobo building in the late afternoon, bringing barely enough food and drink for one meal. This time neither of them suggested sharing what they'd found with the keeper or the others.

Rushing inside, she found the bonobos still in the interaction area, safe (their faces all turning to her, upset at the long delay) and she sat down fast, breathing. Mama knuckled forward, chattering at her with frustration, so Frankie grabbed her by the shoulders and hugged her, pressing her face hard for a moment into Mama's grey neck. How had this happened—shambling apes transformed into individuals so very dear to her?

Stotts moved down the hall to get some cups and the baby bottle, and she began to pull bottles of water out of her bag.

Houdina was the only one who wouldn't take the water from Frankie. In her arms, she held Id who was still sleeping. So Frankie handed the water to Stotts. Instantly Houdina put Id down and knuckled over to sit in his lap and drink, playing flirtatiously with his shirt buttons. Even wearing a turtleneck and a down vest, she was clearly skinnier than just a few days ago. Breastfeeding took calories. Stotts gave her a double serving of water.

Meanwhile Frankie picked Id up and had to jostle her awake, then placed the baby bottle of water to her lips. Id, feeling the nipple against her mouth, latched on and nursed with intensity, her eyes staring into Frankie's. When the water was gone, prying the bottle out of her mouth was difficult. Id arched and began to scream, thrashing with thirst. At her cry, Houdina rushed over and grabbed Id, baring her teeth at Frankie.

Mama barked in response, all of their tempers fraying.

*

As the sun set, Frankie and Stotts clambered up the climbing structure, surveying the horizon for movement. Hunger focused her vision, everything bright and sharp-edged.

When Stotts spotted something, she felt the change and turned, searching. Four deer at the far end of the nearest field picked their way through dusty flowers, lowering their heads to eat.

Other than that, the landscape was empty. The absence loud. The space between Frankie and Stotts warm and muscled.

*

That night, she woke to what she thought was fireworks. A small popping noise in the distance. Her first assumption was rescue personnel and she felt such physical relief. She raised her head, listening.

It took her a moment to understand gunfire.

The shots were close enough, she could hear the report and a slight echo, but too far away to hear anything else. It was difficult to pinpoint the direction from inside the building. In the dry air, with no background hum of traffic or machinery, the sound could travel far.

Now a dog in the distance began baying at the shots. Perhaps the beagle-mutt.

Imagining that dog alone out there in the dark, she realized the commotion might not involve rescue personnel. Instead, whatever was happening might include only the kind of people who disobeyed evacuation orders, these people desperate for food and water.

A bonobo woke at the noise and bolted out of bed, wailing.

One of the females. She rocketed around the room, searching for safety, stampeding over the others, hysterical. Woken this way, the other bonobos keened in communal terror, even though they couldn't hear the gunfire over her wails. Whoever the bonobo was, it seemed likely she had lived in the wild at one point, had seen what guns can do.

A blinding light came bouncing down the hall, Stotts wearing his headlamp. In the cold he was wearing every bit of clothing he'd had on during the day. The bonobo catapulted herself straight into his arms—Houdina. She clung to him, rocking and screaming, pressing her face into his chest. He took a seat on the mattress and held her. The others clustered in, patting her and crying.

Exiled outside the scrum, Frankie patted their backs and said, *shh shh*, but was utterly ignored. The wailing continued, so she draped blankets around them to at least keep them warm. Bit by bit the crying subsided as most of them realized they weren't sure what they were upset about. Frankie walked down the hall to Stotts' mattress, wobbling slightly with exhaustion. Along the way she paused to rest her forehead against the cold glass of a window, listening. Over the still-whimpering bonobos, she couldn't hear anything outside, had no idea if the gunfire had stopped or was moving closer.

Too apprehensive to fall asleep away from the rest of them, she carried the mattress and blankets back and dropped them down next to the huddle of bonobos. They peeped with happiness and spread out across both mattresses, tugging the blankets over them. She shoved her way in. In the center of the pile, Houdina still clung to Stotts. He sighed and clicked off his headlamp. In the dark, there was a rustling as the bonobos moved to let him lie down. All of them together, as though each other's company and some blankets might protect them from whatever was outside.

Houdina quieted except for the occasional hiccup. One by

one they began to fall asleep, their breathing deeper. Frankie felt conscious of Stotts only few inches away. In spite of her exhaustion, sleep felt distant. Listening to his breathing, she believed he was awake too. She could hear no more gunshots. Probably they'd stopped a while ago.

Goliath's hand in hers, Mama exhaling against the back of her head, Frankie gradually began to drift off, thinking that people who had guns like that here were likely to be hunters, not criminals as they would be in Manhattan. Maybe they'd been shooting at the deer she'd seen earlier, wanting the venison.

Sliding deeper into sleep, she wondered what else they could hunt around here. Perhaps some birds—geese or turkeys. Raccoons, sure, but who would want to eat that?

This was when she startled awake.

The Foundation was well-known in the area. Everyone aware of what was penned up inside.

Most people, of course, would shoot the nearby cattle first, preferring to eat steak rather than a body with two hands. However hunters loved trophies. The kind of people who disobeyed a mandatory evacuation might not worry about other rules.

She imagined someone stepping into the interaction area, cradling the gun—the bonobos trotting forward, peeping at the sight of someone new.

She lay there for a long time, listening, trying to sense the slightest movement outside or at the doors.

In the end, in order to sleep, she wiggled her head forward until the corner of her forehead touched Stott's shoulder. At this, his breathing paused. He didn't move away.

She whispered, Is it gonna to be alright?

His arms around Houdina, he whispered, Yes.

She settled her forehead there, letting it rest against his shoulder, breathing in the warmth of the bonobos and him. In a pile, they all fell asleep on the mattresses. Even in her sleep, she listened.

Forty

Early in the morning, just after dawn, the keeper thumped on the door to the interaction area and called them outside for a meeting.

By the time Frankie and Stotts stumbled out, still rubbing the sleep from their eyes, the other humans were already there, clustered near the Eco-Center, where tourists used to gather for lectures on the behavior and original habitat of the apes. Frankie could see the change in the keeper, Rita and Martin: their hair greasy and clothes dirty. All around them lay the dust, the rolling of sine waves. The door to the Snack Shack slapped and thunked in the wind.

She searched the horizon for any rescue vehicles or people with guns. There was no sign of either, but there was the scent of something animal on the wind. She tilted her nose up, sniffing, before she realized it was the other unwashed humans near her, scented with the apes they took care of.

Martin, the man who took care of the chimps, asked, Why the hell haven't the cleanup crews arrived? Is it the cutbacks?

The smell was unsettling: a combination of human and non-human, familiar and not. Frankie wondered how badly she smelled.

Rita who took care of the orangutans said, They probably sent out only one sand-plow.

Martin snorted, Or a teenager with a vacuum cleaner.

Rita said, A toddler and a dustpan.

Their laughter was pitched a little high.

When they stopped, the keeper spoke.

She said, It doesn't matter. What's important is we've emptied the local buildings of food and drink. The apes are dehydrated. We can't transport enough supplies for them to stay here.

They all went still.

The keeper said, Since we can't get water to them, we have to get them to the water.

How, asked Martin.

The keeper said, Release them.

A chickadee called, a whistled rising question. The call seemed more understandable than the words the keeper had spoken.

Martin and Frankie said simultaneously, What?

Rita said, You can't . . . That's not . . .

The keeper asked quietly, When's the last time you saw one of them urinate?

The silence stretched out. They looked around the small circle, staring at one another.

Rita said, Help will arrive in a day or two.

The keeper said, Dehydration's fast. It starts with the juveniles.

She spoke one sentence at a time, so they could absorb the meaning. She said, We have to release the apes while they are still strong enough to move on their own.

She said, We can't carry them.

She said, You must lead them to water.

Martin asked, And what happens when the cleanup crews get here?

You help the crews recapture them.

You kidding? said Rita, That's your plan?

The keeper asked, What's yours?

Rita held her hands out and looked around, waiting for words to be dropped into her palms, an idea, a solution. She

said, Look, the orangutans won't stay together or follow anyone.

The keeper said, With them, you just open the door. They'll
leave on their own.

Rita stared at the keeper.

Martin said, The chimps can be dangerous. We can't just
release them.

The keeper said, The area's been evacuated. There should
be no people around for them to hurt. The only other choice
is to let them die.

That last word, *die*, hung in the air for a while.

The keeper asked a little louder as though the problem
might be with their hearing, Anyone have a better idea?

Looking around, Frankie saw not just their clothing and
hair looked different, but their expressions also, their eyes big
and focused far away. Like daguerreotypes of Sitting Bull and
his war chiefs, they stared into the shutter of the future, all the
rules changed.

The wind whistled by and some of the dust rose and twirled
in the sun. She found herself watching the dust devils with
attention, as though help might be buried nearby, about to be
revealed by the wind.

They emerged from the other side of that silence as different people.

The chimps, said Stotts.

Yes, said the keeper.

He said, Give us a little time, to get the bonobos away. Give
us a head start.

You'll go with them?

Of course.

Martin looked back and forth between the two of them. He
seemed at a loss. He asked, Where do we go?

The keeper looked around, searching the horizon, then
jerked her chin to the right. She said, Head the chimps that way.

Martin looked in that direction, a blank expression on his face, and then back to the keeper.

Try, said the keeper, Try to head them that way. You've been with them for years. You can do it.

The keeper pointed to the left and said, Stotts, you lead the bonobos that way.

Stotts shook his head and instead pointed straight ahead. East, he said.

They all remembered his daughter. Frankie blinked at the illogic of this—that walking in the direction of Tess would speed up the time until he saw her next.

However the keeper looked serious as she said, Ok.

She pointed in a third direction, halfway between East and the chimps. She said, I'll take the gorillas that way.

Rita said, Rescue will get here. Soon. I'll wait for it.

The keeper watched Rita, her expression revealing nothing. She said, When people get here, tell them we're out there. That we need help. Make them bring tranquilizer guns, not guns.

The keeper added, Please no guns.

Good luck, she said, To all of us.

*

Stotts was methodical about packing, considering every item, its weight and potential use. He chose the empty soda bottles, the lighter fluid, a small bottle of bleach, the remaining matches. He hefted the hibachi, then left it. He packed the blankets, then unpacked them, then packed them again. His eyes skittered over the tools in the closet, the pots in the pantry, searching for everything of value.

She fussed with the bonobos, wrapping as much clothing as she could around their upper halves to keep them warm. There was an endless surprise at all of this, this new world she'd traveled to without moving at all.

Tooch stepped into Houdini's lap to nurse. Since Id was

curled up in Houdina's lap, Tooch stepped onto her. She made a small groan but kept sleeping. He nursed from Houdina's left breast and then the right, with Mama and Adele nearby watching. Houdina looked away from him, her face tight. She kept one hand on Id.

Stotts bungeed everything down, then pulled the sled forward a few feet to check the weight. Then removed a few items. He was a man who needed to be prepared. Frankie watched him.

He looked around again for what he might be missing. Their eyes met and locked. Partners on a high wire, the wind from the height tugging at her.

Someone thumped on the door to the offices. The keeper yelled through the door, Hurry. Martin needs to let the chimps out.

Stotts straightened and, pulling the sled, walked to the door to open it. The keeper led the way down the hall to the exit. He paced after her, the door open behind him, the sled bumping and scraping along the floor.

At the end of the hall, the keeper unlatched the front door and stepped outside, heading for her gorillas. Stotts followed her, leaving that door open also.

Frankie and the bonobos remained in the interaction area, peering down the hall to the bright outdoors. She gestured the bonobos forward, calling, It's alright. Come on. We're going to find something to drink. Some food. Drink. Come on.

She walked down the hall, following Stotts, stepping outside into the sunlight. The bonobos followed, one by one, pausing by the door, sniffing the air. Mama peered in every direction, then knuckled out cautiously.

Adele galloped past her, heading around the corner for the basketball court.

Adele, Frankie called, Adele!

The rest took that as the signal to scatter in every direction, scooting up the trees or pawing through the dust searching for flowers to eat.

Adele, called Frankie, Come. This way. Come.

From around the building came the thunk of a basketball hitting the backboard. Sweetie disappeared into the Snack Shack. Marge trotted over to the sign language kiosk to slap at the buttons.

Sweetie, we're leaving, called Frankie, Marge, come. Let's move move.

Stotts pulled the sled and Frankie grabbed Mama's and Goliath's hands and tugged them forward.

Come, please, she called looking back over her shoulder to see if the chimps' door had opened yet. Please, she said, Please. *Adele*, we're leaving.

Stotts dragged the sled along, parallel to the road, heading in the direction the keeper had pointed in. Frankie followed, walking backwards and calling.

It was like attempting a forced march with kittens. The bonobos had no concept of purpose or wasted time. They gamboled in every direction, thrilled and exploring. After 20 minutes, the only way Adele would leave the basketball court was if she got to carry the basketball, clutched to her chest, while she whined and stared back at the hoop.

Hearing the tension in Frankie's voice, Sweetie followed, chirping, trying to make Frankie happy. Not used to distance, within a few hundred yards, most of the bonobos began to fall behind, peeping and shuffling through the dust. As they tired, they'd drop whatever toys they'd picked up—the basketball, a branch, a plastic bag—and walk on for a bit before starting to wail and knuckle back for the object. Frankie kept calling them and looking back at the door to the chimps' building.

Houdina was the only one who didn't run or play. She plodded on, head down and concentrated, following Stotts. Id was a small bump, tucked into her vest. Anytime Stotts stopped, Houdina sat down where she was and stared at the ground.

At one point Frankie turned back and saw the keeper stepping out with the gorillas, the silverback in front, the keeper's hand on his shoulder, his wives and children clustered behind. They wore winter hats with pom-poms and short ponchos, probably made out of blankets. The silverback walked along, sniffing the air and peering about, the keeper beside him.

Next time Frankie looked back, she was far enough away that she believed the door to the orangutans' building might be open, although she couldn't see any of them moving about. These, the hermits of the great apes, would slip away one by one during the night.

Once they got out of sight of the Foundation, she exhaled in relief. She figured now the chimps wouldn't know where they were. She took comfort in Stotts beside her.

However Stotts kept looking back, his eyes concerned. She turned each time he did, but saw no movement.

She knew in the jungle that chimps sometimes killed other animals: small deer or monkeys or other chimps. Now she began to wonder how they found their prey. Did they just stumble upon them or did they have a way of locating them?

After a time Stotts and she lost track of the road, buried somewhere under the dust. They just continued in what they hoped was a straight line with the bonobos trailing behind, peeping sadly.

*

Lucy was the one to find water. She raised her chin and froze, listening or perhaps smelling, then bolted through some bushes and down a small gully. A moment later they heard her splashing in. They all followed as fast as they could. Sliding down the gully, Frankie skidded into a mud flat, her shoes and the bottom of her pants instantly soaked.

Stotts trailed after them, calling, Wait, I brought bleach.

The mud made sucking noises. She struggled forward, trying to reach the water. She had to curl her toes, holding onto her shoes in the muck. Around her, the bonobos stood up on two legs. Moving forward, they leaned from side to side and yanked each leg out in turn. The clean water was just a few feet further, rippling over some rocks.

Stotts stood in the mud behind them, saying, Wait wait. We need to disinfect it first.

She didn't stop moving toward the water.

Reaching the stream itself, the riverbed beneath her feet was muddy and bubbled with her movements, but in Frankie's hand the water was clear. On the far side a red-winged blackbird took off, trilling.

He said, We put the water in a bottle, add a few drops and . . . Ahh crap.

The bonobos were bent over, slurping up long draughts of water, the front of their clothes soaked. Frankie drank the water in her hand. It tasted so sweet and cool in the throat that she crouched down, like the bonobos, to suck it straight from the stream. After drinking for a while, she paused, breathing, her eyes closed, feeling the water inside her. Then she drank more.

Stotts waded in deep enough to fill up the bottles he'd brought and add a few drops of bleach to each. He didn't drink yet, his lips pressed together.

Houdina stayed in the river, drinking and drinking long after the others had finished. She gasped in between her gulps. Stotts splashed over to her and scooped the still-sleeping Id out of her vest, then handed her to Frankie. He said, We can give her water in a bit, once the bleach has had a chance to work.

Frankie tucked Id into her sweater and struggled out of the mud to the shore.

The bonobos climbed out too, one by one and huddled in

close, their fur and clothes soaked. Frankie moved from bonobo to bonobo, pulling off any wet clothes and dropping them onto the ground. The bonobos shivered. Without their clothes, their fur wet, they looked so small—tiny gymnasts trembling in their tights.

She said, We need to warm them up.

Let's move then, Stotts said.

He got up and started walking, pulling the sled now filled with bottles of water.

Please, signed Frankie and then made the bonobo begging gesture, her palm up and extended. She said, Please come.

She took Mama's hand.

The bonobos, trembling, knuckled along, whining.

It began to drizzle. Like cats, the bonobos hunched their spines, picking their way forward through the rain.

Forty One

Two fields away, they came upon a barn and stepped cautiously inside, out of the rain. The space was dark and cavernous, the smell of hay and motor oil. The doors at the far end were open, motes floating in the light. In the center of the barn, a tractor lay on its side, half dismantled like a carcass.

As Frankie's eyes adjusted, she saw a wall of tools and a work-table covered with glass jars full of neatly sorted screws, nuts and bolts. The bonobos wandered deeper into the barn. Frankie walked with them, watching in case they picked up anything dangerous.

Marge found a stall full of hay and burrowed into it, peeping happily. The others pressed in after her, cuddling in and warming up. From deep in the straw came the squeaks of some very startled mice.

With the bonobos pulling the straw in around them like blankets, getting comfortable, Frankie searched deeper in the barn for dry clothes and especially shoes. Walking, her sneakers made squelchy noises, her toes numb from the cold. She peeked into a doorway where the only light came from a small dusty window. Clicking on her headlamp, she saw boxes, filing cabinets and beat-up furniture. With a few minutes of searching, next to a 20-gallon container of fungicide and a child's plastic bouncy horse, she found a box filled with sweatshirts, all extra large and neon green, ConAgra embroidered over the heart.

She carried the carton over to the bonobos and waded into the straw to dress them one by one. They chirped and patted the soft material, then buried themselves deeper into the hay to nap.

When she turned around, Stotts was wearing a pair of rain pants, bright yellow and with an elastic waist. He handed her the matching jacket and boots.

Best I could find, he said and headed toward the front of the barn.

She stepped back into the office to shuck off her wet pants, shoes and socks and pulled the raincoat on, buttoning it. It reached her knees. Walking in the oversized boots, she had to slide her feet forward as though skating.

When she came out, he was in the doorway to the barn, breaking up a small table to make a fire, a bushel of potatoes beside him.

Seeing her in the raincoat, her bare legs and oversized boots beneath, he said, You look like Paddington Bear.

She said, I was thinking more of a flasher.

He piled the wood on the dirt floor away from anything flammable, then stuffed hay beneath. He snapped a match against its box and held it to the straw. The flames climbed quickly. Frankie and he dragged an old radiator as close to the fire as possible, then wrung their socks and pants out and draped them on the radiator, propping their shoes in front. Wearing the raincoat and pants, they both rustled like shower curtains.

Stotts took several water bottles off the sled and handed the baby bottle to her. He said, The bleach must have worked by now. The water should be safe.

He sat down and closed his eyes, drinking water in long gulps.

Frankie sat beside him and pulled Id out of her sweater. Id didn't wake easily and her mouth felt dry. Frankie squeezed drops from the bottle's nipple into Id's mouth.

Id woke up and began to nurse, gulping down the water as quickly as she could. Soon she was shivering from the chill of the water, so Frankie tucked her back into her sweater.

Meanwhile Stotts began to cook the potatoes by dumping them into a dog's metal bowl that he shoved into the fire. He stirred the potatoes with a stick whenever they began to burn. Outside the rain came down harder, occasionally a sheet of mud hissed off the roof to thump onto the ground. Frankie and Stotts huddled close to the fire, blinking in the heat.

The smell of the cooking potatoes gradually woke the bonobos, who knuckled over, covered in hay and whining. When Frankie pulled the potatoes off the fire, the bonobos reached for each other with more intensity than normal, perhaps happy they weren't thirsty or shivering.

Stotts looked down at his hands, his face intent with his effort to keep his eyes away. Frankie, on the other hand, stared. At this moment, sitting near him, the mating of beetles would have drawn her attention.

Marge was the first to throw back her head to cry, *Ahh huh huh*. Since she wasn't ovulating, her climax was loud and obvious. The details of her desire programmed to toggle back and forth from public sex to private sex, depending on what would serve the best interests of her offspring.

The illogic of human sex struck Frankie. Unlike other animals, human couples were so secretive and took a sweaty long time to finish—dangerous to do with the children running around free and predators potentially nearby. There had to be a reason.

She imagined a hairless version of Marge stepping into a bar, wearing a dress and heels, eyeing the options. She saw her dating and then marrying. Later on, when Marge was ovulating, it was possible she'd look around again.

As a human, any time Marge had sex, with her husband or someone else, the act would be clandestine, doused with attachment hormones, but this time for the couple alone. Women (the same as female bonobos) were physically persuading the male to protect any potential offspring. Since the work of raising children was such an endurance event—two grueling decades of work shouldered by the couple alone—it made sense that this physical persuasion, this nomination of the dad, was extra long and intense. How else could the bond last? And given the difficulty and duration of parenting, the woman might need to nominate more than one dad. A dad for genetics, a dad for resources, perhaps a back-up dad just in case.

The act, Frankie realized, had to be covert so if there were more than one dad, none of them was forced to face the true scope of their role.

Her eyes had come to rest on her own hand, cupping a single warm potato, the skin smooth and tight. The last time she'd engaged in that slow physical act and been healthy enough to enjoy it, she'd been with JayJay—the knee-wall closet, the heat of the summer, the pigeons on the roof cooing. Four years ago or five? She looked over at Stotts and then away.

Deliberately she crushed the potato in her hands, breaking it into pieces and handing them out.

This was part of the process of getting healthy, she thought, these feelings. As soon as they were rescued, she'd get away from this married man. She'd head back to Manhattan for a break. There must be 100,000 single men in the city.

Once each piece was cool enough, the bonobos gobbled it down, making little huffy noises at the warmth in their mouths. All of them got some of the potatoes. Frankie scooped out the softest bits on her finger for Id, who now seemed to have more energy. Id gummed the food eagerly until it was all gone, then fell asleep inside Frankie's sweater, exhaling through her mouth like a tiny machine.

The rain outside had stopped, but they weren't yet ready to

move on. The bonobos spread out, exploring. Frankie tested her pants for dryness, then pulled them back on underneath the rain jacket. Stotts took his pants back into the office to get dressed. When he returned, they checked their shoes, but found them still damp so left them by the fire for another few minutes. Both of them pulled on several of the ConAgra sweatshirts for warmth.

And this was when it happened. Perhaps the fire had been a mistake. The smoke, the smell of food. Or maybe it was just bad luck.

Picture it. Stotts and Frankie standing in the doorway, Stotts shoveling dirt onto the fire to put it out. They turned at Mama's happy squealing.

Mama, near the far end of the barn, was waving a lone corn cob she'd found, walking on two feet toward them, Tooch on her shoulder jumping up and down.

Behind Mama, summoned by her squeals, her familiar voice, a group of foreign bonobos appeared, galloping around the corner into the barn. They were strangely muscled, hair unkempt and wet.

Time slowed down.

Frankie kept trying to understand, to recognize the intruders. Whoever was in the front, he must know Mama, be an old friend to be running at her like that, reaching out to hug her.

Stotts yelled. Having lost language in the speed of the moment, he was reduced to just a sound, mostly a vowel, *Aaa!*

The chimp wasn't distracted at all, but Mama was, looking at Stotts, wondering what was wrong. On her shoulder, Tooch had started to turn, gaping at the chimp.

The chimp grabbed her from behind—not her arms or shoulder, but the sides of her head—and twisted, hard. Her shoulders jerked, following her head, a dance partner that wasn't keeping up.

A wet crack.

Her body fell, a thing, a puppet with the strings cut. Her neck at a very wrong angle. Dead before the back of her skull bounced on the ground.

Tooch, knocked off by the fall, bolted for the bonobos, squealing. A small ball of fur galloping with all his might.

The chimps chased, howling with victory. A giant mob of them, sharp canines gleaming.

The approaching horror.

And Stotts threw his shovel. It arced, a wobbling spear. The blade of it clanged into the lead chimp's temple, knocking him back and to the left. The chimps behind twisted in midair, trying to avoid a collision, tumbling and landing, howling and confused. The forward charge stopped.

Tooch reached safety, disappearing into the crowd of *waa*-barking bonobos.

Fifteen feet away, the chimps shrieked, crabbing forward and back, sharp rushes of muscle and fur, working themselves up, preparing to charge again.

The lead chimp got to his feet, dazed, blood on his cheek, and knuckled a wobbling step forward. Stotts hurled a jar full of screws, a driving missile. It slammed into a different chimp, an explosion of glass and metal bits. All of them screamed and flinched and stepped back.

From the wall of tools beside them, Frankie grabbed wrenches and pliers and whipped them. Stotts threw hammers. They hit with fleshy thumps. The chimps shrieked and retreated further.

Adele charged in from the side, karate-kicking a chimp in the head. Her hair erect, barking, she was three times bigger than before. She bolted back to safety, Marge defending her retreat, whirling a broken chair over her head.

Then Stotts threw a sledgehammer, his whole body swinging as a counterweight, his shoulders engaged, his wrists flicking. It sideswiped two chimps and knocked them back several feet.

The two shrieked and fled, leading the way, one of them moving now with a sickening lurch in its stride. The rest of the chimps galloped after them.

Frankie and Stotts followed them to the far door, panting and holding hammers. They watched the chimps flee into the trees and disappear, their cries trailing away.

Nowhere was there any sign of Martin, the human who was supposed to lead them.

Forty Two

When Frankie and Stotts turned around, looking back through the barn, the bonobos were tiny and in the distance, galloping away across the field. On all fours they could move inhumanly fast. Marge trailed the rest, dragging Mama's body, the limbs bouncing along as though she were waving, gesturing to them to hurry.

Hey, yelled Stotts and chased after them, barefoot.

He grabbed the rope for the sled as he ran by, but it was partly unpacked, the blankets and bungee cords on the ground beside it. Dragged along, items flipped out with every bump: the antibiotic cream, the bleach, the lighter fluid and matches. Within 20 feet, the whole sled flipped over and he let got of the rope and simply sprinted, chasing the bonobos who by now had disappeared from sight.

Come, he yelled back to Frankie, *Hurry*.

Frankie's giant boots galumphed with every stride, slowing her, so she kicked them off. Holding a hammer, she ran, terror making her faster than she'd ever been.

He grabbed her hand to pull her along, kept looking back to check the chimps weren't in sight. She was too scared to look, huffing, arms working.

They followed the bonobo tracks through the mud: the feet and knuckle prints, Mama's drag marks. Within half a mile, the humans had slowed to a trot, both of them barefoot and limping, holding nothing but the two hammers. The tracks didn't head in a straight path, the way people would travel. Instead they curved according to the landscape, always heading for the nearest cover—trees, gullies, hedges. Soon, Frankie wasn't sure at all what overall direction they were heading in, except that it wasn't the one the keeper had pointed them in.

Within a mile, they spotted the bonobos in the distance, plodding along now. The humans struggled to catch up.

When the bonobos finally stopped it was on a flat rocky ridge with a good view. They clustered around Mama's body, keening and picking her hands up to press her palms flat against their faces. At all times, at least two bonobos were standing up and looking back the way they had come, keeping watch.

Stotts and Frankie approached cautiously. The bonobos barked, skittish. Their hair bristled, a feral glint to their eyes. The wind had blown the ridge clean of dust sometime before it started raining, so at least there was no mud here. Frankie and Stotts crouched down on the wet ground 30 feet back and waited, watching.

Bit by bit, they eased their way forward, getting closer to the group.

Mama's body was battered, the head twisted. Tooch clung to her chest, his face a half inch from hers, motionless, as though waiting for her to speak, to whisper anything at all. He stared at her, listening, then leaned back and howled at the sky.

He shoved Mama's cheek with the back of his knuckles. The head rolled loosely.

Frankie began to cry. Stotts put his arm around her. She rested against him, pressing her face into his chest, her breath shuddering. He laid his cheek on her hair.

Then, even in this moment, they became aware of the heat and weight of the other. They pulled away and looked off into the distance, blinking.

Stotts stood up and moved away from her, busying himself picking rocks up and putting them in his pockets—things to throw in case the chimps turned up again.

She turned her focus back to Mama's body and inched her way up to it. The bonobos moved out of her way, watching. She sat next to the body for a while, simply looking, then gently touched the motionless ribs and cooling hand. She'd never seen death up close. Mama's mouth open and eyes dry. She looked smaller and harder. The transformation complete.

She sat there beside the body and rocked back and forth on her heels, staring. Adele moved over and wrapped her arms around Frankie. Frankie held her back. Tooch crawled into her lap.

Stotts continued to stay away from them all, searching for rocks.

After a few minutes though they began to get uneasy, looking around, searching the landscape for chimps.

Stotts said, Time to move, alright? Stay on the ridge. Out of the mud.

Frankie asked, Why?

He jerked his chin to their prints and said, I don't want to leave tracks.

She looked at the tracks and then at him, You think they can follow tracks?

She didn't use the word, *chimps*, because the bonobos were listening.

He looked at the group of them and answered, An abundance of caution, alright?

She didn't like making noise now, not since Mama's call had summoned the chimps. So she simply started walking, beckoning to them and signing *please*, watching to make sure they headed in her direction. If they got too close to the edge of the ridge, where the mud started, she made a clicking noise with her tongue to get their attention, then gestured for them to come closer.

At one point, Marge headed off to the side, toward the mud, ignoring Frankie's clicks and waves, so Frankie uttered her best imitation of a *waa*-bark and stamped toward Marge, glaring.

Marge looked uncertain, moving her eyes from Frankie to the others and back. Then she sidled back into line, following the rest.

Frankie led on. Confused and leaderless, they complied.

A few minutes later, Petey got close to the mud, so Stotts tried *waa*-barking, but Petey barked back, teeth showing—all of them edgy. Stotts stepped away.

Frankie yelled, Petey!

She glared and stamped toward him. Remembering how Mama, when angry, would drag the milk crate after her to make an intimidating clatter, Frankie whacked the hammer down onto the rock in front of her, the sound as loud as a shot. Petey flinched and moved back into line, used to obeying a female.

After that Stotts said nothing, except occasionally making a *pssst* noise at Frankie to get her to notice a straying bonobo. He paced along behind them, keeping watch.

Adele carried Mama, tucked under her arm, parts of the body dragging. Sometimes the head hit a boulder with a meaty thud. After Adele tired, Stella carried the body, then Mr. Mister.

After twenty minutes of walking along the bare rocks, the ridge came to an end, and they stepped out across the mud. Frankie looked back at Stotts for his suggestion of a direction and he looked up at the sun then jerked his head to the left. She headed them that way, eastward. The bonobos followed her. All of them glanced occasionally over their shoulders, watching behind them.

By this point, Frankie didn't think she could find her way back to the Foundation if she wanted to.

*

After an hour they paused at a stream. There was no more bleach, so all of them, even Stotts, drank the water straight from the stream. They were travelling pretty slowly by this point, tired.

Before Marge drank any water herself, she dropped the whole front of Mama's torso in. Perhaps she was trying to give her a drink. On Mama's scalp, there were long gashes and scrapes that didn't bleed at all.

After drinking, Marge dragged the body back out and cradled it in her lap, grooming what little hair existed on the body's back and arms. Tooch knuckled over to sit on the chest and rock back and forth, sucking his thumb. Frankie dribbled water into Id's mouth. Id coughed a lot but did drink the water down. She was awake more often now and looking around. At least Houdina was getting more liquids. She'd be able to produce more milk for both Tooch and Id.

They moved on.

*

Partway through the afternoon, Lucy glanced back over her shoulder and stopped dead, staring at something. They all jerked around, bristling. There was only one small creature, way back there. Frankie saw that whatever the creature was, it didn't lope forward using its shoulders, head high, like a chimp. Instead it trotted, low and tireless, close to the ground. A dog, perhaps the beagle.

The bonobos *waa*-barked at it and the distant dog ducked behind a bush. When it didn't come out after a while, they knuckled on, looking back. Half an hour later, they spotted it again, following. They barked again. It hid. And so through the afternoon, the beagle padded after them, 300 feet back, trotting in and out of bushes, stopping occasionally to investigate something, disappearing entirely at times, but always popping back up.

Late afternoon, the stink of rotting meat drifted by on the wind. Looking in the direction of the stench, they spotted a barn through some trees. They skirted it, uneasy. Inside, Frankie knew there'd be empty automatic watering troughs, the pens full of bodies.

Maybe half a mile further on, they stepped over a guardrail onto some muddy pavement. Down the road a bit, on the far side was a 7-Eleven and a lonely parking lot.

Stotts said, Keep them back. I want to make sure no one's in there.

She sat down on the guardrail, used sign language and clicked, holding out her arms. Exhausted and muddy, the bonobos pressed in against her, snuffling.

There was no cover to hide behind, but Stotts still ran in low and fast, a soldier. The front door was locked so he trotted around the back. Soon they heard the sound of wood breaking. A few minutes later, they spotted him through the glass inside the store, moving down the aisles, carrying bags. When he left, he came out the front door and the banner inside fluttered in the wind declaring a sale on Big Gulps. He carried six bags full of dried fruit and Hostess Twinkies, a gallon of Coke under his arm. For once the bonobos were too tired to have sex. They clustered around Mama's body, eating intently. Lucy pressed a Twinkie to Mama's mouth, cream smeared across her lips.

Frankie fed Id the cream filling from several Twinkies, scooping it out on her finger. Id ate every bit of it, then the spongy cake part too, gumming her way through it all, determined.

They moved on. That whole day, they saw no humans anywhere.

*

As dusk started, they stepped around a hedge and came upon a house. The bonobos hurried forward, peeping with happiness, wanting to be inside.

The humans trailed behind, clicking and hissing, *Hey come back. Heyyyy!*

This tired and cold, the bonobos ignored even Frankie,

some of them disappearing around the corner of the house, whining, searching for a way in.

Stotts peeked in the windows, warily. Seeing some motion through the glass, he jerked back flat against the wall.

Not having been trained to react quickly, Frankie just froze there, gaping into the window, to see Goliath's face appear, grinning down at her. Behind him somewhere was an unlocked back door.

Inside, the bonobos slurped water straight out of the toilets. The humans searched the building, confirming it was empty, then returned to the kitchen to pop open jars of applesauce and strawberry jam and spoon the contents into pans on the floor, along with whatever else looked edible. Then Frankie and Stotts gulped soda from the bottles and ripped open bags of Wonder Bread to stuff the food in their mouths, the slices appearing perfectly fresh.

After they'd eaten enough, Frankie pulled off their muddy sweatshirts and handed out blankets. Stotts tugged two mattresses down from upstairs and placed them on the living room floor, equidistant from both exits. The bonobos chirruped and knuckled onto the mattresses, cuddling in and wrapping the blankets tight around them.

Frankie wrapped a blanket around herself and sat down with them. The pleasure of being off her feet brought back a long-ago memory, perhaps 10 years old, trying downhill skiing for the first time. All day in the snow, falling again and again, wrists raw, clothing wet, the slow exhaustion. Only once it began to get dark did her parents allow her back into the ski lodge, where they handed her a cup of hot chocolate. She remembered that pleasure of sitting in the warm building and raising the drink to her lips—the sweet steam, that first sip.

She lay down, pressing in against Goliath. He wrapped his arm around her and she rocked her head into a good spot on his chest. He patted her face. She pulled the blanket tighter, grateful. On the floor nearby lay the dark lump of Mama—her limbs stiff, her head canted.

A foot away, on the other side of Goliath, she heard Stotts shifting about, getting comfortable. She eased her hand forward until her knuckles touched his ribs. She heard him exhale, letting air go, as though her touch helped.

One by one, they fell asleep there, in the dark.

*

Throughout the night, the beagle whined outside. At one point, it scratched at the door and Adele charged out of the bed, *waa*-barking. The dog ran away outside, its yips receding into the distance. Later, they heard it baying in the night, high pitched and alone.

Forty Three

In the morning, they ate the rest of the food: all the cereal, the crackers and bread, the canned tomatoes and sardines and every one of the 15 containers of baby food.

Sitting on the counter Frankie asked, We can't stay here, can we?

Stotts snorted and looked around. The kitchen ransacked, the cupboards open and emptied, the water in the toilets gone. The stench of feces and urine was pungent. All around them were the windows where it was possible at any moment the chimps would appear.

Before they left, Frankie called the bonobos upstairs. She dumped all the clothes she could find onto the floor and let them take what they wanted. She assisted those who couldn't dress themselves, helping them layer the clothes on for warmth. Goliath pulled on a spaghetti-strap dress over his ConAgra sweatshirt. He patted the sequins on the bodice and cooed. Frankie tugged hats onto their heads, zipped jackets and buttoned sweaters. None of the gloves—not even the stretchy ones—would fit over their huge hands.

She and Stotts also changed out of their very soiled clothes. Their choice of what to wear was restricted to what remained. She tugged a pink terrycloth bathrobe on over two button-down shirts and a pair of very large jeans. In order to keep the pants on, she had to use a belt and poke a new hole in it with scissors. Stotts wore an oversized antique tux over a sweatshirt and a pair of overalls. Shoes were more difficult. She chose a pair of Timberlands two sizes too big, had to wear several pairs of socks and yank the laces tight. He pulled on old sneakers. From his slightly mincing step, she guessed they were at least half a size too small.

Stotts packed a knapsack with a gallon of Fanta and a bag of marshmallows, then shouldered it. He moved from room to room inside the house, staring out the windows, searching for any movement before easing himself silently out the back door. They watched him through the windows. He circled the house, occasionally stopping to listen, looking for movement. The tails of his tux flapped in the wind.

When he signaled the all-clear, Frankie opened the door and motioned them forward.

On the porch, she left a bag of dog food ripped open for the beagle, hoping the food would persuade the dog to stay behind. However halfway through the day, the beagle reappeared behind them again, padding along, closer than yesterday. Anytime it got within 100 feet, Adele or Marge would charge and it would flee, howling.

The bonobos continued to drag Mama's body. Each time one of them put the body down, tired of carrying it, the others would cluster around, patting it, until another picked it up.

Stotts had no compass, but walked in the direction of the rising sun. She followed him and they followed her. (Later on, during the middle of the day he would begin to walk with the sun more to his right and then, once it began to set, he'd walk with his back to it. Probably throughout the day, their tracks curved all over the place like the tracks of any animal, but the overall direction was always east, in the direction of his daughter.) He had his head tilted up a lot of the time, watching the sky. Sometimes he turned around as he walked to scan the sky there too. His expression intent.

Regularly she tugged her eyes away from him to look

around for danger. Then let her eyes slide back. She didn't like it when he got too far ahead of the rest of them.

By midmorning, he was 20 feet or so ahead. To slow him up, she called out, It's beginning to freak me out. Where *is* everyone?

He turned, startled.

Evacuated, he answered.

How big was the evacuation zone, she asked.

Five counties.

How far do we have to go to get out of it?

He looked around thinking, 100? 150 miles?

She blinked, How far have we come?

Yesterday we wandered all over the place. As the crow flies, we're probably only three miles from the Foundation, maybe five.

Where are the sand-plows? What the hell's happened?

He held his hands out palms up, watching the sky, moving a little faster with every passing hour.

*

In the early afternoon, they found an orchard that still had a few apples, some in the trees and some on the ground, smeared with mud from the dust and rain. The bonobos scrambled through the trees, peeping as they ate, while Frankie and Stotts ate the bag of marshmallows he had packed.

In another field, they found a few corncobs and spent time searching for more, bonobos and humans shucking corn and eating.

There was always one of them standing up and looking around, keeping watch. Frankie listened also, her head cocked like a dog. She swiveled at the slightest noise, the distant rumble of thunder or the rising rustle of wind, knowing even as she turned that this was not rescue.

Stotts seemed to recognize the sounds faster. His eyes roved across the horizon and sky, searching for the glint of metal, a wispy contrail or the blurred dot of a rescue drone.

When they started moving again, he got ahead of them, wanting to go faster. However the bonobos didn't move quickly. Carrying Mama's body, chasing the dog, following the lay of the land and investigating anything that might result in food or water, they were not a species that marched.

Partway through the afternoon, they heard gunshots, the echo faint, at least a mile away. All of them paused. Listening, exposed in a field, no shelter in sight, the sound such a final one. Houdina galloped forward to jump into Stotts' arms, whining there until the sounds had stopped.

*

By late afternoon, she and the bonobos were trailing so far behind Stotts, she called to him to wait. He looked back, as though surprised to see them. She didn't like the distance in his expression at all. She ran to him, taking his hand to slow him down, looking back at the bonobos who trailed behind, peeping with exhaustion.

Behind them came the dog, sniffing the ground for scraps.

Forty Four

Mama's body gradually looked less and less like Mama, or like a bonobo, or actually like anything except a battered grey doll made of meat. By the middle of the day, whoever was carrying it would occasionally put it down to search for food or to drink some water, wandering 10 or 20 feet away, then abruptly would turn, chirping with distress and rush back to pick it up.

*

That afternoon, stepping past some trees, they came upon a driveway and mailbox. Hanging from the bottom of the mailbox, swaying lightly in the wind, was a steel sign saying COEXIST. In New York, Frankie had seen this sign before, the letters formed from different religious symbols. With this sign, the letters were constructed out of the silhouettes of handguns, rifles, bullets and the NRA logo.

Frankie looked at the sign only for an instant before she clicked her tongue at the bonobos and began backing up.

Stotts however stayed still, staring at the sign and then up the driveway, his eyes narrowed.

With a serious expression, he pointed at her and circled his finger in the air to add all of the bonobos in as the subject of his silent sentence. As the verb, he gestured emphatically twice toward the shelter of the trees. He tapped his wrist to indicate time and held up five fingers.

This, she understood, was commando speak. She however did not want to wait anywhere near this house, not even for a moment. She shook her head *No*.

He nodded at her—Yes—his gesture firm.

She held up her middle finger and shook her head again.

Glaring, he pointed at her and at the trees and then turned and trotted up toward the house.

She stared. The beagle bounded after him through the shrubbery, off to the side, giving the bonobos a wide berth.

The bonobos started to knuckle after Stotts, but she clicked and motioned them back into the trees. They looked from her to Stotts, then moved toward her. She stared after him, her breathing loud.

As he got closer to the rise, Stotts began to run, bent over, using bushes and trees as cover. The dog ran beside him, wagging its tail. Stotts stopped, crouched behind a shrub and the dog slid to a stop, rump in the air. It kicked off to gallop around in a tight figure-eight, then paused in front of him, panting.

Stotts ignored the dog. He sprinted forward 20 feet to flatten himself against a tree trunk. The dog ran too, but when Stotts stopped, the dog trotted on, disappearing over the rise. Stotts didn't move for several minutes. Frankie could see the tail of the dog waving as it wandered by a few times. Stotts occasionally glanced around the trunk in the direction of the house.

The dog came back, something in its mouth. It lay down with a thump near Stotts to gnaw on the object.

Stotts crouched down and ran forward to disappear from sight.

Frankie looked at the spot where he'd disappeared, then at the bonobos, then back. All sound seemed to have disappeared except her breath. What she felt at the moment was no longer anything like a gentle ache in her gut. Instead the feeling was piercing, like glass working its way into her lungs.

She tried to tiptoe away from the bonobos, sneaking up through the trees. They watched with interest, chirped and began to follow. She flapped her hands at them, waving them back, but they continued to amble after her.

Still she couldn't stop herself, running up the rise until she could see the house, pausing there to stare. The bonobos did not pause, but knuckled forward through the trees toward the lawn. Still no movement came from the home.

The bonobos stepped out onto the lawn, blinking in the sun. From the far side of the house came the sound of glass shattering.

Sweetie and Houdina climbed onto the swing set and began pumping their legs, trying to remember this action from long ago. The swing squeaked noisily.

Frankie watched the bonobos and the windows, her mouth open. Listening for a gunshot.

Instead a few moments later Stotts opened a window on the top floor and waved them inside.

Seeing him—framed in the window there, healthy and alive—was the moment when things shifted for her. His wife and child no longer mattered, or the possible pain she risked.

She ran across the lawn and in through the back door, the bonobos filing in behind. She ripped open a box of Oreos and a canister of oatmeal, tossing the food across the floor for them, then bolted upstairs to find Stotts.

He stood in front of the gun cabinet. Unhurt. She slammed into him from behind and wrapped her arms around him. Jesus, she said, Don't do that again.

He froze, his body breathing, not moving away or turning to face her.

She paused, allowing herself to feel the balance of their bodies together. Then let go and backed up.

He watched the floor. In his hand was a small metal sculpture—a reproduction of a Degas ballerina. Visibly he refocused himself on the gun cabinet and tapped the sculpture's head through the glass, running the shoulders round the frame to clear it of shards. He reached in to open the cabinet from inside.

He stood there, considering the different guns before selecting a smaller rifle and a box of ammo. His breath was steadier by now.

He cleared his throat before speaking, Night scope. Lightweight. Fast action.

He slid a clip in. It clicked into place. The way he handled the rifle, she saw he had had a whole different life before her.

He asked, Want one?

Hell no, she said.

They left the house, too uneasy to stay the night there, even when it was deserted. He wore the rifle around his chest, the clips of ammo tucked in his pocket. They ended up in the next house down the road.

Houdina slept with her arms around Stotts; she would never steal from him. Still Stotts unloaded the rifle before lying down, sleeping with one hand on it, the ammo inside his shirt.

That night each time the dog bayed outside, they woke up and breathed there quietly. Stotts stood up to peek out the window, loading the rifle.

Frankie watched, staring at the silhouette of his exposed head.

Forty Five

The next morning, Frankie arranged Mama's body outside on the porch in a rocking chair, a blanket around it. Bye bye, she said, Bye bye. She waved to it and backed away.

The body didn't look like Mama anymore. It no longer smelled like her. Gravity was flattening it bit by bit, its joints sprawled, its flesh slack.

Most of the bonobos paid no attention. They knuckled outside, narrowing their eyes into the sun, then headed off after Stotts. Only Marge, Adele and Tooch stayed, looking from Frankie to the body and back. They prodded the body with their knuckles and grunted low in their chests.

Looking back and forth from the body to the others who were ambling off, Marge abruptly got angry. She charged and slapped the body hard in the chest, knocking it out of the chair. It hit the ground with a thud.

Together she and Adele barked and displayed, kicking the body, the chair and the porch railing.

Their rage abruptly spent, they sat down to groom the body.

Bye bye, said Frankie and picked up Tooch. He stared dully at Mama.

Frankie walked away a few feet, then a few more. She said, Bye bye.

Marge knuckled after her, Adele following. They loped back to touch the body, before following Frankie farther away, looking back and whining.

They turned back many times to see Mama still sprawled there, her head to the side. Her body getting smaller.

Finally the house was out of sight.

*

This morning Stotts seemed more anxious. He would march forward at a fast walk, until almost out of sight, in order to see over the next ridge. Waiting there, he'd glance back for the bonobos, impatient, scanning the landscape and sky for planes or vehicles.

Holding the hands of different bonobos, she urged them on, watching to make sure he didn't step forward over the rise and disappear.

*

Late that morning, they drank the last of the water they carried. Houdina was still thirsty, kept shaking the bottle and raising it to her lips as though there was the chance it might fill itself on its own.

A few minutes later they came upon a line of utility poles, extending into the distance. Frankie tapped Goliath on the shoulder, looked him in the eye and then pointed her eyes to the top of a pole. For clarity, she repeated her eye movements and added the gesture for *please*.

Goliath followed her gaze and grunted, obligingly wrapped his large hands on either side of the pole and shouldered his way up, his feet ascending as easily as up a ladder. The rest of the bonobos sat down and began to groom each other. Ahead of them, Stotts leaned against a fence, keeping watch, one leg jittering. At the top, Goliath paused and looked around, admiring the view. She watched to see if he stared in any direction for a beat longer. He did keep his face turned for a moment in one direction, but when she stepped back a bit, she noticed his face was tilted to the sun and his eyes closed.

Once he descended, she asked him, Water? Which way?

He wrapped an arm around her and rested his head on her shoulder, sighing with happiness.

She touched his chin and looked into his eyes. She cupped an imaginary drink to her mouth, her eyebrows raised to show a question. She wished she'd paid more attention to the avatar so she knew more signs.

Drink, she asked, Where? Water?

Happy with her attention, he stood up with an erection and waggled it around in front of her. Obediently, she patted it.

She asked, Which way? Water?

She stood up and took his hand, waiting for him to lead. He shambled downhill toward some trees. It wasn't to the east, the direction Stotts wanted. She didn't know why Goliath chose this direction, but had to hope he was answering her question and not just wandering off.

She kept watch over her shoulder to make sure Stotts followed.

A few minutes later the dog bolted past them, 20 yards away, thrashing through the undergrowth until they could hear it lapping up water. The bonobos followed and they emerged on a small lake. Wading in to drink, the bonobos slapped at the surface to scare the beagle away, claiming the lake as their own.

Frankie stood on the shore, amazed. Stotts stepped through the underbrush to pause next to her. The sun shimmered on the waves. It had been over a week since either of them had showered.

Stotts said, I'm stripping down and getting in. I really need to get clean. I'll be fast.

His dignity complete, he said, Please look away.

She turned away, but could hear every rustle of his clothing being tugged off. The tuxedo jacket, the overalls, the sweatshirt.

There was the sound of him sloshing forward into the water, then the splash of him diving in. Surfacing, he coughed at the cold.

She turned. Twenty feet out, he was standing, the water to his chest, scrubbing his face, no soap except motion.

She said, I'm coming in too.

The splashing stopped. He said, No you're not.

Fuck you, she said, I'm smelly. You don't like me getting in there, you get out.

She stripped, head down. Her body hadn't been interesting to her for years, tendoned and bony. It was an envelope that had been poked and prodded by so many medical personnel, each of them labeling it faulty. Her belly and thighs were still red from the boiling water. Naked, she splashed forward to her thighs, then dove in, the water startlingly cold and black. Her heart *shh-thump*ed *shh-thump*ed in her ears. She swam under-water—a background hiss and the clink of pebbles shifting. Then she exploded out, sucking in air and slapping forward into a crawl to keep warm.

Only as she turned around, heading back, did this begin to feel different. Drawn to him.

She stopped five feet away and stood there. Neither of them said a word, her head turned precisely. As with a wild creature, she did not look.

So long as she stood here, near him, she felt no fear, not of anything. She didn't think about the cold water. She wasn't waiting for rescue. Her blood pulsing in her skin.

He whispered, Tess.

That single word pushed them apart as distinctly as if the child herself were there, shoving with her hands.

Without a word, Frankie backed up, then waded out onto the shore to get dressed. He followed a moment later, heading for his clothes, as much pale dignity as though he still wore the tux.

They dressed quickly. Afterward, filled with nervous energy, she huffed and ran circles round the bonobos, clapping her hands, trying to warm up. Stotts did jumping jacks with a true ferocity, his eyes closed.

Then he marched again toward the east, moving even faster than before, all of them following.

*

Stotts was 50 yards ahead climbing a small hill, when he reached the top and stared in amazement, still as a statue. He strode forward and disappeared. Without him in sight, she felt terror and calling the bonobos, ran after him.

She saw the ditch first.

A trough of earth ripped into the field, 30 feet wide, arrow straight to disappear into the distance, a wave of dirt and boulders shoved out of the way, a furrow for a seed too big to be imagined.

At the far end of the field, the giant wing of a plane gleamed, the shattered end cantilevered up on the broken trunk of a tree. She walked that way, mesmerized, face canted to the side, sucking air through her mouth, the stench now rising.

On the other side of the tree, the furrow slewed hard to the right, debris beginning, scattered suitcases and plastic cups, fabric fluttering. Walking so slowly now, unwilling, heading toward Stotts who sat in the field, legs sprawled.

Closer now, she saw a shoe—a blue sneaker, a thick river of ants flowing along the shard of bone. She stopped, staring. The bonobos were spreading out, on the periphery of the stench, investigating the detritus.

Stotts held a paper boarding pass—must have been an unaccompanied child on board, young enough not to have BodyWare. His mouth open, he stared blindly in the direction of the airplane tail rising in the distance. He was making a panting sound.

She reached forward and wiggled the pass from his hand.

COSTA RICA AERLINIA C52   SAN JUAN A CHICAGO
HALL / NICK   OCT 28 8:45 A.M.   E7

She glanced at him, relieved this couldn't have been his

daughter's plane. Wrong direction. Wrong day. This wasn't why he was reacting this way.

She turned back to the ticket, trying to understand what he'd seen. The date and time, she studied for a while, tracking the days backward, before understanding.

This plane had been in flight at the point the avatar had started talking gibberish.

No, she said.

Stotts had his hands over his head now, rocking.

She looked around at the debris, frantic to disprove the thought rising inside her. She began to lope across the field, searching the littered objects for proof of any kind. She found the bloated arm with the retro watch still on it.

Using the corner of a tray table, she turned the arm to see the shattered watch face. She held her breath and got close enough to peer through the broken glass. Time frozen at 10:51.

She could see the scene: the human backup pilot dozing in his seat, the plane droning on, boring and calibrated. Then on the dashboard screen, the avatar of the autopilot appeared, stated the time—10:48— and began to speak nonsense. By this point it was too late. No time to warn the passengers, each of them left terribly alone for these final few minutes as the pilot struggled for control, yelling commands and slapping buttons while the plane lurched through the sky, overhead compartments popping open, the frame juddering, seats squealing, luggage and water bottles pinwheeling by, until the engines just cut out, a whistling silence where the roar had been, that final slide beginning, the destination apparent.

She said, Everywhere?

She stared out at this new world she'd been walking through for days without realizing it. Scattered garbage on a desolate landscape, apes wandering about, picking up whatever caught their fancy. On the airplane tail was the logo of a palm tree waving in the wind.

Stotts' wife and daughter were in England.

How helpless we are without technology, naked and defenseless, a soft-limbed creature without wings or fins, our oversized cerebellum able only to grasp the sheer expanse of an ocean.

Her thumbs, she realized, were rubbing the edges of the tray table as though she could absorb this information like braille—its importance, the full scope of its meaning. The rasp of her skin over broken plastic.

Forty Six

T his was where she lost track of time. Days passed.
Stotts walked on wooden and mechanical, his face
frozen. He still headed to the east—there was no other
direction in which he would walk—but he no longer moved
quickly. If she talked to him, he took a moment before turning,
as though listening to something inside that was taking all his
attention, some inner voice relaying complicated information
at a speed he couldn't absorb, neither the details nor the basic
premise, no matter how hard he concentrated.

Normally moving with an attentive power, at times now he
stumbled. She held his hand, helping him along. She talked to
him, telling him what she could. Watching his face.

England, she said, doesn't get all that cold. Winter there is
easy.

She looked around to the bonobos to make sure they were
all in sight and added, A thick sweater is all you need.

She turned around to walk backwards for a moment to
make sure nothing other than the dog followed. She said,
What do they call them? A jumper? One or two thick Fair-Isle
jumpers and you're fine.

*

That night, in the house they'd broken into, she asked,
They in the countryside?

There was a delay before her words reached him. He nodded.

What area?

That delay again, as though he wasn't actually here, but far away, trying to hear her words faint with distance. He answered, Norfolk.

She ripped open a bag of beef jerky and dumped the contents onto the plate between them. She didn't know a thing about Norfolk, so she bluffed. She said, Carrot farms everywhere.

She handed him a piece of jerky. She said, The carrots would be ready for harvest now. Anyone could walk into a field, grab the leaves and yank one out.

He listened, staring at the food in his hand.

She nudged it closer to him and said, Wouldn't take much strength. A child could do it.

*

Each night they slept in a different house. Since it was getting colder, they stayed inside later each day, until the sun was well up. The bonobos wore jackets or sweaters on the top half of their bodies and, before they went out, she helped them pull clothes onto the bottom half also—sweatpants or skirts. Their legs were short so she had to roll the pants up. Children's pants fit them the best.

When they did leave, the bonobos hustled forward through the cold, knuckling only so far as the next house to the east that had water in the toilet tanks, more food and a fireplace. Each day they managed only a mile or two.

Adele found a wedding dress she loved, refusing to take it off for days. It had narrow sleeves and a low-cut bodice that showed off her hairy décolletage. Frankie cut the skirt short in front so Adele's back legs didn't get tangled. Wearing the dress, Adele loved galloping across the fields, the white train fluttering over the ground behind her—Guinevere cantering forward on her charger, only in this case the horse wore the dress. The train was gradually ripped to shreds, plastic pearls littering the ground.

Each day the dog eased in a little closer to the group. It

wanted attention, whining and dancing on its feet, twisting itself into a U so both its head and wagging tail faced them. Still, any time it got within 20 feet, Marge or Adele coughed and it would flee.

In the afternoon, breaking into whatever new house they'd selected, Frankie would light a fire while the bonobos searched for blankets and food. For the dog, she'd dump a can of something edible outside—sardines, spam, cat food.

The next morning they'd leave that house, heading east again. She always tried to ease Stotts' direction slightly south. If she did this for long enough, it might make a difference.

*

She said, Let's talk about potatoes.

After a slight delay, he turned.

She said, The Irish are famous for eating potatoes, right? It's a classic. They grow all over the British Isles.

His eyes were pointed in her direction, not quite focused.

She said, You can dig them out with your hands. Some serious calories in a potato.

Perhaps he heard her. From his expression, she wasn't sure.

*

When she ran out of things to say about England, she talked about whatever else she was thinking, what she was worried about, anything so long as she was talking and his head bent toward her voice, some counterpoint to his terrible thoughts. He might not listen to the words, but he would hear at least the tune of her caring.

She said, I've been watching Sweetie.

Behind her, she heard Sweetie chirp at his name, happy to be mentioned.

She said, He's always grooming others or offering them food or cuddling with them.

She said, It's neoteny. Not only does it give him a baby's oversized eyes, it makes him more social, more gentle.

She looked at Stotts and said, Kindness and nice eyes. What more could a gal want?

*

Manhattan was something she tried not to think about, the restaurants and stores and classrooms, the noisy hustle of its streets, its chaotic drive. She didn't want to imagine what it might be like now.

*

At times she talked about what could have gone wrong, naming the possibilities. EMP. Cyberwar. Poly-roach. Catastrophic solar storm. Each day she came up with a few more ideas, felt strangely reassured by each. She might not be able to control their situation, change it back to the way it was, but at least she could understand the likely causes.

She considered the options, turning them over in her mind, coming up with variants. Her imagination open now, the scope of the empty horizon in front of her, she felt surprise that the society she'd known, had grown up with, had lasted as long as it did.

*

At mealtime, she offered him a glass of water and said, Cows. Lots of cows in Norfolk.

She wrapped his hand around the glass and raised it to his mouth, then continued, It's easy to milk a cow. Even a child can do it. Milk's filled with protein.

She waited, eyebrows raised. She wouldn't speak until he started drinking.

He took a sip, like an android would touch its lips to liquid, obedient and without interest.

She said, The cows *need* to be milked. It hurts otherwise. They'll stay still for anyone to do it.

The bonobos seemed to understand something was wrong, especially Houdina. When Stotts was sitting, she'd knuckle forward to hold his ears and peer into his face, clucking. She'd sit beside him and rest her head on his shoulder.

Each morning when they left one house to walk to the next, Houdina would hand Id to him. Id would crawl into his shirt for warmth and Stotts actually responded, cupping his hand under her rump and resting his nose in the hair on top of her head, his eyes shutting for a moment. Id patted his cheek, running her fingers over his growing whiskers while Houdina stood up to take his other hand, leading him along, every few feet glancing at his face.

Houdina didn't look like a zoo animal anymore, well fed and sleepy in her cage. Breastfeeding two now, she'd lost weight, stripped down to muscle in a way she hadn't been before, her stride loose and feral, her eyes alert. She was somehow so much more present. When she spotted food, she moved toward it with speed. Lately, with her feeding Tooch, the others didn't bark at her as much. They shared their food with her.

At night, Frankie lay down on one side of Stotts, Houdina on the other. Frankie rested her head on his chest, so if he stirred, she'd wake. Once in awhile Houdina shoved at Frankie's head with her elbow, but Marge and Adele would grunt, irritated, and she'd settle down.

Each night Frankie fell asleep listening to his heart.

*

She said, Cows means milk and cheese. You know how many British cheeses there are?

He cocked his head, maybe listening to her or perhaps to his own thoughts.

Stilton, she said counting them off on her fingers, Shropshire, Gloucestershire . . .

He looked at her with blank eyes.

She said, You're right. I've no idea. Let's just say lots.

*

She did no recognizable work anymore: no reading, no note-taking, no experiments, no meetings. Instead she slept when she was tired, ate when she had food. She was never alone. She was always holding someone's hand, getting her hair groomed, Tooch tucked inside her sweater.

She watched the bonobos, letting her eyes run over them, checking they were fine. She spent a lot of time counting, making sure there were still 13 of them. As the days went by, they began to play again, chasing each other, cantering, such slender hairy people.

*

At night Tooch woke at the slightest noise; perhaps he was listening for Mama. He and the dog had become the watchmen for the group. Whenever the dog bayed outside or Tooch whimpered, the rest of them would wake. Stotts would get to his feet and walk to the window. The rifle in his hand, he became Stotts again, for the moments while he stared out into the dark.

In every house, Frankie first searched for matches or anything made of paper in order to light the fire, occasionally discovering a set of paper books, part of the decor like candlesticks and probably used as often. One day, she grabbed a book and was ripping out a handful of pages, when she saw it was a Boy Scout Handbook. She paged through it—how to identify poisonous plants, track animals, fight hypothermia— then put it to the side to read later. Instead she started the fire with a book about the Beatles.

*

Sweetie was sharing a box of raisins with Stotts. Each time he handed Stotts a raisin, he waited, brows raised, for Stotts to put the raisin in his mouth.

Frankie said to Stotts, I wish we were more like Sweetie.

Sweetie peeped at his name.

She explained, Us humans should be more like him.

Stotts chewed on the raisin with little interest, as if it were old gum.

She said, Especially the person who made this happen.

She said, Someone probably did it. Some leader of a country ordered the cyberwar or a programmer created the polyroach. Someone built the EMP device. Someone *decided* this should happen to all of us. I just . . . I wish that person had been nicer.

Stotts turned to her.

She said, Maybe if the mom of that person had chosen someone like Sweetie, someone with big eyes and a generous soul, maybe then he would have been born a little different, wouldn't have done what he did.

Stotts watched her from so far away.

*

She was surprised by how good food tasted—prepared in a rush, without the right ingredients, sometimes just served raw. Perhaps it was the cold air or the walking or that she wasn't sure when she would get to eat again.

Even water tasted better. She'd never thought much about water before, never paid much attention, how its taste varied depending on where it came from: sweet, coppery or flat. The origin in her mouth. A gift running down her throat.

Maybe the difference came partly from how time had shifted. She'd been accustomed to waking at seven each morning to the beep of her EarDrums, her head already filled with a predetermined schedule, tasks to accomplish. Now, without messages scrolling across her Lenses or her next appointment highlighted, without graphs to analyze and papers to write, time began to stretch, became rubbery and intense. Each morning the group left when they were ready, traveled until they found a house they liked, ate whenever they discovered food.

Perhaps it was the simple action of being able to flip forward through a calendar from this year to the next that had seemed to her essentially a promise, luring her into a sense of life as predictable and safe as a long hallway stretching toward an always-distant vanishing point.

At times she heard the wet crack of Mama's neck breaking, the crunch of vertebrae. It came most often when she was eating, biting into an apple or a cracker. Strangely enough, the sound acted like salt, making the flavor pop in her mouth. She tasted so clearly the finite amount of food she would eat in this life, the water she could swallow, the air she could breathe. She closed her eyes to chew.

Throughout her life, she'd been accustomed to waking each day in her own bed, knowing she would be warm and dry, assured of her morning shower and time on the toilet.

Now without any certainty, each object she passed became worth noting, worth exploring. Each morning she left behind an entire building's worth of useful objects—blankets, pans, food—hoping by nightfall to find others. Under these circumstances, just sitting down felt like a prize.

She knew now the experience of loss was a prerequisite to holding anything tight enough to feel it. Each day she lay down next to Stotts, her head on his chest, hearing his heart, smelling the heat of him. She wrapped her arm around him and waited.

Forty Seven

All of the bonobos could now pull on their own clothes before the walk. Outside they peered about with interest, no more plexiglass between them and the world. They cantered toward interesting objects, their energy returning, their physical grace. They trotted through each field and orchard, searching for leftover produce, climbing through the trees. No longer grooming each other all day, bored and waiting to be fed, they were waking up. They smelled water from a distance, loping toward it, noses raised. They recognized fields of potatoes (Frankie wasn't even sure how, the withered plants, the smell?) and would dig into the earth, searching. They learned something new every day, how to open the toilet tank to get to the water or to blow on cooked food to cool it. Marge kept trying to use a can opener to open cans of fruit and got a little closer to managing it every day.

In the afternoon, in whatever home they had found, the fire roaring in the fireplace, the doors closed, they pulled the blankets around them, cooing as they warmed up. Frankie heated the food in the fire, shoving the pans into the cinders, Houdina watching her every action, attentive and hungry.

And always Frankie would search for books, examining any she found. She'd start the fire with books about automotive repair or interior decor. Others she would keep for the evening, flipping through them, trying not to be distracted by the glossy photos of the past as she searched for useful information: local maps, edible plants, first aid.

*

Knuckling along in snowsuits or sweatpants, wearing cowboy hats or knitted toques, the bonobos chased each other, playing a variant of tag. They galloped, their speed inhuman, rushing straight up a tree to hang there by one hand.

Marge grabbed Frankie's hat and bolted away. At the slowness of Frankie's two-legged chase, several of them fell on the ground, their laughter huffing white in the cold. Playing the situation for all it was worth, Marge cantering slowly around Frankie, wearing her hat and grinning, Frankie unable to catch her even then.

She now laughed the way they did, a huffing through the mouth, a quiet sound that didn't carry. Still, the motion shook her bones and emptied the fear from her veins.

When Marge handed back the hat, she stood up and gave Frankie an open-mouthed kiss on the side of her face, the generous size of her mouth slobbering her from her temple down to her jaw.

Something in this moment—perhaps the fondness with which Marge poked fun at Frankie's clear disability—made Frankie feel in her gut how much the bonobos *loved* her. She blinked, surprised. Into her mind flashed a distant image of that first day she'd seen them: bald Mama standing in the enclosure, evaluating her with a cold stare, the rest of them behind her, a mass of hairy indistinguishable animals.

At this change in Frankie's expression, Marge kissed her again. This time some of her slobber got in Frankie's ear so she couldn't hear for a while out of her right side.

*

Three times, dogs appeared. Packs of them roamed free, purebreds and mutts, bony and desperate, reverting to their origins. Their beagle gave them notice, baying as it fled. The bonobos flew up into the nearest trees. Frankie and Stotts were slower, had to search for a tree they could scale or a shed they could clamber up on, but in the end they also got out of the way. They always kept a few rocks in their pockets just in case.

Each time there was danger, Stotts returned, become present. He wouldn't use the gun unless necessary. It was a waste of ammo, the noise could attract unwanted attention and Houdina would howl with terror.

So from the safety of their perch, Frankie and Stotts threw rocks until the dogs ran away. Then they'd lean back against the trunk and nap in the tree, until they were sure the dogs had left the area.

*

One night, they took shelter in a ranch house on the outskirts of a small town. Moving through the house, exploring, Stotts stopped motionless in the doorway of a room.

She stepped fast to his side, scared of what he might have found, but there was only an empty crib sitting there under the window, a wind-up mobile above it. He coughed, the start of sobs, his body jerking with them as though each sound was yanked on a rope out of his gut. He pressed two fists to his face.

The bonobos hustled to him, wrapping their arms around him. Kind souls, they howled with empathy, no need to know what was the matter, only that he was sad. She leaned in against him, against all of them.

He slid to the ground, the bonobos holding onto him.

*

This was the house in which she found that old dog-eared paperback, *Kon-Tiki*.

Now a Major Motion Picture, said the cover, True Story. Across the Pacific in a Raft.

She held the book in her hands for a long time, staring at it, before tucking it into her bag, burying it deep, not willing to leave it behind or show it to him.

*

Walking outside, heading toward a farmhouse, they all heard the noise. At first, on the wind, it sounded a bit like crows, loud and cawing.

It took a moment for Frankie to identify the voices as human.

As soon as she understood, she held her palms up in a signal for everyone to stop, bouncing her hands desperate in the air. The bonobos looked from her gesture to the voices. It was unclear how much they comprehended. Maybe, if they'd been given more time, it might have worked. Meanwhile the humans appeared around the corner of the barn, five of them, calling to each other. One of them wore a rifle.

Spotting the bonobos, they froze. The man with the rifle had two dead rabbits strapped to the side of his knapsack, front paws swaying. The metal of his weapon shone, riveting the attention.

The bonobos grunted and stood up on two feet, sniffing the wind.

Both Stotts and the man stood still, a hand on the stock of their guns.

Frankie yelled, The apes are tame. They won't hurt you.

The group stared, with fear or perhaps hunger.

She yelled again, Tame. They're tame. Gentle.

Frankie held Tooch close, tightening her hand round Goliath's fingers, ready to run.

There was a long moment.

Then the small boy holding onto the mom began to cry, to wail, tugging back on her hand. Watching the bonobos for the slightest move, the strangers began to back up, one foot after the other, following the child and mom, until they were out of sight.

Only then did Stotts speak.

Wait, he yelled desperate, gesturing Frankie and the bonobos back toward the nearby bushes. He yelled, Wait. Give us the news.

The trees were silent, the wind rustled the leaves. No one reappeared.

He ran to the barn, looking around the corner, cautious. He yelled, What happened? Tell me. Please.

He circled on his heels, watching for any movement, the rifle in his hands. He yelled up toward the sky with all his strength, Are any devices working? Did this happen everywhere? Is the Quark gone?

Echoing with distance came the voice of one of the women, We don't know.

A minute later, from further back, came her voice again, the wind loud enough to tug at the words, erasing some of the consonants. It sounded like what she yelled was, It just stopped.

Frankie bellowed as loud as she could, Is it gone for good?

There was only silence in return.

She pulled the bonobos back into the bushes. Stotts followed, looking all around them. The bonobos sat there quietly. Several curled up and fell asleep. Stotts stood, ammo loaded, both hands on the rifle, circling slowly, watching and listening for the slightest movement.

*

Later that afternoon he asked, Did you see the kid?

She was so surprised at his words, at him talking, that she turned to stare.

Stotts asked, He seemed alright, didn't he? In spite of everything, the kid was fine.

Frankie stepped in close to peer into his face the way the bonobos did. Since the day he'd sobbed beside the crib, at times his face had emotion in it again.

She said, People always care for kids first. People everywhere will do that.

He looked at her, his eyes big. He seemed to really be there, hearing her words, seeing her.

She told him, In England they have no guns. No rifles. It's much safer.

Forty Eight

The bonobos had begun to recognize logos and packaging, ripping open boxes of Froot Loops and anything with a picture of mangos on it.

Knuckling through the fields or climbing through the orchards, they were accomplished now at finding unharvested food. The beagle trotted near them, its head down and sniffing through the grass, occasionally flipping field mice into the air with its nose to catch them with a wet clap of its mouth.

In one of the houses, Frankie found a box of powdered milk. She carried it in her knapsack, mixing up a cup of it each morning for Id and Tooch. With the combination of this with Houdina's breast milk and the solid food that Frankie prechewed for them, both of them had gained weight.

At times Id played again. When they traveled outside, she stared at this large world from inside Stotts' shirt, her eyes bright.

In the morning Frankie sometimes tickled Id. She wiggled and pant-laughed, slapping at Frankie's hands, protesting. If Frankie stopped, Id would pause, her belly jutted out, waiting for more.

*

One morning there was the light sheen of ice on the grass. By late morning it had melted. They stayed inside a little longer each day. When they did leave, they moved at a speed that was almost a jog. She always eased their direction slightly south, hoping over time to get to someplace warm enough for the bonobos.

Each time they entered a new house, Houdina and a few others headed straight for the kitchen, opening the cupboards. Others would knuckle upstairs and drag down the pillows and blankets to make a nest on the floor. After checking that all of the food they'd pulled out was actually edible, Frankie would start the fire.

Houdina could now use a spatula to drag the pan back from the fire. With Frankie coaching her, she sometimes lit the fire with a gas lighter, clicking the button again and again until the flame appeared at the end of the nozzle and then she held the lighter to the paper.

*

One day the wind was blowing in the wrong direction and the beagle didn't give them notice. The pack of dogs just appeared, charging forward through the orchard. The one in front was a Newfoundland, its coat billowing loose around its frame, like a person in a badly fitted costume.

Adele shrieked a warning and jumped into one of the apple trees; the rest of them leapt into whatever tree was closest. Frankie scrambled up a trunk, desperate. Stotts climbed behind her, lacking urgency, distant in his thoughts.

The Newfoundland grunted as it leapt. She felt Stotts jerk behind her. Twisting around, she saw him dangling by two hands. Id, inside his shirt, screamed so hard he chinned himself up into the tree. Below him, the dog spat his empty sneaker onto the ground and leapt again.

Stotts settled on that branch, his feet tucked up, not bothering to climb higher, staring down mesmerized, at the dog's teeth snapping a few inches beneath him.

Rage filled Frankie's body, her vision tunneling red. Not at the dog, but at Stotts.

She leaned down from her perch above and said in the

voice she used to use with her doctors, the hard voice, Do you *want* to see her again?

He turned to her.

She asked, Your daughter. Do you?

His eyes dilated.

You're not acting like it, she said.

He stared, utterly present.

She settled her weight back against two branches and yanked items out of her knapsack, searching for the Kon-Tiki book, dropping everything else to the side.

Below her, the Newfie stood on its hind legs, snapping at the candy bars and apples falling from above. A poodle darted off with a potato. A smaller mutt bolted by to grab a pack of peanuts.

She found the book and slapped it into Stotts' hand.

She yelled into his face, It's your choice. You want to see her again, here's how to do it.

He looked down at the book, its cover showing people crossing an ocean by sail.

A moment in which everything changed.

The book in his hand, her choice made, she exhaled, You're going to need to start planning, start learning, like you did with flint knapping.

He looked at her, understanding the depth of this gift.

She said, It's a long way.

*

He read most of the book that first night, his forehead creased with concentration. At times he blinked up and around at the room they were in—the fire crackling in the fireplace, the bonobos cuddled in their blankets, and at her—as though surprised at how different everything looked with this book in his hand.

Every night from then on he studied it, reading and rereading it, writing notes in the margins.

*

From that day on, he began to eat again, to drink, without being urged.

She handed him a packet of beef jerky and said, Peter Rabbit—you know that's a story that came from over there, right?

He bit into the dried meat, chewing.

Rabbits, she said, They're everywhere in Norfolk. Easy to catch. Just set a trap for them. A net, a propped-up box. Good protein.

Water, she said when he picked up his glass, Norfolk is full of water.

He closed his eyes then and drank and drank, imagining his daughter drinking too.

*

He held the first practice. He wanted the bonobos to learn to be quiet and stay still.

She was supposed to make the gesture, a palm jerked down twice, while whispering, *Quiet. Stay.* The bonobos were supposed to sit down and wait for a full minute.

The first time they tried it, Petey and Lucy and Sweetie sat there, not so much obeying as busy grooming each other. However Stotts rewarded them as though they'd obeyed, handing them each a Twizzler, telling them they'd done a great job. They squeaked with surprise and popped the treat straight into the mouth to suck on it. Within a few seconds they pulled their treat out and passed it on to another bonobo to suck on for a while, who then handed it on to a third, subverting the lesson.

In spite of this, Stotts had them practice many times, until all the Twizzlers were gone, until they sometimes sat still at the gesture.

After that first practice, she said, They aren't dogs.

He answered, I'm treating them like soldiers, not dogs.

He was becoming focused again. He looked at her, in her

eyes, the intent way he had for those days before the airplane wreck. If anything his gaze held something more in it, an awareness of her gift.

That night, in bed with all of them, he put his arm around her and held her close. She pressed herself in against him, conscious of his body.

Then Houdina, on the other side of him, pinched the back of her hand, hard.

Yow, Frankie yelled and yanked her hand away.

Adele barked and the rest protested, howling. In the dark, there was the *thwap* of someone getting hit and Houdina yiped.

It took a while for them to settle back down. Frankie sighed and just rested her head on his chest.

It took a long time for the two of them to fall asleep.

Forty Nine

In the morning, Frankie and Stotts walked with the bonobos, a house visible in the distance. He reached over and took her hand. In the cold air, the rasp of his glove against hers was an intimate sound. He rotated her wrist slightly to cradle her arm against his side, tucking her hand with his into the pocket of his jacket.

Chaperoned by 13 apes, they held their heads down, concentrating on the feel of holding hands.

*

Goliath was in the front, knuckling up the hill, when he got to the top and stopped, staring.

Stepping up next to him, Frankie saw a Walgreens 100 yards away, tents set up in the parking lot, the doors to the store propped open, people moving in and out, children playing. Clothes hung up on lines strung from car to car.

The first snow had fallen that morning, so they'd stayed inside until it melted. She didn't know how close they might be to the limits of the evacuation zone. This was the first settled group of people they'd seen.

Frankie's group stood there, staring, heads cocked like they'd caught the strain of a song that had been familiar long ago.

She was the first one to look away, resting her chin on top of Tooch and Id who were tucked into her sweater. She knew her allegiance by now. Stotts stared at the humans for longer. She figured he was watching to make sure none of them had spotted the bonobos. She took a step back and then another, gesturing to the bonobos to follow, assuming he'd bring up the rear.

When she was 20 feet back, Stotts stepped forward instead, taking off his rifle as he moved, dropping it on the ground behind him. She wasn't fast enough. He strode down the hill. She froze, a high pitch in her ear, her feet so far away. If she ran down, all the bonobos would follow. Several of the people wore rifles across their chests. If a bunch of apes cantered out of the underbrush toward them, there was no question about how they would react.

Houdina knuckled forward, starting to follow Stotts, but Frankie said, *No*, and Marge coughed a warning. Houdina stopped, whining.

Stotts stepped out of the shrubbery and stood there, calling out a greeting and holding his hands up in the air like a prisoner. He spoke loudly enough that she could hear him. He said, I've come in peace.

The people turned to stare, their hands on their guns, scanning him and the trees behind.

He kept his hands up, staying still and talking with them. His head turned at times to look at the children. He wasn't talking as loudly now, so she couldn't hear his words, just see that he was speaking and they were replying, their shoulders relaxing, their hands easing away from the rifles.

He gestured behind him and the humans scanned the trees again, surprised. They shook their heads. He spoke a while longer. He reached his hands forward, palms cupped upward.

They shook their heads again.

He turned slowly away and walked back up the hill.

She sprinted to him, slapping her body into his. He wrapped his arms around her and pressed his face against her head.

Then she kicked him hard in the calf, yelling, Don't ever do something like that again.

The kick felt so good that she kicked again, much harder.

He danced away on his other leg, grimacing, telling her all their devices and avatars had gone crazy at 10:48 on the same day. After the dust storm ended, the group had gradually collected in the store; there was safety in numbers and all the supplies were there. Nothing in the store worked, except one old battery-powered radio. They turned it on for a few minutes a day and searched the dial, but hadn't heard any broadcasts yet.

He put his foot down cautiously. He said they'd offered to let him and Frankie join them, but not the 13 apes. They were worried about the food lasting through winter.

Did you see, he asked, Did you see how many of the kids were doing fine?

Limping slightly he led the way, circling widely around the encampment and then heading on toward the southeast.

Every house they entered, he searched systematically for books, looking for anything that might be helpful: astronomy, currents, sailing. He moved with energy now—not with the desperate speed of a sprinter, but with the determined pace of a marathoner.

*

That night, in a ranch house with a wood stove, sitting on the couch, she leaned in against him. He put his arm around her and rested his chin on her hair.

She could feel every fiber in her body, the tendons and flesh. She raised her face toward him, he was leaning down.

Then Houdina screamed and backhanded her head hard from behind.

Marge and Adele attacked Houdina. A table knocked over, a chair broken, the mayhem intense.

Ten minutes later when all the wailing and sobbing had quieted, Stotts and Frankie sat back down on the couch, staring at each other, a foot of space between them.

*

That night, as always, Tooch slept on top of Frankie. He heard something outside and tensed, waking her. The dog outside whined. The group of them woke, their breathing paused. Stotts stood up, pulling the rifle out from under the pillow and sliding the ammo clip in. They lay there still, while he stepped toward the window.

After a few minutes of silence, watching and listening, he looked back at Tooch, who blinked at him, sleepy. Stotts got back into bed.

She didn't know if bonobos normally slept this lightly. They seemed in general more aware, more awake. During the day, exploring the world, their eyes so bright, they searched for trees to climb, toys to play with. She walked alongside them, present to the possibility of food or danger, every detail sharp, the colors shimmering. She watched Stotts—his rangy body, his stride—felt she'd never seen anyone as clearly before.

Since she'd given him the Kon-Tiki book, he no longer stumbled. His face was thinner, older now and worried, but at least his expression was alert, emotion in his eyes when he looked at them, when he looked at her.

As he lay down against her, she curled in and wrapped her arm around him.

*

That morning, Id woke before dawn and slid out of Frankie's arms. She was eating and drinking enough to have energy again. Frankie turned over, hoping for a little more sleep, assuming Id was heading to Houdina to nurse. However when she woke up later, Houdina was staring at her. Neither of them had Id. They jolted out of bed and started searching.

Id, Frankie called, Id!

Houdina hooted, dashing this way and that. The others spread out, squealing.

Frankie looked under the beds and in the closets. Stotts

sprinted into the basement, searching for where the bleach or other poisons might be.

It was only when she ran back to the living room that she saw Houdina stood now by the couch, still hooting for Id, but no longer with alarm. Instead she was slapping the cushions and rustling them around, searching theatrically, moving every pillow except the one that wiggled with laughter, Id's toes visible underneath.

When Stotts came charging back up from the basement, Frankie pointed.

He looked, his face pale and fierce.

Houdina scooped Id up from behind the pillow. Id's face so delighted with her trick.

In the end, he laughed the loudest, laughing until he had to cover his eyes with his arm.

*

While the bonobos were distracted by breakfast, Stotts pulled her behind the fridge to kiss her. They ground in close against each other, the slow heat rising.

Intent, it took them a bit to feel the silence all around. They pulled back to look. The bonobos had knuckled forward around the fridge, staring.

They let go of each other and backed away.

*

Her hope was by the time they reached the coast, they would have traveled far enough south for it to be livable for the bonobos. Some place that by then, next summer or fall, might be less populated than before. She imagined a national park, something with orchards nearby: Georgia peaches or Florida oranges. Once they'd found the right site, she'd search with Stotts for a nearby sailboat and start to equip it: food, water, fishing supplies. The two of them taking short trips with it up and down the coast for practice.

Each time, before they left on one of these sailing trips, she would pump her palm down, telling the bonobos, *Stay*. Telling them, *Here*. Telling them that again and again.

One day, she'd leave with Stotts in the boat for the journey, the trip across the ocean. Hoping to come back. Hoping that when she returned—with or without him—she could walk through the forest where she'd left them, walking and hooting up into the trees, until they heard her and came flying through the branches like furry superheroes, peeping with joy, to land on the ground and canter into her arms.

*

They spent that night in a house on a hill. This was a bigger home than most of the others, newly painted and gleaming. No sign of anyone having come close to it in a long time, except the prints of one wandering rabbit.

The front hall was covered with photos—children on a swing set, a couple grinning in front of a lake, an older man in a hospital bed. Halloween with one child dressed as an Oompa Loompa, the other wearing ears and a collar (A dog? A cat?). In the photos the people were so clean and relaxed, grinning. On their foreheads, their Bindis gleamed.

Stotts and she walked down the hall, staring, examining each photo in turn. He looked at the pictures of the children, his eyes warm.

The furniture was untouched, perfectly placed, the velvet throw folded over the back of the couch. She patted it, then moved to the kitchen. He opened the dishwasher to peer inside at its silence. She touched the sink faucet. The gleaming weight. Cold as a cadaver.

After they'd finished a feast of Cap'n Crunch and Vienna sausages, crackers and strawberry jam, she took his hand and led him gently upstairs. She didn't need to say a word. He followed. She pulled him into the bedroom and closed the door. Somehow all the light in the room seemed concentrated in his face. Even in the dark she could see it perfectly.

She leaned against him and said, Now.

Then Goliath opened the door. The other bonobos were clustered behind. She shooed Goliath out and locked the door, but on the other side Tooch began to howl with terror, the rest joining in, the wails echoing with the rising screams, loud enough the noise could be heard outside, echoing in the night.

So Stotts opened the door and let them enter.

They looked at each other, over the crowd of bonobos wandering in, moving through the room, patting the pillows and opening the closets. In spite of this, the two of them stepped in to each other and kissed. The press of his body, the flesh, nothing else mattered. They pushed in closer, their hands moving.

Around them, she became aware of movement and grunting—the bonobos companionably commencing sex.

Before she'd even gotten his shirt off, the females started to squeal their orgasms, the males following. Then the bonobos knuckled over to the bed to snuggle in, chirping and pulling the blankets over them.

Meanwhile the humans (the determined tortoise of sexuality) kept at it, while easing their way bit by bit toward the door until they were around the corner and in the hall. As the bonobos began to breathe deeper in sleep, Frankie and Stotts leaned against the wall and the side of a bureau, awkward but motivated, working to get a balance and a rhythm, making enough noise so the bonobos knew they were still there.

The need stronger than anything, the rising heat, time slowing, space compressing.

In the end she cried out, somehow surprised. Stotts' noise followed, low in his chest. From inside the room, they heard Tooch coo back at them.

They stood there, leaning against each other, steaming in the night, feeling the slow breath of the other. Only as they began to get cold did they pull on clothes and move into the room, pushing the bonobos over far enough to claim a spot on the bed.

She settled against him, holding on, the feeling different now.

Home, she'd always considered an object, an address, something permanent, a structure with a roof. Lately, sleeping in a new building each night, she'd come to think of home in a different way. She understood that nothing, absolutely nothing, was permanent. All the buildings she'd occupied through her life had been only temporary shelters in which she'd laid down her head—to be forced out after a while. Her childhood house in Canada, that first apartment on 107th, her freshman dorm, the knee-wall closet on Staten Island, there'd been so many. Having to leave each now after a single night was just an acceleration of that life.

She no longer thought of "home" as anything to do with drywall or a door. She appreciated the feeling all the more for knowing there was a limit to the time she could reside within it.

She listened to his heart. His thumb ran down her spine.

Goliath rolled over and draped an arm over both of them. Marge patted Stotts' head. Id and Tooch nursed on their thumbs with an audible suck. The slow respiration of them all.

RESEARCH APPENDIX

In this novel, I use details, stories and research from experts in order to bring to make the book as vivid and real as possible. Of course the human characters in this novel are not based on these real life experts in any way.

Below are books for you to read if you want to learn more about bonobos and the research.

Bonobos and Chimps
Any book at all by Frans de Waal
A Dutch primatologist living in the States, Frans de Waal describes the differences between the great apes with the gentle distance of a foreigner surveying an adopted land. He's one of the world's leading researchers of bonobos and his books are a joy.

Many of the stories and much of the research in this novel came from his books including the name of Mama, who was a relatively hairless chimpanzee at the Arnhem Zoo in the Netherlands. Another chimpanzee at the same zoo was taught to bottle feed her babies because she couldn't supply enough breast milk for them. De Waal also describes a bonobo at Twycross Zoo in England who found a wounded bird, climbed to the highest point in her enclosure, unfolded the bird's wings and threw it toward the sky.

If you aren't sure which book of his to start with, try *The Ape and the Sushi Master*.

Bonobo Handshake, Vanessa Woods

Vanessa Woods tells the story of herself and her researcher husband, Brian Hare, who move to the Democratic Republic of Congo to study the differences between bonobos and chimps. Woods and Hare developed the experiment described in this book where food can be tugged into reach if two apes cooperate, as well as the experiment where a bonobo can choose to let another bonobo into a room to share the food.

Before a male bonobo would participate in the research, he'd frequently insist Woods touch his penis. Woods realized this touch for bonobos functioned as a greeting, like a handshake.

Many of the details in this novel come from Woods' book, such as the bonobos imitating hairstyles from fashion magazines, playing basketball or drinking dish soap in order to burp bubbles. Perhaps most importantly, Woods described how the bonobos can fall in love with a human, flirting intensely with that person, while kicking out anyone they consider competition.

Empty Hands, Open Arms, Deni Béchard

Béchard traveled to the Bonobo Conservation Initiative in the Democratic Republic of Congo. His book describes the struggle of this remarkable nonprofit to support local initiatives to conserve land for bonobos and humans.

The Chimps of Fauna Sanctuary, Andrew Westoll

Westoll spent a summer as a volunteer caring for chimps at a chimp sanctuary outside Montreal. He found everyone he talked to who worked with great apes had dreams at night of those apes talking and driving cars.

Kanzi, PBS, RadioLab

The *Kanzi* RadioLab episode explores the relationships between humans and bonobos at the Great Ape Foundation (now called the Iowa Primate Learning Sanctuary). The Foundation was started and run by the remarkable researcher Sue Savage-Rumbaugh. The Great Ape Foundation in this book is named after that research center. If you ever get a chance, go visit. It's in Des Moines.

Some of the bonobos who Savage-Rumbaugh worked with, such as Kanzi, have vocabularies of several thousand words, and can light fires, cook food and play Pacman. Some of them even struggle to speak English as best as their different vocal cords and physiology will allow. In very high-pitched, hard to understand voices, they say words such as "play," "run" and "chase me."

http://www.radiolab.org/story/91708-kanzi/

Flint Knapping

Making Silent Stones Speak, Kathy D. Schick & Nicholas Toth

To learn how stone tools were developed, Kathy Schick and Nick Toth traveled to Tanzania to make and use stone tools to butcher animals (including an elephant).

Toth also taught the bonobo Kanzi from the Great Ape Foundation to flint knapp. At one point, Kanzi, frustrated with the difficulty of trying to flint knapp, rolled back the rug in order to throw the rock on the cement floor and break it in hopes that he'd have created a shard sharp enough to use.

Songs of the Gorilla Nation, Dawn Prince-Hughes

The scene of gorillas eating pumpkins in this novel came from Prince-Hughes' autobiographical book. As a woman with autism, she learned how to relate better to other humans by watching how a gorilla family related to each other.

Woman, An Intimate Geography, Natalie Angier

If you're a female and think you know your own body, try reading this book. One of the many studies Angier describes is where Professor Nancy Burley from University of California, Irvine, gave male zebra finches hats and stockings of various kinds to find out how the hats and stockings affected mating and parenting.

Pain

The Body in Pain, Elaine Scarry

Harvard Professor Elaine Scarry brilliantly analyzes the way pain affects our culture, literature, art, medicine and politics. When a person is in pain, she notes, language disappears.

Understanding Pain, Fernando Cervero

Cervero examines the history of pain and what is known about it medically. Aristotle was the one to define our five senses and he decided to leave pain off the list.

Cervero points out that while other senses gradually get desensitized (i.e. you stop noticing a smell after a time), pain tends to increase. Long-term pain can change the look of that part of the body. A fingernail begins to grow differently; muscle tone can change; the color of the skin shifts.

Human Reproduction

A Mind of Her Own, Anne Campbell

Campbell describes the active role women play in evolution and reproduction, explaining the research in a clear and thought-provoking way. She points out how women act differently when ovulating and how infidelity might help our species stay healthy.

Claus Wedekind

Wedekind is the Swiss researcher who pioneered the

"sweaty T-shirt study." The study had women rank the attractiveness of the smell of T-shirts that had been worn by different men. The results showed women are attracted to men who have the most dissimilar immunities from their own. To read about his work, you have to plow through science journals.

Deafness
Mean Little Deaf Queer, Terry Galloway
As a child, Galloway gradually lost her hearing. She learned to cope, becoming a successful actress in Australia. This is a funny intimate look into Galloway's experience.

Catching Fire, Richard Wrangham
Harvard Professor Wrangham believes once early humans learned to cook—making food easier to digest—we were able to afford the extra calories necessary to have larger brains.

Other Great Books
The Rational Optimist, Matt Ridley
Living Well with Endometriosis, Kerry-Ann Morris
The Righteous Mind, Jonathan Haidt
Chimpanzee Cultures, Richard Wrangham, W.C. McGrew, Frans de Waal & Paul Heltne
Rattling the Cage, Steven Wise
Great Ape Societies, edited by William C. McGrew, Linda F. Marchant & Toshisada Nishida
Among the Great Apes, Paul Raffaele
Gorilla Society, Alexander H. Harcourt & Kelly J. Stewart

ACKNOWLEDGMENTS

This novel would not have been possible without my editor, Kent Carroll. Without his encouragement, I would not have written another novel.

My great gratitude also goes to the writers who helped me: Beth Castrodale, Grace Talusan, Gilmore Tamny, Mary Sullivan, Talaya Delaney, and Leah De Forest.

Finally, a deep thank you to Doug and my children, who got second fiddle while I worked.

About the Author

Audrey Schulman is the author of four previous novels: *Three Weeks in December* (Europa, 2012), *Swimming with Jonah*, *The Cage*, and *A House Named Brazil*. Her work has been translated into eleven languages. Born in Montreal, she now lives in Cambridge, Massachusetts, where she runs HEET, a non-profit dedicated to the understanding of clean and efficient energy.